美国亚裔文学研究丛书

总主编　郭英剑

An Anthology of West Asian American Literature
美国西亚裔文学作品选

主编　郭英剑　张成文　冯元元

本研究受中国人民大学科学研究基金资助，系 2017 年度重大规划项目“美国亚裔文学研究”（编号：17XNLG10）阶段性成果。

中国人民大学出版社
·北京·

图书在版编目（CIP）数据

美国西亚裔文学作品选：英文、汉文 / 郭英剑，张成文，冯元元主编. -- 北京：中国人民大学出版社，2022.10

（美国亚裔文学研究丛书 / 郭英剑总主编）

ISBN 978-7-300-31090-9

Ⅰ. ①美… Ⅱ. ①郭… ②张… ③冯… Ⅲ. ①文学—作品综合集—美国—英、汉 Ⅳ. ① I712.11

中国版本图书馆 CIP 数据核字（2022）第 186166 号

美国亚裔文学研究丛书

美国西亚裔文学作品选

总主编 郭英剑

主　编 郭英剑　张成文　冯元元

Meiguo Xiyayi Wenxue Zuopinxuan

出版发行	中国人民大学出版社		
社　址	北京中关村大街 31 号	邮政编码	100080
电　话	010-62511242（总编室）		010-62511770（质管部）
	010-82501766（邮购部）		010-62514148（门市部）
	010-62515195（发行公司）		010-62515275（盗版举报）
网　址	http://www.crup.com.cn		
经　销	新华书店		
印　刷	唐山玺诚印务有限公司		
规　格	170 mm × 240 mm 16 开本	版　次	2022 年 10 月第 1 版
印　张	15.5	印　次	2022 年 10 月第 1 次印刷
字　数	292 000	定　价	68.00 元

总 序

美国亚裔文学的历史、现状与未来

郭英剑

一、何谓“美国亚裔文学”？

“美国亚裔文学”（Asian American Literature），简言之，是指由美国社会中的亚裔群体作家所创作的文学。也有人称之为“亚裔美国文学”。

然而，“美国亚裔文学”这个由两个核心词汇——“美国亚裔”和“文学”——所组成的术语，远没有它看上去那么简单。说它极其复杂，一点也不为过。因此，要想对“美国亚裔文学”有基本的了解，就需要从其中的两个关键词入手。

首先，“美国亚裔”中的“亚裔”，是指具有亚裔血统的美国人，但其所指并非一个单一的族裔，其组成包括美国来自亚洲各国（或者与亚洲各国有关联）的人员群体及其后裔，比如美国华裔（Chinese Americans）、日裔（Japanese Americans）、菲律宾裔（Filipino Americans）、韩裔（Korean Americans）、越南裔（Vietnamese Americans）、印度裔（Indian Americans）、泰国裔（Thai Americans）等等。

根据联合国的统计，亚洲总计有 48 个国家。因此，所谓“美国亚裔”自然包括在美国的所有这 48 个亚洲国家的后裔，或者有其血统的人员。由此所涉及的各国（以及地区）迥异的语言、不同的文化、独特的人生体验，以及群体交叉所产生的多样性，包括亚洲各国由于战争交恶所带给后裔及其有关人员的深刻影响，就构成了“美国亚裔”这一群体具有的极端复杂性。在美国统计局的定义中，美国亚裔是细分为“东亚”（East Asia）、“东南亚”（Southeast Asia）和南亚（South Asia）。[1] 当然，也正由于其复杂性，到现在有些亚洲国家在美国的后裔或者移民，

1　参 见：Karen R. Humes, Nicholas A. Jones, Roberto R. Ramirez (March 2011). “Overview of Race and Hispanic Origin: 2010” (PDF). United States Census Bureau. U.S. Department of Commerce.

尚未形成一个相对固定的族裔群体。

其次，文学主要由作家创作而成，由于“美国亚裔”群体的复杂性，自然导致“美国亚裔”的“作家”群体同样处于极其复杂的状态，但也因此使这一群体的概念具有相当大的包容性。凡是身在美国的亚裔后裔、具有亚洲血统或者后来移民美国的亚裔作家，都可以称之为“美国亚裔作家”。

由于亚裔群体的语言众多，加上一些移民作家的母语并非英语，因此，“美国亚裔文学”一般指的是美国亚裔作家使用英语所创作的文学作品。但由于历史的原因，学术界也把最早进入美国时，亚裔用本国语言所创作的文学作品，无论是口头作品还是文字作品——比如19世纪中期，华人进入美国时遭到拘禁时所创作的诗句，也都纳入“美国亚裔文学”的范畴之内。同时，随着全球化时代的到来，各国之间的文学与文化交流日益加强，加之移民日渐增加，因此，也将部分发表时为亚洲各国语言，但后来被翻译成英语的文学作品，同样纳入“美国亚裔文学”的范畴。

最后，“美国亚裔”的划分，除了语言、历史、文化之外，还有一个地理的因素需要考虑。随着时间的推移与学术界研究【特别是离散研究（Diaspora Studies）】的进一步深化，“美国亚裔”中的“美国”（America），也不单单指“the United States”了。我们知道，由于全球化时代所带来的人口流动性的极度增加，国与国之间的界限有时候变得模糊起来，人们的身份也变得日益具有多样性和流动性。比如，由于经济全球化的原因，美国已不单单是一个地理概念上的美国。经济与文化的构成，造就了可口可乐、麦当劳等商业品牌，它们都已经变成了流动的美国的概念。这样的美国不断在“侵入”其他国家，并对其他国家产生了巨大的影响。当然，一个作家的流动性，也无形中扩大了“美国”的概念。比如，一个亚洲作家可能移民到美国，但一个美国亚裔作家也可能移民到其他国家。这样的流动性拓展了“美国亚裔”的定义与范畴。

为此，“美国亚裔文学”这一概念，有时候也包括一些身在美洲地区，但与美国有关联的作家，他们用英语进行创作；或者被翻译成英语的文学作品，也会被纳入这一范畴之内。

应该指出的是，由于“亚裔”群体进入美国的时间早晚不同，加上“亚裔”群体的复杂性，那么，每一个“亚裔”群体，都有其独有的美国族裔特征，比如华裔与日裔有所不同，印度裔与日裔也有所不同。如此一来，正如一些学者所认为那样，各个族裔的特征最好应该分开来叙述和加以研究。[2]

---

2 参见：Chin, Frank, et al. 1991. “Preface” to *Aiiieeeee! An Anthology of Asian American Writers*. Edited by Frank China, Jeffery Paul Chan, Lawson Fusao Inada, and Shawn Wong. A Mentor Book. p.xi.

二、为何要研究“美国亚裔文学”?

虽然上文中提出,“美国亚裔”是个复杂而多元的群体,“美国亚裔文学”包含了极具多样化的亚裔群体作家,但是我们还是要把“美国亚裔文学”当作一个整体来进行研究。理由有三:

首先,“美国亚裔文学”与“美国亚裔作家”(Asian American Writers)最早出现时,即是作为一个统一的概念而提出的。1974 年,赵健秀(Frank Chin)等学者出版了《哎咿!美国亚裔作家选集》。[3] 作为首部划时代的“美国亚裔作家”的文学作品选集,该书通过发现和挖掘此前 50 年中被遗忘的华裔、日裔与菲律宾裔中的重要作家,选取其代表性作品,进而提出要建立作为独立的研究领域的“美国亚裔文学”(Asian American Literature)。[4]

其次,在亚裔崛起的过程中,无论是亚裔的无心之为,还是美国主流社会与其他族裔的有意为之,亚裔都是作为一个整体被安置在一起的。因此,亚裔文学也是作为一个整体而存在的。近年来,我国的“美国华裔文学”研究成为美国文学研究学界的一个热点。但在美国,虽然有“美国华裔文学”(Chinese American Literature)的说法,但真正作为学科存在的,则是“美国亚裔文学”(Asian American Literature),甚至更多的则是“美国亚裔研究”(Asian American Studies)。

再次,1970 年代之后,“美国亚裔文学”的发展在美国学术界逐渐成为研究的热点,引发了研究者的广泛关注,为此,包括耶鲁大学、哥伦比亚大学、布朗大学、宾夕法尼亚大学等常青藤盟校以及斯坦福大学、加州大学系统的伯克利分校、洛杉矶分校等美国众多高校,都设置了“美国亚裔研究”(Asian American Studies)专业,也设置了“美国亚裔学系”(Department of Asian American Studies)或者“亚裔研究中心”,开设了丰富多彩的亚裔文学与亚裔研究方面的课程。包括哈佛大学在内的众多高校也都陆续开设了众多的美国亚裔研究以及美国亚裔文学的课程,学术研究成果丰富多彩。

那么,我们需要提出的一个问题是,在中国语境下,研究“美国亚裔文学”的意义与价值究竟何在?我的看法如下:

第一,“美国亚裔文学”是“美国文学”的重要组成部分。不研究亚裔文学或者忽视甚至贬低亚裔文学,学术界对于美国文学的研究就是不完整的。如上文所说,亚裔文学的真正兴起是在二十世纪六七十年代。美国六七十年代特殊的时

3 Chin, Frank, Chan, Jeffery Paul, Inada, Lawson Fusao, et al. 1974. *Aiiieeeee! An Anthology of Asian-American Writers*. Howard University Press.

4 参见:Chin, Frank, et al. 1991. “Preface” to *Aiiieeeee! An Anthology of Asian American Writers*. Edited by Frank China, Jeffery Paul Chan, Lawson Fusao Inada, and Shawn Wong. A Mentor Book. pp.xi–xxii.

代背景极大促进了亚裔文学发展，自此，亚裔文学作品层出不穷，包括小说、戏剧、传记、短篇小说、诗歌等各种文学形式。在当下的美国，亚裔文学及其研究与亚裔的整体生存状态息息相关；种族、历史、人口以及政治诉求等因素促使被总称为“亚裔”的各个少数族裔联合发声，以期在美国政治领域和主流社会达到最大的影响力与辐射度。对此，学术界不能视而不见。

第二，我国现有的“美国华裔文学”研究，无法替代更不能取代“美国亚裔文学”研究。自从 1980 年代开始译介美国亚裔文学以来，我国国内的研究就主要集中在华裔文学领域，研究对象也仅为少数知名华裔作家及长篇小说创作领域。相较于当代国外亚裔文学研究的全面与广博，国内对于亚裔的其他族裔作家的作品关注太少。即使是那些亚裔文学的经典之作，如菲律宾裔作家卡罗斯·布鲁桑（Carlos Bulosan）的《美国在我心中》（*America Is in the Heart*，1946），日裔女作家山本久惠（Hisaye Yamamoto）的《第十七个音节及其他故事》（*Seventeen Syllables and Other Stories*，1949）、日裔约翰·冈田（John Okada）的《不–不仔》（*NO-NO Boy*，1959），以及如今在美国文学界如日中天的青年印度裔作家裘帕·拉希莉（Jhumpa Lahiri）的作品，专题研究均十分少见。即便是像华裔作家任璧莲（Gish Jen）这样已经受到学者很大关注和研究的作家，其长篇小说之外体裁的作品同样没有得到足够的重视，更遑论国内学术界对亚裔文学在诗歌、戏剧方面的研究了。换句话说，我国学术界对于整个“美国亚裔文学”的研究来说还很匮乏，属于亟待开发的领域。实际上，在我看来，不研究“美国亚裔文学”，也无法真正理解“美国华裔文学”。

第三，在中国“一带一路”倡议与中国文化走出去的今天，作为美国文学研究的新型增长点，大力开展“美国亚裔文学”研究，特别是研究中国的亚洲周边国家如韩国、日本、印度等国在美国移民状况的文学表现，以及与华裔在美国的文学再现，使之与美国和世界其他国家的“美国亚裔文学”保持同步发展，具有较大的理论意义与学术价值。

三、“美国亚裔文学”及其研究：历史与现状

历史上看，来自亚洲国家的移民进入美国，可以追溯到 18 世纪。但真正开始较大规模的移民则是到了 19 世纪中后期。然而，亚裔从进入美国一开始，就遭遇到来自美国社会与官方的阻力与法律限制。从 1880 年代到 1940 年代这半个多世纪的岁月中，为了保护美国本土而出台的一系列移民法，都将亚洲各国人民排除在外，禁止他们当中的大部分人进入美国大陆地区。直到 20 世纪 40 至 60 年代移民法有所改革时，这种状况才有所改观。其中的改革措施之一就是取消了

国家配额。如此一来，亚洲移民人数才开始大规模上升。2010年的美国国家统计局分析显示，亚裔是美国社会移民人数增长最快的少数族裔。[5]

"美国亚裔"实际是个新兴词汇。这个词汇的创立与诞生实际上已经到了1960年代后期。在此之前，亚洲人或者具有亚洲血统者通常被称为"Oriental"（东方人）、"Asiatic"（亚洲人）和"Mongoloid"（蒙古人、黄种人）。[6]美国历史学家市冈裕次（Yuji Ichioka）在1960年代末期，开创性地开始使用Asian American这个术语，[7]从此，这一词汇开始被人普遍接受和广泛使用。

与此时间同步，"美国亚裔文学"在随后的1970年代作为一个文学类别开始出现并逐步产生影响。1974年，有两部著作几乎同时出版，都以美国亚裔命名。一部是《美国亚裔传统：散文与诗歌选集》，[8]另外一部则是前面提到过的《哎咿！美国亚裔作家选集》。[9]这两部著作，将过去长期被人遗忘的亚裔文学带到了聚光灯下，让人们仿佛看到了一种新的文学形式。其后，新的亚裔作家不断涌现，文学作品层出不穷。

最初亚裔文学的主要主题与主要内容为种族（race）、身份（identity）、亚洲文化传统、亚洲与美国或者西方国家之间的文化冲突，当然也少不了性别（sexuality）、社会性别（gender）、性别歧视、社会歧视等。后来，随着移民作家的大规模出现，离散文学的兴起，亚裔文学也开始关注移民、语言、家国、想象、全球化、劳工、战争、帝国主义、殖民主义等问题。

如果说，上述1974年的两部著作代表着亚裔文学进入美国文学的世界版图之中，那么，1982年著名美国亚裔研究专家金惠经（Elaine Kim）的《美国亚裔文学的创作及其社会语境》[10]的出版，作为第一部学术著作，则代表着美国亚裔文学研究正式登上美国学术界的舞台。自此以后，不仅亚裔文学创作兴盛起来，而且亚裔文学研究也逐渐成为热点，成果不断推陈出新。

同时，人们对于如何界定"美国亚裔文学"等众多问题进行了深入的探讨，

5 参见：Wikipedia 依据"U.S. Census Show Asians Are Fastest Growing Racial Group" (NPR.org) 所得出的数据统计。https://en.wikipedia.org/wiki/Asian_Americans。

6 Mio, Jeffrey Scott, ed. 1999. *Key Words in Multicultural Interventions: A Dictionary*. ABC-Clio ebook. Greenwood Publishing Group, p. 20.

7 K. Connie Kang, "Yuji Ichioka, 66; Led Way in Studying Lives of Asian Americans," *Los Angeles Times*, September 7, 2002. Reproduced at ucla.edu by the Asian American Studies Center.

8 Wand, David Hsin-fu, ed. 1974. *Asian American Heritage: An Anthology of Prose and Poetry*. New York: Pocket Books.

9 Chin, Frank, Chan, Jeffery, Paul, Inada, Lawson Fusao, et al. 1974. *Aiiieeeee! An Anthology of Asian-American Writers*. Howard University Press.

10 Kim, Elaine. 1982. *Asian American Literature: An Introduction to the Writings and Their Social Context*. Philadelphia: Temple University Press.

进一步推动了这一学科向前发展。相关问题包括：究竟谁可以说自己是美国亚裔（an Asian America）？这里的 America 是不是就是单指“美国”（the United States）？是否可以包括“美洲”（Americas）？如果亚裔作家所写的内容与亚裔无关，能否算是“亚裔文学”？如果不是亚裔作家，但所写内容与亚裔有关，能否算在“亚裔文学”之内？

总体上看，早期的亚裔文学研究专注于美国身份的建构，即界定亚裔文学的范畴，以及争取其在美国文化与美国文学中应得的席位，是 20 世纪七八十年代亚裔民权运动的前沿阵地。早期学者如赵健秀、徐忠雄（Shawn Wong）等为领军人物。随后出现的金惠经、张敬珏（King-Kok Cheung）、骆里山（Lisa Lowe）等人均成为了亚裔文学研究领域的权威学者，他 / 她们的著作影响并造就了第二代美国亚裔文学研究者。20 世纪 90 年代之后的亚裔文学研究逐渐淡化了早期研究中对于意识形态的侧重，开始向传统的学科分支、研究方法以及研究理论靠拢，研究视角多集中在学术马克思主义（academic Marxism）、后结构主义、后殖民、女权主义以及心理分析等。

进入 21 世纪以来，“美国亚裔文学”研究开始向多元化、全球化与跨学科方向发展。随着亚裔文学作品爆炸式的增长，来自阿富汗、印度、巴基斯坦、越南等族裔作家的作品开始受到关注，极大丰富与拓展了亚裔文学研究的领域。当代“美国亚裔文学”研究的视角与方法也不断创新，战争研究、帝国研究、跨国研究、视觉文化理论、空间理论、身体研究、环境理论等层出不穷。新的理论与常规性研究交叉进行，不但开创了新的研究领域，对于经典问题（例如身份建构）的研究也提供了新的解读方式与方法。

四、作为课题的“美国亚裔文学”研究及其丛书

“美国亚裔文学”研究，是由我担任课题负责人的 2017 年度中国人民大学科学研究基金重大规划项目。“美国亚裔文学研究丛书”，即是该项课题的结题成果。作为“美国亚裔文学”方面的系列丛书，将由文学史、文学作品选、文学评论集、学术论著等组成，由我担任该丛书的总主编。

“美国亚裔文学”研究在 2017 年 4 月立项。随后，该丛书的论证计划，得到了国内外专家的一致认可。2017 年 5 月 27 日，中国人民大学科学研究基金重大规划项目“美国亚裔文学研究”开题报告会暨“美国亚裔文学研究高端论坛”在中国人民大学隆重召开。参加此次会议的专家学者全部为美国亚裔文学研究领域中的顶尖学者，包括美国加州大学洛杉矶分校的张敬珏教授、南京大学海外教育学院前院长程爱民教授、南京大学海外教育学院院长赵文书教授、北京语言大学

应用外语学院院长陆薇教授、北京外国语大学潘志明教授、解放军外国语学院石平萍教授等。在此次会议上，我向与会专家介绍了该项目的基本情况、未来研究方向与预计出版成果。与会专家对该项目的设立给予高度评价，强调在当今时代加强“美国亚裔文学”研究的必要性，针对该项目的预计研究及其成果，也提出了一些很好的建议。

根据最初的计划，这套丛书将包括文学史 2 部:《美国亚裔文学史》和《美国华裔文学史》；文学选集 2 部:《美国亚裔文学作品选》和《美国华裔文学作品选》；批评文选 2 部:《美国亚裔文学评论集》和《美国华裔文学评论集》；访谈录 1 部:《美国亚裔作家访谈录》；学术论著 3 部，包括美国学者张敬珏教授的《静默留声》和《文心无界》。总计 10 部著作。

根据我的基本设想，《美国亚裔文学史》和《美国华裔文学史》的撰写，将力图体现研究者对美国亚裔文学的研究进入了较为深入的阶段。由于文学史是建立在研究者对该研究领域发展变化的总体认识上，涉及文学流派、创作方式、文学与社会变化的关系、作家间的关联等各方面的问题，我们试图通过对亚裔文学发展进行总结和评价，旨在为当前亚裔文学和华裔文学的研究和推广做出一定贡献。

《美国亚裔文学作品选》和《美国华裔文学作品选》，除了记录、介绍等基本功能，还将在一定程度上发挥形成民族认同、促进意识形态整合等功能。作品选编是民族共同体想象性构建的重要途径，也是作为文学经典得以确立和修正的最基本方式之一。因此，这样的作品选编，也要对美国亚裔文学的研究起到重要的促进作用。

《美国亚裔文学评论集》和《美国华裔文学评论集》，将主要选编美国、中国以及世界上最有学术价值的学术论文，虽然有些可能因为版权问题而不得不舍弃，但我们努力使之成为中国学术界研究“美国亚裔文学”和“美国华裔文学”的重要参考书目。

《美国亚裔作家访谈录》、美国学者的著作汉译、中国学者的美国亚裔文学学术专著等，将力图促使中美两国学者之间的学术对话，特别是希望中国的“美国亚裔文学”研究，既在中国的美国文学研究界，也要在美国和世界上的美国文学研究界发出中国学者的声音。“一带一路”倡议的实施，使得文学研究的关注发生了转变，从过分关注西方话语，到逐步转向关注中国（亚洲）话语，我们的美国亚裔（华裔）文学研究，正是从全球化视角切入，思考美国亚裔（华裔）文学的世界性。

2018 年，我们按照原计划出版了《美国亚裔文学作品选》《美国华裔文学作品选》《美国亚裔文学评论集》《美国华裔文学评论集》。2022 年上半年，我们出版了学术专著《文心无界——不拘性别、文类与形式的华美文学》。2022 年下半年，还将出版《美国日裔文学作品选》《美国韩裔文学作品选》《美国越南裔文学作品选》《美国西亚裔文学作品选》《美国南亚裔文学作品选》等 5 部文学选集。

需要说明的是，这 5 部选集是在原有计划之外的产物。之所以在《美国亚裔文学作品选》之外又专门将其中最主要的国家与区域的文学作品结集出版，是因为在研究过程中我发现，现有的《美国亚裔文学作品选》已经无法涵盖丰富多彩的亚裔文学。更重要的是，无论在国内还是在美国，像这样将美国亚裔按照国别与区域划分后的文学作品选全部是空白，国内外学术界对这些国别与区域的文学创作的整体关注也较少，可以说它们都属于亟待开垦的新研究领域。通过这 5 部选集，可以让国内对于美国亚裔文学有更为完整的了解。我也希望借此填补国内外在这个领域的空白。

等到丛书全部完成出版，将会成为一套由 15 部著作所组成的系列丛书。2018 年的时候，我曾经把这套丛书界定为“国内第一套较为完整的美国亚裔文学方面的系列丛书”。现在，时隔 4 年之后，特别是在有了这新出版的 5 部选集之后，我可以说这套丛书将是“国内外第一套最为完整的美国亚裔文学方面的系列丛书”。

那么，我们为什么要对“美国亚裔文学”进行深入研究，并要编辑、撰写和翻译这套丛书呢？

首先，虽然“美国亚裔文学”在国外已有较大的影响，学术界也对此具有相当规模的研究，但在国内学术界，出于对“美国华裔文学”的偏爱与关注，“美国亚裔文学”相对还是一个较为陌生的领域。因此，本课题首次以“亚裔”集体的形式标示亚裔文学的存在，旨在介绍“美国亚裔文学”，推介具有族裔特色和代表性的作家作品。

其次，选择“美国亚裔文学”为研究对象，其中也有对“美国华裔文学”的研究，希望能够体现我们对全球化视野中华裔文学的关注，也体现试图融合亚裔、深入亚裔文学研究的学术自觉。同时，在多元化多种族的美国社会语境中，我们力主打破国内长久以来专注“美国华裔文学”研究的固有模式，转而关注包括华裔作家在内的亚裔作家所具有的世界性眼光。

最后，顺应美国亚裔文学发展的趋势，对美国亚裔文学的研究不仅是文学研究界的关注热点，还是我国外语与文学教育的关注焦点。我们希望为高校未来“美国亚裔文学”的课程教学，提供一套高水平的参考丛书。

五、“美国亚裔文学”及其研究的未来

如前所述，“美国亚裔文学”在20世纪70年代逐渐崛起后，使得亚裔文学从沉默走向了发声。到21世纪，亚裔文学呈现出多元化的发展特征，更重要的是，许多新生代作家开始崭露头角。单就这些新的亚裔作家群体，就有许多值得我们关注的话题。

2018年6月23日，“2018美国亚裔文学高端论坛——跨界：21世纪的美国亚裔文学”在中国人民大学隆重召开。参加会议的专家学者将近150人。

在此次会议上，我提出来：今天，为什么要研究美国亚裔文学？我们要研究什么？

正如我们在会议通知上所说，美国亚裔文学在一百多年的风雨沧桑中历经“沉默”“觉醒”，走向“发声”，见证了美国亚裔族群的沉浮兴衰。21世纪以来，美国亚裔文学在全球冷战思维升温和战火硝烟不断的时空背景下，不囿于狭隘的种族主义藩篱，以“众声合奏”与“兼容并蓄”之势构筑出一道跨洋、跨国、跨种族、跨语言、跨文化、跨媒介、跨学科的文学景观，呈现出鲜明的世界主义意识。为此，我们拟定了一些主要议题。包括：1. 美国亚裔文学中的跨洋书写；2. 美国亚裔文学中的跨国书写；3. 美国亚裔文学中的跨种族书写；4. 美国亚裔文学中的跨语言书写；5. 美国亚裔文学中的跨文化书写；6. 美国亚裔文学的翻译跨界研究；7. 美国亚裔文学的跨媒介研究；8. 美国亚裔文学的跨学科研究等。

2019年6月22日，“2019美国亚裔文学高端论坛”在中国人民大学举行，会议的主题是“战争与和平：美国亚裔文学研究中的生命书写”。那次会议，依旧有来自中国的近80所高校的150余位教师和硕博研究生参加我们的论坛。

2020年年初，全球疫情大暴发，我们的“2020美国亚裔文学高端论坛”一直往后推迟，直到2020年12月5日在延边大学举行，会议的主题是“疫情之思：变局中的美国亚裔文学”。因为疫情原因，我们劝阻了很多愿意来参会的学者，但即便如此，也有近百位来自各地的专家学者与研究生前来参会。

2021年6月26—27日，“相遇与融合：2021首届华文/华裔文学研讨会”在西北师范大学举行。这次会议是由我在延边大学的会议上提出倡议，得到了中国社会科学院文学所赵稀方教授的积极响应，由他和我一起联合发起并主办，由西北师范大学外国语学院承办。我们知道，长期以来，华裔文学和华文文学分属不同的学科和研究领域，其研究对象、传统和范式都有所不同，但血脉相承的天然联系终究会让两者相遇、走向融合。从时下的研究看，虽然两者的研究范式自成体系、独树一帜，但都面临着华裔作家用中文创作和华人作家用外文创作的新趋势，这给双方的学科发展与研究领域都带来了新的挑战，也带来了新的学科发

展机遇。我们都相信，在学科交叉融合已成为实现创新发展必然趋势的当下语境中，华裔 / 华文文学走到了相遇与融合的最佳时机。为此，我们倡议并搭建平台，希望两个领域的学者同台进行学术交流与对话，探讨文学研究的新发展，以求实现华裔文学和华文文学的跨界融通。

事实上，21 世纪以来，亚裔群体、亚裔所面临的问题、亚裔研究都发生了巨大的变化。从过去较为单纯的亚裔走向了跨越太平洋（transpacific）；从过去的彰显美国身份（claiming America）到今天的批评美国身份（critiquing America）；过去单一的 America，现在变成了复数的 Americas，这些变化都值得引起我们的高度重视。由此所引发的诸多问题，也需要我们去认真对待。比如：如何在“21 世纪”这个特殊的时间区间内去理解“美国亚裔文学”这一概念？有关“美国亚裔文学”的概念构建，是否本身就存在着作家的身份焦虑与书写的界限划分？如何把握“美国亚裔文学”的整体性与区域性？“亚裔”身份是否是作家在表达过程中去主动拥抱的归属之地？等等。

2021 年年底，国家社会科学基金重大招标课题揭晓，我申请的“美国族裔文学中的文化共同体思想研究”喜获中标。这将进一步推动我目前所从事的美国亚裔文学研究，并在未来由现在的美国亚裔文学研究走向美国的整个族裔文学研究。

展望未来，“美国亚裔文学”呈现出更加生机勃勃的生命力，“美国亚裔文学”的研究也将迎来更加光明的前途。

2018 年 8 月 28 日定稿于哈佛大学
2022 年 8 月 28 日修改于北京

前 言

“美国亚裔文学”研究，是由中国人民大学“杰出学者”特聘教授郭英剑先生担任课题负责人的 2017 年度中国人民大学科学研究基金重大规划项目。“美国亚裔文学研究丛书”，是该项课题的结题成果。由郭英剑教授担任该套丛书的总主编。这是国内第一套最为完整的“美国亚裔文学”方面的系列丛书，由文学史、文学作品选、文学评论集、学术论著等所组成。

所谓“美国西亚裔文学”，是指具有西亚各国血统的美国人（即西亚裔）用英语创作的文学作品。这里的西亚裔不仅指在美国出生的有西亚裔血统的移民，也包括在美国本土以外出生后来到美国的移民作家（包括成年之后的移民者），如雷哈尼、纪伯伦、阿扎尔 · 纳菲西等。“美国西亚裔文学”的题材不仅局限于反映西亚裔在美国的经历，也可以是关于西亚地区乃至世界的故事。

“美国西亚裔文学”无疑是“美国亚裔文学”版图中不可或缺的一部分，它在一百多年的发展历程中不断壮大。“美国西亚裔文学”最初主要反映西亚移民族群的形成和发展历史，随着西亚地区国际局势的发展变化和西亚裔移民大量涌入美国，美国西亚裔文学开始蓬勃发展。现在，“美国西亚裔文学”已经成为观察美国社会历史与现实的平台之一，有助于人们了解这个国家在短短历史中所发生的许多重大变化，以及西亚裔移民在美国的生活经历和文化思想，同时作为观照，也可促使我们进行自我文化反思。

美国西亚裔的移民史可以追溯到 19、20 世纪之交。这一时期的移民主要来自被称为大叙利亚或黎巴嫩山的地区，代表性作家包括 19 世纪后期的阿米恩 · 雷哈尼和卡里 · 纪伯伦。雷哈尼被认为是美国阿拉伯裔文学的奠基人，他 1911 年出版的《哈立德之书》奠定了美国阿拉伯裔叙事文学的传记性传统。

20 世纪 60 年代以后，随着民权运动、女权运动等多元文化思潮的风起云涌，“美国西亚裔文学”得到了长足的发展，尤其是 20 世纪 80 年代以来，“美国西亚裔文学”的影响力日趋显著，代表作家有埃特尔 · 阿德南、娜奥米 · 希哈布 · 奈等。

虽然“美国西亚裔文学”属于“美国亚裔文学”的一部分，但是由于历史的原因，“西亚”总是被西方人常用的具有强烈地缘政治色彩的“中东地区”这一概念所取代。一直以来，“美国亚裔文学”主要指生活在美国的华裔、日裔、韩裔、菲律宾裔、越南裔等主要群体创作的文学作品，其他族裔的文学创作情况，尤其是西亚裔美国人的文学创作，并未被纳入亚裔文学的范畴之中。然而，鉴于越来越多的西亚裔作家涌上文坛及其愈加显著的影响力，我们认为还是应该将“西亚裔文学”单独列出来，并且作为亚裔群体的组成部分，编写这部《美国西亚裔文学作品选》，便于人们领略更多美国西亚裔作家的风采。

《美国西亚裔文学作品选》以历史为发展脉络，精选了 35 位美国西亚裔作家的作品，并以作家的出生年代为顺序进行编目排列。作品选力图反映美国西亚裔文学一百多年间的发展历程和变化，深刻反映抗争、身份认同与文化冲突所构成的西亚裔文学传统的重要议题。作品选努力求新，体现更大的兼容性。作家群体涵盖老中青三代，既对已经获得普遍认可的老一代作家的经典之作给予重点选介，也对影响力与日俱增的新生代作家群体给予关注，特别收录了一些 80 后、90 后作家的作品，以彰显美国西亚裔文学最近几十年的发展与繁荣，同时也表明美国西亚裔文学创作后继有人，潜力无穷。

《美国西亚裔文学作品选》所选作品虽然仍以长篇小说、短篇小说、诗歌、戏剧几大体裁为主，但在具体作品选取方面，我们也将科幻小说、奇幻文学、儿童文学、复合型体裁等类型的作品收纳其中，以反映美国西亚裔文学发展的整体概貌。

遗憾的是，由于篇幅所限，《美国西亚裔文学作品选》中的部分作品只是节选片段，而且因为各种历史与现实的原因，一些作家的作品仍未能囊括其中。但通过这些选文展现出的冰山一角，大家可以按图索骥继续挖掘，进而探寻西亚裔文学的广袤空间。

无论如何，我们都希望《美国西亚裔文学作品选》能够成为中国学术界研究“美国亚裔文学”特别是“美国西亚裔文学”的重要的参考书目。

编者

2022 年 8 月 28 日

目 录

1

(Ameen Rihani, 1876—1940)
阿米恩·雷哈尼

作者简介

阿米恩·雷哈尼（Ameen Rihani, 1876—1940），生于黎巴嫩弗莱克（Freike, 当时是奥斯曼帝国的一部分），美国黎巴嫩裔作家、知识分子和政治活动家，他也是北美阿拉伯移民发展起来的马哈尔文学（Adab Al-Mahjar，即阿拉伯旅美派文学）运动的主要人物，这个文学流派在文化和特征上是阿拉伯的，在语言上是英语的，在精神和平台上是美国的。他是第一个用英语写散文、诗歌、小说、短篇故事、艺术评论和游记的阿拉伯人，被认为是美国阿拉伯裔文学的奠基人。

雷哈尼一生出版了 30 部阿拉伯语作品和 35 部英文作品。受惠特曼的影响，雷哈尼将自由诗引入阿拉伯诗歌，这使得自由诗在 20 世纪的其他阿拉伯诗人中流行开来。雷哈尼的三本英文诗集在其去世后出版：《我生命的波澜和其他诗歌》（*Waves of My Life and Other Poems*，写于 1897 至 1937 年，2009 年出版）、《神秘圣歌和其他》（*Chant of Mystics and Other Poems*，写于 1904 至 1921 年，1970 年出版）以及《桃金娘和没药》（*Myrtle and Myrrh*, 写于 1905 年，2005 年出版）。《桃金娘和没药》是一本押韵诗集，这部开创性的作品为美国阿拉伯裔文学中的英语诗歌铺平了道路。雷哈尼的其他作品包括 1947 年首次以阿拉伯语出版的《黎巴嫩之心》（*The Heart of Lebanon*），这是对雷哈尼穿越祖国旅行的记述，于 2021 年被译成英文出版；他在 1911 年出版的第一部美国阿拉伯裔小说作品《哈立德之书》（*The Book of Khalid*），奠定了美国阿拉伯裔叙事文学的传记性传统。它将现实与虚构、东方与西方、唯灵论与唯物主义、阿拉伯人和美国人、哲学与文学结合在一起，形成一种独特的语言风格，其中阿拉伯隐喻和英语语言结构结合在一起，试图创造一条两种语言都可以触及的抽象线条。

本部分内容节选自雷哈尼的第一部英文小说《哈立德之书》第一章。小说主人公哈立德出身于巴勒贝克，从黎巴嫩雪松林地出发，一路移民到纽约，面临着东方软弱背景和西方严酷现实的矛盾。他憧憬着虚拟的大城市，想象着理想的帝国，并寻找一个将东方的精神、欧洲的艺术和美国的科学结合在一起的超人。

作品选读

The Book of Khalid

(CHAPTER I PROBING THE TRIVIAL)

By Ameen Rihani

The most important in the history of nations and individuals was once the most trivial, and vice versa. The plebeian, who is called to-day the man-in-the-street, can never see and understand the significance of the hidden seed of things, which in time must develop or die. A garter dropt in the ballroom of Royalty gives birth to an Order of Knighthood; a movement to reform the spelling of the English language, initiated by one of the presidents of a great Republic, becomes eventually an object of ridicule. Only two instances to illustrate our point, which is applicable also to time-honoured truths and moralities. But no matter how important or trivial these, he who would give utterance to them must do so in cap and bells, if he would be heard nowadays. Indeed, the play is always the thing; the frivolous is the most essential, if only as a disguise. —For look you, are we not too prosperous to consider seriously your ponderous preachment? And when you bring it to us in book form, do you expect us to take it into our homes and take you into our hearts to boot? —Which argument is convincing even to the man in the barn.

But the Author of the Khedivial Library Manuscript can make his Genius dance the dance of the seven veils, if you but knew. It is to be regretted, however, that he has not mastered the most subtle of arts, the art of writing about one's self. He seldom brushes his wings against the dust or lingers among the humble flowers close to the dust: he does not follow the masters in their entertaining trivialities and fatuities. We remember that even Gibbon interrupts the turgid flow of his spirit to tell us in his

Autobiography that he really could, and often did, enjoy a game of cards in the evening. And Rousseau, in a suppurative passion, whispers to us in his Confessions that he even kissed the linen of Madame de Warens' bed when he was alone in her room. And Spencer devotes whole pages in his dull and ponderous history of himself to narrate the all-important narration of his constant indisposition, —to assure us that his ill health more than once threatened the mighty task he had in hand. These, to be sure, are most important revelations. But Khalid here misses his cue. Inspiration does not seem to come to him in firefly-fashion.

He would have done well, indeed, had he studied the method of the professional writers of Memoirs, especially those of France. For might he not then have discoursed delectably on The Romance of my Stick Pin, The Tragedy of my Sombrero, The Scandal of my Red Flannel, The Conquest of my Silk Socks, The Adventures of my Tuxedo, and such like? But Khalid is modest only in the things that pertain to the outward self. He wrote of other Romances and other Tragedies. And when his Genius is not dancing the dance of the seven veils, she is either flirting with the monks of the Lebanon hills or setting fire to something in New York. But this is not altogether satisfactory to the present Editor, who, unlike the Author of the Khedivial Library MS., must keep the reader in mind. 'Tis very well to endeavour to unfold a few of the mysteries of one's palingenesis, but why conceal from us his origin? For is it not important, is it not the fashion at least, that one writing his own history should first expatiate on the humble origin of his ancestors and the distant obscure source of his genius? And having done this, should he not then tell us how he behaved in his boyhood; whether or not he made anklets of his mother's dough for his little sister; whether he did not kindle the fire with his father's Korân; whether he did not walk under the rainbow and try to reach the end of it on the hill-top; and whether he did not write verse when he was but five years of age. About these essentialities Khalid is silent. We only know from him that he is a descendant of the brave sea-daring Phœnicians—a title which might be claimed with justice even by the aborigines of Yucatan—and that he was born in the city of Baalbek, in the shadow of the great Heliopolis, a little way from the mountain-road to the Cedars of Lebanon. All else in this direction is obscure.

And the K. L. MS. which we kept under our pillow for thirteen days and nights, was beginning to worry us. After all, might it not be a literary hoax, we thought, and might not this Khalid be a myth. And yet, he does not seem to have sought any material or worldly good from the writing of his Book. Why, then, should he resort to deception? Still, we doubted. And one evening we were detained by the sandomancer, or sand-diviner, who was sitting cross-legged on the sidewalk in front of the mosque. "I know your mind," said he, before we had made up our mind to consult him. And mumbling his "abracadabra" over the sand spread on a cloth before him, he took up his bamboo-stick and wrote therein—Khalid! This was amazing. "And I know more," said he. But after scouring the heaven, he shook his head regretfully and wrote in the sand the name of one of the hasheesh-dens of Cairo. "Go thither; and come to see me again to-morrow evening." Saying which, he folded his sand-book of magic, pocketed his fee, and walked away.

In that hasheesh-den, —the reekiest, dingiest of the row in the Red Quarter, —where the etiolated intellectualities of Cairo flock after midnight, the name of Khalid evokes much resounding wit, and sarcasm, and laughter.

"You mean the new Muhdi," said one, offering us his chobok of hasheesh; "smoke to his health and prosperity. Ha, ha, ha."

And the chorus of laughter, which is part and parcel of a hasheesh jag, was tremendous. Every one thereupon had something to say on the subject. The contagion could not be checked. And Khalid was called "the dervish of science" by one; "the rope-dancer of nature" by another.

"Our Prophet lived in a cave in the wilderness of New York for five years," remarked a third.

"And he sold his camel yesterday and bought a bicycle instead."

"The Young Turks can not catch him now."

"Ah, but wait till England gets after our new Muhdi."

"Wait till his new phthisic-stricken wife dies."

"Whom will our Prophet marry, if among all the virgins of Egypt we can not find a consumptive for him?"

"And when he pulls down the pyramids to build American Skyscrapers with their stones, where shall we bury then our Muhdi?"

All of which, although mystifying to us, and depressing, was none the less reassuring. For Khalid, it seems, is not a myth. No; we can even see him, we are told, and touch him, and hear him speak.

"Shakib the poet, his most intimate friend and disciple, will bring you into the sacred presence."

"You can not miss him, for he is the drummer of our new Muhdi, ha, ha, ha!"

And this Shakib was then suspended and stoned. But their humour, like the odor and smoke of gunjah, (hasheesh) was becoming stifling. So, we lay our chobok down; and, thanking them for the entertainment, we struggle through the rolling reek and fling to the open air.

2

(Kahlil Gibran, 1883—1931)
卡里·纪伯伦

作者简介

卡里·纪伯伦 (Kahlil Gibran, 1883—1931)，美国黎巴嫩裔诗人、画家，他出身于马龙派天主教家庭，幼年未受正规学校教育。1885 年，纪伯伦与他的母亲和兄弟姐妹移居美国，在马萨诸塞州波士顿的一个庞大的叙利亚和黎巴嫩社区定居下来。纪伯伦在美国上学时显露出艺术天赋，后兴趣转向文学。他初期用阿拉伯语，后改用英语进行写作。

1911 年，纪伯伦定居美国纽约，并于 1918 年出版了他的第一本英文书——诗歌寓言集《疯子》(*The Madman*，1918)。此后，纪伯伦于 1923 年在美国首次出版他最著名的作品《先知》(*The Prophet*，1923)，该书成为有史以来最畅销的书籍之一，已被翻译成 100 多种语言。现在已经卖出了 1000 多万册，使纪伯伦成为世界上最畅销的诗人之一。纪伯伦的主要作品还包括《泪与笑》(*A Tear and a Smile*，1914)、《沙与沫》(*Sand and Foam*，1923) 等。

纪伯伦活跃于纽约的美国阿拉伯裔文学团体“笔会”(Pen League)，该团体的成员提倡用阿拉伯语和英语写作。在他的一生中，他出版了 9 本阿拉伯文和 8 本英文书，这些书对爱、渴望和死亡进行了反思，并探讨了宗教主题。纪伯伦是阿拉伯文学的主要奠基人之一，也是 20 世纪阿拉伯新文学道路的开拓者之一，被称为黎巴嫩文坛骄子、艺术天才。纪伯伦和鲁迅以及拉宾德拉纳特·泰戈尔一样是近代东方文学走向世界的先驱。他的文学作品受到尼采思想的影响，蕴含了丰富的社会性和东方精神，不以情节为重，旨在抒发丰富的情感。

在《先知》这部包含 26 篇散文诗歌的寓言书里，涵盖了爱情、婚姻、孩子、给予、吃喝、工作、喜怒哀乐、房屋、衣服、买卖、罪与罚、法律、自由、理性与激情、痛苦、自我知识、教导、友谊、谈话、时间、善恶、祈祷、快乐、美丽、宗教和死亡等主题。

本书选取了《先知》中的部分诗篇，分别代表了纪伯伦借先知之口表达的对于爱情和美的看法。

作品选读

The Prophet

(On Love)

By Kahlil Gibran

Then said Almitra, speak to us of ***Love***.

And he raised his head and looked upon the people, and there fell a stillness upon them. And with a great voice he said:

When love beckons to you, follow him,

Though his ways are hard and steep.

And when his wings enfold you yield to him,

Though the sword hidden among his pinions may wound you.

And when he speaks to you believe in him,

Though his voice may shatter your dreams as the north wind lays waste the garden.

For even as love crowns you so shall he crucify you. Even as he is for your growth so is he for your pruning.

Even as he ascends to your height and caresses your tenderest branches that quiver in the sun,

So shall he descend to your roots and shake them in their clinging to the earth.

Like sheaves of corn he gathers you unto himself.

He threshes you to make you naked.

He sifts you to free you from your husks.

He grinds you to whiteness.

He kneads you until you are pliant;

And then he assigns you to his sacred fire, that you may become sacred bread for …'s sacred feast.

All these things shall love do unto you that you may know the secrets of your heart, and in that knowledge become a fragment of Life's heart.

But if in your fear you would seek only love's peace and love's pleasure,

Then it is better for you that you cover your nakedness and pass out of love's threshing-floor,

Into the seasonless world where you shall laugh, but not all of your laughter, and weep, but not all of your tears.

Love gives naught but itself and takes naught but from itself.

Love possesses not nor would it be possessed;

For love is sufficient unto love.

When you love you should not say, "… is in my heart," but rather, "I am in the heart of …."

And think not you can direct the course of love, for love, if it finds you worthy, directs your course.

Love has no other desire but to fulfil itself.

But if you love and must needs have desires, let these be your desires:

To melt and be like a running brook that sings its melody to the night. To know the pain of too much tenderness.

To be wounded by your own understanding of love;

And to bleed willingly and joyfully.

To wake at dawn with a winged heart and give thanks for another day of loving;

To rest at the noon hour and meditate love's ecstacy;

To return home at eventide with gratitude;

And then to sleep with a prayer for the beloved in your heart and a song of praise upon your lips.

The Prophet

(On Beauty)

By Kahlil Gibran

And a poet said, Speak to us of ***Beauty.***

And he answered:

Where shall you seek beauty, and how shall you find her unless she herself be your way and your guide?

And how shall you speak of her except she be the weaver of your speech?

The aggrieved and the injured say, "Beauty is kind and gentle.

Like a young mother half-shy of her own glory she walks among us."

And the passionate say, "Nay, beauty is a thing of might and dread.

Like the tempest she shakes the earth beneath us and the sky above us."

The tired and the weary say, "Beauty is of soft whisperings. She speaks in our spirit. Her voice yields to our silences like a faint light that quivers in fear of the shadow."

But the restless say, "We have heard her shouting among the mountains,

And with her cries came the sound of hoofs, and the beating of wings and the roaring of lions."

At night the watchmen of the city say, "Beauty shall rise with the dawn from the east."

And at noontide the toilers and the wayfarers say, "We have seen her leaning over the earth from the windows of the sunset."

In winter say the snow-bound, "She shall come with the spring leaping upon the hills."

And in the summer heat the reapers say, "We have seen her dancing with the autumn leaves, and we saw a drift of snow in her hair." All these things have you said of beauty,

Yet in truth you spoke not of her but of needs unsatisfied,

And beauty is not a need but an ecstasy.

It is not a mouth thirsting nor an empty hand stretched forth,

But rather a heart enflamed and a soul enchanted.

It is not the image you would see nor the song you would hear,

But rather an image you see though you close your eyes and a song you hear though you shut your ears.

It is not the sap within the furrowed bark, nor a wing attached to a claw,

But rather a garden for ever in bloom and a flock of angels for ever in flight.

People of Orphalese, beauty is life when life unveils her holy face.

But you are life and you are the veil. Beauty is eternity gazing at itself in a mirror.

But you are eternity and you are the mirror.

3

(Etel Adnan, 1925—2021)

埃特尔·阿德南

作者简介

埃特尔·阿德南（Etel Adnan，1925—2021），美国黎巴嫩裔诗人、散文家和画家，出生于贝鲁特（Beirut）。她曾就读于贝鲁斯高等文学学院（Ecole Supérieure de Lettres de Beyrouth），在那里她创作了她的第一首诗。阿德南还曾在巴黎大学（Sorbonne）、加州大学伯克利分校（UC Berkley）和哈佛大学（Harvard University）学习哲学。

黎巴嫩内战开始后，阿德南移居巴黎，在那里她写出了首部法语小说《西特·玛丽·罗斯》（*Sitt Marie Rose*，1977），获得了法国–阿拉伯友谊大奖（the France-Pays Arabes Award）。这部小说是阿德南最为著名的作品，集中体现了她政治批评、女性主义和文学实验相结合的创作特点，并被翻译成多种语言，为作者带来了世界声誉。1979 年，阿德南回到美国加利福尼亚。

阿德南的大部分诗歌作品用英语写就。受法国诗人兰波（Rimbaud）、美国女诗人琳·海基尼安（Lyn Hejinian）和黎巴嫩作家贾拉勒·陶菲克（Jalal Toufic）的影响，阿德南的诗歌融合了超现实主义意象和强大的隐喻跳跃，以及基于语言和形式的实验，使用意想不到的实验技巧来洞察流亡、政治、社会和性别不公正的本质。她的许多诗集包括《转移沉默》（*Shifting the Silence*，2020）、格里芬诗歌奖获奖作品《时间》（*Time*，2019）、《奔涌》（*Surge*，2018）、《夜晚》（*Night*，2016）、《四季》（*Seasons*，2008）、《那里：在自我与他人的光明与黑暗中》（*There: In the Light and the Darkness of the Self and the Other*，1997）、《春天的花朵和航行的表现》（*The Spring Flowers Own and the Manifestations of the Voyage*，1990）、《印第安人从来没有马》(*The Indian Never Had a Horse*, 1985)和《登月》(*Moonshots*, 1966)。

阿德南一生曾获有多项文学大奖，除了法语小说《西特·玛丽·罗斯》获得法国–阿拉伯友谊大奖之外，2020 年，阿德南凭借其英语故事集《日蚀大师》(*Master of the Eclipse*, 2009)获得年度美国阿拉伯裔图书奖(The Arab American Book Award); 2013 年，她的诗集《海与雾》(*Sea and Fog, Nightboat Books*, 2012)获得美国加州诗歌图书奖(The California Book Award for Poetry)。她还获得了美国阿拉伯裔作家终身成就奖(RAWI Lifetime Achievement Award from the Radius of Arab-American Writers)。2003 年，阿德南被学术期刊《美国多民族文学》(*MELUS*)评为“当今最著名、最有成就的阿拉伯裔作家”。

除了文学作品外，阿德南还在各种媒体上创作了视觉作品，如油画、电影和挂毯，这些作品已在世界各地的画廊展出。

本书节选诗歌《我死后的早晨》(*The Morning After My Death*)和《我童年的未竟事业》(*This Unfinished Business of My Childhood*)均选自诗集《春天的花朵和航行的表现》。这两首诗充分体现了阿德南所主张的诗歌和哲学之间的连续性，她不回避自我审视，其诗歌感觉像是一种大声思考，她在这两首诗中热切地接受并表述抽象概念，如爱、死亡、“别处”、痛苦、精神信仰或思考本身。

作品选读

The Spring Flowers Own and the Manifestations of the Voyage

(The Morning After My Death)

By Etel Adnan

The morning after
my death
we will sit in cafés
but I will not
be there
I will not be
*

There was the great death of birds
the moon was consumed with
fire
the stars were visible
until noon.
Green was the forest drenched
with shadows
the roads were serpentine
A redwood tree stood
alone
with its lean and lit body
unable to follow the
cars that went by with
frenzy
a tree is always an immutable
traveller.
The moon darkened at dawn
the mountain quivered
with anticipation
and the ocean was double-shaded:
the blue of its surface with the
blue of flowers
mingled in horizontal water trails
there was a breeze to
witness the hour
*
The sun darkened at the
fifth hour of the
day
the beach was covered with
conversations
pebbles started to pour into holes
and waves came in like
horses.
*
The moon darkened on Christmas eve
angels ate lemons
in illuminated churches
there was a blue rug

planted with stars
above our heads
lemonade and war news
competed for our attention
our breath was warmer than
the hills.
*
There was a great slaughter of
rocks   of spring leaves
of creeks
the stars showed fully
the last king of the Mountain
gave battle
and got killed.
We lay on the grass
covered dried blood with our
bodies
green blades swayed between
our teeth.
*
We went out to sea
a bank of whales was heading
South
a young man among us a hero
tried to straddle one of the
sea creatures
his body emerged as a muddy pool
as mud
we waved goodbye to his remnants
happy not to have to bury
him in the early hours of the day
We got drunk in a barroom
the small town of Fairfax
had just gone to bed
cherry trees were bending under the
weight of their flowers:
they were involved in a ceremonial
dance to which no one
had ever been invited.

*

I know flowers to be funeral companions
they make poisons and venoms
and eat abandoned stone walls
I know flowers shine stronger
than the sun
their eclipse means the end of
times
but I love flowers for their treachery
their fragile bodies
grace my imagination's avenues
without their presence
my mind would be an unmarked
grave.

*

We met a great storm at sea
looked back at the
rocking cliffs
the sand was going under
black birds were
leaving
the storm ate friends and foes
alike
water turned into salt for
my wounds.

*

Flowers end in frozen patterns
artificial gardens cover
the floors
we get up close to midnight
search with powerful lights
the tiniest shrubs on the
meadows
A stream desperately is running to
the ocean

The Spring Flowers Own and the Manifestations of the Voyage
(This Unfinished Business of My Childhood)

By Etel Adnan

This unfinished business of my
childhood
this emerald lake
from my journey's other
side
haunts hierarchies of heavens

a palm forest
fell overnight
to make room for an unwanted
garden
ever since
fevers and swellings
turn me into a river

the streets were steep
winds were running ahead
of ships ...

There was indeed the death of birds
the moon had passed away.

*

The morning after his death
pursuing him beyond his bitter end
his mother came to
his grave:
she removed his bones out of
their pattern
and ditched them into mud:
women came at night

and claimed Rimbaud their own

that night there was much
thunder   it was awesome

*

Laurels and lilacs
bloom around my head
because I stood up to the sun

You see   the Colorado River runs
between flowered banks
I repeat my journeys to seek the
happiness that overcame
your absence
I was happy not to love you anymore
until the sunset reached
the East
and broke my raft apart
there were other rivers underground
covered with dead flowers
it was cold it was cold yes it was
cold.

*

Under a combination of pain
and machine-gun fire
flowers disappeared
they are in the same
state of non-being
as Emily Dickinson

We the dead have conversation
in our gardens
about our lack of
existence.

*

The gardener is planting
blue and white
flowers
some angel moved in with me
to flee the cold
temperature on earth are
rising
but we wear upon us some
immovable frost
everyone carries his dying as
a growing shadow.

*

I left the morning paper
by the coffee cup
the heat was 85 like the
year
and I went to the window to find
that flowers had bloomed overnight
to replace the bodies
felled in the war

the enemy had come with fire
and ruse
to stamp the names of the dead
in the gardens of Yohmor
It is not because spring
is too beautiful
that we'll not write what
happens in the dark.

*

A butterfly came to die
between two stones
at the foot of the Mountain

the mountain shed shadows
over it
to cover the secret of
death.
*

4

(Samuel John Hazo, 1928—)
塞缪尔·约翰·哈佐

作者简介

塞缪尔·约翰·哈佐（Samuel John Hazo，1928— ）是美国黎巴嫩裔诗人、剧作家、小说家，于1928年出生于宾夕法尼亚州匹兹堡（Pittsburgh, Pennsylvania），父母是难民，母亲是黎巴嫩人，父亲是耶路撒冷的亚述人（Assyrian）。他以优异的成绩在圣母大学（University of Notre Dame）获得文学学士学位，在杜肯大学（Duquesne University）获得文学硕士学位，在匹兹堡大学（University of Pittsburgh）获得博士学位。

哈佐在圣母大学读本科期间开始写诗，他最初的几部作品是在偶然的灵感下或专门为了在文学杂志中得到认可而写就的。直到朝鲜战争时期担任美国海军陆战队上尉时，他才开始回顾自己以前的工作，反思自己的人生——这成了他写作的关键转折点。在那之后，他的作品主题变得更加明显——主要包括哈佐认为与他自己的生活相关的事物：家庭、基督教、战争、苦难、生活的荒谬和死亡的奥秘。

塞缪尔·约翰·哈佐出版的一些主要作品包括《此刻的神圣惊喜》（*The Holy Surprise of Right Now*）、《感谢无聊的天使》（*Thank a Bored Angel*）、《睡前小记》（*Jots Before Sleep*）和《扬帆起航》（*As They Sail*，诗歌）、《剧照》（*Stills*，小说）、《羽毛》（*Feather*）、《短兵相接》（*Mano A Mano*）、《看火，看雨》（*Watching Fire, Watching Rain*，戏剧）、《为……做间谍》（*Spying For ...*，散文）和《留在你心中的匹兹堡》（*The Pittsburgh That Stays Within You*，回忆录）。

他的译作包括丹尼斯·德·鲁盖蒙（Denis de Rougemont）的《深水咆哮》（*The*

Growl of Deeper Waters)、纳迪亚·图埃尼（Nadia Tueni）的《黎巴嫩：二十首诗为一爱》(*Lebanon: Twenty Poems For One Love*）和阿杜尼斯（Adunis）的《白天和黑夜的书页》(*The Pages of Day And Night*)。

哈佐是宾夕法尼亚州匹兹堡国际诗歌论坛（the International Poetry Forum in Pittsburgh, Pennsylvania）的创始人和主任。从1966年到2009年，哈佐博士接待了来自世界各地的800多位杰出的诗人和表演者，将匹兹堡确立为文化和艺术的神经中枢。

哈佐的作品以诗人娜奥米·希哈布·奈(Naomi Shihab Nye)所描述的"巨大的智慧、抒情和人性"来审视家庭和信仰、死亡和爱以及时间的流逝等主题。节选部分为他的诗歌《下一次我们看到巴黎》(*The Next Time We Saw Paris*)、《守夜》(*Vigil*）和《恋人的双眸》(*The Eyes of Lovers*)。

作品选读（一）

The Next Time We Saw Paris

By Samuel John Hazo

THE NEXT TIME WE SAW PARIS
"The next time was the last time"
One morning we saw de Gaulle
himself in uniform chauffeured
alone in an open Peugeot.
He seemed to dare assassination
as he did near Notre Dame
during the Liberation parade.
On house fronts and doors we noticed
small bronze plaques with names
followed by *Victime de Nazis.*
We'd read reports that *Enfants*
des Boches reached 100,000
during the Occupation.
"Horizontal
Collaborators" were shorn bald,

spat upon and marched naked
through the streets.
De Gaulle
pronounced all executed traitors
justly punished.
We focused
on Paris of the postcards: Sacre-
Coeur, the Eiffel Tower,
the Champs-Elysees, the Louvre.
The Folies-Bergere booked sellouts.
The Bateau Mouche was packed.
Lounging by the Seine, a fisherman
propped his rod against
a bench and smoked a Gitanes

as if catching a fish meant
little or nothing at all.

作品选读（二）

Vigil

By Samuel John Hazo

VIGIL
Darkness is illiterate.
You
wait for a word, but there's
nothing;
You wait for a sound
and there's nothing.
Midnight's
a time of its own.
Whatever
it hides is yours to imagine.
You almost hear a voice

you loved above all others.
You'll hear it in your dreams.
But now there's only midnight
and silence.
                    You close your eyes
and keep them closed, and listen.

作品选读（三）

The Eyes of Lovers

By Samuel John Hazo

THE EYES OF LOVERS
They'll look at each other
until whatever prompts them
to keep staring surrenders.
They'll learn that all they ever
hope to see stays near
as here but hiding.
                    Their eyes
will fence to a final draw
that neither even wants
to win.
          They'll think no more
of elsewhere or yesterday
or anything ahead to interrupt
the marriage of their eyes, mating.

5
(Evelyn Shakir, 1938—2010)
伊芙琳·莎基尔

作者简介

伊芙琳·莎基尔（Evelyn Shakir, 1938—2010）是美国黎巴嫩裔文学学者。她在西罗克斯伯里（West Roxbury）的一个黎巴嫩移民家庭长大，1956年毕业于波士顿女子拉丁学校（Girls' Latin School in Boston）后，她在韦尔斯利学院（Wellesley College）学习英语并在那里获得学士学位，莎基尔分别获有哈佛大学的硕士学位和波士顿大学的博士学位。

伊芙琳·莎基尔是美国阿拉伯裔文学研究的先驱，发表了一些最早将美国阿拉伯裔文学命名为一个领域的学术论文。她的主要著作包括《请代我向黎巴嫩问好：美国黎巴嫩妇女的故事》（*Remember Me to Lebanon: Stories of Lebanese Women in America*，2007），这部短篇小说集为她赢得2007年度美国阿拉伯裔国家图书奖（The Arab American National Book Award）。她的回忆录在死后出版，名为《教阿拉伯人写作自我：一位阿拉伯裔美国妇女的回忆录》（*Teaching Arabs, Writing Self: Memoirs of an Arab-American Woman*，2014）。她被波士顿女性遗产之路（The Boston Women's Heritage Trail）铭记，美国阿拉伯裔国家图书奖非小说奖也以她的名字命名。

莎基尔的短篇小说集《请代我向黎巴嫩问好：美国黎巴嫩妇女的故事》以不同的时代为背景，从20世纪60年代跨越到现在，有时甚至回溯到20世纪之交。从抗拒父亲对荣誉的理解的少年，到从坟墓中归来试图最后一次整顿家庭的老年妇女，主人公的年龄各不相同。大多数故事都戏剧化地讲述了涉及代际和文化之间谈判的个人问题。但另一些则有政治方面的因素——一个是以黎巴嫩内战为背景；另一个是对“9 · 11”事件的回应，由一位整天监视隔壁阿拉伯家庭的女人讲述。

节选部分出自《教阿拉伯人写作自我：一位阿拉伯裔美国妇女的回忆录》，在这本精心打磨的死后回忆录中，部分内容是童年记忆，部分内容是她向阿拉伯青年教授英语文学的经历。在这本回忆录中，作者讲述了自己的性格对黎巴嫩人的意义，以及她后来认识到的父母的旧世界中许多熟悉的特征：爱家庭、尊重父母的意愿、谦逊、骄傲和慷慨。

作品选读

Teaching Arabs, Writing Self: Memoirs of an Arab-American Woman

（I Childhood）

By Evelyn Shakir

At Home and Away: Thirteen Takes on Growing Up Arab in America

1

It's my experience that Arabs and psychiatrists are natural enemies. One says, "Family first." The other says, "Only neurotics call home every day." Another difference is that Arabs don't want to hear a word about psychiatry It hurts their ears. "Ooft," they say. "What's this craziness!" But psychiatrists are eager to pry into Arab psyches— expecting to find a house of horrors. Each group calls the other bonkers.

My mother and father were immigrants from Lebanon. I was born in the United States. In the eighties, when Americans were being kidnapped in Beirut, a therapist explained to me the source of my unhappiness: "Your family is holding you hostage," she said. She was being clever. She was pleased with herself.

2

My Uncle Yusuf a gentle man, loved America but hated Catholics, Democrats, and Jews. Mention the pope to him, he'd come close to spitting. Jews, of course, were the usurpers, planting themselves on Arab land. Which also explained his venom toward Democrats and Harry Truman, in particular, who'd waited all of 11 minutes before saying *yes* when Jews in Palestine declared themselves a state.

My Uncle Yusuf loved his suburban garden. He grew vegetables for his wife, and flowers for the joy of it. Flashy blooms—dahlias, giant chrysanthemums, and ruffled peonies. He cradled their heads in his huge hands. He cooed to them like a lover. Their enemies were his enemies. He picked off Japanese beedes with his bare fingers and drowned them in a can of kerosene. He called them "Trumans."

My Uncle Yusuf loved me. One day when it was just the two of us in his car, he asked the standard question. "What do you want to be when you grow up?" To be funny, I said, "President." He said, "Why not?" A window in my mind flew open. I began to think things I'd never thought before.

3

To American diplomats who urged Truman to hold off on recognizing Israel, he cited the wishes of American Jews: "I am sorry, gentlemen, but I have to answer to hundreds of thousands who are anxious for the success of Zionism: I do not have hundreds of thousands of Arabs among my constituents."

On a Christmas show back in the fifties, Perry Como croons carols on TV but also works in Jewish folk songs. My father, passing through the living room, overhears. "Jews!" he explodes. "Do they control everything?" I go into my bedroom and slam the door. Only years after he died did I begin to understand what it felt like for my father to be an Arab in the United States, reminded in every editorial, on every channel, that on matters that mattered, he could have no political voice.

Good that he didn't live to see '67 and Israel's six-day blitzkrieg against Syria and Egypt, when newsmen and even comics on American TV gloated openly at Israel's victory when Arabs were mocked pitilessly.

4

The early seventies. Palestinians are hijacking airliners and planting bombs. After one horrific attack, I'm on a bus, riding through a Boston neighborhood where Syrians and Lebanese have lived for decades. An old man climbs on. He is drunk and disheveled. "Oh, Arabs," he cries out in Arabic, swaying from one overhead strap to another. His tears spill. "Oh, brothers, what have you done!" The driver, who has understood nothing, mutters an ethnic epithet and puts him off the bus.

5

My father's best fishing buddy was Mr. Rosenfield who sold silk ties and held his pants up with suspenders. Before dawn on a Saturday his black Pontiac would drive down our street, and my father, who'd been at the window watching for headlights, would flick off the porch light and be out the door. Gear loaded, the two were off for the day, out after white perch and striped bass—freshwater fish. Forget the sea. Cape Cod had 365 bodies of water, my father claimed, a new one for each day of the year. When they arrived at their special spot, the sun just rising, the morning mist still on the lake, they spread out along the shore in opposite directions. Mirror images. Clumsy figures in waist-high fishermen's boots, wading cautiously into water. Product of shted or mountain, neither man knew how to swim. But they knew rule number one: don't talk, don't call out, don't scare the fish.

At noon, under a fringe of trees, they unrolled a patchwork blanket of wool remnants my mother had pieced together on her sewing machine. Pulled out sandwiches wrapped in wax paper (fried eggplant for my father, something that smelled of fish for Mr. Rosenfield), hard-boiled eggs, whole tomatoes they bit into like apples, thermoses of sweetened black coffee, cinnamon buns picked up the day before from a favorite bakery. Afterwards, my father puffing on his pipe, ME Rosenfield on his cigarette, they relaxed into conversation. What did they talk about then, this Arab and this Jew? Rods and reels, maybe. Lures and live bait. Irish politicians.

6

Riding the bus to work or waiting for the fish to bite, my father must often have dreamed of home. That would be Zahle, a good-sized town in a fertile patch of Lebanon set down between two mountain ranges. Born in the 1880s, an émigré by 1901, he thought well all his life of anybody—himself included—who had roots there. It went beyond a natural attachment. As late as 1960, an historian could write that people from Zahle "exhibit an intense, almost fanatic pride in family, status, and in place of origin." It drove my mother crazy: "These men from Zahle, who do they think they are!"

The Zahlawi, explained the historian, has a personal relationship with God and with the saints, whom he approaches "as he would an equal." That sounded right to me. America might snub them, hold them of no account, but it never occurred to my father, my uncle, and their cousins that they were not in excellent standing with the Almighty;

Standing among their own kind mattered, too. The Zahlawi men I knew demanded respect and were quick to take offense. ("She asked me how many eggs did I want for breakfast," my uncle Jiryes sputtered. "I was a guest in her house, and she was counting eggs.") Like boys in the 'hood, they thought rep was everything. In the old country, their ancestors—those they chose to remember, those whose framed photos hung over the divan—had been *abaday* who galloped through town and down hillside, ready for battle should anyone dis them or their clan. But honor also demanded that, however much or little they had, Zahlawis give without stint to kinsmen, guests, and others under their protection. In America, the sons still harbored that obsession. The grandiose gesture was what they lived by; the open hand was their family crest. When the offering plate came round, heavy with coins, they tossed in dollar bills. When wedding invitations arrived, they didn't stoop to Mixmasters or pressure cookers. Hand-embroidered linens were more their style; brass trays from Tripoli, designs hammered by master craftsmen; end tables from Damascus, inlaid with rosewood, olivewood, and alabaster.

My father ran a one-man printing press, turning out invoices, stationery, ad books, and volumes of Arabic poetry. It was the poetry he cared about. Which may be why he never got ahead. But he handed out what he could, basins of tomatoes and string beans and blackberries from his garden. In the coffee shop, he slapped away any hand that reached for the check.

Recently in Boston a young Lebanese cabbie picked me up at the airport. It turned out he was from Zahle and thrilled that I had connections there, too. I told him my father's surname. "A small fkmily" he said, "but respectable." I told him my grandmother's maiden name. "A very good fkmily," he said. At my door, he made the grand gesture. "Auntie, pay whatever you wish." If I'd played by the rules of his game, he would have made out like a bandit and I would have walked into my house a princess, a queen. When I fell short, he shook his head sadly. Did he write home about me? Did he send word: "In America, how the children of the Zahlawi are fallen!"

My brother saw the advantage in keeping to the old ways. As a little boy, he refused to help weed the garden. "It's below my dignity," he explained. That's when my mother knew to her frustration, that her son was more Zahlawi than her husband. Physical labor, a necessity for most immigrants in America but among the *abaday* in Zahle a source of shame. "A Zahlawi," one of their own has said, "is so proud that, if he bought something and it had to be put in a bag, he would hire a servant to carry it."

But when I needed a typewriter for college, my father found one downtown and lugged it home after work, on the subway and then on the bus and then down the street to our house. Though by then he was 70. "No," I said after I'd pecked out a few letters. "I want larger type."

7

My parents could not get anything right:

Couldn't talk right. *Beoble,* they sometimes said when tired, stymied by the letter *p.* Or else they overcompensated. *pumper.*

Couldn't eat right: okra, eggplant, bulgur, and yogurt—my mother made her own. Bread with pockets. Hummus and tabouli. "Don't put that stuff in my lunch box," I said.

Went to the wrong church. Not Catholic, not Protestant, not even Jewish. "Huh?" the kids said when I said, "Orthodox."

Were too old. One parent over 40 when I was born, the other over 50. "Is this your granddaughter?" the saleslady said.

Smoked, drank. Miss Young, my fifth grade teacher, said those were things the better class of people didn't do.

Were eccentric. My father had a bald head and a Groucho mustache that strangers stared at. And an inch-long nail on the little finger of one hand—back home, a sign of aristocracy. My mother, odd in her own way had a job. Miss Ybung said that was wrong for a married lady. And then it got worse. In April that year, my mother rented a storefront a quarter mile from school and installed two banks of sewing machines, some Singer, some Wilcox and Gibbs, all second-hand. She was going into business for herself just like a man.

6

(Mahmoud Saeed, 1939—)
马哈茂德·赛义德

作者简介

马哈茂德·赛义德（Mahmoud Saeed, 1939— ）是伊拉克出生的美国小说家，写过二十多部小说和短篇小说集，以及数百篇文章。他从小就开始写短篇小说。1956 年，他在《伊拉克法塔报》（*Fata Al-Iraq*, Newspaper）上写了一篇获奖短篇小说。1957 年，他出版了一本短篇小说集《赛义德港和其他故事集》（*Port Saeed And Other Stories*，1957）。1963 年，政变摧毁了他的两本小说手稿:《旧案》（*The Old Case*）和《罢工》（*The Strike*），另外三部遗失。

1968 年，他的小说《节奏与痴迷》（*Rhythm and Obsession*）被政府审查机构禁止出版；1970 年，他的阿拉伯语小说《路本巴尔卡》（*Rue Ben Barka*）被禁止出版，15 年后该书分别于 1985 年、1992/1993 年和 1997 年在埃及、约旦和黎巴嫩出版。从 1963 年到 2008 年，当局禁止出版该作者所写的任何书籍。他最重要的小说是《雅各布家的女孩儿们》（*The Girls of Jacob*，2007）、《天使眼中的世界》（*The World Through the Angel's Eyes*，2006）、《我是看见的人》（*I am the One Who Saw*，1981）和《芝加哥三部曲》（*Trilogy of Chicago*，2008）。他的小说《天使眼中的世界》获得了 2010 年度法赫德国王阿拉伯文学翻译中心奖（The King Fahd MEST Center for Arabic Literature Translation Award）。

马哈茂德·赛义德著名的英文小说《本·巴尔卡巷》（*Ben Barka Lane*，2013），由其 1970 年被禁的阿拉伯语小说《路本巴尔卡》翻译而来。在《本·巴尔卡巷》中，透过一位来自伊拉克的年轻政治流亡者的眼睛，读者可以看到 20 世纪 60 年代末的摩洛哥——那里的美丽与苦难，那里令人难忘的人民。在这部当代经典中，马哈茂德·赛义德向读者呈现了一个时代和地点的独特肖像，以及发生在那里的激情、政治、复仇和背叛的故事。

节选部分出自马哈茂德·赛义德的英文小说——《本·巴尔卡巷》第一章。1964 年，伊拉克政治难民沙奇（Sharqi）来到摩洛哥小城 al-Mohammediya 教高中，他发现这里虽陷入政治动荡之中，但也不乏一些小乐趣，其中包括他和遭受软禁的朋友哈比卜（Habib）之间的友谊以及他们在本·巴尔卡巷的生活。

作品选读

Ben Barka Lane

(Chapter 1)

By Mahmoud Saeed

Chapter 1

The vacation is defined in my mind by an event that seems at the very least more important than the usual. During the days of that tense summer I spent in Mohammediya (Fadala) in 1965, the weavings of chance made me feel I was confronting the experience of a lifetime, the excitement every young man pictures in his dreams.

A year before, I had found an apartment in a building of three floors belonging to a Chinese man. It was pretty and pleasant, and blessed by the warm rays of the sun at about twelve o'clock, after the last fragments of the midday call to prayer rasped from some worn-out throat. The sound was not far away, as it came from the Casbah, behind its wall of reinforced brick. Storms had played havoc with the wall, turning its strength and form into red earth, constantly eroded. That had brought those responsible for monuments to think about protecting it, for fear that it might collapse and leave only the Casbah Gate, that exemplary historical monument, to bear witness to the grandeur of an ancient edifice adorned by rare arabesque designs.

The building belonging to the Chinese man, M. Bourget (who had confused me at first by his multiple names and his origin), stood at the head of Zuhur Street, as Si Sabir calls it, or Ben Barka Lane, as al-Qaidiri calls it. It is a street that divides the small city in two, beginning from the Bab al-Tarikh Square and ending in the new port and the fish market, passing by the most important and beautiful features of the city—the lovers' garden, the nature walk, the large casino, and the Miramar Hotel—until it nears its end and the space is allotted on every side to the Samir petroleum refinery, to canning and printing plants, and to the unending farms stretching left and right, until the city ends at the rocky sea shore, on which one looks down from a great height. The lethal rocks had once brought a Spanish steamer to grief by night, destroying everyone in it and leaving only a small part of the frame, rusting and still bathed by the ocean waves.

A Bata shoe store shines on the ground floor of the building with its refinement, its gleaming glass and modern decor. Across from it is a row of modern, elegant shops: a bakery that made my mouth water over its delicious displays every morning, a store selling stamps, another selling lottery tickets, a butcher, a *brasserie* serving everything from bottles of soda to various kinds of drinks, then the largest store, for luxury goods and furniture, belonging to Si 1-Wakil and his brother, and another *brasserie*.

At the head of the street the new city begins, splitting off from the old Casbah, proud of its radiant youth and smiling at the future, after the last vestiges of domination had disappeared and the French would no longer burn alive any Moroccan they found wandering in their streets after dark. This city embraced the newcomer as soon as he stepped of the bus from Rabat or Casablanca.

More than anything else, my heart was gladdened by the presence of a busy coffee shop, where grains of idle time dissolved in a singular haze of pleasure, melting in the aroma of fine black coffee and visions of the past and of time yet to come.

From the first moment, I fell in love with this unique apartment, its floor a single expanse of gray and soft yellow mosaic, rising on the walls in every direction to the height of a yard, attempting to rival the colored arabesque tiles rising to about the same height on the walls of the Casbah. What more could I ask for? Could the stranger ask for more than to find everything he needs no more than ten steps away, from the bar to the butcher? After twenty-five years of deprivation, persecution, hardship, political struggle, prison, dismissal, and unemployment, I felt as if I had stumbled on a paradise that Adam himself would envy.

What attracted me to this spot was its peacefulness, as well as its beauty and its history, but also the pigeons which clustered in flocks near the wall and its gate. They paced serenely and securely, delving in the cracks of the ancient brick for some stray seed, from time to time fluttering over each other, descending calmly or rising noisily, at times bestowing on the observer a pleasure akin to the early, eternal pleasures of sex.

When I gaze in the afternoon to where the sun immolates itself in a strange calm over the sea hidden from my sight, I feel a strong longing for something I dream of without attaining, wrapped in a captivating, wine-like pleasure flowing through my body and numbing my limbs. I am barely aware of anything in my surroundings until the sudden, daily reversal occurs, and all at once I find myself in a light gray darkness which pushes me with gentle fingers stroking my back, driving me to where I can find all the small pleasures I dreamed of. Others might consider them trifling, but in my particular situation they are enough to justify a happy life.

The Chinese man lived in the adjacent building, on the other street, which formed the second side of the equilateral triangle, in which Bata represented the main angle, across from Bab alTarikh. He rented the rest of it to a Jewish tailor and peddler, and to a few French and other foreigners.

One warm, sunny morning at the end of April, Si Ibrahim motioned to me, so I crossed the street. Si 1-Wakil caught me and asked me to please take a rare stamp to Si Sabir. Si Ibrahim spoke to me, proudly raising a box of strawberries in his hand:

"Do you plant them in your country?" "No."

"A private farm ripened them three months before their time."

"What are they called in Arabic?"

He began to look for the Arabic word, and I thought his head would explode before he found it, so I said first:

"*Shaliik.*"

He nodded his head as he repeated: "*Shaliik.*"

"Put them on my account."

I was on my way to the school. It was a vacation day, and the guard at the end of the hall raised his right hand in greeting and picked up the broom with his left.

I saw no one but Si Sabir. I held out the strawberries. "I brought you breakfast."

He laughed. "How much did you drink last night?"

I put the small box on the table. The red heads of the berries glowed enticingly.

"Please have some, Si."

But he stood back and said, "First, let me present to you... Si 1-Habib."

I was surprised to see the man, sitting calmly of to one side, and looking at me searchingly. I shook his hand. He got up a little and bowed.

Si Sabir threw away his cigarette and took one of the strawberries with the tips of his fingers. I urged Si 1-Habib. He took one, and I burst out: "One isn't enough. Have more."

Si 1-Habib had been forced to stay in Mohammediya after the stormy events that had crushed the country at the beginning of the '60s. He had been fleeing to the east when he was arrested. All that saved him from the noose was a severe heart attack that flattened him for a long time, leaving him suspended between life and death in the prison hospital, in the care of doctors and nurses who hid their sympathy behind the frowning mask of someone doing a duty. When the crisis ended he was encompassed in the supreme neglect of the authorities. Afterwards he played the game of living with a weakened heart, under strict orders that warned him away from any exertion or activity or shock that could lead to his death. His illness cut the hangman's noose but left him in bitter banishment from activities he believed he was made for, without which his life was no more than death itself in slow motion.

The arduous struggle against the French before independence, and against apathy and internecine feuding afterwards, had tempered him, bringing him to a degree of glory reached by only a few notable personalities in a few countries.

As Si Sabir said, "Politics is like commerce in a free country: it chokes the children it has created." But I was always thinking of the feelings of those who had attained tremendous heights in their past and had fallen from them obscurely and suddenly.

What was the true nature of their feelings? Did any of them dream of returning to the dais of true glory, untouched by troubles or falsity? With respect to Si 1-Habib in particular, I wondered, as I watched him pick another strawberry from the box, if his weak heart could bear the surprise of a happy moment.

He was confined to Mohammediya in compulsory residence. Had he been allowed to choose the place? I did not ask. All the coastal cities are surpassingly beautiful. Yet I knew he loved Mohammediya, preferring its old name of *Fadala*, the hidden pearl of the coast whose value had been discovered more than half a century earlier by people from all over the wide world. Still, even in his state of compulsory fixed residence and exclusion from politics, he was unable to keep from commenting sharply when he saw the lofty castles of the great side by side with the huts of the wretched.

7

(Nahid Rachlin, 1946—)
纳希德·拉克林

作者简介

纳希德·拉克林（Nahid Rachlin, 1946—）是美国伊朗裔小说家，她被称为“可能是美国出版作品最多的伊朗作家”。拉克林生于伊朗阿巴丹（Abadan, Iran），曾在美国林登伍德学院（Lindenwood College）获得学士学位，并于1969年入籍成为美国公民。

20世纪70年代初，她开始了研究生阶段的创意写作学习，为哥伦比亚大学的理查德·汉弗莱斯（Richard Humphries）和纽约城市学院（City College of New York）的唐纳德·巴塞尔姆（Donald Barthelme）的一个班级写短篇小说。这些故事为她赢得了斯坦福大学（Stanford University）的斯特格纳奖学金（Stegner Fellowship）。1976年，拉克林在12年后第一次回到伊朗，并将这段经历写进了她的处女作《外国人》（*Foreigner*，1978）。

她的著作包括一本回忆录《波斯女孩》（*Persian Girls: A Memoir*，2006），以及《跳过火》（*Jumping over Fire*，2005）、《外国人》（*Foreigner*）、《嫁给一个陌生人》（*Married to A Stranger*，1983）、《悲伤的人群》（*Crowd of Sorrows*，2015）、《心愿》（*The Heart's Desire: A Novel*, 1995）等五部小说和一部短篇小说集《面纱》（*Veils: short stories*，1992）。她的短篇小说出现在50多本杂志上，包括《冬至文学杂志》（*Solstice Literary Magazine*）、《弗吉尼亚季刊》（*The Virginia Quarterly Review*）、《草原篷车》（*Prairie Schooner*）、《南方人文评论》（*Southern Humanities Review*）、《雪兰多杂志》（*Shenandoah*）等。她的一个故事被《交响空间》（*Symphony Space*）、《短篇选集》（*Selected Shorts*）收录，并在全国公共广

播电台播出；有三个故事被提名手推车奖（Pushcart Prize）。她曾为《纽约时报》（*The New York Times*）、《新闻日报》（*Newsday*）、《华盛顿邮报》（*The Washington Post*）和《洛杉矶时报》（*Los Angeles Times*）撰写评论和文章，其作品在主要杂志和报纸上受到好评，并被翻译成葡萄牙语、波兰语、意大利语、荷兰语、德语、捷克语、阿拉伯语和波斯语。她还获得了班纳特·瑟夫奖（The Bennett Cerf Award）、笔会小说项目奖（Pen Syndicated Fiction Project Award）和一项国家艺术基金资助（National Endowment For The Arts Grant）。

节选部分分别来自其回忆录《波斯女孩》第二部分和小说《外国人》第一章。《波斯女孩》选段中作者描述了初到美国林登伍德学院读书时的印象，在那里她并没有得到之前想象中的生活，并且开始发现其在美国的不公遭遇与自己的少数族裔身份有关；而在《外国人》第一章，当主人公菲莉（Feri）从美国波士顿回到伊朗的时候，却发现自己面临着文化冲突所带来的诸多不确定性。

作品选读（一）

Persian Girls: A Memoir

(PART TWO America)

By Nahid Rachlin

Nineteen

I stood by the window of my room in Green Hall, one of the five dormitories that accommodated Lindengrove College's four hundred students. It was as if years, not just a day, had gone by since I left Iran and only hours since Parviz picked me up from the St. Louis Airport and dropped me off on the campus in St. James. I was so remote now from my family and Ahvaz. The campus, with its colonial and Greek Revival architecture, wide old shady trees, flowers in bloom in rectangular beds, and sets of swing chairs in different spots, looked glorious in the pale, late-afternoon sunlight. I watched with fascination the girls walking about the campus or sitting on the swings. They reminded me of the women I had seen in American movies with Pari, or on the other side of the river. One girl with curly short hair and dimples was an older version of Shirley Temple. Another, with pale blond hair, the color of straw, and milkwhite skin, reminded me of Marilyn Monroe. I couldn't wait to write to Pari and tell her all about them.

I pulled out a photograph of Pari from my suitcase and put it on the desk. Then I spread the paradise tapestry, which I had brought without its frame, on the back of a chair until I could frame it and hang it on the wall. I didn't have a good photograph of Maryam-—only a small one with her hair covered in a black chador, only her eyes showing. After taking a shower in the common bathroom, I sat in bed and wrote a long letter to Pari and one to Maryam. I went to bed early, exhausted from the eighteen-hour Hight from Iran. I fell into a dreamless sleep.

I woke late the next morning and made my way to the college dining room. It was nearly empty. I took some food from the buffet and sat at a table with two other girls. I asked one of them, in broken English, what I had put on my plate.

She stared at me for a moment. "Grits," she said, pointing to a white lump. Then pointing to a hunk of bread, she said, "Corn bread."

In a moment they got up and left. I lingered in the large room by myself.

I registered for as many courses that didn't require fluent English as possible—piano, swimming, home economics. In home economics, the professor taught us how to set a table and seat guests. She also taught us "charm"—not much different from *taarof* in the Iranian culture. We should always say, "Yes, ma'am," she said, when addressing a woman older than ourselves; we should write a thank-you note to our hostess and it should be phrased in a certain way. At the required introduction to English literature, I could absorb only some of the lecture. The one English course I had taken in high school hadn't prepared me adequately. Between classes I sat in my room or on a swing chair and tried to understand the assignments and make sense of my notes, poring over my Farsi-English dictionary.

After dinner I went to my room, leaving the door half open to create a draft with the breeze coming through the window. As the evening wore on other students began to come back, holding Cokes or instant coffee, cellophane-wrapped crackers, cheese, and cookies. Some of them stood in the hall in clusters and talked. When the weekend came most of the girls went out together or on dates with boys from nearby colleges. I stayed in the dormitory, studying.

My isolation felt like freedom at first. But soon the reality of the college and my separation from the other students began to hit me.

Beauty contests, mixers with boys the school invited from colleges in the area, sermons in the Presbyterian chapel at which attendance was required no matter what your religion—all just floated around me without meaning. The ideal young girl, one whom the staff and parents approved of and promoted, was a good Christian who dressed properly and was agreeable and sociable. If a student didn't go on frequent dates with, boys she was "antisocial" or "a loser." If a student had plans with a female friend and then a boy called and asked her out at the same time, she would automatically accept the date and cancel plans with the girlfriend. If a student dated a boy from outside her religion it created problems. Smiling was compulsory. One girl in my dormitory said, "Smile," every time we passed in the hall.

The pocket money Father sent me through Parviz shrank when converted from *toomans* to dollars. The other girls flew home often for family gatherings or to reunite with a high school sweetheart. They had their hair done in expensive beauty salons in St. Louis, then went shopping and returned with packages of hats, gloves, blouses, shoes. They often skipped dormitory meals to buy their own food. The girls who didn't have cars took taxis everywhere, rather than buses, which ran infrequently on limited routes. They decorated their rooms with their own personal furniture.

I was out of the prison of my home, but I was here all alone. I didn't have easy access to my brothers. I didn't know a single other person.

One day toward the end of the semester I found a note from the dean in my mailbox inviting me, along with the three other foreign students on campus, to participate in Parents' Day. She asked that I stop by her office. The dean was wearing a linen suit, her blond hair set in neat short curls. She greeted me with a warm smile. "I'm telling this to all the foreign students on campus," she said. "You should wear your native costumes on Parents' Day."

I was silent, feeling awkward. I had no costume. She was waiting.

"In Iran, some women cover themselves in chadors, but they wear them on top of regular clothes, similar to what people wear here," I said.

"Then wear a chador," she said.

My awkwardness only increased.

"I never wore one in Iran," I said finally, my voice drowned in the sound of laughter and conversation in the hall.

"I still want you to wear it for this occasion, to show a little of your culture to us," she said, smiling cheerfully.

To me the chador had come to mean a kind of bondage, as religion had. It felt ridiculous to wear it in this American college. "Maybe I can think of something else to wear," I mumbled.

"No, no, the idea of the chador is excellent. I've seen pictures of women in Islamic countries wearing them. It fascinates me. What is the point?"

"Well, in Islam, exposed hair and skin is considered to be seductive to men."

"I wish I felt my hair and skin were so seductive that I had to cover them up," she said with a chuckle. But her attempt at humor only made me more insecure in this unexpectedly alien environment. I was realizing quickly how different this place was from my expectation of America.

That afternoon after classes I walked to St. Louis's Main Street to buy fabric for the chador. On one side of the street was a pharmacy, a post office, a small department store, a small supermarket, and a diner. Several residential streets branched off it and led to the Mississippi River, a muddy and turbulent body of water, with traffic racing on the wide street running alongside it. I thought of standing on the bank of the Karoon River and looking at the Americans on the other side. Here I was among them and feeling cut off and insecure.

In the department store I looked at stacks of fabric in one corner. I wondered what to buy, a lightweight bright fabric like Maryam and other women wore around the house when a man was there, or the more somber black material they wore outside. Finally I decided on a few yards in blue with floral designs in paler blue. I also bought thread, scissors, and a needle.

Back in my room, I spread the fabric on the floor, cut it in the shape of a chador, and hemmed the edges. It was hard to cut it right; I went very slowly. Maryam used to have hers made by a seamstress. As a child, I chose not to wear the chador. Now cutting one felt almost like making a shroud, as I had seen Maryam and her tenants doing. My mind went to my grandmother telling me that Reza Shah, the father of the present Shah, had forbidden women to wear the chador. The police used to pull it off the heads of women who wore it outdoors. He wanted the world to see Iran as modern. Then the present Shah, who had the same idea of modernizing Iran, as a compromise to please the clergy made wearing it optional. Women like Maryam, who were totally observant, wore it; some, who were less religious, wore head scarves; more Westernized women like Mohtaram didn't cover their heads. The whole notion of the chador was very strange to Americans; I could tell by the dean's reaction, yet she wanted me to wear it.

On Parents' Day I put the chador on and looked at myself in the mirror. I was reminded of the times 1 wore it to passion plays and to a mosque Maryam took me to. I didn't connect to the chador and the realization had made me sad—at one time Maryam and I were so much alike. Now, here I was in this land of freedom and more or less forced to wear it. I tried to brush off my thoughts, to not be so easily dissatisfied.

I went to the room where the reception was taking place. Framed photographs of various benefactors hung on the walls. As I stood with Margarita, from Greece, who was wearing a full embroidered skirt and blouse; Rachel, from Turkey, in something similar; and Bharti, from India, in a sari, everyone's eyes focused mainly on me.

"Isn't that pretty," one young mother said, with a Southern drawl. "But it must be difficult to move around in."

"Does everyone dress like that in Iran?" another woman asked.

"No," I said, "it's optional; only about half the women wear it."

"I can't imagine wearing it."

Though I didn't accept the chador, I felt insulted, thinking of Maryam always enclosed in one, by choice.

After enduring more questions from mothers, the foreign students and I left together. Outside, sitting on facing swings, we talked among ourselves. Margarita, dark-haired and plump, was a sophomore; she said she disliked the college and planned to return home as soon as the year was over. Rachel, redhaired and pale, with a quiet manner, said she was happy enough so far, this being her first year. On the plane ride to the United States she had met a man from her own country who attended a nearby college; the two of them spent a lot of time together. And Bharti, thin and dark and serious, was unhappy but intended to stay on until she graduated. I told her I also intended to finish, although I was beginning to feel the college wasn't the right place for me and wasn't what I had imagined it to be like.

作品选读（二）

Foreigner

(Chapter 1)

By Nahid Rachlin

As I boarded the plane at Logan Airport in Boston I paused on the top step and waved to Tony. He waved back. I pulled the window curtain beside me and closed my eyes, seeing Tony's face falling away, bitten by light....

In the Teheran airport I was groggy and disoriented. I found my valise and set it on a table, where two customs officers searched it. Behind a large window people waited. The women, mostly hidden under dark *chadors*, formed a single fluid shape. I kept looking towards the window trying to spot my father, stepmother, or stepbrother, but I did not see any of them. Perhaps they were there and we could not immediately recognize each other. It had been fourteen years since I had seen them.

A young man sat on a bench beside the table, his task there not clear. He wore his shirt open and I could see bristles of dark hair on his chest. He was making shadow pictures on the floor—a rabbit, a bird—and then dissolving the shapes between his feet. Energy emanated from his hands, a crude, confused energy. Suddenly he looked at me, staring into my eyes. I turned away.

I entered the waiting room and looked around. Most people had left. There was still no one for me. What could possibly have happened? Normally someone would be there—a definite effort would be made. I fought to shake off my groggy state.

A row of phones stood in the corner next to a handicraft shop. I tried to call my father. There were no phone books and the information line rang busy, on and on.

I went outside and approached a collection of taxis. The drivers stood around, talking. "Can I take one of these?" I asked.

The men turned to me but no one spoke.

"I need a taxi," I said.

"Where do you want to go?" one of the men asked. He was old with stooped shoulders and a thin, unfriendly face. I gave him my father's address.

"That's all the way on the other side of the city." He did not move from his spot.

"Please ... I have to get there somehow."

The driver looked at the other men as if this were a group project.

"Take her," one of them said. "I would take her myself but I have to get home." He smiled at me.

"All right, get in," the older man said, pointing to a taxi.

In the taxi, he turned off the meter almost immediately. "You have to pay me 100 *tomans* for this."

"That much?"

"It would cost you more if I left the meter on."

There was no point arguing with him. I sat stiffly and looked out. We seemed to be floating in the sallow light cast by the street lamps. Thin old sycamores lined the sidewalks. Water flowed in the gutters. The smoky mountains surrounding the city, now barely visible, were like a dark ring. The streets were more crowded and there were many more tall western buildings than I had remembered. Cars sped by, bouncing over holes, passing each other recklessly, honking. My taxi driver also drove badly and I had visions of an accident, of being maimed.

We passed through quieter, older sections. The driver slowed down on a narrow street with a mosque at its center, then stopped in front of a large, squalid house. This was the street I had lived on for so many years; here I had played hide-and-seek in alleys and hallways. I had a fleeting sensation that I had never left this street, that my other life with Tony had never existed.

I paid the driver, picked up my valise, and got out. On the cracked blue tile above the door, "Akbar Mehri," my father's name, was written.

I banged the iron knocker several times and waited. In the light of the street lamps I could see a beggar with his jaw twisted sitting against the wall of the mosque. Even though it was rather late, a hum of prayers, like a moan, rose from the mosque. A Moslem priest came out, looked past the beggar and spat on the ground. The doors of the house across the street were open. I had played with two little girls, sisters, who lived there. I could almost hear their voices, laughter. The April air was mild and velvety against my skin but I shivered at the proximity to my childhood.

A pebble suddenly hit me on the back. I turned but could not see anyone. A moment later another pebble hit my leg and another behind my knee. More hit the ground. I turned again and saw a small boy running and hiding in the arched hallway of a house nearby.

I knocked again.

There was a thud from the inside, shuffling, and then soft footsteps. The door opened and a man—my father—stood before me. His cheeks were hollower than I had recalled, the circles under his eyes deeper, and his hair more evenly gray. We stared at each other.

"It's you!" He was grimacing, as though in pain.

"Didn't you get my telegram?"

He nodded. "We waited for you for two hours this morning in the airport. What happened to you?"

I was not sure if he was angry or in a daze. "You must have gotten the time mixed up. I meant nine in the *evening*."

My father stretched his hands forward, about to embrace me but, as though struck by a shyness, he let them drop at his sides. "Come in now."

I followed him inside. I too was in the grip of shyness, or something like it.

"I thought you'd never come back," he said.

"I know, I know."

"You aren't even happy to see me."

"That's not true. I'm just..."

"You're shocked. Of course you are."

He went towards the rooms, arranged in a semicircle, on the other side of the courtyard. A veranda with columns extended along several of the rooms. Crocuses, unpruned rosebushes, and pomegranate trees filled the flower beds. A round pool of water stood between the flower beds. The place seemed cramped, untended. But still it was the same house. Roses would He went towards the rooms, arranged in a semicircle, on the other side of the courtyard. A veranda with columns extended along several of the rooms. Crocuses, unpruned rosebushes, and pomegranate trees filled the flower beds. A round pool of water stood between the flower beds. The place seemed cramped, untended. But still it was the same house. Roses would blossom, sparrows would chirp at the edge of the pool. At dawn and dusk the voice of the muezzin would mix with the noise of people coming from and going to the nearby bazaars.

We went up the steps onto the veranda and my father opened the door to one of the rooms. He stepped inside and turned on the light. I paused for a moment, afraid to cross the threshold. I could smell it: must, jasmin, rosewater, garlic, vinegar, recalling my childhood. Shut doors with confused noises behind them, slippery footsteps, black, golden-eyed cats staring from every corner, indolent afternoons when people reclined on mattresses, forbidden subjects occasionally reaching me—talk about a heavy flow of menstrual blood, sex inflicted by force, the last dark words of a woman on her death bed.

My father disappeared into another room. I heard voices whispering and then someone said loudly, "She's here?" Footsteps approached. In the semidarkness of a doorway at the far end of the room two faces appeared and then another face, like three moons, staring at me.

"Feri, what happened?" a woman's voice asked, and a figure stepped forward. I recognized my stepmother, Ziba. She wore a long, plain cotton nightgown.

"The time got mixed up, I guess." My voice sounded feeble and hesitant.

A man laughed and walked into the light too. It was my stepbrother, Darius. He grinned at me, a smile disconnected from his eyes.

"Let's go to the kitchen," my father said. "So that Feri can eat something."

They went back through the same doorway and I followed them. We walked through the dim, intersecting rooms in tandem. In one room all the walls were covered with black cloth, and a throne, also covered with a black cloth, was set in a corner—for monthly prayers when neighborhood women would come in and a Moslem priest was invited to give sermons. The women would wail and beat their chests in these sessions as the priest talked about man's guilt or the sacrifices the leaders of Islam had made. They would cry as if at their own irrevocable guilt and sorrow.

We were together in the kitchen. Darius, Ziba, my father—they seemed at once familiar and remote like figures in dreams.

Ziba, her eyes still shrewd and slipping frequently into disapproval, lips thin and prim, hair frizzy from a permanent, breasts flat under the loose, white robe. A woman in her late forties but looking older, with deep frown lines on her forehead and creases all over her face as if a layer of anxiety had imprinted itself on her. Darius, wearing his stained work clothes— his dark, persistent gaze, protruding forehead, heavy sensual lips. The last I had heard, he worked as a garage mechanic instead of in my father's fabric shop in Sabzi Bazaar as they had once both hoped. And my father, crouching on a chair, eyes almost hidden under his thick eyebrows as if he were trying to avoid confrontation with me.

"I'd have had something better for you to eat if I knew you'd be here tonight," Ziba said, mixing with a spoon the leftover *abgoosht* she was warming on the stove.

"Don't worry about me. I'm not hungry." Although I had eaten little on the plane I had no appetite.

"She isn't a stranger," Darius said.

But I *was* a stranger, with people I had not seen for so long and hardly knew any more. I looked around the imitation modern kitchen—redone since I had left—with plastic chairs made to look like wood, a brown formica table, a flimsy gas stove and, instead of the wooden icebox, an old refrigerator with its enamel chipped. The gold-colored curtains were soiled with spots of grease.

"What did you do that for, not come back for so long?" my father said, his eyes still cast downward.

"I was busy, time went by—it didn't seem like so long." I couldn't seem to find the words. "And my work—it's hard to get away from it." I was a biologist, a researcher in a consulting firm near Boston. Although I worked hard, building a career, my refusal to return for visits, in spite of my father's pressure, had taken an effort on my part. I had tried to forget my past. But gradually, after years, that had no longer been possible. Little by little I had been filled with a sense of futility and restlessness. Vague dissatisfactions with work, with Tony, with people I knew had set on me.

"You're back now," my father said, as though trying to avoid unpleasantness.

"It seems she never left," Darius said, punching me gently on my side.

"But you look different," my father said. "You look Western."

My hair was short, just to the nape of my neck in a blunt cut. I had plucked my eyebrows so that they were almost straight, making my eyes seem larger than they were and my face more angular. I wore a silk blouse, a scooped-neck sweater, and slacks.

"You don't expect me not to have changed," I said.

"She's just as thin as she used to be," Ziba said, putting a bowl of *abgoosht* and a slab of gravel-baked bread before me.

I began to eat reluctantly.

"She was thin as a child," my father said. "Thin as a reed."

"We'll have to feed her well," Darius said.

"Why didn't you bring your husband with you?" my father asked.

"He had work to do."

"He teaches college, right?"

I nodded. Tony taught urban planning at a university in Cambridge.

"A college professor," Darius said with a touch of mockery. "Do you have any pictures of him? You never sent one us."

My father had objected so strongly to the news that I wanted to marry Tony—an American—that I had kept most of the business to myself.

8

(Azar Nafisi, 1948—)

阿扎尔·纳菲西

作者简介

阿扎尔·纳菲西（Azar Nafisi，1948—）是美国伊朗裔作家，出生于伊朗德黑兰（Tehran），她是伊朗著名学者、小说家和诗人赛义德·纳菲西的侄女，她的父亲曾做过德黑兰市市长。1961年，她在英国的兰开斯特（Lancaster）完成学业，后又移居瑞士，并于1963年短暂返回伊朗。自1997年以来她一直居住在美国，并于2008年成为美国公民。她曾在俄克拉荷马大学（University of Oklahoma）研习英美文学并获得博士学位。

阿扎尔·纳菲西最出名的是她2003年出版的《在德黑兰阅读洛丽塔：书中的回忆录》（*Reading Lolita in Tehran: A Memoir in Books*），这本书描述了革命后，她作为一名世俗女性在伊朗伊斯兰共和国生活和工作的经历。该书在《纽约时报》（*The New York Times*）畅销书排行榜上保持了117周，并获得了多个文学奖项，包括2004年度非小说类图书奖（Non-fiction Book of the Year Award from Booksense）。

除了《在德黑兰阅读洛丽塔》之外，2008年，纳菲西写了一本关于她母亲的回忆录，名为《我一直沉默的事情：浪子的回忆》（*Things I've Been Silent About: Memories of a Prodigal Daughter*）；2014年10月，纳菲西撰写了《想象共和国：三本书中的美国》（*The Republic of Imagination: America in Three Books*）一书。在这本书中，纳菲西借鉴了《哈克贝利·费恩历险记》（*The Adventures of Huckleberry Finn*）、《巴比特》（*Babbitt*）和《心是一个孤独的猎人》（*The Heart Is a Lonely Hunter*），以及詹姆斯·鲍德温和其他许多人的作品，回答了一位伊朗读者关于美国人是否关心或需要他们的文学的问题；2019 年，她的《另一个世界：纳博科夫与流亡之谜》（*That Other World: Nabokov and the Puzzle of Exile*）的英译本由耶鲁大学出版社（Yale University Press）出版；她的最新著作《危险阅读：乱世文学的颠覆力量》（*Read Dangerously: The Subversive Power of Literature in Troubled Times*）已于 2022 年 3 月出版。

1979 年，伊朗革命后，纳菲西回到伊朗，在德黑兰大学（Tehran University）教授英国文学。1981 年，她因拒绝戴伊斯兰教强制规定的面纱而被大学开除。多年后，在自由化时期，她开始在阿拉姆·塔巴塔巴依大学（Allameh Tabataba'i University）任教。1995 年，纳菲西试图辞职，但大学不肯接受她的辞呈。在多次拒绝上班后，他们最终将她开除，但依然拒绝她的辞职。

从 1995 年到 1997 年，纳菲西邀请她的几名女学生每周四早上在她家参加例行学习。他们讨论了她们作为女性在革命后伊朗社会中的地位，并研究了部分文学作品，包括一些被视为"有争议"的作品，例如《洛丽塔》（*Lolita*）和《包法利夫人》（*Madame Bovary*）等。她还教授菲茨杰拉德、亨利·詹姆斯和简·奥斯汀等著名作家的小说，试图从现代伊朗的角度理解和解释它们。《在德黑兰阅读洛丽塔》讲述的便是这一段时期她们阅读的书目和发生的故事。革命后，纳菲西在伊朗住了 18 年后，于 1997 年 6 月 24 日返回美国，并继续在那里居住。

本文节选自《在德黑兰阅读洛丽塔》第二部分，讲述的是纳菲西和她的几名女学生一起阅读菲茨杰拉德的小说《了不起的盖茨比》（*The Great Gatsby*），并试图从现代伊朗的角度对这部小说进行理解和解释。

作品选读

Reading Lolita in Tehran: A Memoir in Book

(PART Ⅱ 17 Gatsby)

By Azar Nafisi

I spoke briefly about the next week's assignment and proceeded to set the trial in motion. First I called forth Mr. Farzan, the judge, and asked him to take his seat in my usual chair, behind the desk. He sauntered up to the front of the class with an ill-disguised air of self-satisfaction. A chair was placed near the judge for the witnesses. I sat beside Zarrin on the left side of the room, by the large window, and Mr. Nyazi sat with some of his friends on the other side, by the wall. The judge called the session to order. And so began the case of the Islamic Republic of Iran versus The Great Gatsby.

Mr. Nyazi was called to state his case against the defendant. Instead of standing, he moved his chair to the center of the room and started to read in a monotonous voice from his paper. The judge sat uncomfortably behind my desk and appeared to be mesmerized by Mr. Nyazi. Every once in a while he blinked rather violently.

A few months ago, I was finally cleaning up my old files and I came across Mr. Nyazi's paper, written in immaculate handwriting. It began with "In the Name of God," words that later became mandatory on all official letterheads and in all public talks. Mr. Nyazi picked up the pages of his paper one by one, gripping rather than holding them, as if afraid that they might try to escape his hold. "Islam is the only religion in the world that has assigned a special sacred role to literature in guiding man to a godly life," he intoned. "This becomes clear when we consider that the Koran, God's own word, is the Prophet's miracle. Through the Word you can heal or you can destroy. You can guide or you can corrupt. That is why the Word can belong to Satan or to God."

"Imam Khomeini has relegated a great task to our poets and writers," he droned on triumphantly, laying down one page and picking up another. "He has given them a sacred mission, much more exalted than that of the materialistic writers in the West. If our Imam is the shepherd who guides the flock to its pasture, then the writers are the faithful watchdogs who must lead according to the shepherd's dictates."

A giggle could be heard from the back of the class. I glanced around behind me and caught Zarrin and Vida whispering. Nassrin was staring intently at Mr. Nyazi and absentmindedly chewing her pencil. Mr. Farzan seemed to be preoccupied with an invisible fly, and blinked exaggeratedly at intervals. When I turned my attention back to Mr. Nyazi, he was saying, "Ask yourself which you would prefer: the guardianship of a sacred and holy task or the materialistic reward of money and position that has corrupted—" and here he paused, without taking his eyes off his paper, seeming to drag the sapless words to the surface—"that has corrupted," he repeated, "the Western writers and deprived their work of spirituality and purpose. That is why our Imam says that the pen is mightier than the sword."

The whispers and titters in the back rows had become more audible. Mr. Farzan was too inept a judge to pay attention, but one of Mr. Nyazi's friends cried out: "Your Honor, could you please instruct the gentlemen and ladies in the back to respect the court and the prosecutor?"

"So be it," said Mr. Farzan, irrelevantly.

"Our poets and writers in this battle against the Great Satan," Nyazi continued, "play the same role as our faithful soldiers, and they will be accorded the same reward in heaven. We students, as the future guardians of culture, have a heavy task ahead of us. Today we have planted Islam's flag of victory inside the nest of spies on our own soil. Our task, as our Imam has stated, is to purge the country of the decadent Western culture and ..."

At this point Zarrin stood up. "Objection, Your Honor!" she cried out.

Mr. Farzan looked at her in some surprise. "What do you object to?"

"This is supposed to be about *The Great Gatsby*," said Zarrin. "The prosecutor has taken up fifteen precious minutes of our time without saying a single word about the defendant. Where is this all going?"

For a few seconds both Mr. Farzan and Mr. Nyazi looked at her in wonder. Then Mr. Nyazi said, without looking at Zarrin, "This is an Islamic court, not Perry Mason. I can present my case the way I want to, and I am setting the context. I want to say that as a Muslim I cannot accept *Gatsby*."

Mr. Farzan, attempting to rise up to his role, said, "Well, please move on then."

Zarrin's interruptions had upset Mr. Nyazi, who after a short pause lifted his head from his paper and said with some excitement, "You are right, it is not worth it ..."

We were left to wonder what was not worth it for a few seconds, until he continued. "I don't have to read from a paper, and I don't need to talk about Islam. I have enough evidence—every page, every single page," he cried out, "of this book is its own condemnation." He turned to Zarrin and one look at her indifferent expression was enough to transform him. "All through this revolution we have talked about the fact that the West is our enemy, it is the Great Satan, not because of its military might, not because of its economic power, but because of, because of"—another pause—"because of its sinister assault on the very roots of our culture. What our Imam calls cultural aggression. This I would call a rape of our culture," Mr. Nyazi stated, using a term that later became the hallmark of the Islamic Republic's critique of the West. "And if you want to see cultural rape, you need go no further than this very book." He picked his Gatsby up from beneath the pile of papers and started waving it in our direction.

Zarrin rose again to her feet. "Your Honor," she said with barely disguised contempt, "these are all baseless allegations, falsehoods..."

Mr. Nyazi did not allow his honor to respond. He half rose from his seat and cried out: "Will you let me finish? You will get your turn! I will tell you why, I will tell you why ..." And then he turned to me and in a softer voice said, "Ma'am, no offense meant to you."

I, who had by now begun to enjoy the game, said, "Go ahead, please, and remember I am here in the role of the book. I will have my say in the end."

"Maybe during the reign of the corrupt Pahlavi regime," Nyazi continued, "adultery was the accepted norm."

Zarrin was not one to let go. "I object!" she cried out. "There is no factual basis to this statement."

"Okay," he conceded, "but the values were such that adultery went unpunished. This book preaches illicit relations between a man and woman. First we have Tom and his mistress, the scene in her apartment—even the narrator, Nick, is implicated. He doesn't like their lies, but he has no objection to their fornicating and sitting on each other's laps, and, and, those parties at Gatsby's ... remember, ladies and gentlemen, this Gatsby is the hero of the book—and who is he? He is a charlatan, he is an adulterer, he is a liar ... this is the man Nick celebrates and feels sorry for, this man, this destroyer of homes!" Mr. Nyazi was clearly agitated as he conjured the fornicators, liars and adulterers roaming freely in Fitzgerald's luminous world, immune from his wrath and from prosecution. "The only sympathetic person here is the cuckolded husband, Mr. Wilson," Mr. Nyazi boomed. "When he kills Gatsby, it is the hand of God. He is the only victim. He is the genuine symbol of the oppressed, in the land of, of, of the Great Satan!"

The trouble with Mr. Nyazi was that even when he became excited and did not read from his paper, his delivery was monotonous. Now he mainly shouted and cried out from his semistationary position.

9
(Fatemeh Keshavarz, 1952—)
法蒂梅·凯沙瓦兹

作者简介

法蒂梅·凯沙瓦兹（Fatemeh Keshavarz，1952—）是美国伊朗裔诗人、鲁米和波斯语研究学者。她在伊朗设拉子市（City of Shiraz）出生长大，1976 年获得设拉子大学（Shiraz University）波斯语言文学学士学位，1981 年获得伦敦大学东方与非洲研究学院（School of Oriental and African Studies, University of London）近东研究硕士学位，并于 1985 年获得博士学位。

法蒂梅·凯沙瓦兹出版了几本著名的书，包括《阅读神秘的歌词：贾拉尔·丁·鲁米的案例》（*Reading Mystical Lyric: the Case of Jalal al-Din Rumi*，1998）、《以红玫瑰的名义背诵》（*Recite in the Name of the Red Rose*，2006）以及将个人回忆录与文学分析和社会评论相结合，打破了西方对伊朗人普遍存在的刻板印象的著作《茉莉花与星星：在德黑兰不只阅读〈洛丽塔〉》（*Jasmine and Stars: Reading more than Lolita in Tehran*，2007）。

《茉莉花与星星：在德黑兰不只阅读〈洛丽塔〉》提供的思想与阿扎尔·纳菲西的《在德黑兰阅读〈洛丽塔〉：书中的回忆录》形成鲜明对比，后者探讨了革命后伊朗文学与社会的关系。凯沙瓦兹认为纳菲西的书呈现了“许多具有破坏性的误解”，更多地依赖于刻板印象和简单的比较，而不是对这个国家和人民的准确描述。2008 年，法蒂梅·凯沙瓦兹作为 2007 年度美国公共媒体特邀嘉宾的广播节目《说信仰：鲁米的狂热信仰》（*Speaking of Faith: The Ecstatic Faith of Rumi*）被授予皮博迪奖（Peabody Award），该奖被认为是美国电子媒体最令人垂涎的大奖。同年，凯沙瓦兹还在联合国大会上发表了题为“文化教育对世界和平的重要性”的演讲。2008 年她还获得了“赫歇尔·沃克和平与正义奖”（The Hershel Walker “Peace and Justice” Award）。

本文节选自《茉莉花与星星：在德黑兰不只阅读〈洛丽塔〉》第五章，在这一部分，法蒂梅·凯沙瓦兹针对阿扎尔·纳菲西在其《在德黑兰阅读〈洛丽塔〉：书中的回忆录》的一些主要观点做出了相反的评论，认为后者对伊朗的新东方主义叙事有失偏颇，她还特别批评了叙事的沉默本质，它反映在选择性记忆、对传统文化的缺乏敏感性和对宗教实践的基本蔑视上。

作品选读

Jasmine and Stars:Reading more than Lolita in Tehran

(5 The Good, the Missing, and the Faceless:

What Is Wrong with Reading Lolita in Tehran)

By Nahid Rachlin

In this chapter, however, I will shift the gaze from my personal stories and focus closely on the work that I have used throughout *Jasmine and Stars* as a typical example of the New Orientalist narrative, namely *Reading Lolita in Tehran* (*RLT*). It is vital to provide a condensed and concrete critique of the aspects of this work that foster otherness and difference. In our close reading, *RLT* 's perspective on contemporary Iran is shown to be one-sided and extreme, in fact as extreme as the views of the revolutionaries it criticizes. Similarly, the book's erasure of the voices of sanity reduces the entire culture to the behavior of its extremists. Before I start the critique, however, let me give you a summary of *RLT*. In particular, it will help for you to see the names of the seven young women in the reading group and those of the major villains, as I shall refer to them repeatedly it this chapter.

A Brief Plot Summary

RLT does not follow a continuous and unfolding plot. The best way to understand the structure of its content is to take a look at its various sections.

Essentially, the book is the author's exchanges with her seven female students embedded in anecdotes that occur in weekly reading sessions. The young women are

Manna, Mahshid, Nassrin, Yassi, Azin, Mitra, and Sanaz, all in their late teens or early twenties. While the group meets between 1995 and 1997, the author's recollection of her life experience in Iran stretches from 1979 to 1997. The main writers read and discussed in the group are Vladimir Nabokov, F. Scott Fitzgerald, Henry James, and Jane Austen. The book devotes a part to each one of them.

Part I attends to Nabokov's *Invitation to a Beheading* first, drawing a parallel between its chilling atmosphere and the environment created by the Islamic Republic. The main focus of this part, however, is *Lolita*, with the seduced girl child presented to us as a metaphor for Iranian society violated by the revolutionary forces.

Part Ⅱ contains discussions of Fitzgerald's *The Great Gatsby* while at the same time touching on social events such as the purging of certain "antirevolutionary" faculty from the universities and the taking of the American hostages.

Part Ⅲ opens with reference to the Iran-Iraq war beginning in 1980. Its literary focus is on James, his personality, and his lobbying Americans to enter World War II in support of Britain. Thereafter, we read about the women characters in Washington Square and Daisy Miller. Like the rest of the book, this part makes many allusions to the misfortunes of the local population, including a female leftist student named Razieh who is executed and an unnamed male student who burns himself to death.

Part Ⅳ, which follows a format similar to that of the preceding part, is centered on female characters from Austen's novels and their rebellion against conventions. This last part winds down with Nafisi's personal thoughts about leaving Iran. Finally, a brief epilogue brings us up to date with the author's current life in the United States. It also touches on the fate of the group since the author's departure and alludes to much that has changed in "appearance" since then

Throughout, the book is peppered with references to Muslim males and/or villains. These are colleagues or students whom we do not get to know but whose behaviors represent the extremist ideals of the revolution. Unlike the female students, we do not learn their first names. Prominent among these are Messrs. Forsati, Ghomi, Bahri, Nyazi, and Nahvi. Like the revolutionaries it criticizes, rlt speaks from a vantage point of moral goodness and superiority. The degree of heroism implied by the author's act of teaching Western fiction writers is astonishing. The students' smiles are described as "meant to tell" how crucial it was for the teaching to continue "at all costs to myself or them" (68). The uninformed reader is hence encouraged to assume that reading Western literature is forbidden in postrevolutionary Iran, an act so risky it could endanger the reader's life.

The extremists' perception of the universe as a black-and-white world of infidelity and faith is replicated by rlt's oversimplified world that posits good on the side of the West and evil squarely in the Muslim camp. The book's villains are often reduced to the basic essence of their primitive otherness: a blind adherence to their faith, hatred for progress (exemplified by the West), and the oppression of women. This last is portrayed as a repressed, savage "sexual frenzy" surfacing at public events such as mourning for dead leaders. In effect, the reader finds a harem filled with beatings, floggings, even an occasional dance behind closed doors (90, 244, 265). In the currently fragmented relations between East and West, such exaggerated and simplistic portrayals are dangerous.

By and large, rlt satisfies mass curiosity and affirms preexisting perceptions. Its central message to the reader, delivered by a member of the native culture, is: Meet the subhumans you always knew were there! Comparing the extremist student Nahvi to Elizabeth Bennet, rlt declares, "you are as different as man and mouse" (290). This assertion reflects the book's central thesis that Iranian Muslim revolutionaries are subhuman. They cannot understand any language other than brute force and do not deserve anything but our "eternal contempt" (288).

*All parenthetical page citations in this chapter refer to Reading Lolita in Tehran.

Flying airplanes into buildings, keeping prisoners of war out of reach of the law, beheading those who might vaguely sympathize with the "enemy," setting of bombs in subway cars, and dragging the largest army of the world halfway across the globe to fight imaginary weapons of mass destruction are signs of big trouble. This environment festering with suspicion and hatred needs a more sophisticated global perspective, one geared toward respect, recognition, and healing.

Let us now turn to specific examples of what I consider serious flaws in *RLT*.

10
(Naomi Shihab Nye, 1952—)
娜奥米·希哈布·奈

作者简介

娜奥米·希哈布·奈（Naomi Shihab Nye，1952—），美国巴勒斯坦裔诗人、小说家、编辑和作曲家。她的父亲是巴勒斯坦人，母亲是美国人。奈于 1974 年在三一大学（Trinity University）获得英语和世界宗教学士学位，此后一直住在圣安东尼奥（San Antonio）。

她 6 岁时开始创作自己的第一首诗，目前总共出版或创作了 30 多部诗集。她的作品包括诗歌、青少年小说、图画书和小说。2019 年，诗歌基金会（Poetry Foundation）授予她 2019—2021 年度“青年桂冠诗人”（Young People's Poet Laureate）称号。

奈把自己描述为“流浪诗人”。她声称自己的很多诗都是受到童年记忆和旅行的启发。圣安东尼奥是她许多诗歌的灵感来源，根源和地方感是她作品的主要主题。她的诗坦率而平易近人，经常以惊人的方式使用普通的形象。

她的第一本诗集《不同的祈祷方式》（*Different Ways to Pray*，1980）探讨了不同文化之间的异同，这成为她一生关注的领域之一。她的其他书籍包括诗集《19 种瞪羚：中东诗歌》（*19 Varieties Of Gazelle: Poems Of The Middle East*，2002）、《红色手提箱》（*Red Suitcase*，1994）和《燃料》（*Fuel*，1998）。这些诗歌探索了“9 · 11”恐怖袭击后中东地区人们的生活。《出版人周刊》（*The Publishers Weekly*）评论这本书是“邀请人们探索和讨论遥远地区发生的事件及其对国内产生的影响的绝佳方式”。

她还著有题为《从不匆忙》（*Never in a Hurry*，1996）的散文集，和讲述

20 世纪 70 年代移居耶路撒冷的美国阿拉伯裔青少年的自传体故事《哈比比》(*Habibi*, 1999), 她因此获得了 1998 年的简·亚当斯儿童图书奖(The Jane Addams Children's Book Award)。奈的前两本章节故事书《文身的脚》(*Tattooed Feet*, 1977)和《眼对眼》(*Eye-to-Eye*, 1978)采用自由诗形式, 主题具有探索性。奈的第一部长篇作品集《不同的祈祷方式》探讨了从加利福尼亚到得克萨斯州, 从南美到墨西哥的不同文化之间的差异和共同经历。她的《拥抱点唱机》(*Hugging the Jukebox*, 1982)是一部获得沃特曼诗歌奖(The Voertman Poetry Prize)的长篇诗集, 它关注不同民族之间的联系以及其他国家人民的观点。《黄手套》(*Yellow Glove*, 1986)则以悲剧和哀伤为主题。诗歌基金会(The Poetry Foundation)认为《燃料》可能是奈最受好评的作品, 涉及各种主题、场景和背景。她的诗《如此多的幸福》(*So Much Happiness*, 1995)被收录在《抛物线》的《幸福版》("Happiness" edition of Parabola)中。

娜奥米·希哈布·奈编辑了许多老少皆宜的诗集, 其中最著名的一本是《同一片天空: 世界各地诗集》(*This Same Sky: A Collection of Poems from around the World*,), 收录了来自 68 个不同国家的 129 位诗人的翻译作品。

她最近的诗歌选集包括《抛弃: 我们时代的诗》(*Cast Away: Poems for Our Time*, 2020)、《小记者》(*The Tiny Journalist*, 2019)、《空中的声音: 给听者的诗》(*Voices in the Air: Poems for Listeners*, 2018)、《转移》(*Transfer*, 2011)、伊莎贝拉·加德纳诗歌奖获奖作品《你和你的》(*You and Yours*, 2005)以及《这是永远, 还是什么?: 来自得克萨斯州诗歌与绘画》(*This Forever, Or What?: Poems & Paintings from Texas*, 2004)。

节选部分分别出自娜奥米·希哈布·奈的三首诗歌:《燃料》、《如此多的幸福》和《许多人叫我不要忘记他们》(*Many Asked Me Not to Forget Them*)。这些诗歌涵盖了各种主题和场景, 但都无一例外地表明, 她相信那些被忽视、被遗忘了一半的人的价值, 她对日常生活和纷争的描写传达出一种微妙的道德关怀和必要的紧迫感。

作品选读（一）

Fuel
(A Poem)

By Naomi Shihab Nye

Even at this late date, sometimes I have to look up
the word "receive." I received his deep
and interested gaze.

A bean plant flourishes under the rain of sweet words.
Tell what you think—I'm listening.

The story ruffled its twenty leaves.

*

Once my teacher set me on a high stool
for laughing. She thought the eyes
of my classmates would whittle me to size.
But they said otherwise.

We'd laugh too if we knew how.

I pinned my gaze out the window
on a ripe line of sky.

That's where I was going.

作品选读（二）

So Much Happiness

(A Poem)

By Naomi Shihab Nye

It is difficult to know what to do with so much happiness.
With sadness there is something to rub against,
a wound to tend with lotion and cloth.
When the world falls in around you, you have pieces to pick up,
something to hold in your hands, like ticket stubs or change.

But happiness floats.
It doesn't need you to hold it down.
It doesn't need anything.
Happiness lands on the roof of the next house, singing,
and disappears when it wants to.
You are happy either way.
Even the fact that you once lived in a peaceful tree house
and now live over a quarry of noise and dust
cannot make you unhappy.
Everything has a life of its own,
it too could wake up filled with possibilities
of coffee cake and ripe peaches,
and love even the floor which needs to be swept,
the soiled linens and scratched records...

Since there is no place large enough
to contain so much happiness,
you shrug, you raise your hands, and it flows out of you
into everything you touch. You are not responsible.
You take no credit, as the night sky takes no credit
for the moon, but continues to hold it, and share it,
and in that way, be known.

作品选读（三）

Many Asked Me Not to Forget Them

(A Poem)

By Naomi Shihab Nye

Where do you keep all these people?
The shoemaker with his rumpled cough.
The man who twisted straws into brooms.
My teacher, oh my teacher. I will always cry
when I think of my teacher.
The olive farmer who lost every inch of ground,
every tree,
who sat with head in his hands
in his son's living room for years after.
I tucked them into my drawer with cuff links and bow ties.
Touched them each evening before I slept.
Wished them happiness and peace.
Peace in the heart. No wonder we all got heart trouble.
But justice never smiled on us. Why didn't it?
I tried to get Americans to think of them.
But they were too involved with their own affairs
to imagine ours. And you can't blame them, really.
How much do I think of Africa? I always did feel sad
in the back of my mind for places I didn't
have enough energy to worry about.

11

(Alev Lytle Croutier, 1954—)
艾芙·丽泰·克罗提尔

作者简介

艾芙·丽泰·克罗提尔（Alev Lytle Croutier，1954—）是享誉国际的畅销书《后宫：面纱背后的世界》（*Haram: The World Behind the Veil*，1989）和《寻水而居：精神、艺术、性感》（*Taking the Waters: Spirit, Art, Sensuality*，1992）的作者。她出生于土耳其，在伊斯坦布尔罗伯特学院（Robert College in Istanbul）学习文学，在美国欧柏林学院（Oberlin College in the US）学习艺术史，现居美国旧金山。

她凭借《告诉我一个谜语》（*Tell Me a Riddle*）获得了古根海姆奖（Guggenheim Fellowship），这也是该奖项有史以来第一个电影剧本奖。

艾芙·丽泰·克罗提尔的书已经被翻译成22种语言，其主要作品还包括小说《泪宫》（*The Palace of Tears*，2000）、《七屋》（*Seven Houses*，2002）和《第三个女人》（*The Third Woman*，2007）。

她的第二部小说《七屋》历时七年完成，于2002年出版，人们将其与加夫列尔·加西亚·马尔克斯（Gabriel Garcia Marquez）、卡洛斯·富恩特斯（Carlos Fuentes）和伊莎贝尔·阿连德（Isabel Allende）相提并论。克罗提尔以自己家族的故事为背景，在《七屋》中假借七所房屋之口讲述了四代杰出女性的故事，从奥斯曼帝国的君主制，到土耳其转变成一个共和政体国家：东西方文明的交汇与扞格、传统与现代化的矛盾，全被融入了小说里。这是一部关于丝绸家族四代杰出女性和她们生活过的七处房屋的传奇。从20世纪早期士麦那的大屋，到奥林匹斯山下的丝绸庄园，从一个不起眼的镇上小屋，到一座现代化高楼中的公寓，家族住所的变迁见证了家族的兴衰。当公共浴室和女眷们让位于电影和手机，四位独特而充满力量的女性也饱尝了生活中的酸甜苦辣。

她写给年轻读者的小说《莱拉：黑色郁金香》(*Leyla: The Black Tulip*)于2003年作为"美国女孩"系列的一部分，与美泰公司（Mattel）生产的土耳其历史玩偶一起出版。

她的文章发表在文学和主流杂志上，如《伦敦电讯报》(*London Telegraph*)、《纽约时报》(*The New York Times*)和《旧金山纪事报》(*San Francisco Chronicle*)等。她为2001年在热那亚（Genoa）举行的G8峰会撰写了《地中海之窗》(*A Window over the Mediterranean*)。

节选部分出自艾芙·丽泰·克罗提尔的小说《七屋》第二部分，作者书中亲切地介绍了家族女性在伊兹密尔（Izmir）的大宅子里的日常生活，包括饮食、服装、传统、迷信、发型、潮流等。作者令人回味的散文风格与经典的东方童话相呼应，使得土耳其的异域风情跃然纸上，但同时又不失讽刺效果。

作品选读

Seven Houses

(Part Ⅱ The Prodigal Daughter's Return)

By Alev Lytle Croutier

1997

Wherever the changes of my life may lead me in the future, it will remain my spiritual home until I die, a house to which one returns not with the certainty of welcoming human beings, nor familiarity in which every lichen-covered rock and rowan tree show known and reassuring faces.

GAVIN MAXWELL, *A Ring of Bright Water*

In a sad state of dilapidation and disrepair, the wooden facade rotten with age, the delicate gingerbread pitifully bug-eaten, I had been on my deathbed for a long, long time. Pallid and peeling, worn out by the elements. The latticed balcony dangled in the air at a dangerous incline from the main facade and the rust had eaten the gutters. Some windows were broken; others boarded up just as it had been during the Great War. Without attention and respect for so long, fragile and brittle, not much hope to be resurrected.

The government official who came to inspect a few months ago declared me unsafe and condemned, but the latest owner, a sleazeball in the black-market trade, bribed him into keeping his mouth shut so that he could sell me and cash in.

The afternoon that the FOR SALE sign was plastered all over me, pedestrians shook their heads in disbelief or laughed at my condition. But then the unexpected wand of change. Once-in-a-lifetime kind of thing. As vivid as the day Esma had first arrived here.

Two women stood across the street and stared at me for a long time—one was fortyish, I'd say, the other less than half her age. Something seemed familiar about the older one, something about the way she tilted her head slightly to the right and those strange paisley eyes. If it weren't for her modern clothes and short hair, she was the spitting image of Esma about the time when she passed on.

They stood there, gazing at me, squinting their eyes, in deep contemplation. I could read their lips.

"That's the house, Nellie. Can you believe it, I was born there," she told the younger one, which made me almost jump out of my skin. I'm older than a century but during all these years and numerous occupations, only one child was born inside me—odd since so many women of child-rearing age had passed through. Amber was her name. Intense little girl. This would explain the uncanny resemblance. But why had she come back?

"How sad," Nellie replied. "It looks so unloved now."

"The poor thing. It looks totally abandoned. I don't think anyone's lived here for a long time."

They walked around to the side, passed through the wobbly gate, followed the small path leading to the water landing.

"I was only five when we left but I still dream about this house," Amber explained.

"I can relate to that. I still dream about the house where we lived in Vermont."

Suddenly, inside me, an anxious stirring and something parting the jalousie shutters upstairs, peering out.

The Adonis tree still stood firm. Amber had told Nellie about the old legend. They saw the nightingale perched on the branches, singing a cheerful, welcoming song. It was a tender day.

They sat at the dock all afternoon, looking out at the promenade across the Bay in Cordelio, watching the water traffic. For hours neither of them uttered a word.

They watched the last sliver of the sun sink into the Aegean when Nellie reached out and touched her mother's shoulder. "We must go," she said. "It's getting dark. Your grandmother will worry."

Amber stood up and followed Nellie through the side portal but she had that sense of not wanting to part. They crossed the street, heading in the direction of the boat landing.

The nightingale thrashed around in the garden, jumping from branch to branch, singing a beckoning song. *Come back. Come back, the heart of my delight*. Of course, no one could understand the words other than me, except maybe the *jinns* who themselves were beginning to stir with restrained curiosity.

The nightingale leapt out of the Adonis tree and flew across the street—a taboo since the fuses of spirits are connected to their domicile where a strict treaty exists on the boundaries of their territories. Dangerous to cross, dangerous for the house spirits and the outdoor spirits to mingle. War among the spirits, the worst hazard.

She landed on Amber's shoulder.

"What a sweet bird," Nellie said enchanted. "Look, it's as if it's trying to communicate with us."

Then, the bird flew back and perched on the portico and began to sing.

"Sounds just like an old lullaby I used to hear when we lived here. *Dandini, dandini, danali bebek*," she began humming.

"It's totally weird."

With instant determination, Amber ran across the street. Sire stopped in front of the sign on the front door.

"Where are you going, mother?" Nellie called back. She caught up with her mother. "What does it say? Condemned?"

"It says, FOR SALE."

Nellie, in a flicker, read her mother's mind. "God," she said, "who'd ever want to buy a dump like this?"

"I'd like to see what shape it's in. The frame looks strong and beautiful."

They sneaked in through the side door, which hung by a single hinge, as the people on the street peered at them suspiciously but refrained from eye contact, making no effort to acknowledge their presence, as if a ghostly secret had veiled their sight.

The back windows were effectively boarded up but one of the doors opening into the cellar gave way. Inside, the walls bulged, the floorboards broken, the windows shattered. Smelled of cat piss, a refuge for the neighborhood strays—skinny toms with enormous balls dangling from side to side, pregnant females rubbing their scent on the posts. A fresh litter of blind devilish black kittens shrieking.

“It’s odd,” Amber said. “This culture that once castrated men, that made eunuchs would not consider doing the same to their cats. All those litters of poor kittens we see at street corners, huddled together at busy intersections. Makes me so sad.”

They opened the doors to various storage rooms. “And here is the little dungeon where they’d send me when I didn’t eat my food, where parents’ will dominated children’s desires. There’s no such thing as an empty room, you know?”

They began climbing up the uneven steps but the door leading up was bolted shut. So they returned to the street.

Amber’s hands were unsteady like an old woman’s as she jutted down the phone number on the “For Sale” sign.

“When are we going back to San Francisco?” Nellie asked.

“When the time is right,” Amber replied. “Tomorrow, I want to come back with the realtor and look inside.”

“You’re not thinking what I’m afraid you’re thinking, are you?”

“Maybe I am. I don’t know what I’m going to do now that you’ll be off to college. I can’t continue living the same old life, trying to fill the missing gap. Anyway, did I ever tell you that my grandmother Esma had paid for this house with a twenty-five-carat sapphire?”

“You might be able to get it for a pair of Adidas now.”

“Come on. Be a good sport.”

12

(Mahbod Seraji, 1956—)
马赫布·塞拉吉

作者简介

马赫布·塞拉吉（Mahbod Seraji，1956—）博士，美国伊朗裔作家，他于1956年10月18日出生于伊朗安扎利班达尔（Bandar Anzali），1976年（19岁时）移居美国。他曾就读于艾奥瓦大学（University of Iowa），在那里获得了电影与广播硕士学位和教学设计与技术博士学位。

马赫布·塞拉吉广受好评的小说《德黑兰的屋顶》（*Rooftops of Tehran*，2009）于2009年5月出版，并被翻译成多种语言。他的这部处女作小说探讨了政治镇压的人力成本。《德黑兰的屋顶》是一部以伊朗前伊斯兰革命为背景的充满激情的哲学小说，讲述了人类状况的普遍性，不分文化、宗教和民族。

《德黑兰的屋顶》讲述了在1973年夏天，17岁的帕夏·沙赫德（Pasha Shahed）和最好的朋友艾哈迈德（*Ahmed*）在自家屋顶上度过了一个夏天，他们梦想着未来，问着关于生活的尖锐问题，同时也在努力解决一个重大秘密。他爱上了他美丽的邻居扎里，而扎里一出生就和另一个男人订婚了。尽管帕夏对她充满了负罪感，但在漫长炎热的日子里，他们短暂的友谊加深成了更丰富的情感纽带。但是，当帕夏不知不觉地成为伊朗国王秘密警察的线人时，这种完美而短暂的夏天的幸福突然在一个晚上被打破。暴力后果使帕夏和他的朋友们意识到生活在一个强大的暴君统治下的现实，并导致扎里做出一个帕夏可能永远无法理解的令人震惊的选择。

这部令人惊叹的处女作以凄美、令人叹为观止的散文揭示了传承了几个世纪的波斯文化中的美丽与残酷，同时重申了我们共同拥有的人类经历：欢笑、泪水、爱、无助，最重要的是，希望。在书末的一次采访中，塞拉吉谈到“在写《德黑兰的屋顶》时，我想让读者了解伊朗，并把几个世纪以来波斯文化的一小部分带到生活中。在我出生的国家经常被新闻媒体描述为‘敌人’的时候，我选择讲述一个友谊和幽默、爱和希望的故事，这是古今中外人们所珍视的普遍经历。”

2009 年 6 月，《德黑兰的屋顶》被美国书商协会（American Booksellers Association）评为 2009 年最佳处女作之一，还被《旧金山纪事报》（*San Francisco Chronicle*）选为 2009 年湾区（Bay Area）50 大著名书籍之一，并且名列 2009 年最受读书俱乐部欢迎的 25 本书之一。

节选部分来自其小说《德黑兰的屋顶》第二章。德黑兰男孩帕夏（Pasha）和他的朋友艾哈迈德（Ahmed）经常坐在屋顶上聊天，两人各自有着心仪的姑娘，但是他们又面临着种种失意和挑战，小人物的戏剧性命运在马赫布·塞拉吉的笔下得以充分展现。他希望读者在德黑兰的夜晚与小巷中的人物一起放松自己，了解这些好人在这个世界上必须经历的麻烦。

作品选读

Rooftops of Tehran

(2 Faheemeh's Tears and Zari's Wet Hair)

By Mahbod Seraji

Rooftops of Tehran

2

Faheemeh's Tears and Zari's Wet Hair

Our summer nights on the roof are spent basking in the wide-open safety of our bird's-eye view. There are no walls around what we say, or fears shaping what we think. I spend hours listening to stories of Ahmed's silent encounters with Faheemeh, the girl he loves. His voice softens and his face quiets as he describes how she threw back her long black hair while looking at him—and how that must mean she loves him. Why else would she strain her neck to communicate with him? My father says that Persians believe in silent communication; a look or a gesture imparts far more than a book full of words. My father is a great silent communicator. When I behave badly, he just gives me a dirty look that hurts more than a thousand slaps in the face.

I listen while Ahmed's voice chatters on about Faheemeh, but my gaze usually wanders into our neighbors' yard, where a girl named Zari lives with her parents and her little brother, Keivan. I've never seen Faheemeh up close, so when Ahmed talks about her I picture Zari in my mind: her delicate cheekbones, her smiling eyes, and her pale, soft skin. Most summer evenings Zari sits at the edge of her family's little hose under a cherry tree, dangling her shapely feet in the cool water as she reads. I'm careful not to let my eyes linger too long because she is engaged to my friend and mentor, Ramin Sobhi, a third-year political science major at the University of Tehran whom everyone, including his parents, calls Doctor. It's low to fancy a friend's girl, and I shove all thoughts of Zari from my head every time I think of Doctor, but Ahmed's lovesick ramblings make it hard for me to keep my mind clear.

Every day Ahmed bikes ten minutes to Faheemeh's neighborhood in the hope of getting a glimpse of her. He says she has two older brothers who protect her like hawks, and that everyone in the neighborhood knows that messing with their sister means getting a broken nose, a dislocated jaw, and a big black eggplant under at least one eye. Ahmed says that if Faheemeh's brothers learned that he fancied their sister, they'd make his ears the biggest parts of his body—meaning that they would cut him into little pieces.

Not one to be thwarted, Ahmed picks a day when Faheemeh's brothers are in the alley and intentionally rides his bike into a wall. He moans and groans with pain, and Faheemeh's brothers take him inside their home and give him a couple of aspirin, then immobilize his injured wrist by wrapping a piece of fabric around it. Faheemeh is only a few steps away, and knows full well what the handsome stranger is up to.

Ahmed now rides his bike to Faheemeh's alley without a worry in the world, spending hours with Faheemeh's brothers and talking about everything from the members of this year's Iranian national soccer team to next year's potential honorees. He says he doesn't mind that her brothers bore him to death as long as he is close to her. They play soccer all afternoon in the alley and Ahmed insists on playing goalie, even though he stinks in that position. While the other kids chase the ball in the scorching heat of Tehran's afternoons, Ahmed stands still. Supposedly he's defending his team's goal, but really he's watching Faheemeh, who watches him from the roof of her house.

After only a few games, Ahmed is forced to abdicate his post as the goalie. He is so preoccupied with Faheemeh that he is never prepared for the opponent's attackers and his team always loses by at least five or six points. When Ahmed begins to play forward his team starts to win again, but now he has to run after the ball, which means he can no longer exchange silent looks with Faheemeh.

So Ahmed comes to me with a plan. I am to accompany him to Faheemeh's alley the next day. He will introduce me to his new friends and will make sure that I end up on the opposite team. I will aim at his knee during a crucial play and he'll fake a bad fall and a serious injury. Then he will have no choice but to play as goalie again. He will be a goalie in agony, playing despite his pain, and that will undoubtedly impress Faheemeh.

I agree to go along but worry deep down about what Faheemeh might think of me after I knock Ahmed down. I feel better when I imagine the day we tell her the whole thing was a setup to get Ahmed back in the goalie position.

"Don't hurt me for real, now," Ahmed warns with a smile on his face.

"Make sure the orthopedic surgeon is on call, pal," I respond, getting into the spirit.

"Oh, come on. You know I have fragile bones. Just touch me lightly and I'll do the rest."

The plan is carried out masterfully. Ahmed deserves an Oscar for his portrayal of a boy in pain, and a gold medal for playing goalie after his dreadful injury. Looking at his face, which glows with the knowledge that Faheemeh is watching, I worry that he might really hurt himself with his courageous dives to the left, to the right, and under the feet of our attackers—all of this on asphalt. We can't score on him. He scrapes his hands and elbows, and tears his pants at the knees. Each time he stops us he grimaces with pain, releases the ball, and looks up toward the roof where Faheemeh is watching attentively. I even see her smile at him once.

One of Faheemeh's brothers notices that I'm looking toward the roof, and I know from that moment on he doesn't like me anymore, just as I don't like Iraj for staring at Ahmed's sister. He doesn't shake my hand when I say good-bye to everyone. I size him up surreptitiously. He's taller and bigger than I am. I leave with the comfort of knowing that I would not be letting down the sacred brotherhood of the boxing fraternity if he ever decided to be an asshole to me or to Ahmed.

A couple of weeks pass, and I'm sitting on our roof in the dark, my ears and eyes filled with the rush and sway of the light wind that bends the treetops, when I hear the door to Zari's yard open, then shut.

Don't look, I think resolutely, but my body resorts to quick, shallow breaths as soon as it recognizes the sound. *It could just be Keivan*, I reason. I decide to close my eyes, but my heart races as I realize that doing so has only sharpened my hearing. Bare feet pad across the yard, then the water in the *hose* begins to murmur with the slow churning of her legs as the pages of her book turn with the soft, rhythmic hiss so familiar from my own hours spent reading. She's read four pages by the time Ahmed arrives on my roof. He sits silently on the short wall that runs between our rooftops and lights a cigarette with shaking hands. The momentary illumination from the match reveals tears in his eyes.

"Is something wrong?" I ask, my chest growing tight at the expression on his face.

He shakes his head no, but I don't believe him. We Persians as a people are too deeply immersed in misery to resist despair when it knocks on our door.

"Are you sure?" I insist;, and he nods his head yes.

I decide to leave him alone because that's what I wish people would do for me when I don't feel like talking.

He sits as still as stone for a few minutes as the cigarette's glowing coal creeps toward his fingers, then whispers, "She has a suitor."

"Who has a suitor?" I ask, glancing below at Zari; her ivory feet stir the moon's reflection on the water's surface so that it shimmers like liquid gold.

"Faheemeh. A guy who lives a couple of doors down from them is sending his parents to her house tomorrow night."

It feels like someone knocked the wind out of me. I don't know what to say. People who insist on sticking their noses into other people's business seldom know what to say or do. I wonder why they ask in the first place. I pretend to study the blinking city lights that sprawl across the shadowy distance.

"When did you find out?" I finally ask.

"After you left this afternoon, her brothers and I went into her yard to get some cool water and that's when they told me."

"Was she around?"

"Yes," he says, looking up hard at the sky to keep the tears from falling down his face. "She was pouring water from a pitcher into my glass when they told me." He remembers his cigarette and takes a big puff. "I was sitting in a chair and she was standing over me, actually bending over me. She looked at my eyes the whole time, never blinked.” Ahmed shakes his head as his lips twist into the ghost of a smile. “She was so close I could feel her breath on my face, and her skin smelled clean—like soap, but sweeter. One of her brothers asked if I was going to congratulate their little sister, but I couldn’t make my voice come out of my throat.” Ahmed lets his face and his tears fall as he drops the spent cigarette and steps on it.

“She’s too young,” I whisper. “For crying out loud, how old is she, seventeen? How can they marry off a seventeen-year-old kid?”

Ahmed shakes his head again, mute.

“Maybe her parents will reject him,” I say, to plant hope in his heart.

“Her family loves him,” he says with a short bitter laugh as he pulls another cigarette from the pack. “He’s a twenty-six-year-old college graduate who works for the Agriculture Ministry, owns a car, and will soon be buying his own home in Tehran Pars. They won’t say no to him.” He lights the cigarette, then holds the pack out in my direction. I picture my father appearing unexpectedly and pinning me down with one of his dirty looks, the ones that hurt more than a thousand slaps in the face. I shake my head no.

I look at Ahmed’s sad face and wish I could do something to help him out. This is a historic night for both of us. We’re experiencing the first major personal crisis of our young lives. It’s sad, but I must admit, on some level it’s also exciting. It makes me feel grown-up.

“Do you know how bad this feels?” Ahmed asks between puffs.

“Well,” I begin, wanting desperately to carry his pain, “I’ve only read about it in books,” I confess, somewhat embarrassed. Then I look toward Zari’s yard, and add, “But I think I can imagine.”

13

(Mona Simpson, 1957—)

莫娜·辛普森

作者简介

莫娜·辛普森（Mona Simpson，1957— ）于1957年6月14日出生在威斯康星州的格林湾（Green Bay, Wisconsin），十几岁时搬到了洛杉矶。父亲是叙利亚裔移民，母亲是一个养水貂的农民的女儿，也是家里第一个上大学的人。莫娜·辛普森是已故苹果联合创始人史蒂夫·乔布斯的妹妹。她曾在加州大学伯克利分校（UC Berkley）学习英语，后在哥伦比亚大学（Columbia University）学习语言与文学。

在读研究生期间，她在《犁头文学杂志》（*The Ploughshares Literary Journal*）、《爱荷华评论》（*The Iowa Review*）和《小姐杂志》（*Mademoiselle*）等刊物上发表了她的第一批短篇小说。她在《巴黎评论》（*The Paris Review*）担任了五年的编辑，同时完成了她的第一部小说《芳心天涯》（*Anywhere But Here*, 1986）。《芳心天涯》大获成功，获得了怀廷奖（The Whiting Award），随后于1999年被改编为同名电影热映。在那之后，她写了续集《失去的父亲》（*The Lost Father*, 1992），再度获得评论界的认可，并获得芝加哥论坛报哈特兰奖（Chicago Tribune Heartland Award）。她还写过《一个普通人》（*A Regular Guy*, 1996）和《离开凯克路》（*Off Keck Road*, 2000）等作品。《离开凯克路》还曾入围笔会/福克纳奖（Pen/Faulkner Award）。她的作品还获得了其他多个奖项：古根海姆奖（Guggenheim Fellowship）、普林斯顿大学的霍德奖学金（Hodder Fellowship of Princeton University）、莱拉华莱士读者文摘奖（Lila Wallace Reader's Digest Fellowship），以及后来的美国艺术与文学学院奖（Literature Award from the

American Academy of Arts and Letters)。

节选部分出自《芳心天涯》第一章。《芳心天涯》讲述的是一个关于母亲和女儿的令人心碎的故事。这部小说对聪明的孩子安·奥古斯特（Ann August）和她的母亲阿黛尔（Adele）进行了感人且充满喜剧色彩的描绘。小说讲述了这两个女人在彼此矛盾的雄心壮志中旅行的故事。这本书精彩地探索了人们即使面临严重迷失方向的风险也要不断前进的长期冲动，它讲述了我们为爱所做的事情，并对家庭纽带进行了强有力的研究。

作品选读

Anywhere But Here

(Chapter 1 ANYWHERE)

By Mona Simpson

We fought. When my mother and I crossed state lines in the stolen car, I'd sit against the window and wouldn't talk. I wouldn't even look at her. The fights came when I thought she broke a promise. She said there'd be an Indian reservation. She said that we'd see buffalo in Texas. My mother said a lot of things. We were driving from Bay City, Wisconsin, to California, so I could be a child star while I was still a child.

"Talk to me," my mother would say. "If you're upset, tell me."

But I wouldn't. I knew how to make her suffer. I was mad. I was mad about a lot of things. Places she said would be there, weren't. We were running away from family. We'd left home.

Then my mother would pull to the side of the road and reach over and open my door."

"Get out, then," she'd say, pushing me.

I got out. It was always a shock the first minute because nothing outside was bad. The fields were bright. It never happened on a bad day. The western sky went on forever, there were a few clouds. A warm breeze came up and tangled around my legs. The road was dull as a nickel. I stood there at first amazed that there was nothing horrible in the landscape.

But then the wheels of the familiar white Continental turned, a spit of gravel hit my shoes and my mother's car drove away. When it was nothing but a dot in the distance, I started to cry.

I lost time then; I don't know if it was minutes or if it was more. There was nothing to think because there was nothing to do. First, I saw small things. The blades of grass. Their rough side, their smooth, waxy side. Brown grasshoppers. A dazzle of California poppies.

I'd look at everything around me. In yellow fields, the tops of weeds bent under visible waves of wind. There was a high steady note of insects screaking. A rich odor of hay mixed with the heady smell of gasoline. Two or three times, a car rumbled by, shaking the ground. Dry weeds by the side of the road seemed almost transparent in the even sun.

I tried hard but I couldn't learn anything. The scenery all went strange, like a picture on a high billboard. The fields, the clouds, the sky; none of it helped because it had nothing to do with me.

My mother must have watched in her rearview mirror. My arms crossed over my chest, I would have looked smaller and more solid in the distance. That was what she couldn't stand, my stubbornness. She'd had a stubborn husband. She wasn't going to have a stubborn child. But when she couldn't see me anymore, she gave up and turned around and she'd gasp with relief when I was in front of her again, standing open-handed by the side of the road, nothing more than a child, her child.

And by the time I saw her car coming back, I'd be covered with a net of tears, my nose running. I stood there with my hands hanging at my sides, not even trying to wipe my face.

My mother would slow down and open my door and I'd run in, looking back once in a quick good-bye to the fields, which turned ordinary and pretty again. And when I slid into the car, I was different. I put my feet up on the dashboard and tapped the round tips of my sneakers together. I wore boys' sneakers she thought I was too old for. But now my mother was nice because she knew I would talk to her.

"Are you hungry?" was the first thing she'd say.

"A little."

"I am," she'd say. "I feel like an ice cream cone. Keep your eyes open for a Howard Johnson's."

We always read the magazines, so we knew where we wanted to go. My mother had read about Scottsdale and Albuquerque and Bel Air. But for miles, there was absolutely nothing. It seemed we didn't have anything and even air that came in the windows when we were driving fast felt hot.

We had taken Ted's Mobil credit card and we used it whenever we could. We scouted for Mobil stations and filled up the tank when we found one, also charging Cokes on the bill. We dug to our elbows in the ice chests, bringing the cold pop bottles up like a catch. There was one chain of motels that accepted Mobil cards. Most nights we stayed in those, sometimes driving three or four hours longer to find one, or stopping early if one was there. They were called Travel Lodges and their signs each outlined a bear in a nightcap, sleepwalking. They were dull motels, lonely, and they were pretty cheap, which bothered my mother because she would have liked to charge high bills to Ted. I think she enjoyed signing Mrs. Ted Diamond. We passed Best Westerns with hotel swimming pools and restaurants with country singers and we both wished and wished Ted had a different card.

Travel Lodges were the kind of motels that were set a little off the highway in a field. They tended to be one or at the most two stories, with cement squares outside your room door for old empty metal chairs. At one end there would be a lit coffee shop and a couple of semis parked on the gravel. The office would be near the coffee shop. It would have shag carpeting and office furniture, always a TV attached by metal bars to the ceiling.

Those motels depressed us. After we settled in the room, my mother looked around, checking for cleanliness. She took the bedspreads down, lifted curtains, opened drawers and the medicine cabinet, and looked into the shower. Sometimes she took the paper off a water glass and held the glass up to see that it was washed.

I always wanted to go outside. My mother would be deliberating whether it was safer to leave our suitcase in the room or in the locked car; when she was thinking, she stood in the middle of the floor with her hands on her hips and her lips pursed. Finally, she decided to bring it in. Then she would take a shower to cool off. She didn't make me take one if I didn't want to, because we were nowhere and she didn't care what I looked like in the coffee shop. After her shower, she put on the same clothes she'd been driving in all day.

I went out to our porch and sat in the one metal chair. Its back was a rounded piece, perhaps once designed to look like a shell. I could hear her shower water behind me, running; in front, the constant serious sound of the highway. A warm wind slapped my skin lightly, teasing, the sound of the trucks on the highway came loud, then softer, occasionally a motorcycle shrank to the size of a bug, red taillights ticking on the blue sky.

I acted like a kid, always expecting to find something. At home, before supper, I'd stood outside when the sky looked huge and even the near neighbors seemed odd and distant in their occupations. I'd watched the cars moving on the road, as if by just watching you could understand, get something out of the world.

14
(Rabih Alameddine, 1959—)
拉比·阿拉梅丁

作者简介

拉比·阿拉梅丁（Rabih Alameddine，1959—）是美国黎巴嫩裔作家和画家。他出生于约旦安曼（Amman），在科威特和黎巴嫩长大。他在17岁时离开黎巴嫩，先在英格兰生活，然后移居美国加利福尼亚。他在加州大学洛杉矶分校（UCLA）获得工程学学位，并在旧金山获得商科硕士学位。

阿拉梅丁的职业生涯始于工程师，然后转向写作和绘画。他的处女作《库拉兹》（*Koolaids*）于1998年由皮卡多出版社（Picador）出版，内容涉及旧金山的艾滋病疫情和黎巴嫩内战。作为6部小说和1部短篇小说集的作者，阿拉梅丁于2002年获得了古根海姆奖学金（The Guggenheim Fellowship）。他曾在旧金山和贝鲁特（Beirut）生活，目前在弗吉尼亚大学（University of Virginia）的创意写作项目任教。

2014年，阿拉梅丁的小说《一个不必要的女人》（*An Unnecessary Woman*）入围了美国国家书评家协会奖（The National Book Critics Circle Award），并成功获得加州图书奖小说金奖（The California Book Awards Gold Medal Fiction）、《华盛顿邮报》（*The Washington Post*）、柯库斯（*Kirkus*）和美国国家公共广播电台2014年度最佳图书奖。他的其他小说包括《历史的天使》（*The Angel of History*，2016）、《哈卡瓦提》（*Hakawati*，2008）和《我乃真神》（*I, the Divine*，2001），另有一本短篇小说集《变态》（*The Perv*，1999）。2017年，阿拉梅丁凭借《历史的天使》获得了美国阿拉伯裔图书奖（The Arab American Book Award）。他的故事《七月战争》入围了2021年星期日泰晤士报短篇小说奖（*The Sunday Times*

Short Story Award）；他的 2021 年小说《望远镜的错端》（*The Wrong End of the Telescope*, 2021）被《出版人周刊》（*The Publishers Weekly*）称为“深刻而精彩”，并获得了 2022 年笔会 / 福克纳小说奖（The PEN/Faulkner Award for Fiction）。

本部分内容节选自拉比·阿拉梅丁成名作《一个不必要的女人》第一章。阿利亚独自住在贝鲁特的公寓里，周围堆满了书籍。没有神、没有父亲、离异、没有孩子，阿利亚是她家人“不必要的附属物”。每年，她都会将一本最喜欢的新书翻译成阿拉伯语，然后将其收藏起来。阿拉梅丁的这部成名作《一个不必要的女人》讲述了生活在饱受战争蹂躏的黎巴嫩妇女兼翻译阿利亚的故事。这部小说“展现了（黎巴嫩）内战的创伤性标志，使它成为不可磨灭的情景，并因此抓住了复杂的心理问题”。

作品选读

An Unnecessary Woman

(Chapter 1)

By Rabih Alameddine

An Unnecessary Woman

You could say I was thinking of other things when I shampooed my hair blue, and two glasses of red wine didn't help my concentration.

Let me explain.

First, you should know this about me: I have but one mirror in my home, a smudged one at that. I'm a conscientious cleaner, you might even say compulsive—the sink is immaculately white, its bronze faucets sparkle—but I rarely remember to wipe the mirror clean. I don't think we need to consult Freud or one of his many minions to know that there's an issue here?.

I begin this tale with a badly lit reflection. One of the bathroom's two bulbs has expired. I'm in the midst of the evening ritual of brushing my teeth, facing said mirror, when a halo surrounding my head snares my attention. Toothbrush in right hand still moving up and down, side to side, left hand reaches for reading glasses lying on the little table next to the toilet. Once atop my obtrusive nose they help me see that I'm neither a saint nor saintly but more like the Queen Mother—well, an image of the

Queen Mother smudged by a schoolgirl's eraser. No halo this, the blue anomaly is my damp hair. A pigment battle rages atop my head, a catfight of mismatched contestants.

1 touch a still-wet lock to test the permanency of the blue tint and end up leaving a sticky stain of toothpaste on it. You can correctly presume that multitasking is not my forte.

I lean over the bathtub, pick up the tube of Bel Argent shampoo I bought yesterday. I read the fine print, squinting even with the reading glasses. Yes, I used ten times the amount prescribed while washing my hair. I enjoy a good lather. Reading instructions happens not to be my forte either.

Funny. My bathroom tiles are rectangular white with interlocking light blue tulips, almost the same shade as my new dye. Luckily, the blue isn't that of the Israeli flag. Can you imagine? Talk about a brawl of mismatched contestants.

Usually vanity isn't one of my concerns, doesn't disconcert me much. However, I'd overheard the three witches discussing the unrelenting whiteness of my hair. Joumana, my upstairs neighbor, had suggested that if I used a shampoo like Bel Argent, the white would be less flat. There you have it.

As I understand it, and I might be wrong as usual, you and I tend to lose short wavelength cones as we age, so we're less able to distinguish the color blue. That's why many people of a certain age have a bluish tint to their hair. Without the tint, they see their hair as pale yellow, or possibly salmon. One hairstylist described on the radio how he finally convinced this old woman that her hair was much too blue. But his client still refused to change the color. It was much more important that she see her hair as natural than the rest of the world do so.

I'd probably get along better with the client.

I too am an old woman, but I have yet to lose many short wavelength cones. I can distinguish the color blue a bit too clearly right now.

Allow me to offer a mild defense for being distracted. At the end of the year, before I begin a new project, I read the translation I've completed. I do minor final corrections, set the pages in order, and place them in the box. This is part of the ritual, which includes imbibing two glasses of red wine. I'll also admit that the last reading allows me to pat myself on the back, to congratulate myself on completing the project. This year, I translated the superb novel *Austerlitz*, my second translation of W. G. Sebald. I was reading it today, and for some reason, probably the protagonist's unrequited despair, I couldn't stop thinking of Hannah, I couldn't, as if the novel, or my

Arabic translation of it, was an inductor into Hannah's world.

Remembering Hannah, my one intimate, is never easy. I still see her before me at the kitchen table, her plate wiped clean of food, her right cheek resting on the palm of her hand, head tilted slightly, listening, offering that rarest of gifts: her unequivocal attention. My voice had no home until her.

During my seventy-two years, she was the one person I cared for, the one I told too much—boasts, hates, joys, cruel disappointments, all jumbled together. I no longer think of her as often as I used to, but she appears in my thoughts every now and then. The traces of Hannah on me are indelible.

Percolating remembrances, red wine, an old woman's shampoo: mix well and wind up with blue hair.

I'll wash my hair once more in the morning, with no more tears baby shampoo this time. Hopefully the blue will fade. I can just imagine what the neighbors will say now.

For most of my adult life, since I was twenty-two, I've begun a translation every January first. I do realize that this is a holiday and most choose to celebrate, most do not choose to work on New Year's Day. Once, as I was leafing through the folio of Beethoven's sonatas, I noticed that only the penultimate, the superb op. 110 in A-flat Major, was dated on the top right corner, as if the composer wanted us to know that he was busy working that Christmas Day in 1821. I too choose to keep busy during holidays.

Over these last fifty years I've translated fewer than forty books—thirty-seven, if I count correctly. Some books took longer than a year, others refused to be translated, and one or two bored me into submission—not the books themselves, but my translations of them. Books in and of themselves are rarely boring, except for memoirs of American presidents (No, No, Nixon)—well, memoirs of Americans in general. It's the "I live in the richest country in the world yet pity me because I grew up with flat feet and a malodorous vagina but I triumph in the end" syndrome. Tfeh!

Books into boxes—boxes of paper, loose translated sheets. That's my life.

I long ago abandoned myself to a blind lust for the written word. Literature is my sandbox. In it I play, build my forts and castles, spend glorious time. It is the world outside that box that gives me trouble. I have adapted tamely, though not conventionally, to this visible world so I can retreat without much inconvenience into my inner world of books. Transmuting this sandy metaphor, if literature is my sandbox, then the real world is my hourglass—an hourglass that drains grain by grain. Literature gives me life, and life kills me.

Well, life kills everyone.

But that's a morose subject. Tonight I feel alive—blue hair and red wine alive. The end of the year approaches, the beginning of a new year. The year is dead. Long live the year! I will begin my next project. This is the time that excites me most. I pay no attention to the Christmas decorations that burst into fruitful life in various neighborhoods of my city, or the lights welcoming the New Year. This year, Ashura falls at almost the same time, but I don't care.

Let the people flagellate themselves into a frenzy of remembrance. Wails, whips, blood: the betrayal of Hussein moves me not.

15

(Diana Abu-Jaber, 1960—)
黛安娜·阿布杰比

作者简介

黛安娜·阿布杰比（Diana Abu-Jaber，1960—）是美国约旦裔作家，她出生在纽约的锡拉丘兹（Syracuse, New York），母亲是美国人，父亲是约旦人。在她的童年时期，她的家人曾几次搬到约旦，她在美国和约旦的经历，以及跨文化问题，尤其是烹饪方面的思考，都在她的作品中有所体现。她经常通过食品和食品生产的文化来书写阿拉伯以及美国阿拉伯裔的文化和身份。

黛安娜·阿布杰比著有八本小说和非小说类书籍，这些作品很受读者欢迎，并为她带了很多文学奖项。她的第一部食谱回忆录《巴克拉瓦的语言》（*The Language of Baklava*，2005），曾入选2005年最佳美食写作，还获得了2006年西北书商奖（The Northwest Booksellers' Award），并被翻译成多种语言。黛安娜的烹饪回忆录《没有食谱的生活》（*Life Without A Recipe*，2016）被描述为“一本关于爱、死亡和蛋糕的书”。她的第一部小说《阿拉伯爵士乐》（*Arabian Jazz*，1994）荣获俄勒冈州图书奖（Oregon Book Award）的文学小说奖，并入围了笔会海明威奖（PEN/Hemingway Award）。第二部小说《新月》（*Crescent*，2003）结合了浪漫故事、民间故事和时事事件来描述美国阿拉伯裔的移民经历。故事以洛杉矶的伊朗和伊拉克移民和流亡者为背景，讲述了美国伊拉克裔移民西尔琳爱上伊拉克流亡者哈尼夫的故事。这部小说获得了美国笔会中心文学小说奖（PEN Center USA Award for Literary Fiction）和美国图书奖（American Book Award），还被《基督教科学箴言报》（*Christian Science Monitor*）评为年度著名书籍。

熟悉黛安娜作品的人都知道她的小说关注美国阿拉伯裔人的文化、美味的食谱和烹饪爱情故事。然而，在她的小说《起源》（*Origin*，2007）中，黛安娜深入探索了文学神秘题材，写了“她不知道的事情”。《起源》是一部心理惊悚文学作品，受到了《出版人周刊》（*The Publishers Weekly*）和《书目》（*Booklist*）的好评，并获得了西北书商奖。

黛安娜的小说《天堂鸟》（*Birds of Paradise*，2011）是一部以当代迈阿密为生动背景，关于家庭与自我、自我放纵与慷慨的多层次、结构优美的小说。它获得了美国阿拉伯裔图书奖，并被《华盛顿邮报》（*The Washington Post*）、美国国家公共电台（NPR）、《芝加哥论坛报》（*The Chicago Tribune*）等媒体评为最佳图书。她的青年小说《银世界》（*Silver World*，2020）是一部以美国阿拉伯裔女孩为核心的奇幻小说，于2020年春天由皇冠图书（Crown Books）/兰登书屋（Random House）出版。这个奇幻冒险故事讲述了一个美国黎巴嫩裔女孩鼓起勇气去救她的祖母的经历。

黛安娜的最新作品《与国王击剑》（*Fencing With the King*，2022）通过对现代政治和家庭动态、精神疾病禁忌以及我们与过去不可避免的关系的敏锐洞察，巧妙地捕捉到了约旦在1990年代中期中东和平进程中的微弱角色，同时发掘了一个家庭被埋葬的秘密，是一部引人入胜的家庭剧。

节选部分分别为黛安娜的小说《天堂鸟》第一章和《新月》第二章。《天堂鸟》中，13岁的菲利斯·穆尔（Felice Muir）因为琐事离家出走，成为街头流浪儿。这给她在迈阿密的上层中产阶级家庭带来了很大的影响。在迈阿密海滩寻找食物、毒品和庇护所五年之后，菲利斯的故事重新开始，因为她18岁生日和卡特里娜飓风都接近脆弱的海岸线和情感脆弱的家庭，每个人都沉浸在自己独特的世界中。

《新月》第一章中，美国伊拉克裔女孩瑟润（Sirine）在叔叔的鼓励下，开始与叔叔部门的新员工——伊拉克移民哈尼夫·伊亚德（Hanif Al Eyad）建立浪漫关系。双方开始分享的亲密世界，不仅是关于他们的童年，还有对故国的记忆。在黛安娜·阿布杰比的笔下，读者读到了一个与当前媒体描述截然不同的伊拉克。

作品选读（一）

Birds of Paradise

(Chapter 1)

By Diana Abu-Jaber

A COOKIE, AVIS TOLD HER CHILDREN, is a soul. She held up the wafer, its edges shimmering with ruby-dark sugar. "You think it looks like a tiny thing, right? Just a little nothing. But then you take a bite."

Four-year-old Felice lifted her face. Avis fanned her daughter's eyes closed with her fingertips and placed it in Felice's mouth. Felice opened her sheer eyes. Lamb slid his orange length against her ankles. Avis handed a cookie to eight-year-old Stanley, who held it up to his nose. "Does that taste good?" she asked. Felice nodded and opened her mouth again

"It smells like flowers," Stanley said.

"*Yes*." Avis paused, a cookie balanced on her spatula. "That's the rosewater. Good palate, darling."

"Mermaids eat roses," Felice said. "Then they melt."

THIS MORNING'S PASTRY poses challenges. To assemble the tiny mosaic disks of chocolate flake and candied ginger,

Avis must execute a number of discrete, ritualistic steps: scraping the chocolate with a fine grater, rolling the dough cylinder in large-grain sanding sugar, and assembling the ingredients atop each hand-cut disk of dough in a pointillist collage. Her husband wavers near the counter, watching. "They're like something Marie Antoinette would wear around her neck. When she still had one."

"I thought she was more interested in cake," Avis says, she tilts her narrow shoulders, veers around him to stack dishes in the sink.

"But really—look at this." Brian holds one on the palm of his hand; it twinkles with the kitchen light. "Shame to eat them."

Avis had shopped for the ingredients two days earlier, driving to Fort Lauderdale, to an Italian import store, to buy the rock sugar and flour. The outlying regions of downtown Miami, Hallandale, Hollywood, seemed esoteric, scribbled over —

inscrutable as an ancient desert. She was offended by the ads painted on the sides of warehouses, hawking lamps and furniture, medical treatments and ice cream, a thirty-foot naked man reclining, selling God-knows-what.

Yesterday she crystallized the ginger, then mixed the ingredients slowly, not to disturb the dough. But even after one full day's work, there were still more steps to complete this morning, including baking and cooling. Avis had hurried, not wanting Brian to notice how much labor has gone into this. Her assistant won't be in for another hour and there's a tower in the sink, open bins of pastry flour, the hair dryer on the counter (just a blast of cool air, to ward off the humidity, before slipping the cookies into tins). Brian slips one of the half-dollar-sized pastries into his mouth. Avis knows it will dissolve mid-chew, fleeting as a wink. "Have I had these before? Do you sell them?"

"Not for years." Avis can't help boasting a little, "Last time I made these, Neiman's sold them for $4.95 apiece in their case."

Brian eyes the three remaining on his plate. "We should stick them in a safe."

Avis admits, "A little labor-intensive." *Gingembre en cristal* was Felice's favorite cookie; Stanley's were homely, proletarian Toll Houses. Avis remembers toiling over the delicate ginger coins for Felice's tenth birthday, only for her daughter to thank her politely and then refuse to eat them. She'd said, "I just like the way they look."

Avis had felt singed by the rejection. Yet there was also a pang of admiration: the purity of Felice's desires—preferring beauty to sugar!

Avis had started baking because there was never anything to eat when she was a child. Her mother—head lowered over Dante, Hegel, C. S. Lewis, reading Voltaire, Bakhtin, Avicenna, in French, Russian, Arabic—would murmur, "Go get yourself something." Avis would hang on the refrigerator door, staring at cans of tomato juice, sticks of butter, bags of coffee. She went for days at a time eating only jam and slices of bread. The women at the Redbird Bakery on the next block gave her free muffins and scones whenever she came in. Her mother was busy: she taught and wrote about private and cultural representations of Heaven, the phoenix the transformation of base materials into gold. Instead of reading storybooks, Avis stood in the kitchen studying the pictures in cookbooks, a more immediate form of alchemy.

Avis asked about the identity of her father when she was ten: Geraldine waved her off, saying, "Oh, who keeps track?" When Avis persisted, she shook her head: "No, no— don't be tedious, dear."

The first time Avis knelt on a chair and stirred eggs into flour to make a vanilla cake, she had an inkling of how higher orders of meaning encircle the chaos of life. Where philosophy, she already intuited, created only thought—no beds made, no children fed—in other rooms there were good things like measuring spoons, thermometers, and recipes, with their lovely, interwoven systems and codes. Avis labored over her pastries: her ingredient base grew, combining worlds: preserved lemons from Morocco in a Provencal tart; Syrian olive oil in Neapolitan *cantuccini*; salt combed from English marshes and filaments of Kashmiri saffron secreted within a Swedish cream. By the time Avis was in college, her baking had evolved to a level of exquisite accomplishment: each pastry as unique as a snowflake, just as fleeting on the tongue: pellucid jams colored cobalt and lavender, biscuits light as eiderdown.

Brian edges in front of the sink, trying to stay out of her way. "Like you don't have enough to worry about today."

"Yes, yes." She glances at him: he's holding the counter as if it were keeping him steady. He's in the kitchen, she knows, because they'd fought earlier—or had what passes for a fight between them—the dart of words: Why are you still doing this? I just don't think...

I'm aware of what you think.

Now he looms, big as an obstacle. Not sure where to put himself. She doesn't like having people in her kitchen, but she does feel a lilt toward him, grateful that he hasn't run out yet. They're trying to stop fighting, but can't quite leave each other alone.

"That kid never ate anything anyway," he says darkly.

Avis begins the cautious and deliberate transfer of cookies to tin, using just the tips of her fingers. "Yes, and I'm crazy to go meet her."

"Now you're angry again."

"No I'm not." Avis places the cookies in concentric rings on parchment layers inside the tin. "I know just what my husband thinks, thank you very much, and I'm not angry. I'm fine."

Brian crosses his arms, the suit fabric bunching in fine soft ripples. She knows he can't stop himself. "But, please, *admit it*. It's what? The first time all *year we* hear from that girl? Light of our lives. You're already exhausted, at your wits' end. Finally you'll see her—if she comes. I don't get why you knock yourself out even more—making some impossible dessert that—I'm sorry, but she probably won't even eat. Am I wrong?"

Avis touches the sides of the tin. Her ribs feel compressed, like a whalebone corset. "No. No. You're right."

He stares at her, a weight in his gaze. He turns and his eyes fall on the Audubon calendar hanging near the door— the only ornamentation in Avis's kitchen. The month of August, Snowy Egret. He looks away.

作品选读（二）

Crescent

(Chapter One)

By Diana Abu-Jaber

CHAPTER ONE

The sky is white.

The sky shouldn't be white because it's after midnight and the moon has not yet appeared and nothing is as black and as ancient as the night in Baghdad. It is dark and fragrant as the hanging gardens of the extinct city of Chaldea, as dark and still as the night in the uppermost chamber of the spiraling Tower of Babel.

But it's white because white is the color of an exploding rocket. The ones that come from over the river, across the fields, from the other side of an invisible border, from another ancient country called Iran. The rockets are so close sometimes he can hear the warning whisk before they explode. The ones that explode in the sky send off big round blooms of colors, pinwheels of fire. But the ones that explode on the ground erase everything: they send out streamers of fire that race across the ground like electric snakes; they light up the donkeys by the water troughs and make their shadows a hundred meters long. They light up every blade of grass, every lizard, and every date; they electrify the dozing palms and set the most distant mountains—the place his uncle calls the Land of Na—on fire. They make his sister's face glow like yellow blossoms, they make the water look like phosphorescence as it runs from the tap. Their report sizzles along the tops of the tallest western buildings and rings against the minarets and domes. They whistle through the orchards and blast acres of olive trees out of the ground. They light up the Euphrates River, knock down the walls of the old churches, the ancient synagogues, the mysterious, crumbling monuments older than the books, monuments to gods so old they've lost their names, the ancient walls dissolving under the shock, waves like dust.

They erase all sleep. For years.

A young boy lies in his bed on the outskirts of town, still not-sleeping. He tries to calm himself by reciting poetry:

"Know that the world is a mirror from head to foot,
In every atom are a hundred blazing suns,
If you cleave the heart of one drop of water,
A hundred pure oceans emerge from it."

Far away, on the other side of town, deep in the city night, behind the Eastern Hotel where all the foreigners stay, there is a pool as round as the moon, where a white-skinned woman waits for him in the phosphorescent water. The night over the pool is undisturbed by bombs, he knows, because nothing can cross into the land of the bright-haired women, their painted nails and brilliant hair and glowing skin. She stands hip-deep and motionless in the shallow end of the water, waiting for him to come to her. Her hair is the color of fire and her eyes are the color of sky and the pool is the round moon above Baghdad. He lies dreaming and awake in his bedroom on the other side of town. He is young but he has not truly slept for years. She can send him to a new place, away from the new president, as far away as the other side of the world, a place where he will no longer have to look at his brother and sister not-sleeping, where he will not have to count his heartbeats, his breaths, the pulse in his eyelids. Where his mouth will not taste of iron, his ears will not ring, his hands and feet will not tingle, his stomach will not foam with the roaring sound that has gotten inside of him and that he fears in his deepest heart will never go away again.

Her uncle in his room of imagined books. Everything smells of books: an odor of forgotten memories. This is the library of imagined books, her uncle says, because he never reads any of them. Still, he's collected them from friends' basements and attics, garage sales and widows' dens, all over Culver City, West Hollywood, Pasadena, Laurel Canyon, picking books for their heft and their leather-belted covers. The actual pages don't matter.

"If you behave," he tells his thirty-nine-year-old niece Sirine, "I'll tell you the whole story this time."

"You always say I'm too young to hear the whole story," Sirine says. She carves a tiny bit of peel from a lemon for her uncle's coffee. They're up in the bluish white predawn, both of them chronically early risers and chronically sleepy.

Her uncle looks at her over his glasses. The narrow ovals slide down his nose; he tries to press them back into place. "Do I say that? I wonder why. Well, what are you now, a half-century yet?"

"I'm thirty-nine. And a half."

He makes a dismissive little flick with his fingers. "Too young. I'll save the juicy parts for when you're a half-century."

"Oh boy, I can't wait."

"Yes, that's how the young are. No one wants to wait." He takes a ceremonial sip of coffee and nods. "So this is the moralless story of Abdelrahman Salahadin, my favorite cousin, who had an incurable addiction to selling himself and faking his drowning."

"It sounds long," Sirine says. "Haven't I already heard this one?"

"It's a good, short story, Miss Hurry Up American. It's the story of how to love," he says.

Sirine puts her hands into her uncombable hair, closes her eyes. "I'm going to be late for work again."

"There you have it—the whole world is late for work, and all faucets leak too—what can be done? So it begins." He situates himself in his storytelling position—elbow on knee and hand to brow. "Abdelrahman Salahadin was a sensitive man. He never forgot to bathe before his prayers. Sometimes he knelt on the beach and made the sand his prayer carpet. He just had the one vice."

Sirine narrows her eyes. "Wait a second—you said this is the story of how to fall in love? Is there even a woman in this one?"

Her uncle tilts back his head, eyebrows lift, tongue clicks: this means, *no, or, wait, or, foolish, or, you just don't understand.* "Take my word for it," he says. "Love and prayer are intimately related." He sighs. Then he says slyly, "So I hear Professor Handsome was in today eating some of your tabbouleh. *Again.*"

Once again, her uncle is speaking of Hanif Al Eyad, the new hire in the Near Eastern Studies Department at the university. Hanif has come into the restaurant four times since arriving in town several weeks ago and her uncle keeps introducing him to Sirine, saying their names over and over, "Sirine, Hanif, Hanif, Sirine."

Sirine leans over the cutting board she has balanced on her knees and steadies the lemon. "I really don't know who you're referring to."

Her uncle gestures with both arms. "He's tremendous, covered with muscles, and shoulders like this—like a Cadillac—and a face like I don't know what."

"Well, if you don't know, I certainly don't," Sirine says as she slices the lemon.

Her uncle lounges back in his big blue chair. "No, really, you can't believe it, I'm telling you, he looks like a hero. Like Ulysses."

"That's supposed to sound good?"

He leans over and picks up the unsliced half of lemon, sniffs it, then bites into one edge.

"I don't know how you do that," Sirine says.

"If I were a girl, I'd be crazy for Ulysses."

"'What does Ulysses even look like? Some statue-head with no eyes?"

"No," he says, indignant. "He has eyes."

"Still not interested."

He frowns, pushes his glasses up; they slide back down. "As you know, if you're fifty-two, that makes me eighty-four—"

"Except that I'm thirty-nine."

"And very soon I won't be here. On this planet."

She sighs and looks at him.

"I would just like to see you with someone nice and charming and all those things. That's all."

16

(Dunya Mikhail, 1965—)
邓娅·米哈伊尔

作者简介

邓娅·米哈伊尔（Dunya Mikhail, 1965—）是美国伊拉克裔诗人，她于1965年生于巴格达（Baghdad），在巴格达大学（University of Baghdad）获得学士学位。在被列入萨达姆·侯赛因的敌对者名单之前，她曾为《巴格达观察报》（*The Baghdad Observer*）担任翻译和记者。她于20世纪90年代中期移民到美国，并在韦恩州立大学（Wayne State University）获得文学硕士学位。

米哈伊尔是几本阿拉伯文诗集的作者。她的第一本英文书《战争艰难》（*The War Works Hard*，2005）由伊丽莎白·温斯洛（Elizabeth Winslow）翻译，获得笔会翻译奖（PEN's Translation Fund Award），后又入围格里芬诗歌奖（Griffin Poetry Prize），并被纽约公共图书馆评选为2005年25本最佳图书之一。2011年，埃琳娜·奇蒂将《战争艰难》翻译成意大利语。米哈伊尔与伊丽莎白·温斯洛联合翻译的《海上海浪日记》（*Diary of a Wave Outside the Sea*，2009）获得了美国阿拉伯裔图书奖（The Arab American Book Award）。米哈伊尔的诗集《伊拉克之夜》（*The Iraqi Nights*，2014）由卡里姆·詹姆斯·阿布·扎伊德（Kareem James Abu-Zeid）翻译成英文。她用阿拉伯语和英语创作了诗集《她的女性符号》（*In Her Feminine Sign*，2019）。她还是非小说类书籍《养蜂人》（*The Beekeeper*，2018）的作者。

米哈伊尔的荣誉包括古根海姆奖（The Guggenheim Fellowship）、骑士基金会奖（The Knights Foundation Grant）、克雷斯基奖（The Kresge Fellowship）、联合国人权写作自由奖（The United Nations Human Rights Award For Freedom Of

Writing），以及入围阿拉伯布克奖（The Shortlist Of The Arabic Booker Prize）。她是密歇根社区美索不达米亚艺术与文化论坛（The Michigan community-based Mesopotamian Forum for Art and Culture）的联合创始人，目前在密歇根州奥克兰大学（Oakland University）担任阿拉伯语特聘讲师。

节选部分分别出自邓娅·米哈伊尔的英文诗集《战争艰难》和《伊拉克之夜》。米哈伊尔以讽刺和颠覆性的简单手法，运用报告文学、寓言和抒情诗等形式，阐述了战争、流亡和损失等主题。尽管她的诗歌记录了战争和流亡的创伤，但她也谈到了审查制度对她的作品的影响，这也是她在创作中使用了很多隐喻和多层含义的原因。

作品选读（一）

The War Works Hard

By Dunya Mikhail

The War Works Hard
How magnificent the war is!
How eager
and efficient!
Early in the morning,
it wakes up the sirens
and dispatches ambulances
to various places,
swings corpses through the air,
rolls stretchers to the wounded,
summons rain
from the eyes of mothers,
digs into the earth
dislodging many things
from under the ruins...
Some are lifeless and glistening,
others are pale and still throbbing...
It produces the most questions

in the minds of children,
entertains the gods
by shooting fireworks and missiles
into the sky,
sows mines in the fields
and reaps punctures and blisters,
urges families to emigrate,
stands beside the clergymen
as they curse the devil
(poor devil, he remains
with one hand in the searing fire)...
The war continues working, day and night.
It inspires tyrants
to deliver long speeches,
awards medals to generals
and themes to poets.
It contributes to the industry
of artificial limbs,
provides food for flies, adds pages to the history books,
achieves equality
between killer and killed,
teaches lovers to write letters,
accustoms young women to waiting;,
fills the newspapers
with articles and pictures,
builds new houses
for the orphans,
invigorates the coffin makers,
gives grave diggers
a pat on the back
and paints a smile on the leader's face.
The war works with unparalleled diligence!
Yet no one gives it
a word of praise.

作品选读（二）

The Iraqi Nights

By Dunya Mikhail

THE IRAQI NIGHTS

PRELUDE

In the land of Sumer, where the houses are packed so closely together that their walls touch, where people sleep on rooftops in the summer and lovers climb the walls to see one another, and where lovers marry young, though their parents always refuse at first... In that land, Ishtar was walking through the souk looking for a gift for Tammuz. She wanted to buy everything, even the skull hanging there like the ring around the neck of a dove—a dove stepping into what it thinks is the fragment of a setting sun. And the card she forgot to pay for contains neither Cupid nor his arrows, neither fire nor water nor air nor earth; it does not show her bending over the grave, and it does not tell her story on the thousand and second night.

On her way back, she was kidnapped by some masked men. They dragged her onward, leaving her mother's outstretched hand behind her forever. They brought her down into the underworld through seven gates. These poems Ishtar wrote on the gates suggest that she wasn't killed at once. Or perhaps her words drew her abductors' attention away from thoughts of murder.

Her hand holding a gift,
her mother's outstretched hand behind her,
the hand of her childhood doll, who sings when you press a button,
the hand of her abductor, dragging her along,
the hand that wipes away a tear,
the hand that turns over the nights
in an old calendar,
the hand that waves in greeting
or farewell
or for help,
the hand with all its lines:
the line of life,

the line of love,
the line of fate...

1.
In the first year of war
they played "bride and groom"
and counted everything on their fingers:
their faces reflected in the river;
the waves that swept away their faces
before disappearing;
and the names of newborns.
Then the war grew up
and invented a new game for them:
the winner is the one
who returns from the journey
alone,
full of stories of the dead
as the passing wings flutter
over the broken trees;
and now the winner must tow the hills of dust
so lightly that no one feels it; and now the winner wears a necklace
with half a metal heart for a pendant,
and the task to follow
is to forget the other half.
The war grew old
and left the old letters,
the calendars and newspapers,
to turn yellow
with the news,
with the numbers,
and with the names
of the players.

2.
Five centuries have passed
since Scheherazade told her tale.
Baghdad fell,
and they forced me to the underworld.
I watch the shadows

as they pass behind the wall:
none look like Tammuz.
He would cross thousands of miles
for the sake of a single cup of tea
poured by my own hand.
I fear the tea is growing
cold: cold tea is worse than death.

3.
I would not have found this cracked jar
if it weren't for my loneliness,
which sees gold in all that glitters.
Inside the jar is the magic plant
that Gilgamesh never stopped looking for.
I'll show it to Tammuz when he comes,
and we'll journey, as fast as light,
to all the continents of the world,
and all who smell it will be cured
or freed,
or will know its secret.
I don't want Tammuz to come too late
to hear my urgent song.

4.
When Tammuz comes
I'll also give him all the lists I made
to pass the time:
lists of food,
of books,
lost friends,
favorite songs,
list of cities to see before one dies,
and lists of ordinary things
with notes to prove that we are still alive.

5.
It's as if I'm hearing music in the boat's hull,
as if I can smell the river, the lily, the fish,
as if I'm touching the skies that fall from the words "I love you,"

as if I can see those tiny notes that are read over and over again,
as if I'm living the lives of birds who bear nothing but their feathers.

6.
The earth circled the sun
once more
and not a cloud
nor wind
nor country
passed through my eyes.
My shadow,
imprisoned in Aladdin's lamp,
mirrors the following:
a picture of the world with you inside,
light passing through a needle's eye,
scrawlings akin to cuneiform,
hidden paths to the sun,
dried clay,
tranquil Ottoman pottery,
and a huge pomegranate, its seeds
scattered all over Uruk.

7.
In Iraq,
after a thousand and one nights,
someone will talk to someone else.
Markets will open
for regular customers.
Small feet will tickle
the giant feet of the Tigris.
Gulls will spread their wings
and no one will fire at them.
Women will walk the streets
without looking back in fear.
Men will give their real names
without putting their lives at risk.
Children will go to school
and come home again.
Chickens in the villages

won't peck at human flesh
on the grass.
Disputes will take place
without any explosives.
A cloud will pass over cars
heading to work as usual.
A hand will wave
to someone leaving
or returning.
The sunrise will be the same
for those who wake
and those who never will.
And every moment
something ordinary
will happen
under the sun.

17

(Khaled Hosseini, 1965—)

卡勒德·胡赛尼

作者简介

卡勒德·胡赛尼（Khaled Hosseini，1965—）是美国阿富汗裔小说家，联合国难民署亲善大使。胡赛尼出生于阿富汗喀布尔（Kabul），在其15岁时加入了美国国籍。胡赛尼直到2003年（时年38岁）才回到阿富汗，这一经历与《追风筝的人》（*The Kite Runner*，2003）中的主人公类似。在后来的采访中，胡赛尼承认自己在苏联入侵和随后的战争之前离开了这个国家，感到了幸存者的罪恶感。大学毕业后，1996年至2004年期间胡赛尼在美国加州（California）成为一名执业内科医生，他把这种情况比作“包办婚姻”。

2001年3月，在行医期间，胡赛尼开始写他的第一部小说《追风筝的人》（*The Kite Runner*，2003），该书于2003年由河源出版社（Riverhead Books）出版。他的这部处女作在评论界和商业上都取得了成功；这本书和他后来的小说都至少部分地以阿富汗为背景，并以一名阿富汗人为主角。《追风筝的人》雄踞《纽约时报》畅销书排行榜（*The New York Times* bestseller list）达101周，其中有3周是位居第一；他的第二部小说《灿烂千阳》（*A Thousand Splendid Suns*，2007）在排行榜上停留了103周，其中排名第一的有15周；而他的第三部小说《群山回唱》（*And the Mountains Echoed*，2013）则停留了33周。胡赛尼的新作《海的祈祷》（*Sea Prayer*，2018）于2018年首次出版，该书以书信体的形式，通过一位叙利亚父亲写信给孩子的口吻，讲述了他们在渡海去往欧洲的夜晚，父亲注视着沉睡中的儿子，对他讲述叙利亚家乡昔日的美景，以及海上漂泊的凶险。作者希望借《海的祈祷》这样的作品，启发人们用人道主义的角度看待难民问题。

除了写作，胡塞尼还高度关注难民问题。2006 年，他被任命为联合国难民署亲善大使。受联合国难民署阿富汗之旅的启发，他后来建立了卡勒德·胡赛尼基金会，这是一个非营利机构，为阿富汗人民提供人道主义援助。

节选部分分别出自卡勒德·胡赛尼的三部小说《追风筝的人》、《灿烂千阳》和《群山回唱》。《追风筝的人》讲述了喀布尔富家少爷阿米尔和仆人哈桑的故事，将阿富汗君主制的终结、塔利班当权、"9·11" 等政治事件融合在小说生活背景中。书中的主人公在成长过程中见证了战争、宗教、爱、愧疚、赎罪等人类永恒话题。第二本小说《灿烂千阳》被认为是"女性版《追风筝的人》"，讲述了两个阿富汗女性如何在婚姻暴力、干旱和贫穷中挣扎求生。《群山回唱》讲述了一对兄妹在 60 年内因贫穷和战争铸成的故事。围绕父母、兄妹，甚至表亲和继母，他们如何去爱，如何被伤害，如何相互背叛，如何为彼此牺牲。小说探索了流亡、自我牺牲以及复杂的家族关系。家庭是胡赛尼写作最重要的主题，《群山回唱》一书的写作便始于家庭概念。

作品选读（一）

The Kite Runner

(Chapter Twenty Five)

By Khaled Hosseini

THEN, FOUR DAYS AGO, on a cool rainy day in March 2002, a small, wondrous thing happened.

I took Soraya, Khala Jamila, and Sohrab to a gathering of Afghans at Lake Elizabeth Park in Fremont. The general had finally been summoned to Afghanistan the month before for a ministry position, and had flown there two weeks earlier—he had left behind his gray suit and pocket watch. The plan was for Khala Jamila to join him in a few months once he had settled. She missed him terribly—and worried about his health there—and we had insisted she stay with us for a while.

The previous Thursday, the first day of spring, had been the Afghan New Year's Day—the *Sawl-e-Nau*—and Afghans in the Bay Area had planned celebrations throughout the East Bay and the peninsula. Kabir, Soraya, and I had an additional reason to rejoice: Our little hospital in Rawalpindi had opened the week before, not the surgical unit, just the pediatric clinic. But it was a good start, we all agreed.

It had been sunny for days, but Sunday morning, as I swung my legs out of bed, I heard raindrops pelting the window. *Afghan luck*, I thought. Snickered. I prayed morning *namaz* while Soraya slept—I didn't have to consult the prayer pamphlet I had obtained from the mosque anymore; the verses came naturally now, effortlessly.

We arrived around noon and found a handful of people taking cover under a large rectangular plastic sheet mounted on six poles spiked to the ground. Someone was already frying *bolani*; steam rose from teacups and a pot of cauliflower *aush*. A scratchy old Ahmad Zahir song was blaring from a cassette player. I smiled a little as the four of us rushed across the soggy grass field, Soraya and I in the lead, Khala Jamila in the middle, Sohrab behind us, the hood of his yellow raincoat bouncing on his back.

"What's so funny?" Soraya said, holding a folded newspaper over her head.

"You can take Afghans out of Paghman, but you can't take Paghman out of Afghans," I said.

We stooped under the makeshift tent. Soraya and Khala Jamila drifted toward an overweight woman frying spinach *bolani*. Sohrab stayed under the canopy for a moment, then stepped back out into the rain, hands stuffed in the pockets of his raincoat, his hair—now brown and straight like Hassan's—plastered against his scalp. He stopped near a coffee-colored puddle and stared at it. No one seemed to notice. No one called him back in. With time, the queries about our adopted—and decidedly eccentric—little boy had mercifully ceased, and, considering how tactless Afghan queries can be sometimes, that was a considerable relief. People stopped asking why he never spoke. Why he didn't play with the other kids. And best of all, they stopped suffocating us with their exaggerated empathy, their slow head shaking, their *tsktsks*, their "*Oh gung bichara*." Oh, poor little mute one. The novelty had worn off. Like dull wallpaper, Sohrab had blended into the background.

I shook hands with Kabir, a small, silver-haired man. He introduced me to a dozen men, one of them a retired teacher, another an engineer, a former architect, a surgeon who was now running a hot dog stand in Hayward. They all said they'd known Baba in Kabul, and they spoke about him respectfully. In one way or another, he had touched all their lives. The men said I was lucky to have had such a great man for a father.

We chatted about the difficult and maybe thankless job Karzai had in front of him, about the upcoming *Loya jirga*, and the king's imminent return to his homeland after twenty-eights years of exile. I remembered the night in 1973, the night Zahir Shah's cousin overthrew him; I remembered gunfire and the sky lighting up silver—Ali had taken me and Hassan in his arms, told us not to be afraid, that they were just shooting ducks.

Then someone told a Mullah Nasruddin joke and we were all laughing. "You know, your father was a funny man too," Kabir said.

"He was, wasn't he?" I said, smiling, remembering how, soon after we arrived in the U.S., Baba started grumbling about American flies. He'd sit at the kitchen table with his flyswatter, watch the flies darting from wall to wall, buzzing here, buzzing there, harried and rushed. "In this country, even flies are pressed for time," he'd groan. How I had laughed. I smiled at the memory now.

By three o'clock, the rain had stopped and the sky was a curdled gray burdened with lumps of clouds. A cool breeze blew through the park. More families turned up. Afghans greeted each other, hugged, kissed, exchanged food. Someone lighted coal in a barbecue and soon the smell of garlic and *morgh* kabob flooded my senses. There was music, some new singer I didn't know, and the giggling of children. I saw Sohrab, still in his yellow raincoat, leaning against a garbage pail, staring across the park at the empty batting cage.

A little while later, as I was chatting with the former surgeon, who told me he and Baba had been classmates in eighth grade, Soraya pulled on my sleeve. "Amir, look!"

She was pointing to the sky. A half-dozen kites were flying high, speckles of bright yellow, red, and green against the gray sky.

"Check it out," Soraya said, and this time she was pointing to a guy selling kites from a stand nearby.

"Hold this," I said. I gave my cup of tea to Soraya. I excused myself and walked over to the kite stand, my shoes squishing on the wet grass. I pointed to a yellow *seh-parcha*. "*Sawl-e-nau mubabrak*," the kite seller said, taking the twenty and handing me the kite and a wooden spool of glass *tar*. I thanked him and wished him a Happy New Year too. I tested the string the way Hassan and I used to, by holding it between my thumb and forefinger and pulling it. It reddened with blood and the kite seller smiled. I smiled back.

I took the kite to where Sohrab was standing, still leaning against the garbage pail, arms crossed on his chest. He was looking up at the sky.

"Do you like the *seh-parcha*?" I said, holding up the kite by the ends of the cross bars. His eyes shifted from the sky to me, to the kite, then back. A few rivulets of rain trickled from his hair, down his face.

"I read once that, in Malaysia, they use kites to catch fish," I said. "I'll bet you didn't know that. They tie a fishing line to it and fly it beyond the shallow waters, so it doesn't cast a shadow and scare the fish. And in ancient China, generals used to fly kites over battlefields to send messages to their men. It's true. I'm not slipping you a trick." I showed him my bloody thumb. "Nothing wrong with the *tar* either."

Out of the corner of my eye, I saw Soraya watching us from the tent. Hands tensely dug in her armpits. Unlike me, she'd gradually abandoned her attempts at engaging him. The unanswered questions, the blank stares, the silence, it was all too painful. She had shifted to "Holding Pattern," waiting for a green light from Sohrab. Waiting.

I wet my index finger and held it up. "I remember the way your father checked the wind was to kick up dust with his sandal, see which way the wind blew it. He knew a lot of little tricks like that," I said. Lowered my finger. "West, I think."

Sohrab wiped a raindrop from his earlobe and shifted on his feet. Said nothing. I thought of Soraya asking me a few months ago what his voice sounded like. I'd told her I didn't remember anymore.

"Did I ever tell you your father was the best kite runner in Wazir Akbar Khan? Maybe all of Kabul?" I said, knotting the loose end of the spool *tar* to the string loop tied to the center spar. "How jealous he made the neighborhood kids. He'd run kites and never look up at the sky, and people used to say he was chasing the kite's shadow. But they didn't know him like I did. Your father wasn't chasing any shadows. He just... knew."

Another half-dozen kites had taken flight. People had started to gather in clumps, teacups in hand, eyes glued to the sky.

"Do you want to help me fly this?" I said.

Sohrab's gaze bounced from the kite to me. Back to the sky.

"Okay." I shrugged. "Looks like I'll have to fly it t*anhaii*." Solo.

I balanced the spool in my left hand and fed about three feet of *tar*. The yellow kite dangled at the end of it, just above the wet grass. "Last chance," I said. But Sohrab was looking at a pair of kites tangling high above the trees.

"All right. Here I go." I took off running, my sneakers splashing rainwater from puddles, the hand clutching the kite end of the string held high above my head. It had been so long, so many years since I'd done this, and I wondered if I'd make a spectacle of myself. I let the spool roll in my left hand as I ran, felt the string cut my right hand again as it fed through. The kite was lifting behind my shoulder now, lifting, wheeling, and I ran harder. The spool spun faster and the glass string tore another gash in my right palm. I stopped and turned. Looked up. Smiled. High above, my kite was tilting side to side like a pendulum, making that old paper-bird-flapping-its-wings sound I always associated with winter mornings in Kabul. I hadn't flown a kite in a quarter of a century, but suddenly I was twelve again and all the old instincts came rushing back.

I felt a presence next to me and looked down. It was Sohrab. Hands dug deep in the pockets of his raincoat. He had followed me.

作品选读（二）

A Thousand Splendid Suns

(26)

By Khaled Hosseini

It was, by far, the hottest day of the year. The mountains trapped the bone-scorching heat, stifled the city like smoke. Power had been out for days. All over Kabul, electric fans sat idle, almost mockingly so.

Laila was lying still on the living-room couch, sweating through her blouse. Every exhaled breath burned the tip of her nose. She was aware of her parents talking in Mammy's room. Two nights ago, and again last night, she had awakened and thought she heard their voices downstairs. They were talking every day now, ever since the bullet, ever since the new hole in the gate.

Outside, the far-off *boom* of artillery, then, more closely, the stammering of a long string of gunfire, followed by another.

Inside Laila too a battle was being waged: guilt on one side, partnered with shame, and, on the other, the conviction that what she and Tariq had done was not sinful; that it had been natural, good, beautiful, even inevitable, spurred by the knowledge that they might never see each other again.

Laila rolled to her side on the couch now and tried to remember something: At one point, when they were on the floor, Tariq had lowered his forehead on hers. Then he had panted something, either *Am I hurting you? or Is this hurting you?*

Laila couldn't decide which he had said.

Am I hurting you?

Is this hurting you?

Only two weeks since he had left, and it was already happening- Time, blunting the edges of those sharp memories. Laila bore down mentally. What had he said? It seemed vital, suddenly, that she know.

Laila closed her *eyes*. Concentrated.

With the passing of time, she would slowly tire of this exercise. She would find it increasingly exhausting to conjure up, to dust off, to resuscitate once again what was long dead. There would come a day, in fact, years later, when Laila would no longer bewail his loss. Or not as relentlessly; not nearly. There would come a day when the details of his face would begin to slip from memory's grip, when overhearing a mother on the street call after her child by Tariq's name would no longer cut her adrift. She would not miss him as she did now, when the ache of his absence was her unremitting companion—like the phantom pain of an amputee.

Except every once in a long while, when Laila was a grown woman, ironing a shirt or pushing her children on a swing set, something trivial, maybe the warmth of a carpet beneath her feet on a hot day or the curve of a stranger's forehead, would set off a memory of that afternoon together. And it would all come rushing back. The spontaneity of it. Their astonishing imprudence. Their clumsiness. The pain of the act, the pleasure of it, the sadness of it. The heat of their entangled bodies.

It would flood her, steal her breath.

But then it would pass. The moment would pass. Leave her deflated, feeling nothing but a vague restlessness.

She decided that he had said *Am I hurting you?* Yes. That was *it*. Laila was happy that she'd remembered.

Then Babi was in the hallway, calling her name from the top of the stairs, asking her to come up quickly.

"She's agreed!" he said, his voice tremulous with suppressed excitement "We're leaving, Laila. All three of us. We're leaving Kabul."

* * *

In Mammy's room, the three of them sat on the bed. Outside, rockets were zipping across the sky as Hekmatyar's and Massoud's forces fought and fought. Laila knew that somewhere in the city someone had just died, and that a pall of black smoke was hovering over some building that had collapsed in a puffing mass of dust. There would be bodies to step around in the morning. Some would be collected. Others not. Then Kabul's dogs, who had developed a taste for human meat, would feast.

All the same, Laila had an urge to run through those streets. She could barely contain her own happiness. It took effort to sit, to not shriek with joy. Babi said they would go to Pakistan first, to apply for visas. Pakistan, where Tariq was! Tariq was only gone seventeen days, Laila calculated excitedly. If only Mammy had made up her mind seventeen days earlier, they could have left together. She would have been with Tariq right now! But that didn't matter now. They were going to Peshawar-she, Mammy, and Babi-and they would find Tariq and his parents there. Surely they would. They would process their paperwork together. Then, who knew? Who knew? Europe?

America? Maybe, as Babi was always saying, somewhere near the sea...

Mammy was half lying, half sitting against the headboard. Her eyes were puffy. She was picking at her hair.

Three days before, Laila had gone outside for a breath of air. She'd stood by the front gates, leaning against them, when she'd heard a loud crack and something had zipped by her right ear, sending tiny splinters of wood flying before her eyes. After Giti's death, and the thousands of rounds fired and myriad rockets that had fallen on Kabul, it was the sight of that single round hole in the gate, less than three fingers away from where Laila's head had been, that shook Mammy awake. Made her see that one war had cost her two children already; this latest could cost her her remaining one.

From the walls of the room, Ahmad and Noor smiled down. Laila watched Mammy's eyes bouncing now, guiltily, from one photo to the other. As if looking for their consent. Their blessing. As if asking for forgiveness.

"There's nothing left for us here," Babi said. "Our sons are gone, but we still have Laila. We still have each other, Fariba. We can make a new life."

Babi reached across the bed. When he leaned to take her hands, Mammy let him. On her face, a look of concession. Of resignation. They held each other's hands, lightly, and then they were swaying quietly in an embrace. Mammy buried her face in his neck. She grabbed a handful of his shirt.

For hours that night, the excitement robbed Laila of sleep. She lay in bed and watched the horizon light up in garish shades of orange and yellow. At some point, though, despite the exhilaration inside and the crack of artillery fire outside, she fell asleep.

And dreamed they are on a ribbon of beach, sitting on a quilt. It's a chilly, overcast day, but it's warm next to Tariq under the blanket draped over their shoulders. She can see cars parked behind a low fence of chipped white paint beneath a row of windswept palm trees. The wind makes her eyes water and buries their shoes in sand, hurls knots of dead grass from the curved ridges of one dune to another. They're watching sailboats bob in the distance. Around them, seagulls squawk and shiver in the wind. The wind whips up another spray of sand off the shallow, windward slopes. There is a noise then like a chant, and she tells him something Babi had taught her years before about singing sand.

He rubs at her eyebrow, wipes grains of sand from it. She catches a flicker of the band on his finger. It's identical to hers-gold with a sort of maze pattern etched all the way around.

It's true, she tells him. *It's the friction, of grain against grain. Listen.* He does. He frowns. They wait. They hear it again. A groaning sound, when the wind is soft, when it blows hard, a mewling, high-pitched chorus.

* * * Babi said they should take only what was absolutely necessary. They would sell the rest.

"That should hold us in Peshawar until I find work."

作品选读（三）

And the Mountains Echoed

(Chapter Two)

By Khaled Hosseini

Two Fall 1952

Father had never before hit Abdullah. So when he did, when he whacked the side of his head, just above the ear—hard, suddenly, and with an open palm—tears of surprise sprung to Abdullah's eyes. He quickly blinked them back.

"Go home," Father said through gritted teeth.

From up ahead, Abdullah heard Pari burst into sobs.

Then Father hit him again, harder, and this time across the left cheek. Abdullah's head snapped sideways. His face burned, and more tears leaked. His left ear rang. Father stooped down, leaning in so close his dark creased face eclipsed the desert and the mountains and the sky altogether.

"I told you to go home, boy," he said with a pained look.

Abdullah didn't make a sound. He swallowed hard and squinted at his father, blinking into the face shading his eyes from the sun.

From the small red wagon up ahead, Pari cried out his name, her voice high, shaking with apprehension. "Abollah!" Father held him with a cutting look, and trudged back to the wagon. From its bed, Pari reached for Abdullah with outstretched hands. Abdullah allowed them a head start. Then he wiped his eyes with the heels of his hands, and followed.

A little while later, Father threw a rock at him, the way children in Shadbagh would do to Pari's dog, Shuja—except they meant to hit Shuja, to hurt him. Father's rock fell harmlessly a few feet from Abdullah. He waited, and when Father and Pari got moving again Abdullah tailed them once more.

Finally, with the sun just past its peak, Father pulled up again. He turned back in Abdullah's direction, seemed to consider, and motioned with his hand.

"You won't give up," he said.

From the bed of the wagon, Pari's hand quickly slipped into Abdullah's. She was looking up at him, her eyes liquid, and she was smiling her gap-toothed smile like no bad thing would ever befall her so long as he stood at her side. He closed his fingers around her hand, the way he did each night when he and his little sister slept in their cot, their skulls touching, their legs tangled.

"You were supposed to stay home," Father said. "With your mother and Iqbal. Like I told you to."

Abdullah thought, She's your wife. My mother, we buried. But he knew to stifle those words before they came up and out.

"All right, then. Come," Father said. "But there won't be any crying. You hear me?"

"Yes."

"I'm warning you. I won't have it."

Pari grinned up at Abdullah, and he looked down at her pale eyes and pink round cheeks and grinned back.

From then on, he walked beside the wagon as it jostled along on the pitted desert floor, holding Pari's hand. They traded furtive happy glances, brother and sister, but said little for fear of souring Father's mood and spoiling their good fortune. For long stretches they were alone, the three of them, nothing and no one in sight but the deep copper gorges and vast sandstone cliffs. The desert unrolled ahead of them, open and wide, as though it had been created for them and them alone, the air still, blazing hot, the sky high and blue. Rocks shimmered on the cracked floor. The only sounds Abdullah heard were his own breathing and the rhythmic creaking of the wheels as Father pulled the red wagon north.

A while later, they stopped to rest in the shadow of a boulder. With a groan, Father dropped the handle to the ground. He winced as he arched his back, his face raised to the sun.

"How much longer to Kabul?" Abdullah asked.

Father looked down at them. His name was Saboor. He was dark-skinned and had a hard face, angular and bony, nose curved like a desert hawk's beak, eyes set deep in his skull. Father was thin as a reed, but a lifetime of work had made his muscles powerful, tightly wound like rattan strips around the arm of a wicker chair. "Tomorrow afternoon," he said, lifting the cowhide water bag to his lips. "If we make good time." He took a long swallow, his Adam's apple rising and dropping.

"Why didn't Uncle Nabi drive us?" Abdullah said. "He has a car."

Father rolled his eyes toward him.

"Then we wouldn't have had to walk all this way."

Father didn't say anything. He took off his soot-stained skullcap and wiped sweat from his brow with the sleeve of his shirt.

Pari's finger shot from the wagon. "Look, Abollah!" she cried excitedly. "Another one."

Abdullah followed her finger, traced it to a spot in the shadow of the boulder where a feather lay, long, gray, like charcoal after it has burned. Abdullah walked over to it and picked it by the stem. He blew the flecks of dust off it. A falcon, he thought, turning it over. Maybe a dove, or a desert lark. He'd seen a number of those already that day. No, a falcon. He blew on it again and handed it to Pari, who happily snatched it from him.

Back home, in Shadbagh, Pari kept underneath her pillow an old tin tea box

Abdullah had given her. It had a rusty latch, and on the lid was a bearded Indian man, wearing a turban and a long red tunic, holding up a steaming cup of tea with both hands. Inside the box were all of the feathers that Pari collected. They were her most cherished belongings. Deep green and dense burgundy rooster feathers; a white tail feather from a dove; a sparrow feather, dust brown, dotted with dark blotches; and the one of which Pari was proudest, an iridescent green peacock feather with a beautiful large eye at the tip.

This last was a gift Abdullah had given her two months earlier. He had heard of a boy from another village whose family owned a peacock. One day when Father was away digging ditches

in a town south of Shadbagh, Abdullah walked to this other village, found the boy, and asked him for a feather from the bird. Negotiation ensued, at the end of which Abdullah agreed to trade his shoes for the feather. By the time he returned to Shadbagh, peacock feather tucked in the waist of his trousers beneath his shirt, his heels had split open and left bloody smudges on the ground. Thorns and splinters had burrowed into the skin of his soles. Every step sent barbs of pain shooting through his feet.

When he arrived home, he found his stepmother, Parwana, outside the hut, hunched before the tandoor, making the daily naan. He quickly ducked behind the giant oak tree near their home and waited for her to finish. Peeking around the trunk, he watched her work, a thickshouldered woman with long arms, rough-skinned hands, and stubby fingers; a woman with a puffed, rounded face who possessed none of the grace of the butterfly she'd been named after.

Abdullah wished he could love her as he had his own mother. Mother, who had bled to death giving birth to Pari three and a half years earlier when Abdullah was seven. Mother, whose face was all but lost to him now. Mother, who cupped his head in both palms and held it to her chest and stroked his cheek every night before sleep and sang him a lullaby:

I found a sad little fairy
Beneath the shade of a paper tree.
I know a sad little fairy
Who was blown away by the wind one night.

He wished he could love his new mother in the same way. And perhaps Parwana, he thought, secretly wished the same, that she could love him. The way she did Iqbal, her one-year-old son, whose face she always kissed, whose every cough and sneeze she fretted over. Or the way she had loved her first baby, Omar. She had adored him. But he had died of the cold the winter before last. He was two weeks old. Parwana and Father had barely named him. He was one of three babies that brutal winter had taken in Shadbagh. Abdullah remembered Parwana clutching Omar's swaddled little corpse, her fits of grief. He remembered the day they buried him up on the hill, a tiny mound on frozen ground, beneath a pewter sky, Mullah Shekib saying the prayers, the wind spraying grits of snow and ice into everyone's eyes.

Abdullah suspected Parwana would be furious later to learn that he had traded his only pair of shoes for a peacock feather. Father had labored hard under the sun to pay for them. She would let him have it when she found out. She might even hit him, Abdullah thought. She had struck him a few times before. She had strong, heavy hands—from all those years of lifting her invalid sister, Abdullah imagined—and they knew how to swing a broomstick or land a well-aimed slap.

But to her credit, Parwana did not seem to derive any satisfaction from hitting him. Nor was she incapable of tenderness toward her stepchildren. There was the time she had sewn Pari a silver-and-green dress from a roll of fabric Father had brought from Kabul. The time she had taught Abdullah, with surprising patience, how to crack two eggs simultaneously without breaking the yolks. And the time she had shown them how to twist and turn husks of corn into little dolls, the way she had with her own sister when they were little. She showed them how to fashion dresses for the dolls out of little torn strips of cloth.

But these were gestures, Abdullah knew, acts of duty, drawn from a well far shallower than the one she reached into for Iqbal. If one night their house caught fire, Abdullah knew without doubt which child Parwana would grab rushing out. She would not think twice. In the end, it came down to a simple thing: They weren't her children, he and Pari. Most people loved their own. It couldn't be helped that he and his sister didn't belong to her. They were another woman's leftovers.

He waited for Parwana to take the bread inside, then watched as she reemerged from the hut, carrying Iqbal on one arm and a load of laundry under the other. He watched her amble in the direction of the stream and waited until she was out of sight before he sneaked into the house, his soles throbbing each time they met the ground. Inside, he sat down and slipped on his old plastic sandals, the only other footwear he owned. Abdullah knew it wasn't a sensible thing he had done. But when he knelt beside Pari, gently shook her awake from a nap, and produced the feather from behind his back like a magician, it was all worth it—worth it for the way her face broke open with surprise first, then delight; for the way she stamped his cheeks with kisses; for how she cackled when he tickled her chin with the soft end of the feather—and suddenly his feet didn't hurt at all.

Father wiped his face with his sleeve once more. They took turns drinking from the water bag. When they were done, Father said, "You're tired, boy."

"No," Abdullah said, though he was. He was exhausted. And his feet hurt. It wasn't easy crossing a desert in sandals.

Father said, "Climb in."

In the wagon, Abdullah sat behind Pari, his back against the wooden slat sides, the little knobs of his sister's spine pressing against his belly and chest bone. As Father dragged them forward, Abdullah stared at the sky, the mountains, the rows upon rows of closely packed, rounded hills, soft in the distance. He watched his father's back as he pulled them, his head low, his feet kicking up little puffs of red-brown sand. A caravan of Kuchi nomads passed them by, a dusty procession of jingling bells and groaning camels, and a woman with kohl-rimmed eyes and hair the color of wheat smiled at Abdullah.

18

(Adina Hoffman, 1967—)
阿迪娜·霍夫曼

作者简介

阿迪娜·霍夫曼（Adina Hoffman, 1967—）是一位美国以色列裔作家，她出生于密西西比州的杰克逊（Jackson, Mississippi），在新罕布什尔州的彼得伯勒（Peterborough, New Hampshire）和得克萨斯州的休斯敦（Houston, Texas）长大，1989 年毕业于卫斯理大学（Wesleyan University）。她的作品融合了文学和纪实的元素。

她的第一本书《窗户之家：耶路撒冷社区的肖像》（*House of Windows: Portraits from a Jerusalem Neighborhood*, 2000）包含了一系列关于她在耶路撒冷的北非犹太人社区的相关文章。2009 年，耶鲁大学出版社（Yale University Press）出版了她的《我的幸福与幸福无关：巴勒斯坦世纪诗人的生活》（*My Happiness Bears No Relation to Happiness: A Poet's Life in the Palestinian Century*），该书记述了巴勒斯坦诗人塔哈·穆罕默德·阿里（Taha Muhammad Ali）的一生和时代。《我的幸福》是有史以来出版的第一本关于巴勒斯坦作家的传记，曾获得了英国 2010 年犹太季刊温盖特奖（Wingate Prize），并被巴恩斯和诺贝尔书评（*The Barnes & Noble Review*）评为 2009 年最佳 20 本书之一，还位列《书目》（*Booklist*）杂志评选的年度十大传记之一。

2011 年，古根海姆基金会研究员（Guggenheim Foundation Fellow）霍夫曼嫁给了麦克阿瑟奖得主、诗人兼翻译家彼得·科尔（Peter Cole）。同年，她和科尔共同出版了《神圣的垃圾：开罗秘籍的失物招领世界》（*Sacred Trash: The Lost and Found World of the Cairo Geniza*）一书并广受好评，哈罗德·布鲁姆（Harold

Bloom）称其为“小杰作”，该书被美国图书馆协会授予年度犹太图书布罗迪奖章（American Library Association's Sophie Brody Medal for Outstanding Jewish Literature）。

她还著有《直到我们建造了耶路撒冷：新城市的建筑师》（*Till We Have Built Jerusalem: Architects of a New City*, 2016）和《本·赫克特：战斗文字，电影》（*Ben Hecht: Fighting Words, Moving Pictures*，2019），后者曾入围 2020 年笔会 / 杰奎琳·博格勒韦尔德传记奖（PEN/Jacqueline Bograd Weld Prize for Biography），并被《星期日泰晤士报》（*The Sunday Times*）评为 2020 年最佳平装书之一，称其为“启示录”。

节选部分出自阿迪娜·霍夫曼的《神圣的垃圾：开罗秘籍的失物招领世界》第一章。《神圣的垃圾》讲述了开罗金尼萨犹太教堂（The Cairo Geniza）的传奇故事，这座犹太教堂收藏着破旧的文本，并被发现里面藏有迄今为止发现的最重要的犹太手稿。阿迪娜·霍夫曼和彼得·科尔展示了地中海犹太教近千年来生机勃勃的全景，将当代读者带进这个鲜为人知的宝藏的核心，其内容被正确地称为“活海古卷”（The Living Sea Scrolls）。《神圣的垃圾》既是一本传记，也是对犹太人长期以来书写在文字中的最高价值的思考，它首先是一个扣人心弦的冒险和救赎的故事。

作品选读

Sacred Trash: The Lost and Found World of the Cairo Geniza

(Chapter 1)

By Adina Hoffman & Peter Cole

Hidden Wisdom

Cambridge, May 1896

When the self-taught Scottish scholar of Arabic and Syriac Agnes Lewis and her no-less-learned twin sister, Margaret Gibson, hurried down a street or a hallway, they moved—as a friend later described them— “like ships in full sail.” Their plump frames, thick lips, and slightly hawkish eyes made them, theoretically, identical. And both were rather vain about their dainty hands, which on special occasions they “weighed down with antique rings." In a poignant and peculiar coincidence, each of the sisters had been widowed after just a few years of happy marriage to a clergyman.

But Mrs. Lewis and Mrs. Gibson were distinct to those who knew them. Older by an entire twenty minutes, Agnes was the more ambitious, colorful, and domineering of the two; Margaret had a quieter intelligence and was, it was said, "more normal." By age fifty, Agnes had written three travel books and three novels, and had translated a tourist guide from the Greek; Margaret had contributed amply to and probably helped write her sister's nonfiction books, edited her husband's translation of Cervantes' *Journey to Parnassus*, and grown adept at watercolors. They were, meanwhile, exceptionally close—around Cambridge they came to be known as a single unit, the "Giblews"—and after the deaths of their husbands they devoted themselves and their sizable inheritance to a life of travel and study together.

This followed quite naturally from the maverick manner in which they'd been raised in a small town near Glasgow by their forward-thinking lawyer father, a widower, who subscribed to an educational philosophy that was equal parts Bohemian and Calvinist—as far-out as it was firm. Eschewing the fashion for treating girls' minds like fine china, he assumed his daughters were made of tougher stuff and schooled them as though they were sons, teaching them to think for themselves, to argue and ride horses. Perhaps most important, he had instilled in them early on a passion for philology, promising them that they could travel to any country on condition that they first learned its language. French, Spanish, German, and Italian followed, as did childhood trips around the Continent. He also encouraged the girls' nearly familial friendship with their church's progressive and intellectually daring young preacher, who had once been a protege of the opium-eating Romantic essayist Thomas de Quincy.

After their father's sudden death when they were twenty-three, Agnes and Margaret sought consolation in strange alphabets and in travel to still more distant climes: Egypt, Palestine, Greece, and Cyprus. By middle age they had learned, between them, some nine languages—adding to their European repertoire Hebrew, Persian, and Syriac written in Estrangelo script. Having also studied the latest photographic techniques, they journeyed extensively throughout the East, taking thousands of pictures of ancient manuscript pages and buying piles of others, the most interesting of which they then set out to transcribe and translate.

As women, and as devout (not to mention eccentric and notoriously party-throwing) Presbyterians, they lived and worked on the margins of mostly Anglican, male-centered Cambridge society—women were not granted degrees at the town's illustrious university until 1948—and they counted as their closest friends a whole host of Quakers, freethinkers, and Jews. Yet Agnes's 1892 discovery at St. Catherine's Monastery in Sinai of one of the oldest Syriac versions of the New Testament had brought the sisters respect in learned circles: their multiple books on the subject ranged from the strictly scholarly *A Translation of the Four Gospels from the Syriac of the Sinai Palimpsest* to the more talky and popular *How the Codex Was Found.* Somehow the rumor spread that Mrs. Lewis had just happened to recognize a fragment of the ancient manuscript in the monastery dining hall, where it was being used as a butter dish. In fact, the codex was kept under tight lock and key, and its very fragile condition—to say nothing of its sacred status— certainly precluded its use by the monks as mere tableware. It took serious erudition and diplomacy for the twins to gain access to the manuscript in the monastery library; they then worked painstakingly over a period of years to decode the codex, as it were. "The leaves," wrote Agnes, "are deeply stained, and in parts ready to crumble. One and all of them were glued together, until the librarian of the Convent and I separated them with our fingers." She and Margaret proceeded to photograph each of its 358 pages and, on their return to Cambridge, processed the film themselves and labored over the text's decipherment. Later they arranged for an expedition of several distinguished Cambridge scholars to travel with them to Sinai, where they worked as a team, transcribing the codex as a whole.

19

(Mohja Kahf, 1967—)
莫哈·卡夫

作者简介

莫哈·卡夫（Mohja Kahf，1967—）出生于叙利亚大马士革（Damascus），是一位叙利亚裔美国诗人、小说家和教授。她随家人于1971年移居美国，获有罗格斯大学（Rutgers University）的比较文学博士学位。

在美国长大的经历塑造了她对自己的家乡和旅居国文化之间的差异和相似之处的看法。她的诗歌融合了叙利亚和美国的影响。卡夫的作品探讨了美国穆斯林和其他宗教和世俗社区之间文化不和谐和重叠的主题。叙利亚、伊斯兰教、伦理、政治、女权主义、人权、身体、性别和情色经常出现在她的作品中。在她的诗集《来自山鲁佐德的电子邮件》（*Emails From Schherazad*，2003）中，卡夫探讨了许多不同的阿拉伯和穆斯林身份和实践，并且经常使用幽默手法。她重新塑造了许多伊斯兰传统中的女性形象，这在《夏格诗集》（*Hagar Poems*，2016）中尤为突出。

她的作品《夏格诗集》在2017年美国阿拉伯裔国家博物馆图书奖（Book Awards of the Arab American National Museum）中获得荣誉奖。卡夫因其创造性的非虚构文章《因沙拉之歌》（*The Caul of Inshallah*，2010）获得“手推车奖”（Pushcart Prize）。这篇文章讲述了她儿子难产的故事，首次发表在2010年的《河牙杂志》（*River Teeth*）上。卡夫的第一本诗集《来自山鲁佐德的电子邮件》是2004年帕特森诗歌奖（Paterson Poetry Prize）的入围作品。她的小说《戴橘色围巾的女孩》（*The Girl in the Tangerine Scarf*，2006）讲述了一个叙利亚女孩在20世纪70年代被移民到美国中西部的故事，描绘了美国印第安纳州穆斯林少女的成长过程以及移民的艰辛。卡夫借用了自己生活中的一些细节——她小时候从叙利亚搬到美国——但她坚持认为这本书不是其自传。

卡夫于2002年因诗歌获得阿肯色州艺术委员会个人艺术家奖学金（The Arkansas Arts Council Individual Artist Fellowship）。她的诗歌曾在美国新概念艺术家珍妮·霍尔泽的系列作品中出现。

节选部分出自莫哈·卡夫的小说《戴橘色围巾的女孩》。叙利亚移民卡德拉·谢米（Khadra Shamy）成长于20世纪70年代的印第安纳州，在一个虔诚、关系紧密的穆斯林家庭中长大，她和哥哥埃亚德（Eyad）以及她的非洲裔美国朋友哈基姆（Hakim）和哈尼法（Hanifa）一起骑自行车在印第安纳波利斯（Indianapolis）的街道上探索“穆斯林”和“美国”之间的分界线。《戴橘色围巾的女孩》文笔优美，人物性格活泼，描绘了美国中部穆斯林的精神和社会风貌。

作品选读

The Girl in the Tangerine Scarf

(Excerpts)

By Mohja Kahf

Danger abounded. Pork was everywhere. At first the young couple thought it was merely a matter of avoiding the meat of the pig. Soon their eyes were opened to the fact that pig meat came under other names and guises in this strange country. Sometimes it was called bacon, other times it was called sausage, or bologna, or ham. Its fat was called lard and even in a loaf of Wonder Bread it could be lurking. Bits of pig might appear in salad-imagine, in salad! Jell-O had pig. Hostess Twinkles had pig. Even candy could have pig.

Pig meat was filthy. It had bugs in it, Khadra's father said. That's why God made it haram, her mother said. If you ate pig, bugs would grow and grow inside your stomach and eat your guts out. Always ask if there is pig in something before you eat anything from kuffar hands.

Mrs. Brown the kindergarten teacher poured the candy corn into a little flowered plastic cup on Khadra's desk.

Khadra said, "I can't eat this," her round, baby-fat face grave.

"Why not, sweetie?" Mrs. Brown said, bending low so her white face was next to Khadra's.

"There's a pig in it."

Mrs. Brown laughed a pretty laugh and said, "Nooo, there isn't a pig in it, dear!"

"Are you sure?"

"I'm positive."

She was so pretty and so nice and so sure. Khadra ate the candy corn and put some in her pocket. But when Eyad saw the candy corn on the bus he said, "Ommm, you ate candy corn. Candy corn has pig!"

"Nuh uh!"

But it did. And it was too late to throw it up. Khadra was tainted forever. If she lived, that is. Too ashamed to tell her parents, she waited in horror for the bugs to grow in her stomach and eat her guts out.

…

One day Khadra's father heard a call in the land and, the love of God his steps controlling, decided to take his family to a place in the middle of the country called Indiana, "The Crossroads of America." He had discovered the Dawah Center.

His wife said that a Dawah worker's job was to go wherever in the country there were Muslims who wanted to learn Islam better, to teach it to their children, to build mosques, to help suffering Muslims in other countries, and to find solutions to the ways in which living in a kuffar land made practicing Islam hard. This was a noble jihad.

"Position open: Chapter Coordinator, Dawah Center. Develop Islamic education programs via logical Islamic methodology. Requirements: Practicing Islamic lifestyle, sound Islamic belief, college degree. Contact: Br. Omar Nabolsy or Br. Kuldip Khan, Indianapolis Home Office, 1867 New Harmony Drive, Simmonsville, Indiana." (Classified in The Islamic Forerunner)

So they loaded up everything they owned on the luggage rack of the station wagon and set off over prairie and dale like pioneers. Tall tall mountains shining in their eyes. Immaculate lakes like God's polished tables. Rivers that churned and frothed. Forests, high-treed and terrifying, and then land so wide and flat it made you lonely.

"Where's Syria?" Khadra asked Eyad, staring at her stubby toes on the back window of the station wagon where they lay on a Navajo blanket. Khadra couldn't remember Syria, although she thought of it whenever she rubbed a little boomerang-shaped scar on her right knee that had been made on a broken tile in Syria. Red blood running down a white stone step. Walay himmek. Ey na'am. Sometimes she had a vague memory of having been on a mountain. Dry sunny days that had a certain smell made her think of Syria, and when she bit into a tart plum or a dark cherry, her mouth felt like Syria.

Eyad, with his serious gray-green eyes, remembered Syria in complete sentences, not flashes of words and tastes. Life there had Aunt Razanne and Uncle Mazen. And their kids, cousin Reem and cousin Roddy, drinking powdered milk from a big tin that said NEEDO. Syria was Mama's daddy called Jiddo Candyman, with his tuft of thick white hair like cotton candy, throwing you up-up while you screamed with delight. The adhan floating down from up in the air. Streets busy with people who spoke Arabic in the same rhythms as his mother and father, ey wallah, people whose faces bore his parents' features. Here in 'Mreeka, no one looked like them and they looked like no one.

"Far away," Eyad said gravely. "Syria's far, far away."

"Where? Point. Where the sky touches the ground, is that Syria?"

"No," he said, with authority. "Farther."

"Like a star?" She squinted at the street lamps, making them send rays of light to her eyes.

The little frontier family trekked the Oregon Trail in reverse, with as much wonder in their hearts as the pioneers of an earlier century heading the other way. Square One itself had been strange enough and new, and now they were going further, over the edge of the known world. At the start of every day, their mother recited the Throne of the Heavens and the Earth Verse, the three "I seek refuge" chapters from the Quran, and her favorite travel prayer: O Thou My God: I seek refuge in Thee from humiliation or humiliating, from being astray or leading others astray, from wronging or being wronged, from ignorance or having ignorance perpetrated upon me.

It has been seven years since the adult Khadra. had set foot in Indi- ananapolis. She'd left in the middle of a college degree, in the middle of a marriage to a nice Muslim guy, in the middle of community ties she cauterized abruptly. The Fallen Timbers Townhouses are coming up on the right and, on a whim, she turns off on General Wayne Drive toward it: the old homestead.

There are laundry lines by the corner wall. There's number 1492 Tecumseh Drive. A caramel-colored girl comes out the door swinging a brown shopping bag full of fancy ladies' shoes. ¡A la casa de Simona!" she shouts over her shoulder.

Khadra, returning to this ground that didn't love her, tries to stave the panic in her gut that is entirely the fault of the state of Indiana and the lay of its flat, flat land, to which she had never asked to be brought. She repeats the favorite prayer of her mother aloud to the windshield of her little car and grips the steering wheel a little tighter, like someone holding a small lantern and going out to investigate, a little afraid of what she might find.

Hoosier \ hii-zha r/ a native or resident of Indiana—used as a nickname.

—Merriam-Webster

... in the eighteenth century, Hoosier was used generally to describe a backwoodsman, especially an ignorant boaster, with an overtone of crudeness and even lawlessness.

—Howard H. Peckham, Indiana, A History

The Shamy family had come to Indiana for God. It wasn't much pay.

"It doesn't matter," Khadra's mother said. "We are not in love with the glitter of this world." But oh, Khadra loved the glitter of the purple banana seat bike at the garage sale. Her father haggled the price down to four dollars.

"How come 'Nifa and them get new bikes, Baba?" she asked, skittering to keep up with her father as he maneuvered the bike to the station wagon.

"When I was your age back in Syria, my folks were so poor I had to work after school till dark. Days we had nothing in the house but bread and olives."

"Yeah, but how come Hanifa and them get new bikes?"

"Say al-hamdu-lilah, Khadra." He hoisted the bike into the cargo space of the station wagon. "Give thanks for what you have."

"Hamdilah. But how come—"

His mother's mother had been a seamstress. In the days of privation and cholera epidemic in Damascus, when menfolk were drafted by the Turks and forced to fight the Safar Barlek, she scraped through by sewing for the neighbors. She pedaled that kettle-black Singer to success. By the 1920s, ladies from all over Damascus would come to her with fashion magazines, point at an outfit, and she'd custom tailor it for them, or delegate it to one of her apprentices—young women vied to be trained by her.

"Like, a fashion designer?" Khadra said, looking at the woman with the arching brows and upswept hair in the faded photo, one of the few pictures the Shamys packed with them from Syria. Her father's grandma eyeballed you, looking kind of magnificent and cheekbony, not like the pictures of Mama's mother, which showed a plump, sweet-faced woman looking like she was about to give you a big cozy hug in shades of black and white.

The Shamy side tended to look heroic and solemn in photographs. Khadra's dad, Wajdy, had a picture of his father, Jiddo Abu Shakker, in his youth, standing at attention in a military uniform. His mother, Sitto Um Shakker, is seated next to him in her bridal dress. Both look brave and sad and serious. Of course they wouldn't have been called Um Shakker and Abu Shakker then, because they hadn't had the first baby, Shakker, yet.

Jiddo the Soldier-Man had died the year before they came to America. It happened when her father's big brother Shakker got put in jail for saying things against the Syrian government. Her father said Syria was a mean government, and that Shakker had told the truth to its face and that's called standing witness and that's what a good Muslim should do. Shakker died a hero. A martyr. In Syria, everyone in the Shamy neighborhood called Wajdy "Shakker's little brother."

The last picture they had of Jiddo Abu Shakker is of him in a fez and a full gray beard, smiling sadly. Baby Khadra is in his lap and little tyke Eyad in a sailor suit at his knee.

"They didn't have such fancy titles as 'fashion designer' in Syria then," her father answered Khadra. "Seamstress is what she called it." He had learned to sew almost by osmosis. 'Burdas"—that's what Wajdy called sewing patterns—"burdas are for beginners."

Little Khadra had only to point to a dress in her Sleeping Beauty Golden Book and her father would whip it up for her on the secondhand Singer. Her friends may have flaunted gorgeous new ghararas from Hyderabad on Eid, with gold-on-red and silveron-green chumki-bordered brocade and matching depattas thrown over their shoulders like glamorous boas. But they had nothing on the fairy-tale gown Khadra's father made for her. It boasted fivecount 'em, five-tiers of ruffles on the full-length violet skirt, and a petal collar with rickrack trim.

20

(Saïd Sayrafiezadeh, 1968—)

赛义德 · 赛拉菲扎德

作者简介

赛义德 · 赛拉菲扎德（Saïd Sayrafiezadeh，1968— ）是美国伊朗裔回忆录作家、剧作家、小说家，出生于纽约布鲁克林（Brooklyn, New York），他曾就读于匹兹堡大学 (University of Pittsburgh)，但在大四辍学。

2010 年，他凭借回忆录《滑板何时自由》(*When Skateboards Will Be Free*, 2009) 获得怀廷奖（The Whiting Award）。他还著有两部故事集：《与敌人的短暂相遇》（*Brief Encounters With the Enemy*，2013）和《美国隔阂》(*American Estrangement*, 2021)。《与敌人的短暂相遇》曾入围 2014 年美国笔会 / 罗伯特 · W. 宾厄姆小说处女作奖（2014 PEN/Robert W. Bingham Prize for Debut Fiction）。

他的戏剧作品包括《纽约流血》（*New York is Bleeding*）、《一个恐怖分子的自传》（*Autobiography of a Terrorist*）、《一切都已消失》（*All Fall Away*）和《夏天的长梦》（*Long Dream in Summer*）。它们曾在南海岸剧目中心（South Coast Repertory）、纽约戏剧工作坊（New York Theatre Workshop）、新美国戏剧节（The Humana Festival of New American Plays）和圣丹斯戏剧实验室（The Sundance Theatre Lab）被制作或阅读。

赛拉菲扎德曾在《纽约客》（*The New Yorker*）、《巴黎评论》（*The Paris Review*）、《纽约时报》（*The New York Times*）、《格兰塔》（*Granta*）和《麦克斯威尼》（*McSweeney's*）等多家媒体发表文章和短篇小说。

赛义德 · 赛拉菲扎德的短篇小说集《与敌人的短暂相遇》，通过八个战争故事，作者讲述了美国看似无休止的战争以及参与其中可能产生的道德矛盾心理。节选部分出自与这本书的名字相同的那个令人难忘的故事：一名士兵在一条荒芜的山间小路上进行最后一次例行巡逻时，终于遇到了他一直想要一睹的“敌人”。

作品选读

Brief Encounters With the Enemy

(Brief Encounters With the Enemy)

By Saïd Sayrafiezadeh

A BRIEF ENCOUNTER WITH THE ENEMY

To get to the hill you have to first take the path. The path is narrow and steep and lined with trees that are so dark they could be purple, and so dense it feels as though you're walking alongside a brick wall. You can't see in and you hope that no one can see out.

The first time I went up the path, it was terrifying. I could barely take a full breath, let alone put one foot in front of the other. If I'd had to run, I wouldn't have remembered how. Besides, I was loaded down with fifty pounds of equipment that clanged and banged with every step. I might as well have been carrying a refrigerator on my back. But after the first month, the fear dissipated and the path started to become fascinating, even charming. I was able to appreciate the "beauty of the surroundings"—as the brochure had said —even the trees that I was constantly bumping against. "What kind of trees are these?" I asked out loud. I wanted to learn everything I could. I wanted to get everything there was to get out of this experience.

"Christmas trees," someone answered back. He was being funny, of course, and everyone laughed, even though we were missing Christmas.

The sergeant wanted to know what was funny. We told him nothing was funny, sir. He said that that was true—nothing was funny, that if you could get shot in the face at any moment, then nothing could be funny.

So we were quiet again, the fifty of us, we were fearful again, but that didn't last too long, because fear can't persist unless you have at least a little evidence to sustain it. Fascination can't persist either. What can persist, however, is boredom. I had come all this way hoping for something groundbreaking to happen, and nothing had happened.

Now twelve months had passed, and tomorrow I was flying back home.

That's what I was thinking about when I walked up the path for the last time.

I was also thinking about Becky. "Ooh," she had said when I told her the news. "You're going on an adventure, Luke!" She'd clapped her hands like a little girl. "I sure am," I said.

We'd run into each other in the lobby. She was coming down with a cigarette and I was going up with a sandwich. I hadn't seen her since the afternoon I'd tried to casually ask her out and she'd said no, point-blank. "Do you want to get some ice cream?" I had said. I'd known her since high school, and the Mister Softee truck was parked right outside.

"No, thanks," she'd told me. "I'm on a diet." I couldn't tell if that was an excuse. Her body looked fine to me.

Six months later, though, she was all smiles, standing close to me in the lobby and batting her eyelashes as the other office workers came and went around us in a big wave of suits.

I was deploying in two weeks, but I tried to make it sound as if it was no big deal. In fact, it *was* no big deal. Everyone thought that the war was coming to an end. Everyone thought that it was only a matter of time. We'd taken the peninsula and we'd secured the border and we'd advanced to within twenty-five miles of the capital. Any day now, everyone said. My main concern had been that I wouldn't make it over in time to see any action.

She said, "You going to keep in touch, Luke?" And she made a pouting face, as if I'd been the one to turn down her invitation for ice cream.

"You know I will," I said.

She had big lips and long lashes. She had a little gray in her hair, but I didn't care about that. She'd been married and was now divorced. I didn't care about that either. I'd just hit twenty-seven and was getting soft around the middle. I was hoping to get back in shape. "Push yourself to your physical limits," the brochure had said.

"You get ten of those, you get court-martialed," the most paranoid among us speculated.

Boots did finally arrive. This was about three months into our tour. They came from Timberland, no less, donated free of charge so that not everything would have to fall on the taxpayers. Half the guys sold their boots right off; they sold them to the other half of the guys who could afford to buy them and have two pairs. Then they used the proceeds to purchase things like cigarettes and instant soup. There was a guy named Chaz who wanted to give me twenty-five dollars for my boots. He acted like he was doing me a favor. "I'll tell you what I'll do," he said. He sat down on my cot and took out his money. "Whaddya say?" He was trying to be chummy about it. He was trying to be down-home. He'd gone to a good college and his parents sent him money every two weeks and we had nothing in common except that we both wanted boots. He was one of those guys who had joined for all the wrong reasons. He had joined not because he believed in anything but because he wanted to put it down on his resume and jump-start his career.

I told him, "You're here for the wrong reasons, Chaz."

He said, "What reasons are those?^{n} As if he didn't know.

He used phrases like "in the long term" regarding my boots. Twenty years from now, I'd probably see him on television, asking for my vote.

I emailed Becky to tell her that we'd gotten new boots from Timberland.

She emailed back:

But what else is going on? xoxo***

It wasn't the rainy season now. It was the hot and dry season. No one needed boots anymore. I made it to the end of the path in fifteen minutes. I could have done it in flip-flops. I could have done it barefoot.

It was getting close to evening, and things were cooling down a bit, but the flies were buzzing and I was sweating badly because I was dressed as if I were heading into battle. I felt less like a soldier and more like I was going trick-or- treating dressed as a soldier; all I needed was a bag for my candy. Everything about me was superfluous and ridiculous—the boots but also the helmet, the jacket, and the backpack, which rattled on my back like a gumball machine. The gun was unnecessary too, but it was the lightest thing on me. That was the contradiction. It was three feet long and looked like it was made of iron, but it felt like plastic. It could have been a squirt gun, except for the fact that it had all sorts of gadgets and meters on it that told you things like the time and the temperature. Plus it could kill a man from a mile away. You hardly even had to pull the trigger. If you put your finger in the proximity of the trigger, it sensed what you wanted to do and it pulled itself. *Poof* went the bullet, and the gun would vibrate gently, as if you were getting a call on your cell phone.

She wrote her email address in purple ink on the bottom of my sandwich bag. When she walked off, I took a long look at her ass. She didn't need a diet.

In the first couple of months, I made a point of emailing her. We were each allotted fifteen minutes a day at the Internet café, and I sent her updates when I could.

"What's going on down there, Luke?" she wanted to know. "Tell me everything." She ended her emails with "xoxo* * *."

"What's that mean?" I had to ask one of the guys.

"Hugs and kisses," he said.

"But what do the asterisks mean?"

He didn't know.

There wasn't much to report about what was going on. The enemy had yet to make his appearance. So I told her that we had an Internet café, and a bowling alley, and a Burger King. "They have everything down here," I wrote.

It wasn't entirely true. They didn't have things like boots. It was the rainy season and it rained every day. To be fair, there were ponchos, but ponchos don't keep you from slipping and sliding when you're going along the path on patrol in Skechers. If you got caught in a particularly bad downpour, you might as well be ice-skating, and you'd come back to base at least an hour late. The sergeant would mark this down in his blue book. He'd make sure you saw him marking it down. What happened after that was anyone's guess.

The first time I'd ever shot a gun was when my dad had taken me and my sister down to the woods to go hunting. This was about ten years ago, when the war had just started. There were supposed to be things like deer and elk lurking around in those woods. At least that was how it had been when my dad was a kid and his dad had taken him hunting. But times had changed, and the factories were up and running for the war effort, and the woods had been dug through to make way for a new train line. Not only were there no deer or elk, there weren't even any chipmunks. So instead of teaching us how to hunt, my dad drew a bull's-eye on the side of a tree using a piece of chalk. Inside the bull's-eye he drew the face of the enemy. It was a surprisingly good representation, although he exaggerated the nose and eyes and ears for comic effect.

"This is how you hold it, Luke," he told me. "This is how you cock it. This is how you aim it."

I remember that the gun was heavy like a brick, and when I pulled the trigger, it felt as if my right hand and ear had caught on fire. "Look what you did, Luke!" my father screamed. Sure enough, I had hit the bull's-eye right in the center. "Try again, Luke," he said, but I didn't want anything more to do with it.

My sister, on the other hand, had a great time. She blasted away at the target, *blam, blani blam,* pretending it was really the enemy. Most of the time she missed everything, including the tree, but she thought the experience was fun and funny. "He's dead!" she kept saying. "The enemy's dead!" She looked like a pro, even though she was only twelve. I threw stones in the river, waiting for the shooting to be over so I could go back home and play video games. By the time evening came and the bullets ran out, she'd blasted a hole through the tree.

"They're all dead," she said.

Ten years later, it was the sergeant asking us if we wanted to end up dead. No sir, we said. He had us at target practice two hours a day. Lying on our bellies, crawling through the mud. We were training like mad because we thought we were going to be doing some real fighting. One week after we arrived, the war had taken a turn for the worse, just like that, and there was no longer a chance that it was going to be ending anytime soon. We had lost the peninsula and we had mishandled the border and we had been forced back from the capital. Each day the reports would come through listing the number of casualties. It always seemed to fall somewhere between two and two hundred, and by the time word spread around the base, no one could be sure if the numbers were being exaggerated up or down. It was anyone's guess how many we were losing. I say "we," but we had nothing to do with it. We had landed on the other side of the country, far from the fighting, and we hadn't lost anything—it was the poor bastards a thousand miles away, trying to push back toward the capital, who had something to worry about.

I wrote to Becky a few times: "Can you tell me what is happening, please?" When her email came back, it would be almost entirely redacted:

XOXO***

According to my state-of-the-art gun, it was now 6:02 and eighty-five degrees. Back home, it was twelve hours earlier and sixty degrees colder. Tomorrow morning we were flying home, and we didn't care that we were going back to cold weather. We were flying home on American Airlines, which had donated the plane free of charge. "Traveling in style," the guys said. They said that it was the least American Airlines could do. The fact was that twelve months had passed and we hadn't done much of anything. Our main accomplishment might have been the bridge that I was walking across. My boots echoed in the valley. It was sturdy, the bridge, and it was steel, and it would no doubt be here, sitting at the end of the path, in ten thousand years, when the war was finally over. We had built the bridge in order to get across the valley. We had to get across the valley so we could get up the hill. The hill was the goal. The hill was where the enemy was waiting for us.

"Eight hundred and eighty hiding," our sergeant had told us. How he'd come up with that number, we didn't know. It was so specific, we thought it must be true.

Ten hours a day we worked on that bridge. We'd wake up in the morning when it was dark, and we'd eat our powdered eggs in darkness, and by the time we walked up the path and reached the valley, the sun would just be rising, and the light would seem to be emanating upward from the valley, golden and warm, with traces of pinks and reds. One of the guys, who worked at a used-car dealership, said that if he was going to make a car commercial, he'd use the valley as a backdrop to portray things like power and eternity, and everyone said that was right, that they'd buy that car for sure.

But the truth was that no one really wanted to get the bridge built, because no one wanted to get over the hill. We didn't say this out loud; instead, we worked as slowly as possible, and as incompetently. We accidentally dropped tools into the valley. I once dropped my blowtorch. It slipped from my hands like a bar of soap and bounced down the cliff until it took flight into the abyss.

"Do you know how much that blowtorch cost?" my sergeant screamed. He screamed like the money was coming out of his own pocket. He screamed like I had dropped his daughter in the valley. He stared at me for so long, one inch from my face, breathing like he'd run a race, his breath smelling like powdered eggs, that I thought he was actually asking if I knew how much it cost.

"A hundred and thirty-five dollars?" I guessed.

This caught him by surprise. "It cost forty dollars," he said.

That didn't seem like all that much.

"I should drop *you* in the valley," he said. He made me do push-ups, right then and there, thirty push-ups. I got down on the ground, but I couldn't do them. He told me to take my backpack off and try again, but I still couldn't do them. This pissed him off even more. He put me to work cleaning the bathrooms, which was fine by me. I could have scrubbed toilets for the rest of my tour and been perfectly content. I could have scrubbed toilets for the rest of my life. Anything not to get over that hill and find eight hundred and eighty enemy waiting. But the next day I was back working on the bridge, bright and early. He needed all the help he could get. His superiors were probably screaming at him an inch from his face. Their superiors were screaming at them, and so on and so forth, until you got all the way up to the president screaming and panting as if he'd just run a race. Meanwhile, on the other side of the country, the casualties were mounting.

Day after day, we hammered and welded. Fifty guys pounding at the same time. The sounds echoed through the valley from morning to night, so that if the enemy didn't know we were coming, they knew now.

21

(Zainab Salbi, 1969—)
扎伊纳布·萨尔比

作者简介

扎伊纳布·萨尔比（Zainab Salbi，1969—）是一位美国伊拉克裔作家、妇女权利活动家和演说家。萨尔比 1969 年出生于伊拉克巴格达（Bagdad）。两伊战争时期，她曾居住在巴格达，亲身经历了战争，与萨达姆·侯赛因关系密切的家人也经历了恐惧和独裁，她 19 岁的时候成功逃离了伊拉克。1990 年，在她来到美国几个月后，第一次海湾战争爆发，她再也没能回到伊拉克。萨尔比的战争经历使她对世界各地战争中妇女的困境感到敏感。当她来到美国几年后得知波黑战争爆发时，她决定采取行动，与第二任丈夫阿姆贾德·阿塔拉（Amjad Atallah）创立了国际妇女组织（Women for Women International），并将自己的一生奉献给战争中的女性幸存者。

扎伊纳布·萨尔比著有多本书，主持了《透过她的眼睛看雅虎新闻》（*Through Her Eyes with Yahoo News*）和公共广播公司《我也是，现在该怎么办?》（*Me Too, Now What?*）系列原创剧集。

萨尔比的主要作品包括:《两个世界之间：逃离暴政：在萨达姆的阴影下长大》（*Between Two Worlds: Escape from Tyranny: Growing Up in the Shadow of Saddam*, 2005）、《隐藏在显而易见的地方：在萨达姆的阴影中成长》（*Hidden in Plain Sight: Growing up in the Shadow of Saddam*，2006）、《战争的另一面：妇女生存和希望的故事》（*The Other Side of War: Women's Stories of Survival & Hope*, 2006）、《如果你知道我，你会关心纽约》（*If You Knew Me You Would Care New York*, 2012），以及《自由是一项内部工作：拥有我们的黑暗和光明来治愈我们自

己和世界》(*Freedom Is an Inside Job: Owning Our Darkness and Our Light to Heal Ourselves and the World*, 2018)。

节选部分出自扎伊纳布·萨尔比的《两个世界之间：逃离暴政：在萨达姆的阴影下长大》第十章。《两个世界之间》是一部引人入胜的对真理的探索，加深了我们对权力、恐惧、性征服等普遍主题的理解，以及一代人问上一代人的问题：你们怎么能让这种事情发生在我们身上？

作品选读

Between Two Worlds: Escape from Tyranny: Growing Up in the Shadow of Saddam

(10 SETTING ME FREE)

By Zainab Salbi

SETTING ME FREE

I DIDN'T SEE MY MOTHER for five years.

We spoke, but international calls were hard to place and strained by my unresolved anger. Even if I'd wanted to, how could we have had a heart-to-heart conversation when I knew there was at least one intelligence agent listening in from Iraq and possibly another in America as well? What conversations there were took on a predictable pattern in which we would edge briefly into emotional topics, then back away, often ending with Mama asking me to come home for a visit and telling me about all the parties she would have for us. The last thing I wanted was a party to prove to her friends that I had made a good marriage after all. Iraqi intelligence was done the old-fashioned way, with someone listening in, and one time our monitor spoke up and took her side. "Be a good daughter, come home for a visit," he said. Even in America Amo's secret police interrupted my phone calls. After that, I always had a perverse urge to speak to our eavesdropper directly and say, "How are you today? How are things in Iraq—everyone still terrified?"

One day in 1997, Mama called to say she wasn't feeling well and had developed a limp that doctors in Baghdad couldn't diagnose—could I help set up doctors' appointments for her in America? Medical care in Iraq, once among the best in the Arab world, was another casualty of sanctions—another punishment for the punished. I helped arrange her visa, set up appointments, and suddenly she was back in my life, sitting in an airport wheelchair in her Nina Ricci mink. Given the limp, it didn't surprise me that they had wheeled her off the plane, but when I hugged her, her old vitality seemed missing. She was no longer the beauty I remembered. The skin around her lips sagged when she smiled, and I realized she had aged.

Amjad and I had bought a one-bedroom condo in Alexandria, Virginia, that we thought of as our "nest." We had a quiet balcony that opened up onto trees and a pool, and friends from around the world had stayed with us. Until now, it had been a refuge from my past. I was nervous as we walked in the door, full of conflicting feelings.

Mama was exhausted from the long flights and went to bed early.

"Noah's Ark?" she asked.

Noah's Ark. I felt that old flutter of love for her. That was what we used to call her king-sized bed when I was little. "Noah's Ark!" she would shout out sometimes when my father was away, especially during the war, and my little brothers and I would all run and jump in her big bed for a sleepover. 1 tried to sleep with her that night, in hope of bringing back some of the trust lost between us, but I found no comfort being near to her anymore, only anxiety. I lay there thinking of all the things I wanted to say to her, then slipped away when she fell asleep, and joined Amjad on the sofa bed.

"I can't even hug her," I said, crying softly into his chest. "I just can't."

Except for the limp, she seemed much better the next day. The image of the dutiful daughter, I served her breakfast in bed and told her about the appointments we had lined up and the sights we were planning to see. This was the first time we had been together in nearly seven years without a marital crisis facing us, but it was obvious from that first day that we had different needs. She wanted to bring back the loving daughter I had been, and I wanted to bring back the strong, independent mother she had been. So we politely danced and parried with each other as Amjad looked on in discomfort. We went to the Smithsonian Institution, and Mama silently made her point by lingering at a portrait of a mother and daughter. We went to the Kennedy Center to see *Phantom of the Opera*, the story of a young opera singer held captive by a hideously deformed phantom in a mask. "Those who have seen your face draw back in fear," the young singer told her tormentor. "I am the mask you wear." There it is Mother, look! I wanted to say. That's the nightmare of my life you created for me. Can't you see it? I was the mask Amo wore. I still have this nightmare that my face will disintegrate and people will see his face underneath mine. Can't you *feel* it, Mama? But all she said was how much she enjoyed the show. Except for one emotional invective against Saddam Hussein by Amjad's father, who had no idea we knew him, no one mentioned the man who had formed, or rather deformed, my life.

One night Mama invited to dinner an Iraqi couple who also happened to be visiting their children in Washington, D.C. My mother got all dressed up for the evening, and as we sat down to eat, I felt the same surge of anxiety I used to feel every time we walked into one of Aunt Sajida's palace parties together, when she would try to show me off and I would have to smile and pretend to be happy to please her. But it was different now. I was twenty-seven years old. This was my house. I had worked so hard to break out of those old habits, and I was not going to let her make me snap right back into them. I stood up politely, went to the stereo, and put on Persian music by a singer named Quoqoosh. Instantly, our dinner table conversation stopped. My mother's face flushed, and drops of sweat formed on her upper lip as they always did when she was angry or embarrassed. Mama gave me a look I would not forget for a long time. Amjad looked puzzled. He was the only non-Iraqi at the table. He didn't know our vocabulary of fear. He didn't understand what it meant to play the music of the enemy. Finally, the tension was broken when the Iraqi man said, "Ahhh, I've missed this music. It has been so long." We all laughed then, recognizing for a brief moment how silly it was to be terrified of a song thousands of miles from Baghdad, years after the war had ended. Yet, after that brief acknowledgment of common ground, we moved to safer topics about the old days in Baghdad. I cringed inside, realizing how insensitive and cruel I had been. I did not know if these visitors were Baathists. They might have been informers, and Mama would have to go back and deal with the consequences of my arrogant disregard for her safety. Instead of sharing my new freedom with her, I was rubbing her face in it and risking her life.

One of the things on my agenda was to show her what I had accomplished despite what she had done to me. I wanted to show her the new me, the women's advocate who had founded an international women's organization, the expert on women survivors of war who published papers on the subject, appeared on television, and was doing her best to make a difference in people's lives. Between doctors' appointments, I took her to our office and explained our program and what we were trying to accomplish. I taught her about the rape camps in Bosnia and the mass rape in Rwanda and showed her pictures of women I had met there. She listened to everything I said and began working as a volunteer, reading and filing letters from women in Bosnia, Croatia, and Rwanda. When I saw how she responded, I knew the mother who had taught me to care about women and their issues was still there inside her. She was the one who had inspired me to do this work, both through her example and through the feminist books she had given me. I decided to give her my own selections of feminist work, some of it about mother-daughter relationships, and I stacked them in the order I wanted her to read them: Amy Tan's *The Joy Luck Club,* Alice Walker's *The Color Purple,* Betty Friedan's *The Feminine Mystique,* and Fatima Marnissi's *The Forgotten Queens of Islam.*

After a single chapter of Amy Tan, she got it.

"Are you trying to tell me that I have not been a good mother to you?" she asked.

It was the opening I wanted, but it was a sunny afternoon, and she had taken me by surprise. For a moment I doubted my resolve.

"*La, la, la*, Mother," I answered in the traditional Iraqi way of repeating things three times. "No, no, no. You are a wonderful mother, and I love you very much."

But Mama knew my plastic smile when she saw it.

"Something is wrong, Zainab," she declared a few days later. "What is wrong? What have I done, Zainab? Why are you so angry with me?"

She was sitting in a chair that she and I had upholstered together. I was sitting on the floor next to her. I felt all the anger, rage, and disappointment rush out in a stream of bitterness and accusations.

"You destroyed everything you had helped me build, Mama!" I said. "Why did you do that to me? Yank me out of my last year of college? Take me away from my family and my friends and marry me off to a man I barely knew—a man who *hurt* me? Why did you abandon me, leave me here in a strange country all alone?"

I burst out in sobbing.

"Oh, Zanooba, you don't—"

"Understand? What is there not to understand, Mama? You used to make fun of people who married strangers! You taught me to finish college, get a career, be a strong woman, and then look what you did to your own daughter! I *believed* in you, Mama, and you sent me halfway around the world into the arms of a man who had no respect at all for anything you brought me up to care about. I trusted you with my life, Mama! You were the one who kept preaching to me that 1 should never let myself be abused by any man, and then what did you do? You married me to a cold, horrible man who didn't think twice about raping me!"

I don't know how to describe the look she gave me. It was a look of devastation, of irredeemable failure. I think I saw her fall apart. Her shoulders collapsed. She leaned over, looking down at her hands, and began crying too.

"I had to get you out, *habibiti!*" she finally said. "I had to! He *wanted* you, Zainab. I didn't see any other way."

"*He?* Who was *he*?"

I had been in America too long. There was only one *he* in Iraq. *He* was Amo.

So Mama hadn't sent me off to America to live her dream? She had married me off to Fakhri because she was afraid Amo was going to rape me? Me? The enormity of this revelation wouldn't sink in.

"But, Mama, I was only nineteen," I said, realizing how naïve that sounded.

"In his eyes, you were a woman, Zainab," she said. "You had been engaged to be married. Then you broke off your engagement. You were a woman."

She beseeched me to understand and went back through times I had spent with Amo that I had tried to put out of my mind, hoping to make me see them as she had.

"Do you remember that night when you were standing out on the balcony by the lake and he and I were watching you? The wind was catching your hair in the moonlight, and he just stood still staring at you, as if he was breathing you in. I was standing next to him, *habibiti*. I knew that look. He didn't even turn around when he said to me, 'Your daughter is so beautiful.' I knew that night I had to keep him away from you until I could get you out."

"But, Mama," I stammered, trying to understand the one crime it had never occurred to me he was capable of. "We were like his family, he couldn't—he wouldn't have hurt *me*, would he?"

"Oh, honey, I hoped never to have to tell you all this! But I could see his infatuation with you. He started using his smile on you, you know the one, his charming smile. I knew that damned smile. Trust me, Zainab. You don't know how he can be."

And I remembered the first night I saw him after I had broken off my engagement, how he had gazed into my eyes for a long time with what I read as sympathy. That was the same night he gave me that shining-eye look for playing the *Blue Danube*, and I had assumed he was punishing Sarah. Had there been more to it than that? Yes, I suddenly knew, there had.

I looked at Mama's beautiful eyes, so red and wrenched in pain from how unfairly I had treated her. I felt such an outpouring of trust and love that I fell into her arms, and we sobbed together at what he had done to both of us and at the years we had lost. I felt her pain and her ragged releasing of it. That was one of the most powerful moments of my life. It was the time I became her daughter again, and the moment she regained her ability to comfort me. I asked for her forgiveness and she asked for mine. How could she possibly have known that to save me from rape, she was sending me into the arms of a rapist?

After we both calmed down, she told me she and the other parents had started to worry about their daughters that day Amo took us off in his sports car without telling them.

"How worried we were for you girls! When you got back, he saw the look on our faces and sent you off. Then he took us aside and lectured us and said, 'How *dare* you think I'd do anything to your daughters!'"

I heard his voice in hers. I knew the intonation, and it chilled me to the bone.

No wonder they were scared, watching Saddam Hussein drive up with their daughters, all in the bloom of young womanhood. They were totally impotent. He could have done anything to us he pleased, and there was nothing they could have done about it. I was totally unaware of any danger. There were only two times I could remember that I had actually enjoyed his company, and that afternoon was one of them. After all these years and all my education, I realized, I had never reconciled the Saddam Hussein who committed genocide with the Amo who drove us around that day in his red sports car. Intellectually, I understood, but emotionally I didn't. The wall between the two was still there in my brain, sturdy as fear.

22

(Eman Quotah, ?—)
伊曼·奎塔赫

作者简介

伊曼·奎塔赫（Eman Quotah，？—）是美国沙特裔作家，出生在沙特阿拉伯的吉达（Jidda, Saudi Arabia），母亲是美国人，父亲是沙特人。她在沙特阿拉伯的吉达和美国俄亥俄州的克利夫兰（Cleveland Heights, Ohio）长大。她于1995年毕业于斯沃斯莫尔学院（Swarthmore College），获得英语文学和语言学学士学位，1997年毕业于塔夫茨大学（Tufts University），获得英语文学硕士学位。

伊曼·奎塔赫写过关于美国穆斯林妇女的经历和沙特阿拉伯妇女的经历的文章。这些文章发表在《华盛顿邮报》(*The Washington Post*)、《今日美国》(*USA Today*)、《祝酒辞》(*The Toast*)、《文学中心》(*Literary Hub*)和《电子文学》(*Electric Literature*)等出版物上。2021年，她出版了自己的小说处女作《海上新娘》(*Bride of the Sea*，2021)，这本书随即入选了《新闻周刊》(*News Weekly*) 2021年最受期待的新书排行榜以及26本"让人迷失其中的小说和非小说类书籍"榜单。

节选部分出自伊曼·奎塔赫的小说《海上新娘》。

《海上新娘》取名伊曼·奎塔赫的出生地吉达，这里被人们称作"红海新娘"。故事讲述的是在一个下雪的二月里，美国克利夫兰两个新婚的沙特裔大学生穆尼尔和赛伊达正期待着他们的第一个孩子，然而丈夫穆尼尔心里却藏着一个秘密：离婚。不久，他们的婚姻走向了结束，穆尼尔将返回沙特阿拉伯，而赛伊达和他们的女儿哈娜迪仍留在克利夫兰。由于越来越担心失去女儿，赛伊达带着女儿消失了，开始了新的秘密生活，而穆尼尔多年来一直在另一个国家拼命寻找他的女儿。这次绑架的影响向外波及，不仅改变了哈娜迪和她父母的生活，也改变了与他们交织在一起的家人和朋友——他们必须选边站队，隐藏自己深藏不露的秘密。当哈娜迪成年后，她发现自己处于这场冲突的中心，在她长大的世界和大洋彼岸的家庭之间左右为难。她应该怎样存在于父母之间，国家之间？这个问题是伊曼·奎塔赫的这部关于文化、移民、宗教和家庭碰撞的引人入胜的处女作的核心，一幅关于失去和治愈的亲密写照，最终证明了我们在爱、距离和心碎中发现自己的方式。

作品选读

Bride of the Sea

(Dreams 2018)

By Eman Quotah

DREAMS

2018

LAST WISH

Hannah prophesies her grandfather's death.

She's always had memories of dreams here and there, like anyone else, but since her forty-eighth birthday two months ago, her dreams have been more vivid. She wakes up with memories of symbolic sheaves of wheat and fat sheep and never-ending stairways and the family in Jidda burying her mother.

Unlike the Prophet Yusuf, she has no one to explain the symbols to her.

For several weeks before the news of her grandfather's illness arrives, she dreams of emaciated animals—dogs, cats, goats, chickens, a lion, a hyena, a zebra. She dreams of wilting fruit trees and straw-brown lawns. At first, she attributes these visions of near-death to the onset of her eleventh New England autumn, the primary intensity of the trees bursting against the deep blue sky, that last gasp before winter. She's no wimp about winter; she grew up with the northern Ohio lake effect, frozen eyelashes, snow boots, snow pants, and snow mittens clipped to her down coat. The time she spent in temperate and tropical places strengthened her fundamental resilience.

Still, fall depresses her. It conjures death. Hamza makes fun of her for saying that, but she knows she's not wrong.

She wakes up on a fall Tuesday morning and digs her sketchbook, which she hasn't touched in years, out of her nightstand drawer. It's the same fat book she took on her first trip to Jidda, set aside when she ditched art school for pre-law. Last night she dreamed she was drawing in it—was it a dream of the past, or the future? She isn't sure. The sketchbook has been hiding under random photos of Fareed as a baby, as a toddler, in first grade; under a half-knitted scarf and smooth wooden knitting needles; boxes of not-her-taste jewelry from aunts and cousins; forsaken cell phones; and an iPod Shuffle.

She sketches, in pencil, trees outside the window and snippets of her dreams, trying to capture in-betweenness: the space between seasons, between waking and sleeping, between life and death.

A few hours later, Aunt Randah sends a WhatsApp message saying Hannah's grandfather is in the hospital and she should visit him one last time. No one knows exactly how old he is, because there were no birth certificates when he was young, when her parents were young. And no one but God knows when a man's time will come, Randah writes. But he's old, and these are possibly his last days.

In between classes at the ESOL school where she teaches, Hannah reads the message. She's alone in the windowless cliché of a teachers' break room, which smells of burnt coffee and reheated spaghetti and chicken.

She does the math in her head to calculate what time it is in Jidda. It's a decent hour, and probably not prayer time. It seems simpler to call Randah than to write back.

There's no debate over whether Hannah will go see her grandfather in the hospital. Randah takes it as a given. Hannah and her grandfather Fareed have grown close in the years since her reunion with her family. A dozen times or so he's come to visit or asked her to meet him wherever he was speaking or attending, when he was younger and more able to travel. She flew to Chicago, New York, and LA to see him. It's been a few years. She liked the light banter they had the times they met for coffee. He brought her clothes and jewelry from her aunts and uncles —sweaters, oddly enough, and rhinestoned things and good, soft gold earrings, and pretty embroidered abayah and tarhah sets in the latest colors (it's not all black anymore). Over the years, he's emailed her articles he wanted her to see, about youth in Saudi, about changes that are coming ("economic diversification") and changes that seemed like they were not, but finally did (women driving). He has a rascally seriousness she washes he could gift to her, instead of the jewelry and clothing. Sometimes, she almost forgets he is her mother's father. He's morc like her dad in many ways. Curious. Opinionated. A truth teller.

Her grandfather has never said whether he sees her mother in her. He never asks about her mother.

And though she named her son after her grandfather, Hannah hasn't told her father about the times she's seen her grandfather Fareed, since the first time she mentioned him in passing. Her father paused so long on the phone she thought the line had dropped.

"That part of the family," he said. "I am not on good terms." She would expect him to be grateful that her grandfather had helped get Fouad out of detention, helped her father get out of Saudi jail. But her father is embarrassed of these favors he can't repay.

She has never wanted to ask her grandfather if her mother spoke to him when they were hiding. She does not want to have to blame him. She will go visit him one last time, though it will be impossible to do that without telling her father she's coming to Jidda.

Randah is intent on complicating her life further with a request that pulls Hannah's heart up into her throat. She chokes a little when she hears it: "Can you convince your mother to come?"

Hannah swallows her heart into the pit of her stomach. "I don't know where she is."

It's a way of not saying: *If I thought I could persuade her, I wouldn't want to.*

Randah has a way of guilting her, though. "Please, habibti. It's your grandfather's last wish."

At home, Hannah pulls the calendar down from the bulletin board in the kitchen to try to find a weeklong break in her schedule. Hamza is browning ground beef for tacos. She wishes Fareed were here to grate the cheese, but he won't be home from University of Washington till the holidays.

"The family must be distraught to be losing their patriarch," Hamza says.

In this kitchen smelling of hamburger and onions, cilantro and Colby-Jack, she feels trapped by Taco Tuesday, the Americanness of her existence.

RELICS

When they moved io Cambridge ten years ago, so Hamza could code for a genetics startup, Hannah told herself one of the benefits would be living closer to W.

A long drive or a quick flight, and they are in Toledo. They see W at least once a year, at Thanksgiving or Christmas or spring break. She visits them or they visit her. She's edging up on seventy, and her accent is as hard-edged and as distant from Hannah's mother's accent as ever.

Hannah hadn't, at the time, thought about how Cleveland lay en route to Toledo, how her mother, as far as she knew, was a mile marker on the way to W. She's never run into her accidentally at Hopkins Airport—the last place they met—but the possibility is a burden. Whenever she thinks of W, her brain has to pass through Sadie on the way there.

Telling Randah she doesn't know Sadie's whereabouts wasn't a lie. Hannah doesn't know her mother's home address or her place of business. She doesn't know if Sadie is dating anyone, or married, or what church—church!—she attends.

But she has a phone number that's probably good. She changed her own number years ago so her mother couldn't reach her, figured out how to keep it private so her mother couldn't find her again, like she always seemed to. But on purpose, in case she ever needed it, Hannah saved her mother's number. Not at Hamza's encouragement; on her own she'd done it. Written it down on a piece of paper because she didn't trust her SIM card. In the end, the SIM card worked. It worked so well, her mother's name is in her contacts twice.

She texts the number. If her father were dying, she would want someone to tell her.

"Your father is in the hospital. I'm going next week. Randah wants me to ask you to come."

Immediately, regret hits her like a hangover. She should have told Hamza to do it, or given the number to Randah. Why hadn't she? Why hadn't she thought of that years ago?

It's a relief and an annoyance that she gets crickets from her mother in return for her message.

"At least she knows," Hamza says over tater tots and pizza on Takeout Friday. "No one expects her to go. Her Saudi passport is probably decades expired."

When Fareed was younger, she rarely talked about her mother in front of him because he worried about everything—his grades, whether his parents would come home or end up in a fiery car crash, whether things cost too much, whether he was coming down with chicken pox (it was acne). So much worry was strange, she thinks, for a kid who grew up with stability she never had. She's never told him about her childhood. She never explained why they didn't see her mom. His Syrian grandparents were doting and visited often. There was no reason to tell him the truth about Sadie.

She wonders if she should tell him now.

Her phone begins to buzz. It's her mom.

"Thank you for the message."

She can't do this alone. She puts the phone on speaker so Hamza can hear.

"What's up, Mom?"

"When are you leaving for Jidda?"

"Monday."

"I think I should go," her mother says. "I think that's probably what I should do. I don't know... How is my father?"

"He's in intensive care. I couldn't book an earlier flight."

The teakettle whistles. Hamza removes it from the stove and pours water into a teapot with mint and two Lipton's tea bags.

She tries to put herself in her grandfather's place. If she were on her deathbed, who would she want there?

"I don't know if I can get a ticket," Hannah's mother says. "I have to go to Washington first, to the consulate, for a temporary passport."

Hannah had hoped her mother would easily say no. She'd asked to please Randah.

Her mother's response sets her ears buzzing. Why, after more than forty years, does her mother want to go home? It's a betrayal. If Sadie goes back, why did Hannah go through everything she went through, as a child?

"Do you want me to come?" Sadie says.

Hamza pours tea into glasses.

"OK, Mama, come." She doesn't mean it, but she doesn't want to be the person she is, the person who wants to say no, who wants to keep Sadie from seeing her own father.

23
(Alia Malek, 1974—)
阿莉亚·玛利克

作者简介

阿莉亚·玛利克（Alia Malek，1974—），1974 年出生于马里兰州巴尔的摩（Baltimore, Maryland），她的父母从叙利亚移民到美国。玛利克于 1996 年毕业于约翰霍普金斯大学（Johns Hopkins University）。随后，她在乔治城大学（Georgetown University）法律中心获得法学博士学位。她曾在美国司法部民权司担任民权律师，后来回到学校获得哥伦比亚大学（Columbia University）新闻学硕士学位。她在 2009 年出版了她的第一本书（*A Country Called Amreeka: Arab Roots, American Stories*）。2011 年至 2013 年，她住在叙利亚大马士革（Damascus）。她的叙事非小说类书籍《曾经是我们国家的家园：叙利亚回忆录》（*The Home That Was Our Country: A Memoir of Syria*，2017）就是以这一时期为基础的。

2011 年 4 月，她移居叙利亚大马士革，并匿名为该国境内的多家媒体撰稿。她在叙利亚的报道为她赢得了 2013 年 11 月的玛丽·科尔文奖（The Mary Colvin Award）。

她于 2013 年 5 月回到美国，参加了美国半岛电视台（Al Jazeera America）的成立，在那里她担任高级作家直到 2015 年 10 月。她还曾是国家研究所的海雀基金会写作研究员（Puffin Foundation writing Fellow at the National Institute）。

2016 年 11 月，玛利克荣获第 12 届年度希尔特人文科学奖（Hilt Prize in human Humanities）。2017 年夏天，纽约艺术基金会（New York Foundation for Arts）任命她为非小说文学研究员。

她还担任过美国半岛电视台的资深作家。她的故事出现在《纽约客》（*The*

New Yorker)、《纽约时报》(*New York Times*)、《基督教科学箴言报》(*The Christian Science Monitor*)和《国家报》(*The Nation*)等出版物上。

本文选自《曾经是我们国家的家园：叙利亚回忆录》第 18 章。《曾经是我们国家的家园》是一部深入研究的个人旅程，它对叙利亚的历史、社会和政治进行了细致而尖锐的阐释。书中充满了深刻的见解，将尖锐的政治分析与一个世纪的亲密家族史交织在一起，最终描绘了一幅令人难忘的正在被抹去的叙利亚肖像。

作品选读

The Home That Was Our Country: A Memoir of Syria

(18 DISPLACED)

By Alia Malek

Atmeh, Syria, April 2013

THERE ARE COUNTRIES THAT ONE CAN IMMEDIATELY RECOGNIZE from the sky because the borders are so natural—formed by deep mountain ranges, mighty rivers, or vast oceans. Italy, for example, is easy: it mostly floats in the Mediterranean Sea, visibly separated from other landmasses. Then there are those borders that are much less organic, having been arbitrarily drawn.

The border between Syria and Turkey's Hatay Province is one of those. Flying to Hatay in April 2013, I couldn't see how Syria would naturally end "here; historically, it never had.

Through successive regimes, Syria has never renounced its claim to what it calls Iskenderun, and Syrian maps continued to show it as a part of Syria. After Bashar al-Assad came to power and relations between Turkey and Syria improved, families divided by the border were allowed to visit each other during both Muslim and Christian holidays. In February 2011, the two countries were about to build a "Friendship Dam" together, and it appeared that perhaps Assad was relinquishing Syria's claim to the land. But with the rapid deterioration between Erdogan and Assad (thus between Turkey and Syria), the project was never actualized, and Syrian state media began to again demand the territory's return.

Now, thousands of Syrians were escaping the violence at home, and many were crossing over daily into Hatay, with an ease that might suggest that the border, at the very least, was not natural at all.

Refugees have never been unfamiliar to Syrians. In the past century alone, Syria took in fleeing Armenians, Palestinians, and Iraqis. As a condition, it afflicted those people's privileged classes as much as their poorest. Wealth could mitigate its indignities, almost hiding it from view. But many suffered from it openly, and the refugee camp became the most visible symbol of this terrible circumstance.

I doubt that many Syrians imagined that such a fate would ever befall them. One of the supposed tradeoffs from living under authoritarian regimes was stability. And yet, by spring 2013, registered Syrian refugees numbered over 1 million. The actual number of Syrians who had left their homes and crossed a border was likely much larger. They had fled mostly to the neighboring countries of Lebanon, Jordan, Turkey, and Iraq. I had come to Reyhanli, a small Turkish border town where many of the Turkish inhabitants were originally Syrian, to cross back into Syria, to rebel-held territory. There in Atmeh, a Syrian American foundation was running a camp for those Syrians who had been internally displaced.

The Maram Foundation had been started by Yakzan Shishakly, the thirty-five-year-old grandson of one of Syria's first presidents, Adib Shishakly. Salma had liked him because he was also from Hama and because she believed he had shakhsiyeh. I wondered now as I prepared to meet Yakzan if he would have it too. I knew very little about him—other than who his grandfather was and that his older brother Adib was a visible member of the opposition.

By the time I arrived from the airport in Antakya, the sun had already begun to set, and Yakzan was back in his office, which was on the Turkish side of the border, after a full day in the camp. From the looks of things, that didn't mean his day had ended. I arrived to what I imagine was a daily scene: Yakzan sitting behind his desk, almost holding court. People were coming in and out with woes, requests, and complaints.

When he rose, I had to admit he had the large physical presence that suggests natural leadership. At six feet four inches, he stood above everyone else there. He could have been a professional athlete. And with a full head of dark, wavy hair, and those light eyes so coveted by Syrians, he could have been an actor. His cargo pants and construction boots—which contrasted with the slacks and loafers (or flip-flops) of the other Syrian and Turkish men—gave him an air of masculinity that seemed much more Texan than Mediterranean. But Yakzan, who was soft spoken, did not particularly seem to like this part of the job—that is, the constant flow of people coming to him because they wanted something. Until Syria began to fall apart, Yakzan had been a content owner of an air-conditioning installation and repair business in Houston, Texas.

Yakzan had left Syria for Texas in 1997 at the age of nineteen, even though he had lived well in Syria, in the toniest of neighborhoods in Damascus. If his lineage sometimes afforded him favor, it also meant that the regime had watched his family closely, lest their historical legacy threaten its grip on the country. They were generally unharmed, though, under certain conditions: basically, stay away from politics, and don't open your mouth. Yakzan's father had long chosen to accede. He used to tell his children, "If we leave the country because of those people, who is going to stay?"

In Texas, Yakzan had been unburdened by his name and expectations. He waited tables at T.G.I. Friday's, putting the money toward English classes. He enrolled in a local community college and earned a degree in air-conditioning installation and repair, a sensible choice in a place as hot as Houston. Eventually, he started his own business, assembling a fleet of seven trucks and vans branded with his "U.S. Refrigeration" decal and the motto "Live Above the Weather."

"So how did you end up here?" I asked him when we met.

He laughed. "I don't know."

I think that was in part true—there was a bit of a bewildered air about him. Still, he was able to describe the sequence of events that had preceded that very moment.

After Syrians began protesting in March 2011, Yakzan had helped organize weekly protests in Houston against the regime's crackdown. From there, he joined efforts to organize Syrian Americans across the United States. Meanwhile, however, more and more Syrians were leaving their homes, and a humanitarian crisis was developing. So, exasperated with what he saw as global indifference, and eager to do more, Yakzan had journeyed in September 2012 to the Turkish side of the border, where he distributed aid gathered in the United States to the refugees. It was there, while looking across to the Syrian side, that he unexpectedly first saw families among the olive trees: hundreds of men, women, and children were living there. Tauntingly close to Turkey, yet refused entry, and with the clashes in their homeland at their backs, they had taken refuge under the silvery leaves of a hilltop grove.

Yakzan snuck across the border to Syria to speak to them. They had already been there a month, they said, having brought what they could carry with them, and aside from a few makeshift tents, they were living in the open. Because they were still in their own country and therefore not "refugees"—who, by definition, cross national borders—these people were in a no-man's land in terms of international aid. Yakzan asked them what they needed. Tents and water tanks, they said, so he crossed back into Turkey, purchased the supplies with his own money, then stole across the border into Syria again to deliver them. For two weeks, Yakzan did what he could for them, then returned to Texas. By then he had decided to start an organization to aid these IDPs or internally displaced persons.

24

(Porochista Khakpour, 1978—)
博罗切斯特·卡普尔

作者简介

博罗切斯特·卡普尔（Porochista Khakpour，1978— ）是美国伊朗裔小说家和散文家，她出生于伊朗德黑兰（Teheran），在加利福尼亚州南帕萨迪纳（South Pasadena, California）和洛杉矶地区（Los Angeles area）长大。卡普尔曾在纽约莎拉·劳伦斯学院（Sarah Lawrence College in New York）攻读文学学士学位，主修创意写作和文学。随后她获得了约翰·霍普金斯大学（Johns Hopkins University）和约翰·霍普金斯写作研讨会（The Johns Hopkins Writing Seminars）的硕士学位。在获得硕士学位后，卡普尔成为约翰·霍普金斯大学的讲师和艾略特·科尔曼研究员（Eliot Coleman fellow）。

卡普尔的处女作《儿子和其他易燃物品》(*Sons and Other Flammable Objects*, 2007)，被认为是对伊朗作家萨德格·希达亚特（Sadegh Hedayat）的《盲猫头鹰》（*The Blind Owl*）的回应和“改写”，曾获《纽约时报》“编辑推选”（*The New York Times* “Editor’s Choice”）、《芝加哥论坛报》“秋季最佳”（*The Chicago Tribune* “Fall’s Best”）和2007年加州图书奖(California Book Award)。它还入选了威廉·萨罗扬国际写作奖候选名单（The William Saroyan International Prize for Writing shortlist）、迪伦·托马斯奖入围名单（The Dylan Thomas Prize long list）、信徒图书奖入围名单（the Believer Book Award longlist）以及其他许多奖项。她的作品还被提名为手推车奖（The Pushcart Prize）。

她的第二部小说《最终幻想》(*Last Illusion*，2014）荣获柯克斯2014年最佳图书（Kirkus Best Book of 2014）和巴兹菲德2014年最佳小说（Buzzfeed Best

Fiction Book of 2014）等殊荣。

卡普尔的第一本回忆录《生病》（*SICK*，2018）被视为“一本关于慢性疾病、误诊、成瘾和完全康复神话的回忆录，记录了她漫长而艰难地发现晚期莱姆病的过程”。

2020 年，卡普尔出版了她的第一部散文集《棕色专辑》（*Brown Album*，2020），这部令人心酸的个人散文集，时而幽默，时而深刻，记录了当代移民和美国伊朗裔移民的生活，揭示了美国的移民生活会给一个人带来的损失和快乐。

节选部分为卡普尔的处女作《儿子和其他易燃物品》第七章：祖国。这本书描述了一个伊朗家庭从伊朗移民到美国后如何努力适应新生活的故事。在成长的过程中，薛西斯·亚当（Xerxes Adam）痛苦地意识到，他对自己的伊朗血统的理解是不同的，从典型的青少年尴尬到悲剧得难以言表。这部小说充满讽刺意味，令人难忘。卡普尔在本书中将民族的历史深深植根于人物的个人历史中，类似于萨德格·希达亚特的《盲猫头鹰》。

作品选读

Sons and Other Flammable Objects

(Part Seven Homelands)

By Porochista Khakpour

Part Seven Homelands

They held the fort on New Year’s 2002. That was their joke. *Oh, we’re not going to do anything—nah, we think we’ll ship it—we hate New Year’s anyway—we’re gonna play it safe—oh, we’re just gonna hold the fort that night, just this year.* Xerxes shrugged it off halfheartedly. *As if the fort could be held*, was what he really thought. The fort couldn’t even be counted on to properly exist, much less be held by anyone.

Still, people expected another worst and pretended they didn’t, as 2001, to the *good riddance* of all, did away with itself.

8:30 p.m., Pacific Time: Lala and Darius’s New Year’s Eve celebration consisted of simply staying tuned. They had stopped making a big deal of it once Xerxes was grown—the young Xerxes after all was the force that would get them to tune in to Dick Clark one minute, that would, the next minute, order them to the balcony to watch the fire in the sky and listen to gunshots while he stayed inside holding his breath, reminding them to hurry back in when he sensed it had to be over, eager to trade in spectacle for normalcy. Their New Year's Eve observance was scheduled for exactly a half hour before the East Coast's New Year's, with the TV on as their link. On every channel the world unabashedly put its concerned eyes on Times Square—everybody was pretending that it was just New York's New Year that year. But the televised Times Square might as well have been a taped video of years before had it not been for the many American flags and the "We Will Never Forget" banners. The still indestructible stubborn hordes gathered in full for that pin to drop. It was as if they had to; if you didn't go on with things, they said, that other *they* had won. Lala loved this spirit, this fierce, blind, backward, overdone investment. It was as if they were burning their dinner on purpose—preferring coal to food. She had lived this way every day of her life—it was her secret to survival. You let your counterintuition take over and they don't win. Neither do you, but nobody's asking.

Midnight, Eastern time (according to Suzanne's watch, still 11:55 according to Xerxes's; but they didn't argue): Suzanne began counting down and Xerxes thought to himself, after correcting her gently once, them twice, finally *Who cares, let her have it*—after all, better she be early, in case. She could still have her countdown. Better, he thought, better that he be counting down negative numbers than having his countdown cheated of its hopefully still-as-hell zero.

9:05 p.m., Pacific Time: Lala and Darius went to bed before their own New Year's. The left coast's didn't matter. Darius reminded her, mumbling as they hit the lights and crawled under the covers, that their own Iranian New Year's was still over two months away anyway.

12:05 a.m., Eastern time: When the clock struck twelve, according to *his* watch, plus an extra second or two, Xerxes sighed. They had gone through two of their midnights—it was certain. They: okay. The fort: held. A New Year. 2002. A nice even number. Palindromic. Stable. Not the first year of a millennium, the second. The children's rhyme, how did it go? *First is the worst, second is the best*. Yes. They could move on.

January 2, 2002: California was fine. New York felt okay.

Nobody on the East Coast took the kind, lesser cold of that January for granted.

They deserved it, New Yorkers said. Things were getting better and the weather, it was throwing them a bone. Suzanne swore she saw people smiling more, she felt that she was breathing better, easier exhales, as if her lungs were clearing themselves of whatever residual scarring they had undergone from the bad air of the last season. *The city is being born again*, Suzanne would declare, *it's as if winter for once means renewal not death*! He was glad, but how could anyone trust it?

Because there were days—perhaps just a few days after the terror threat level had been heightened, when the news had some new tidbit to dash like extra oil onto an already burning skillet—when Xerxes would get a wave of the old tension. One time in particular that January. Suzanne and Xerxes were taking a very packed rush hour subway uptown to meet Suzanne's friends for dinner. Xerxes, rarely having had the sort of employment that would require seeing what 5:30 p.m. on the New York subways looked like, was a bit horrified at the overcrowding. There was no chance of a seat so they crammed into each other in a corner, and he held her tight to him when noticing she was also crammed against three other men. He could hear waves of conversation, some louder than others, some whispers, many coughs. So many suits, he noticed. And police. One particularly fat cop, who was in the corner talking to a thin old cop, lifted his shirt for a second in a casual scratching gesture and, totally unembarrassed and unconcerned, revealed a whole network of wiring all across and up his fat white belly. Xerxes closed his eyes—*Maybe it would just be better to close your eyes*, he told himself. But Suzanne was going on and on about Valentine's Day, where they could spend it, an island, upstate, a different state, the other coast. *Doesn't sound doable, too extreme, dunno*, Xerxes was mumbling, while opening his eyes periodically and making some worrying eye contact with someone who happened to be staring right at him. *We could get off now, take a ca*b, he thought to himself, but he imagined what hell it would be to make it through all those hordes to get to the door. Even when the door opened and the train stopped it seemed as if nobody was getting off or getting in. He did not think it was a horrible exaggeration to consider them all trapped. All it would take, after all, was a tragedy outside, a tragedy beyond the glass—hell, a tragedy inside, anywhere—for their situation to register as potentially fatal entrapment. He could feel himself growing hot, then cold, then hot, over and over. In a sort of distance, spiraling gingerly through his right ear, he could just barely make out Suzanne's almost motorized rambles. The crowd was squirming, arranging and rearranging like a snake taking the shape of its route, making way, making some natural way, apparently, for a blind man to get off. His guiding stick was helping but still, in a crowd like that, people were getting prodded and poked and trying their best not to hiss. With his free hand, the blind man grabbed for poles and when he got close to them, he actually grabbed Suzanne's shoulder by mistake. *Hey*, Xerxes accidentally snapped. Several people, including Suzanne, shot him dirty looks—*What's wrong with you, he was, you know,* Suzanne whispered, upset—but the blind man was off, and the train was rumbling on. It sounded louder than usual to Xerxes. *We could get off and try a different train, maybe they're not all so bad*, he thought to himself. But he couldn't imagine making it through. It was not until they were a stop away that the train actually froze, stalling between stops—something that Xerxes was well used to in the city, but this time, he panicked. *Great*, he snapped, *what do we do?!* Hot, cold, cold, hot. Suzanne looked at him perplexed, *No big deal, Xerxes. It's just a usual stall.* Xerxes waited for the conductor, even an automated one, but nothing. He never understood why the conductors didn't communicate better. Had they seen it all? Was that it? Nothing moved them? They had forgotten that the public might not think like them? Xerxes scanned the eyes of the passengers. The cops were chuckling loudly to themselves, all the others just reading their books, eying their papers, staring at their feet, a few still looking over at him. He couldn't take it. He was burning. It had been a long time. He was freezing. *What the hell, how long has this been*, he snapped under his breath.. Suzanne kissed his cheek and told him to calm down, asked if he'd ever been to the Vineyard, maybe that was a good romantic possibility? Xerxes shook his head and stared at the door's glass. Pitch-black. He could vaguely hear another train zoom by on the other tracks, without a hitch. Where were they? Were they not telling them what was going on because they were worried about public reaction? Live not telling a kid bad news to prevent crying? Were they going to be surprised? Xerxes was irate; this lack of information, this black nothing, this entrapment—they were entitled to more. He wanted to stand up and scream, *What are we all doing here anyway?* But instead, he muttered, a light mutter that Suzanne either didn't hear or found it easy enough to ignore, *I don't get it, Su, why won't it open. ...* He suddenly felt half his body turning into ice while the other was melting into ash, perfectly splitting off each other, as if sense and nonsense, heaven and hell, were trying to tear him apart in a second. He endured it. Giving up made his panic more manageable. *What do I have to live for anyway?*—he ran that question through his head all the while the train sat immobilized. Eventually it got moving again and once out and back up and in the New York air, Xerxes, like a spring, bounced back into form—that was what New York did to you, you were Gumby, you were superhuman, you could forgive and forget, because *if you could take it there, you could take it anywhere*—and like the rest of the residents of the island, he forgot moments like those enough to take it from day to day.

25

(Randa Jarrar, 1978—)

兰达·贾拉尔

作者简介

兰达·贾拉尔（Randa Jarrar，1978—），美国巴勒斯坦裔作家、翻译家。1978年出生于芝加哥（Chicago），母亲是埃及人，父亲是巴勒斯坦人。她在科威特和埃及长大。1991年海湾战争后，她和她的家人回到美国，住在纽约地区。贾拉尔在莎拉劳伦斯学院（Sarah Lawrence College）学习创意写作，获有德克萨斯大学奥斯汀分校（University of Texas at Austin）中东研究硕士学位和密歇根大学（University of Michigan）创意写作硕士学位。

兰达·贾拉尔写过非虚构类和虚构类作品，并于2004年秋天在著名的《犁头文学杂志》（*The Ploughshares Literary Journal*）上发表了她的第一个短篇小说。她凭借短篇小说《你是一个14岁的阿拉伯女孩，第一次搬到得克萨斯州》（*You Are a 14-Year-Old Arab Chick Who First Moved to Texas*，2004）获得第一届网络小说百万作家奖（The First Million Writers Award for Online Fiction）。她还在《纽约时报杂志》（*The New York Times Magazine*）上发表了两篇生活专栏，探讨她自己作为单身母亲的过去。

她的第一部小说，成长故事《家的地图》（*A Map of Home*，2008）为她赢得了霍普伍德奖（Hopwood Award for Best Novel）和美国阿拉伯裔图书奖（The Arab American Book Award）。《基督教科学箴言报》（*The Christian Science Monitor*）这样评论这部小说："兰达·贾拉尔在她充满活力、讽刺幽默的处女作《家的地图》中，把所有关于'你把帽子挂在哪里'的愚蠢的、受人追捧的陈腔滥调文章都击成碎片。"

此后，她先后出版了故事集《他、我、穆罕默德·阿里》（*Him, Me, Muhammad Ali*，2016）和回忆录《爱是一个前国家》（*Love Is an Ex-Country*，2021）。前者为她赢得了笔会奥克兰奖（PEN Oakland Award）、故事奖聚焦奖（Story Prize Spotlight Award）和美国图书奖（American Book Award）。

《他、我、穆罕默德·阿里》在现实主义和神话、历史和现在之间无缝地移动，捕捉了穆斯林男女跨越无数地理和环境的生活。贾拉尔以尖刻的风趣、深沉的柔情和无限的想象力生动地刻画了一群令人难忘的人物，其中许多人都是“偶然的过客”——一个术语，指迷路的候鸟，它们在寻找回家的迂回路线。《他、我、穆罕默德·阿里》是面对爱、失去和流离失所时生存的见证。

节选部分为贾拉尔的成长故事《家的地图》第一章。在这本小说中，主人公妮妲莉（Nidali）讲述了她在科威特的童年，她在埃及的青少年时期，以及她的家人最后一次飞往得克萨斯州（Texas）的故事，为一个古怪的中产阶级家庭提供了一个幽默、犀利但充满爱的肖像。

作品选读

A Map of Home

(ONE OUR GIVEN NAMES)

By Randa Jarrar

ONE
OUR GIVEN NAMES

I DON'T REMEMBER HOW I CAME TO KNOW THIS STORY, AND I don't know how I can possibly still remember it. On August 2, the day I was born, my *baba* stood at the nurses' station of St. Elizabeth's Medical Center of Boston with a pen between his fingers and filled out my birth certificate. He had raced down the stairs seconds after my birth, as soon as the doctor had assured him that I was all right. I had almost died, survived, almost died again, and now I was going to live. While filling out my certificate, Baba realized that he didn't know my sex for sure but that didn't matter; he'd always known I was a boy, had spoken to me as a boy while I was tucked safely in Mama's uterus amid floating amniotic debris, and as he approached the box that contained the question, NAME OF CHILD, he wrote with a quivering hand and in his best English cursive, Nidal (strife; struggle). It was not my grandfather's name, and Baba, whose name is Waheed and who was known during his childhood as Said, was the only son of the family, so the onus of renaming a son after my grandfather fell squarely upon his shoulders. It was an onus he brushed off his then-solid shoulders unceremoniously, like a piece of lint or a flake of dandruff; these are analogies my grandfather would the next day angrily pen in a letter sent from Jenin to Boston.

And why was my dear baba filling out my birth certificate so soon after my birth? Because before his birth, he'd had three brothers who had all evaporated like three faint shooting stars before anyone could write them a birth, let alone a death, certificate. His superstitions superseded his desire to hold me so soon after my emergence, and besides, he told himself now, we had the rest of our lives for that.

When he'd filled out the entire form, Baba regally relayed it to the black nurse, who he remembers was called Rhonda, and she stared at the name and sighed, "Damn." Then Baba, in flip-flops, turned around and raced up the white tiled hallway, bypassed the elevator, ran up the three floors to the maternity ward, and burst into the birthing room. Mama was nursing me and I was eagerly sucking the colostrums, now and then losing her nipple.

"How is my queen?" said Baba, caressing my mother's face.

"She's lovely," Mama said, thinking he meant me, "and eight whole pounds, the buffalo! No wonder my back was so ..." Baba's brow furrowed, and Mama couldn't finish her complaint, because, eager to correct his mistake, Baba was already out the door and running down the white-tiled hallway, past new mothers and their red-faced babies, past hideous robes in uncalled-for patterns, bypassing the elevator, and sliding down the banister of the staircase, landing smack on his balls at the end of it. But he raced on, doubtlessly feared by the hospital's patients and nurses who saw an enormous mustache with limping legs, which, upon its arrival at its destination, was screaming for Rhonda, where is Rhonda, help me, Rhonda, an outcry that provided the staff with three weeks' worth of endless laughter and snickering.

Why had Baba assumed, no, hoped, that I was a boy? Because before his birth, his mother had had six daughters whose births all went uncelebrated. He'd watched his sisters grow up and go away, each one more miserable than the last, and didn't want to have to be a spectator to such misery ever again: to witness his own girl's growing and going.

Rhonda, who'd expected Baba to come back and try the naming thing again, emerged with the birth certificate already in hand, and Baba, who is not usually known for laziness, grabbed a pen and added at the end of my name a heavy, reflexive, feminizing, possessive, cursive, cursing "I."

Moments later, Mama, who had just been informed of my *nom de guerre*, and who was still torn up in the nether regions, got out of bed, flung me into a glass crib, and walked us to the elevator, the entire time ignoring my baba, who was screaming, "Nidali is a beautiful name, so unique, come on Ruz, don't be so rash, you mustn't be walking, your, your… *pussy*"—this in a whispered hush, and in Arabic, *kussik*—"needs to rest!"

"*Kussy? Kussy ya ibn ilsharmoota?*"—My pussy, you son of a whore? "Don't concern yourself with my pussy, you hear? No more of this pussy for you, you ... ass!"

"Ruz, enough, have you gone mad cussing in public that way?"

"You think these people understand a word we're saying? You!" she shouted in Arabic, and pointed at a white woman nursing her child in the hallway, "your kid looks like a monkey's ass." The woman smiled at her in English. Mama looked at Baba again. "Aaah, there are surely hundreds of Arabs in Boston!"

"Actually, my love, this is where Arabs first arrived, in the 1800s, and called themselves Syrians."

Mama stared at him incredulously. Her brown IV-ed hand rested on her enormous hip, colostrum leaked into her nightshirt, and her large eyes, which were fixed at Baba as though poised to shoot death rays, were still lined with kohl.

"Impossible! You're giving me a lesson in history, you ass, and you named our daughter Nidali?"

"Yes, and another curious thing: the immigration officers would change the Arabs' names, so the Milhems would become the Williams, the Dawuds the Daywoods, the Jarrars the Gerards, and so on." Baba was trying to calm Mama down by distracting her.

"It's good that you are mentioning name changes, my dear; Pm changing the girl's name right this instant! First you give her a stock boy's name, as though she'll be raised in a refugee camp, as though she's ready to be a struggler or a diaper-warrior, then you add a letter and think it's goddamn unique." A nurse who had been following Mama presently gave up, and Mama continued. "No, brother, over my dead body and never again will you get pussy, I'm not forecasting this girl's future and calling her 'my struggle'! She'll be my treasure, my life, my tune, so don't tell me my pussy needs to rest!"

The elevator announced its arrival with a hushed DING, as though begging my parents to give up.

"Your tune?" Baba said, boarding the elevator with Mama. "Don't tell me, don't tell me: you wanted to call her Mazurka? Or Sonatina? Or Ballade? Or, or ... Waltz?" Baba was giggling, amusing himself while angering Mama to unnamable extremes, a skill he was just beginning to master.

"There's nothing wrong with Sonatina!" Mama said, and the elevator made another DING, and she walked out.

Baba stood in the elevator still, pondering the idea of Sonatina Ammanr, and finally he released a giant, expanding, white-tile-hallway-shaking laugh.

Mama must not have fought longer after Baba's laugh, or who knows: maybe she went to the nurses' station and talked to Rhonda, and maybe Rhonda told her that the birth certificate was already sent out—that Mama would have to go to the office of the City of Boston clerk and see the registrar of vital statistics, where they keep the birth *and* death certificates—and maybe Mama, who is the most superstitious of all humans (even more than Baba, and to that she'll attest) shuddered at the thought of taking me, a newborn, through the heat and the Boston traffic to a place where, she must've imagined, people went to fill out death certificates, and she must've further imagined that going on such a trip, to such a place, would surely bring about my death—because I still have my name.

MAMA LIKED TO say you could never judge how people might have turned out. For her—aforementioned superstitionist *par excellence*—if things hadn't happened exactly the way they'd happened, one out of three people involved would invariably be dead. "If we'd stayed in America the first time," she'd say, "maybe I would have believed that women's liberation thing and left your baba. Then we would have lived off my pitiful salary as a concert pianist at the local TGIF. Ah, no, no, this is a nightmare already, my daughter, no, things always turn out for the better in the end, Allah wills it so."

26

(Dina Nayeri, 1979—)

迪娜·纳耶里

作者简介

迪娜·纳耶里（Dina Nayeri，1979—）是美国伊朗裔小说家、散文家和短篇小说作家。她出生于伊朗伊斯法罕（Esfahan）并在那里生活了8年。1988年纳耶里与母亲和兄弟丹尼尔一起逃离伊朗，因为她的母亲皈依了基督教，伊斯兰共和国的道德警察威胁要处决她。纳耶里、她的母亲和弟弟在迪拜（Dubai）和罗马寻求庇护，并最终在美国的俄克拉何马州（Oklahoma）定居，而她的父亲留在了伊朗。

纳耶里拥有普林斯顿大学（Princeton University）的文学学士学位和哈佛大学（Harvard University）的教育硕士和MBA学位。她还拥有艾奥瓦州作家研讨会的文学硕士学位。

她的第一部小说《一茶匙的土地和海洋》（*A Teaspoon of Earth and Sea*, 2014）于2014年由河源出版社（Riverhead Books）出版，并被翻译成14种语言。她的第二部小说《避难所》(*Refuge*, 2017）也于2017年由同一家出版社出版。《避难所》是一部半自传体小说，其章节是从移民到美国的伊朗妇女尼鲁·哈米迪和她的父亲巴赫曼·哈米迪的角度交替撰写的。在小说撰写时，尼鲁·哈米迪正在阿姆斯特丹（Amsterdam）的一所大学教人类学，巴赫曼·哈米迪是一名牙医和口腔外科医生，住在伊朗伊斯法罕（Esfahan）。尼鲁的章节以第三人称叙述了她目前在荷兰的生活，巴赫曼的章节也是如此，而关于尼鲁与父亲在四个不同城市的四次访问的倒叙章节则由尼鲁以第一人称叙述。这部小说部分是关于父女关系，部分是关于影响整个欧洲的难民危机，特别关注荷兰的伊朗难民社区。

纳耶里凭借非虚构作品《忘恩负义的难民》(*The Ungrateful Refugee*，2019)获得格施维斯特·斯科尔·普赖斯奖(Geschwister Scholl Preis)，并入围洛杉矶时报图书奖(Los Angeles Times Book Prize)、柯克斯奖(Kirkus Prize)和电气大奖赛(Elle Grand Prix des Electrices)。这部作品被《卫报》(*The Guardian*)称为“一部具有惊人、持续重要性的作品”她的同名文章是《卫报》2017年阅读量最大的长篇读物之一，在世界各地的学校教授，并被各类文学作品选集收录。迪娜是巴黎哥伦比亚创意与想象力研究所(Columbia Institute for Ideas and Imagination in Paris)2019—2020年研究员、2018年联合国教科文组织文学之城保罗·恩格尔奖(UNESCO City of Literature Paul Engle Prize)获得者，她获得了国家艺术基金会创意写作奖学金(National Endowment for the Arts Creative Writing Fellowship)、欧·亨利奖(O. Henry Prize)和最佳美国短篇小说(Best American Short Stories)等荣誉。她的作品已在20多个国家发表，并在《纽约时报》(*The New York Times*)、《卫报》(*The Guardian*)、《华盛顿邮报》(*The Washington Post*)、《纽约客》(*The New Yorker*)、《格兰塔》(*Granta*)等出版物上发表。

节选部分分别来自其小说《一茶匙的土地和海洋》和《避难所》。《一茶匙的土地和海洋》讲述了一个年轻的伊朗女人因强大的想象力和对西方文化的热爱而摆脱悲伤的故事，也是一部讲述记忆和掌握自己命运重要性的故事，人物阵容丰富，将东方故事的节奏与现代西方散文融合在一起，以迷人的声音娓娓道来。

《避难所》通过全球移民的视角，描绘了父亲和女儿之间感人的一生关系。小说文笔优美，充满洞察力、魅力和幽默，巧妙地揭示了我们在散居后被遗忘的部分，并最终提出了这样的问题：家必须永远是一个实体的地方，还是我们可以在另一个人身上找到它？

作品选读（一）

A Teaspoon of Earth and Sea

[It's All in the Blood (Khanom Basir)]

By Dina Nayeri

It's All in the Blood

(*Khanom Basir*)

Saba may not remember clearly, but I do. And yes, yes, I will tell you in good time. You can't rush a storyteller. Women from the North know how to be patient, because we wade in soggy rice fields all day, and we're used to ignoring an itch. They talk about us all over Iran, you know ... us *shomali,* northern women. They call us many good and bad things: fish-head eaters, easy women with too much desire, *dehati*. They notice our white skin and light eyes, the way we can dismiss their city fashions and still be the most beautiful. Everyone knows that we can do many things other women can't— change tires, carry heavy baskets through fast rains, transplant rice in flooded paddies, and pick through a leafy ocean of tea bushes all day long—we are the only ones who do real work. The Caspian air gives us strength. All that freshness—*green Shomal*, they say, *misty, rainy Shomal*. And yes, sometimes we know to move slowly; sometimes, like the sea, we are weighed down by unseen loads. We carry baskets of herbs on our heads, swaying under coriander, mint, fenugreek, and chive, and we do not rush. We wait for the harvest to saturate the air, to fill our scattered homes with the hot, humid perfume of rice in summer, orange blossom in spring. The best things take time, like cooking a good stew, like pickling garlic or smoking fish. We are patient people, and we try to be kind and fair.

So when I say that I don't want Saba Hafezi to set hopeful eyes on my son Reza, it is not because I have a black heart. Even though Saba thinks I hate her, even though she gives all her unspent mother love to old Khanom Omidi, I've been watching out for that girl since she lost her mother. Sitill, just because you cook a girl dinner on Tuesdays doesn't mean you hand her your most precious son. Saba Hafezi will not do for my Reza, and it salts my stomach to think she holds on to this hope. Yes, Saba is a sweet enough girl. Yes, her father has money. God knows, that house has everything from chicken's milk to soul of man—that is to say, everything that exists and some things that don't; everything you can touch, and some things you can't. I know they are far above us. But I don't care about money or schoolbooks. I have a more useful kind of education than the women in that big house ever had, and I know that a bigger roof just means more snow.

I want my son to have a clearheaded wife, not someone who is lost in books and Tehrani ways and vague things that have nothing to do with the needs of today, here in one's own house. And what is all this foreign music she has given him? What other boy listens to this nonsense, closing his eyes and shaking his head as if he were possessed? God help me. The other boys barely know there is a place called Amcrica. ... Look, I want Reza to have friends without jinns. And Saba has jinns. Poor girl. Her twin sister, Mahtab, is gone and her mother is gone and I don't mind saying that something troublesome is going on deep in that girl's soul. She makes a hundred knives and none have any handles—that is to say, she has learned how to lie a little too well, even for my taste. She makes wild claims about Mahtab. And why shouldn't she be troubled? Twins are like witches, the way they read each other's thoughts from far away. In a hundred black years I wouldn't, have predicted their separation or the trouble it would cause.

I remember the two of them in happier days, lying on the balcony under a mosquito net their father had put up so they could sleep outside on hot nights. They would whisper to each other, poking the net with their painted pink toes and rummaging in the pockets of their indecent short shorts for hidden, half-used tubes of their mother's lipstick. This was before the revolution, of course, so it must have been many months before the family moved to Cheshmeh all year round. It was their summer holiday from their fancy school in Tehran—a chance for the city girls to pretend to live a village life, play with village children, let worshipful village boys chase them while they were young and such things were allowed. On the balcony the girls would pick at bunches of honeysuckle that grew on the outer wall of the house, suck the flowers dry like bees, read their foreign books, and scheme. They wore their purple Tehrani sunglasses, let their long black hair flow loose over bare shoulders browned by the sun, and ate foreign chocolates that are now long gone. Then Mahtab would start some mischief, the little devil. Sometimes I let Reza join them under the mosquito net. It seemed like such a sweet life, looking out from the big Hafezi house onto the narrow winding dirt roads below and the tree-covered mountains beyond, and, in the skirt of it, all our many smaller roofs of clay tiles and rice stalks, like Saba's open books facedown and scattered through the field. To be fair, the view from our window was better because we could see the Hafezi house on its hilltop at night, its pretty white paint glowing, a dozen windows, high walls, and many lights lit up for friends. Not that there is much to see these days—now that nighttime pleasures happen behind thick music-muffling curtains.

Some years after the revolution, Saba and Mahtab were put under the head scarf and we could no longer use the small differences in their haircuts or their favorite Western T-shirts to tell them apart in the streets—don't ask me why their shirts became illegal; I guess because of some foreign *chert-o-pert* written on the front. So after that, the girls would switch places and try to fool us. I think that's part of Saba's problem now—switching places. She spends too much time obsessing about Mahtab and dreaming up her life story, putting herself in Mahtab's place. Her mother used to say that all life is decided in the blood. All your abilities and tendencies and future footsteps. Saba thinks, if all of that is written in one's veins, and if twins are an exact blood match, then it follows that they should live matching lives, even if the shapes and images and sounds all around them are different—say, for argument's sake, if one was in Cheshmeh and the other was in America.

It breaks my heart. I listen to that wishful tone, lift her face, and see that dreamy expression, and the pit of my stomach burns with pity. Though she never says out loud, "I wish Mahtab was here," it's the same stew and the same bowl every day. You don't need to hear her say it, when you see well enough, her hand twitching for that missing person who used to stand to her left. Though I try to distract her and get her mind on practical things, she refuses to get off the devil's donkey, and would you want *your* son to spend his youth trying to fill such a gap?

The troubling part is that her father is so unskilled at understanding. I have never seen a man fail so repeatedly to find the way to his daughter's heart. He tries to show affection, always clumsily, and falters. So he sits at the hookah with his vague educated confusions, thinking, *Do I believe what my wife believed? Should I teach Saba to be safe or Christian?* He watches the unwashed children in Cheshmeh—the ones whose mothers tuck their colorful tunics and skirts between their legs, hike up their pants to the knee, and wade in his rice fields all day long—and wonders about their souls. Of course, I don't say anything to the man. No one does. Only four or five people know that they are a family of Christ worshippers, or it would be dangerous for them in a small village. But he puts eggplant on our plates and watermelons under our arms, so, yes, much goes unsaid about his Saba-raising ways, his nighttime jinns, his secret religion..

Now that the girls are separated by so much earth and sea, Saba is letting her Hafezi brain go to waste under a scratchy village play chador, a bright turquoise one lined with beads she got from Khanom Omidi. She covers her tiny eleven-year-old body in it to pretend she belongs here, wraps it tight around her chest and under her arms the way city women like her mother never would. She doesn't realize that every one of us wishes to be in her place. She wastes every opportunity. My son Reza tells me she makes up stories about Mahtab. She pretends her sister writes her letters. How can her sister write letters? I ask. Reza says the pages are in English, so I cannot know what they really say, but let me tell you, she gets a lot of story out of just three sheets of paper. I want to shake her out of her dreamworld sometimes. Tell her we both know those pages aren't letters—probably just schoolwork. I know what she will say. She will mock me for having no education. "How do you know?" she will goad. "You don't read English."

That girl is too proud; she reads a few books and parades around like she cut off Rostam's horns. Well, I may not know English, but I am a storyteller and I know that pretending is no solution at all. Yes, it soothes the burns inside, but real-life jinns have to be faced and beaten down. We all know the truth about Mahtab, but she spins her stories, and Reza and Ponneh Alborz let her go on and on because she needs her friends to listen—and because she's a natural storyteller. She learned that from me—how to weave a tale or a good lie, how to choose which parts to tell and which parts to leave out.

Saba thinks everyone is conspiring to hide the truth about Mahtab. But why would we? What reason would her father and the holy mullahs and her surrogate mothers have for lying at such a time? No, it isn't right. I cannot give my son to a broken dreamer with scars in her heart. What a fate that would be! My younger son twisted up in a life of nightmares and what-ifs and other worlds. Please believe me. This is a likely enough outcome ... because Saba Hafezi carries the damage of a hundred black years.

作品选读（二）

Refuge

(A NEW-YEAR WORLD)

By Dina Nayeri

A NEW-YEAR WORLD

JUNE 2009 *Isfahan, Iran*

When two thuggish ill-wishers who have much to gain financially from one's death enter one's bedroom unannounced, it's natural to indulge in a little deathbed dysteria. Bus Bahman didn't.He had seen such plays at aggression, the chest-thumping puffery and swagger of certain Iranian men (usually anxious ones with a little money and not much education, the kind from South Tehran), and he knew the limits of Sanaz's hurt and resentment. So not death, but they would hurt him.

The queasy paralysis of the withdrawal helped. He had been slipping in and out of a long stupor, and the painful spasms racking his body seemed wholly unrelated to any physical impetus. The entire event might have been a dream. Oh, how the universe turns on itself! How nimbly some infections spread, unseen until their work is done. Soleimani had once been his friend—had he harbored hatred for him in those days? Before Bahman married Sanaz, Soleimani's family had hosted him and his children in London. Now the same man shoved a pillow over his face, putting on a show to intimidate him. He leaned on top of him and spoke into his ear, promising to kill him if he touched Sanaz again. Bahman choked into the cottony mound, fabric filling his mouth and crushing his nose. He felt the man's cold spit in his ear but didn't struggle. Though his heart was pounding out a fitful rhythm, the weary organ threatening to explode out of his chest, he knew how much to expect. Mostly he thought, *How did my life come to this? I was the cleverest student in medical school*. And then, an unbidden thought, out of the ether: *Why did I become a dental surgeon instead of trying for more? Why did teeth seem to matter so much more than the heart or the brain? Was I lazy? Did I not trust myself?* Even as a young man, he had a special reverence for the human mouth. He had always been attracted to a flawless smile, and teeth fascinated him, these instruments of tearing that tie us to our primal ancestors, and yet are signals of modem refinement and grace. Now these thoughts came to him as he endured the pillow over his face, his body too weak and unwilling to engage in the drama of a few seconds without oxygen.

Soleimani lifted the pillow. He stared at Bahman with a cold gaze and said, "I would break your hand." Something writhed in Bahman's stomach. This was a credible threat—hadn't he once accused him of arrogance, claiming that all his pride would be gone with one fracture of the hand? "But your prospects are Sanaz's too." He punched Bahman in the gut. Bahman heaved clear acrid bile onto his pillow.

Then the two men left. On his way out, the bearded man cast an apologetic glance around the girlish room, eyeing the apricot wallpaper, the yellow plastic wastebasket. Bahman waited half an hour (or was it five minutes?). He sat up in his bed, panting, wiping his brow, and staring at the black television screen. He swallowed some water. He felt no pain in his stomach but his legs itched badly. And he sensed that the diarrhea phase was about to begin. He called to Fatimeh. She hadn't heard Sanaz let the men in. "That shit-eating snake!" Fatimeh said. "Please let me put some turmeric in the princess's face soap." Bahman chuckled. He had forgotten Fatimeh's rural humor. He gave her some cash and asked her to take it to the guards. "Tell them they could at least protect us from break-ins." Of course, Bahman knew that the intruders had also paid the guards. But what he was offering was undoubtedly more. How foolish he had been not to pay them from the start.

When she had carried out his errand, Fatimeh cleaned his sheets and helped him change his pajamas. A distinctive fresh scent, like lilac and tea leaves, filled the room as soon as the new sheets were on, and Bahman realized how much grime he had been living in, layers of sweat after a day of vomiting. The indignity of allowing Fatimeh to clean his soiled linens didn't bother him. This was his third detox attempt. And Sanaz had been the only woman from whom he had tried to hide the disgraces of being human, and of growing older.

Maybe Fatimeh, with her hardworking village sheen, was his only true friend. As she was leaving, he called to her, panting between words as a wave of nausea hit: him in the throat, making his mouth water. These animal spasms repulsed him. "Fatimeh joon ... when this is all over ... let me repair your teeth."

Her brown and broken smile died and deep grooves settled on her cheeks, bracketing her face. Her marble blue eyes, a sign of northern blood like his ginger hair, clouded over, and she said, "Go to sleep," and closed the door gently behind.

For three days, he suffered. The diarrhea came and went. The shivers intensified and receded. The itching stopped. Waves of pain and wooziness and delirium crashed down on him, possessed his body, then released him. For an entire day, his face seemed to be melting, as every crevice began to stream, eyes and nose and mouth becoming loose spigots of mucus and water and blood.

Meanwhile, the women fought. Sometimes Bahman saw it, and tried to understand their individual grief. Had Sanaz never been confronted by a supposed rival who refuses to compete? Did Fatimeh hold out hope of returning to this house?

"What do you want here?" Sanaz would shriek when she couldn't think of any new cruelties to fling at Fatimeh, no more pots to salt or medicines to throw out. Once Sanaz threw out Fatimeh's spice jar from Ardestoon, and Fatimeh wept alone in her room, because each year the spice is different. That year's special taste had ended early for her, only three months after the New Year.

Fatimeh's tactic was often just stony silence. She only answered on every fourth outburst, and even then it was usually an under-the-breath "God help you" or an impish reedy-voiced reference to Sanaz's blood pressure.

Sometimes, when he was feeling well, Bahman entertained himself by goading them. "Why are you here?" Sanaz would ask Fatimeh again at lunchtime.

Bahman would grin wide, forgetting about the missing tooth in the back. "I like her food," he'd say. "It's full of butter."

"It's full of butter," Fatimeh would drone, hiding a smirk, keeping her eyes on her cross-stitch or on Shirin's coloring book. Shirin often sat in her lap as they ate.

"Come now! You like it too," Bahman would prod Sanaz. "Look how much we've both grown." And Sanaz's arm would circle her waist and she would glare.

"Who wants to do recitations?" Bahman would say. Then he would offer up an easy one for Sanaz, something from the Rubaiyat perhaps. "*Here with a loaf of bread beneath the bough,*" he would murmur to himself, pretending to be stuck.

Sanaz would sit silently chewing, refusing the bait. But as soon as Fatimeh opened her mouth, Sanaz would say, as if she were doing him a favor, "*A flask of wine, a book of verse, and thou*?"

He would tap his chin and nod as if saying, *Oh yes, now I remember*, then with feigned difficultly, "*Beside me singing in the wilderness*."

They always let Shirin do the last line. She would scream, "*And wilderness is paradise enow!*" At such times, Bahman always thought of the girl's natural father.

On the fourth morning, while the women and Shirin were food shopping, Bahman phoned Donya Norouzi. This woman's appearance in his life was a sign from whatever pitiless gods might exist. Regardless, he wasn't certain what hope he sought from her. He told himself he wanted to help.

A man answered on the second ring. Given Bahman's gruff, aged voice like smoky scotch, and his title, and his presence, he had no trouble getting her on the phone. A quick, "I'm Dr. Hamidi, DDS, please put Ms. Norouzi on" was enough. The trick of getting these rural men to put their women on the phone with another man was the cloak of the professional: no apologies, no explanations, and, most important, the ability to endure the silence that followed with a kind of ease that carries through the phone. He chuckled, thinking if only he had known this trick when he was twenty, a ginger university student with a footballer physique and a married lover he could never get on the phone. That was before he met Pari in a waiting room and fell instantly in love.

Donya seemed cautious, her voice breathless and low, her mouth obviously pressed to the receiver. Someone must have been listening, because instead of asking, “Who is this?” she pretended to know him. “Doctor?” she said.

He realized now that he had no sane reason for calling, and, yes, surely some man (or his nosy mother) was listening. He couldn’t speak openly this way. He said, “Khanom Norouzi, I need to change your gum graft to four p.m. tomorrow. Can you come to my office then?” In his office, he could find out her situation, maybe try to help.

“Your office?” she repeated.

He gave her the address, making sure to specify thrice that it was a dental office. As he spoke, he strained to make his voice older, more jolly and foolish. With the listener handled, he added, to convince her, “I’m sorry I didn’t say hello at the courthouse. I saw you, and I thought, who wants to be reminded of their receding gums in the middle of their legal matter. I hope whatever papers you were signing weren’t too tiresome, and that there’s not too much pain in your mouth.”

“No, Doctor,” she mumbled. Somewhere far off, he heard a click. It seemed the listener found Donya’s gums too boring to wait for the pleasantries to end.

He was sure she would come. He hung up and congratulated himself. He hadn’t been involved in a good scheme in years. When he was young, he created fun out of thin air. He used to play pranks on Pari every day. Why did he stop?

He thought, *Maybe I’ll play a joke on Fatimeh*. But he couldn’t think of any.

He wandered out to the front door and waved a guard to him. He was still ill, his hair stuck to his head from the constant sweating. “*Agha*” he said, holding out a handful of bills. “I need to visit my dental office tomorrow at tour. Can you call the judge and get permission?”

“Call him yourself,” said the guard, annoyed at having been made to stand and walk. “If he agrees, we’ll take you.” He took the money and returned to the car.

Ali secured the judge’s permission. Again, it required money, but Ali’s charm was unparalleled and he got some extra information too: the court was finding very little evidence of Bahman’s guilt, and the judge would illuminate his fate soon. Not that a lack of evidence ever stalled a guilty verdict in this country: the judge must have hobbled to the realization that Bahman was harmless, not a plausible criminal to be made an example of, and useful to the economy and to the judge personally.

27

(Deepak Unnikrishnan, 1980—)
迪帕克·乌尼克里希南

作者简介

迪帕克·乌尼克里希南（Deepak Unnikrishnan，1980—）是一位来自阿拉伯联合酋长国阿布扎比（Abu Dhabi，United Arab Emirates）的美国作家，曾在新泽西州的蒂内克（Teaneck, New Jersey）、纽约的布鲁克林（Brooklyn, New York）和伊利诺伊州的芝加哥（Chicago, Illinois）生活过。他曾在芝加哥艺术学院（the Art Institute of Chicago）学习并任教，现任教于纽约大学阿布扎比分校（New York University Abu Dhabi）。

迪帕克·乌尼克里希南是一位作家、大学讲师和策展人。作为作家，他尝试各种文学形式，关注身份、移民和流亡问题。他的第一部作品《临时的人》（*Temporary People*, 2017）获得了首届新移民写作永不休止图书奖（The Restless Books Prize for New Immigrant Writing），以及 2017 年度印度奖（The Hindu Prize），并且入围了纽约小说中心第一小说奖（New York Center for Fiction Award for Fiction's First Novel Prize）。

在第 57 届威尼斯双年展（Venice Biennale）上，他的作品登上了阿联酋国家馆（The National Pavilion of the United Arab Emirates）的书面出版物：《石头、剪刀、布：游戏中的位置》（*Rock, Paper, Scissors:Positions in Play*）。2004 年，迪帕克·乌尼克里希南创作并出版了一本名为《骆驼茶杯上的咖啡渍》（*Coffee Stains in a Camel's Teacup*，2004）的故事集。这本书被他有趣地描述为"构成一本书的东西的第一次尝试"。他曾于 2013 年至 2016 年间担任迪拜《国家报》（*The State*）的编辑和特约撰稿人。

节选部分出自迪帕克·乌尼克里希南的小说《临时的人》第一章、第三章和第四章。《临时的人》是迪帕克·乌尼克里希南的一部引人入胜的处女作集，由28篇短篇小说组成，风格各异。讲述了在阿拉伯联合酋长国得不到公民身份的客工们的生活遭遇和多重身份，以及他们渴望回家的心理，并探讨了“临时身份如何影响心理、家庭、记忆、寓言和语言”。

作品选读

Temporary People

(Chapter 1、3、4)

By Deepak Unnikrishnan

LIMBS

There exists this city built by labor, mostly men, who disappear after their respective buildings are made. Once the last brick is laid, the glass spotless, the elevators functional, the plumbing operational, the laborers, every single one of them, begin to fade, before disappearing completely. Some believe the men become ghosts, haunting the facades they helped build. When visiting, take note. If you are outside, and there are buildings nearby, ghosts may already be falling, may even have landed on your person.

—NAME WITHHELD BY REQUEST

CHAPTER ONE:
GULF RETURN

IN A LABOR CAMP, somewhere in the Persian Gulf, a laborer swallowed his passport and turned into a passport. His roommate swallowed a suitcase and turned into a little suitcase. When the third roommate, privy and vital to the master plan, ran away the next morning with the new suitcase and passport, he made it past the guard on night duty, onto the morning bus to the airport, past the bored ticket agent at check-in, past security, past pat down and a rummage through his suitcase, past using the bathroom once, twice, thrice, to pee, to shit, to sit, past Duty Free, where he stared at chocolates and booze and magazines and currencies, past families eating fast food in track suits or designer wear, past men and women sleeping on the floor, past his past, past his present, past the gold in the souks, the cranes in the sky, petrol in the air, dreams in his head, past God and the devil, the smell of mess halls, past humidity and hot air, past it all, until he found an empty chair in the departures lounge, where he sat and held his future in his hands. It was then the little suitcase sprouted legs and ears, and the passport developed palms and long fingers as well as a nose and a mustache, and soon after the boarding call, at the very moment the stewardess checked his documents, the third laborer was asked to wait.

The stewardess needed time to figure out what protocol she should follow or what precedent there was for the man and his possessions. The man preferred not to wait and ran as fast as he could through the door to boarding, past passengers who had already gone through and formed a line inside the tube with the little windows, waiting like blood in a syringe, now followed at an animal's pace by the little suitcase on legs, ridden like a horse by the passport with the long fingers, a sight that both fascinated and terrified and caused personnel, propelled by some odd sense of duty, to stand in the way of the trio and block their path, to protect the plane and its pilots and cabin crew from what they couldn't define. It didn't matter what they did, it wouldn't have mattered what they did, because the man leading the charge, in an act of despair, opened his mouth wide to ask them all to get away get away, wide wide wider, until he swallowed the first person in his path, then the next, and the next, refusing to stop running, as the little suitcase did the same, opening and closing itself, running into people, sucking people in like a sinkhole, aided by the passport jockey, who assisted by stuffing in those who fought desperately to escape. It happened so quickly, the running, the swallowing, the stuffing, the madness, that when the three of them reached the aircraft doors, they seemed at first surprised rather than jubilant, then relieved as the pilots and cabin crew stared from the other end of the tube, where everyone, including the remaining passengers, had now run to watch them like cats watching dogs.

The little suitcase, the little passport, and the man caught their breath, inhaling and exhaling raggedly, as though nails filled the air, while in the distance, with the sound of a million horses, well-meaning men with guns and gas rushed the gate where the stewardess had screamed and then fainted. The trio realized it was now or never, abhi ya nahi, do or die, so they rushed into the empty plane, locked its door, and the little suitcase and the little passport found seats in First Class and put on their seat belts, while the man ran to the back of the plane and began swallowing everything in sight, starting with the two lavatories, the trolleys with the veg and non-veg options, the apple juice and the Bloody Mary mixes, the seats and the magazines, the tray tables and the blinking lights, the blankets and the overhead bins, the socks and the TV monitors, the cabin air, with its lingering halitosis and mint-candy smell, swallowing everything in sight, moving expertly from Economy to Business to First, swallowing even the little suitcase and the little passport, swallowing the carpets, the emergency exits, the airplane controls and smudged windows and the odor of pilots, slipping down the aircraft's nose and continuing to swallow as he moved from the aircraft's beak towards its base, swallowing wings, wheels, luggage, fuel, skin, presence, until the man was not recognizable anymore and had turned into an enormous jumbo, observed from the cordoned-off terminal by dumbstruck passengers and the men armed with guns and gas, whose leader wondered on his walkie-talkie what sort of protocol ought to be followed here, but he needn't have bothered. The plane had begun taxiing down the runaway, past other waiting aircrafts, ignoring pleas from the control tower to desist, to wait a minute, to let's talk this through, to whadabout the hostages, but the plane didn't care, it went on its merry way, picking up speed, lifting its beak, tucking in its mighty wheels, returning its cargo.

CHAPTER THREE: PRAVASIS

Expat. Worker.
Guest. Worker.
Guest Worker. Worker.
Foreigner. Worker.
Non-resident. Worker.
Non-citizens. Workers.
Workers. Visa.
People. Visas.
Workers. Worker.
A million. More.
Homeless. Visiting.
Residing. Born.
Brought. Arrived.
Acclimatizing.
Homesick,
Lovelorn. Giddy.

Worker. Workers.
Tailor. Solderer.
Chauffeur. Maid.
Oil Man. Nurse.
Typist. Historian.
Shopkeeper. Truck driver.
Watchman. Gardener.
Secretary. Pilot.
Smuggler. Hooker.
Tea boy. Mistress.
Temporary.
People.
Illegal. People. Ephemeral. People.
Gone. People.
Deported. Left.
More. Arriving.

CHAPTER FOUR: FONE

NEAR JAWAZAT ROAU, THERE used to be an ordinary looking kadakaran who owned a little kada. In the back, where he kept the surplus Basmati rice, the colas, the cooking oil, and the hardcore porn, was what some customers sought him out for, a fone. The device resembled a rotary phone, but it wasn't a phone; it was a *fone*. The fone did the one thing you would expect a phone to do: it could make calls. However, it couldn't receive any. The fone's main purpose was teleportation. A man could use the fone to talk to his wife, and as his wife cried softly into the neighbor's phone, her husband would hover over her, like a giant bee, seeing his wife cry like that, feeling satisfied that his wife could cry like that, content that he could see her cry like that, even though she wouldn't be able to see him, or even know that he was there, so close he could see the dirt on the back of her neck. And he was so happy he could see her cry like that. Or a woman could be speaking to her daughter, a daughter who hasn't learned to form words yet, but is instead biting the phone, like it's meant to be bitten, drooling into it, as her father steadies her wobbling body, coaxing her to talk, to speak, pleading with her to perform something worthy for her mother, and the woman sees all of this, her husband encouraging their child to say something, anything, as long as it's a word, any word, it didn't matter as long as it was a word. Or the phone simply rang and rang and no one picked up, even though the fone caller was in a state of bliss, itching to tell someone that he'd been promoted, that he was happy, that he needed to tell people he was happy to feel happy, that he needed to see people pretending to be happy in order to be happy. So the fone had its uses, but its usage was regulated by the kadakaran. It would break if too many people used it, he said, and. I don't know how to fix it if it breaks. So a person could use the fone only once a year. One couldn't tell one's friends about the fone. They had to find it. Stumble across it and the kada itself was like stumbling across a Kurdish-speaking macaw or a wizard in a bar. Then once one knew what the fone did, one put oneself on a list and chose a date and time. If one were smart, one didn't choose religious or public holidays, or a late-evening time. One wanted to be sure the person one was calling was home, because one only got one fone call and it had to count. On the appointed day, one cut work by calling in sick, made one's way to the kada, and made that call. Then when one hung up, one would make an appointment for the next year.

If Johnny Kutty hadn't called his wife, maybe the fone would still be in operation.

Johnny Kutty was married only a month before a distant relative found him a job as a car mechanic's apprentice in Dubai. Johnny Kutty bought phone cards and called his wife once a week. He called his friend Peeter's STD booth, and Peeter sent a helper to fetch Johnny Kutty's wife and they talked frantically until the card ran out. When Johnny Kutty discovered the fone, he couldn't wait; he made an appointment for the next available date. On that fateful day, as Johnny Kutty hovered over his wife in his friend Peeter's STD booth, he noticed Peeter sat there, smiling at her, and she at him. He offered her cold cola, which she sipped using a straw, blushing as she did so, blushing, Johnny Kutty couldn't be sure, at Peeter's attentiveness or because of what Johnny Kutty was telling her, of the things he wanted to do to her—dirty, dirty things —and she nodded and blushed, and blushed then nodded, smiling all the time, smiling until it drove the hovering Johnny Kutty crazy, until the phone card ran out. Quickly, Johnny Kutty made the next available appointment for the following year, but he continued to call his wife every week using a regular pay phone. It wasn't enough anymore. He imagined all sorts of things: that she was drinking cola, that Peeter had bought bottles of cola only for her, that he put the straw in himself, that he sucked on that straw after Johnny Kutty's wife left, that he licked the tip where her lips and spit had been. When his young wife shared she was pregnant a few weeks later, Johnny Kutty knew then that his life was ruined. That night, he broke into the kadakaran's kada and called Peeter. The phone rang and rang and rang, and Johnny Kutty was sure Peeter wasn't managing the STD booth, which was also the front portion of his house. Peeter, Johnny Kutty knew, was busy with Johnny Kutty's wife, and had no time to answer phone calls from his best friend, too busy cuckolding his best friend with his friend's young wife, the bitch who loved cola. As he realized what his wife had done, Johnny Kutty started hating his once-happy life, destroyed now by his cheating wife and his once-best friend. He wished he wasn't in that kada by himself, standing next to that fone, the fone that broke his heart, a device that may have done the same for countless others, and thus needed to be put down. Exterminated. So he got to work. Johnny Kutty poured fifteen liters of cola into a bucket the kadakaran used to clean his kada, and dropped the fone into the fizzing liquid, holding it down as it were a person, drowning it, drowning the people it contained. Then he looked for match boxes, piled them next to the bucket with the dead fone, then poured three tins of cooking oil on the floor for good measure. He lit one match and watched it drop. When the shurtha at the police station told Johnny Kutty that he could make one phone call, he told them they could do whatever they wanted to him, but if they asked him to phone someone or brought a phone to him, he would die, and for a man to die so many times in one year was not normal, and he said he probably wouldn't survive that, which would be a shame, because he had been through a lot.

28

(Stephen Karam, 1980—)
斯蒂芬·卡拉姆

作者简介

斯蒂芬·卡拉姆（Stephen Karam，1980—），美国剧作家、编剧、导演。卡拉姆出生在一个信奉马龙派（Maronites）的美国黎巴嫩裔家庭，在宾夕法尼亚州的斯克兰顿（Scranton）长大。卡拉姆曾就读于布朗大学（Brown University），主修英语。在大学期间，他获得了第一份专业戏剧工作，为三一剧团（Trinity Repertory Company）的文学系朗读剧本。2002 年从布朗大学毕业后，卡拉姆在犹他州莎士比亚节上当学徒，在那里他遇到了 P.J. 帕帕雷利（P.J. Paparelli），并与他共同创作了卡拉姆的第一部专业作品《哥伦比纳斯》（*Columbinus*），这本书改编自 1999 年科罗拉多州哥伦比纳高中大屠杀事件。

从那时起，卡拉姆写了两部戏剧：《先知之子》（*Sons of the Prophet*，2011）记录了两个美国黎巴嫩裔兄弟在父亲去世后努力应对生活的故事，《人类》（*The Humans*，2014）讲述了一个爱尔兰裔美国家庭在感恩节晚餐上应对"衰老、疾病和不断变化的经济"的场景。他的这两部戏剧分别入围了 2012 年和 2016 年普利策戏剧奖（Pulitzer Prize for Drama）。凭借《人类》这部独幕剧，卡拉姆获得了 2016 托尼奖最佳戏剧奖（Tony Award for Best Play）和奥比杰出剧本奖（Obie Award for Playwriting）。该剧在 2015 年与外百老汇签约后，于 2016 年在百老汇上演。2021 年，由卡拉姆本人执导的这部剧本的同名电影公开上映。

卡拉姆也是一位杰出的编剧，他将自己的作品《演讲和辩论》（*Speech & Debate*，）改编成电影，还改编了安东·契诃夫（Anton Chekhov）的《海鸥》（*The Seagull*）。卡拉姆表示，他的戏剧是"情感自传"，因为他对人类状况有着无尽的迷恋。

本部分节选自斯蒂芬·卡拉姆的独幕剧《人类》。贯穿全剧的动作和人物的选择都不同程度地反映了“只有抓住希望并付诸行动，才能战胜恐惧”的主题。从它的第一个时刻开始——即主角埃里克（Erik）对舞台下一声巨响的反应，戏剧的动作和角色的故事都是由恐惧体验定义的。在戏剧的结尾，主人公（埃里克）做了一个决定，从字面上和视觉上来说，这是一个远离恐惧、走向希望和可能性的决定：他走出了他和家人正在庆祝感恩节的黑暗公寓，走进了灯光明亮的走廊。通过这些方式，同一枚硬币的两面（恐惧和希望）构成了戏剧叙事和主题进展的基础。

作品选读

The Humans

(Excerpts)

By Stephen Karam

A turn-of-the-century ground-floor/basement duplex tenement apartment in New York City's Chinatown. It's just big enough to not feel small. It's just small enough to not feel big.

The two floors are connected via a spiral staircase. Each floor has its own entrance.

The apartment's pre-war features have been coated in layers of faded off-white paint, rendering the space curiously monotone. The rooms are worn, the floors are warped, but clean and well kept.

The layout doesn't adhere to any sensible scheme; the result of a mid-century renovation in which two autonomous apartments were combined.

UPSTAIRS: two rooms divided by an open entryway. The room with the staircase also has the apartment's lone, large deep-set window with bars. The window gets no direct sunlight. An urban recliner is the only piece of furniture upstairs. The other room has a door that leads to the duplex's sole bathroom.

DOWNSTAIRS: two windowless rooms divided by an even larger open entryway—with a different floorplan than upstairs. A small kitchen alley is wedged awkwardly behind the spiral staircase. The other room is dominated by a modest folding table.

The table is set with six paper plates and napkins with turkeys on them. Plastic silverware. Scattered moving boxes. Not much else.

The apartment is a touch ghostly, but not in a forced manner; empty pre-war basement apartments are effortlessly uncanny.

At lights:

Erik is upstairs, alone, some plastic bags in his hands. Beside him is an empty wheelchair. He takes in the space. The main door is open. Beat.

A sickening thud sounds from above the ceiling. Erik looks up.

ERIK

[What the hell was that?]

He recovers.

Gradually his attention shifts away from the noise; he continues to explore the space when—

Another sickening thud sounds from above, startling him. He looks up.

ERIK

[God, what the hell is that?]

A toilet flush.

Aimee and Brigid enter through the main door carrying a few plastic bags.

AIMEE

This is the last of the goodies ...

BRIGID

(To Erik)

I told you guys not to bring anything.

Deirdre and Momo exit the bathroom; Momo is shaky on her feet.

Erik helps her into her wheelchair.

DEIRDRE

Mission accomplished...

BRIGID	ERIK
It's pretty big, right?	I gotcha, Mom, there you go...

AIMEE

Definitely bigger than your last place.

ERIK

Is there some kinda construction going on upstairs?

BRIGID

Oh, no that's our neighbor, we think she drops stuff? Or stomps around?
—we don't know…

DOWNSTAIRS: *Richard emerges from the kitchen alley.*

RICHARD

(*Calling up*)

Everyone okay up there?

BRIGID

We're fine, babe, just keep an eye on the oven, we'll be down in a minute.

RICHARD

You got it.

ERIK

Have you complained to her about the noise?

BRIGID

No, Dad, she's a seventy-year-old Chinese woman, / I'm not gonna—

DEIRDRE

Well, Brigid, I'm sixty-one—older people can still process information, we're / still able to—

BRIGID

I'm saying she means well, she's older so I don't wanna disturb her if I don't have to /... hey, here, I'll take your coats…

MOMO

(*Mumbled*)

You can never come back… you can never come back /… you can never come back… can never you come back…

DEIRDRE

All right... you're all right, Mom…

Momo's mumbling is not: directed to anyone—her primary focus is down, toward the floor, lost; she is passive and disconnected.

BRIGID

What's she saying?

DEIRDRE

She's—[who the hell knows]—
even when she is saying real
stuff… what's been coming
out is still all… [muddled]…

MOMO

…fernall here sullerin…
werstrus um black… sezz it
bigger… fernal down /
black… sorn it all...

ERIK

Mom, hey Mom, this is Brigid's new apartment…

BRIGID

How are you, Momo?

DEIRDRE

We're gonna have Thanksgiving at your granddaughter's new place, / that sound good?

MOMO

(Mumbled)

… you can never come back… you can never come back…

BRIGID

Momo, you can absolutely come back, any time you want.

Deirdre moves into the room with the recliner.

ERIK

This is a decent layout, Bridge… / good space…

DEIRDRE

Really nice…

BRIGID

It's good, right?—I can set up my music workspace downstairs so I won't drive Rich crazy.

29
(Atia Abawi, 1982—)
阿提娅·阿巴维

作者简介

阿提娅·阿巴维（Atia Abawi，1982—）是美国阿富汗裔作家和电视记者。她出生在西德（West Germany），父母是阿富汗人，他们在苏联入侵阿富汗后逃离阿富汗并在美国定居。从安纳代尔高中（Annandale High School）毕业后，阿巴维进入了弗吉尼亚理工大学（Virginia Tech）。大学毕业后，阿巴维曾在阿富汗的喀布尔（Kabul）为美国有线电视新闻网（CNN）工作了近5年，并以在写作和报道中对女性赋权的强烈支持而闻名，她还为《国家评论》（*The Nation Review*）和《赫芬顿邮报》（*The Huffington Post*）写过关于伊斯兰教和阿富汗的文章，并曾公开谈到女性记者在战区和冲突地区所面临的困难。

2014年9月，基于她在阿富汗的经历，企鹅图书（Penguin Books）出版了阿巴维的第一本书《神秘的天空：阿富汗禁忌之爱》（*The Secret Sky: A Novel of Forbidden Love in Afghanistan*，2014）。这部青少年小说讲述了两个阿富汗年轻人的禁忌之爱：哈扎拉女孩法蒂玛和普什图男孩萨米乌拉。《神秘的天空》因其对阿富汗、伊斯兰激进组织的准确刻画，以及包括多种角色，尤其是一名坚强的女性而受到好评。《神秘的天空》被英国《卫报》（*The Guardian*）选为展示世界青少年生活的7部青少年小说之一。

阿提娅·阿巴维的第二本书《永别之地》（*A Land of Permanent Goodbyes*，2018）于2018年1月23日出版。柯克斯书评（*Kirkus Reviews*）将其描述为“令人难忘的小说，让读者直面全球难民危机”。2018年，这本小说被评为亚马逊年度最佳青少年书籍（Amazon’s Best Young Adult Book of The Year）。

作为切尔西·克林顿（Chelsea Clinton）和亚历山德拉·博伊格尔的（Alexandra Boiger）《纽约时报》（*The New York Times*）畅销书《她坚持不懈》系列（*She Persisted* series）的一部分，阿提娅·阿巴维撰写的第三本书《她坚持不懈：萨莉·莱德》（*She Persisted: Sally Ride*，2021）由企鹅出版社（Penguin Books）于2021年3月出版发行。

节选部分分别为阿提娅·阿巴维的第一本书《秘密天空：阿富汗禁忌之爱》第一章和她的第二本书《永别之地》第三章。

在《神秘的天空》里，法蒂玛（Fatima）是一个哈扎拉（Hazara）女孩，从小被教导要听话、孝顺。萨米乌拉（Samiullah）是一个普什图族（Pashtun）男孩，从小就被教导要捍卫自己部落的传统。碍于世俗原因，他们本不该坠入爱河。但是他们做的事和接下来的故事展现了当今阿富汗的美丽与暴力，法蒂玛和萨米乌拉为了团结一致，与家人、文化和塔利班做斗争。这本令人惊叹的小说以阿提娅·阿巴维在阿富汗近五年里所遇到的人和她所报道的事件为基础，是任何经历过美国在阿富汗战争的人的必读之书。

《永别之地》基于正在发生的难民危机，将故事发生地设在饱受战争蹂躏的叙利亚，讲述了“一名叙利亚少年在空袭中失去了大部分家人后，开始了与妹妹前往欧洲的痛苦旅程”。虽然这是一个家庭的故事，它也是所有战争、所有悲剧和所有冲突的永恒故事。当你是难民时，成功比失去更重要。

作品选读（一）

The Secret Sky: A Novel of Forbidden Love in Afghanistan

(Chapter One Fatima)

By Atia Abawi

I know this worn path better than I know myself. As I walk through the nut-colored haze, I can taste the salty bitterness of the parched ground meeting the air and then meeting my mouth. Since I was a child, I've always tried to walk in front of everyone, so the dirt wouldn't hit my clothes. There's nothing worse than the smell of earth on your clothing when you are lying on your mat and trying to sleep at night. It lingers, making its way into your dreams.

But still, the path brings me comfort. It's something I am familiar with. I don't know the new curves on my body the way I know the bends on the footpath.

I look down and am glad that I can hide myself under an oversized payron. I'm jealous of my three-year-old sister, Afifa. She doesn't have to worry about becoming a woman. At least, not yet. I turn and see her behind me, jumping onto the footprints I've made, carefree like I used to be.

"What are you doing, crazy girl?" my best friend, Zohra, asks my little Afifa.

"I'm jumping so I don't drown!" she says with determination, sticking her tongue out to the side as she lands on another print.

"Drown in what? We're walking on dirt." Zohra shakes her head.

"No, it's a river!" Afifa responds. "And Fato's footprints are the rocks I need to jump on so I don't drown!"

"Okay, you dewanagak," Zohra says, laughing. "Fatima, your sister has a lot of imagination. I don't think we were that colorful when we were her age."

"I think we were," I say. "At least I was. You were always so scared of everything, including your own shadow." I can't help but laugh.

"What do you know?" Zohra pouts, just as I thought she would. The best part about teasing her is that she is horrible at pestering back. She's my best friend for many reasons, and that is definitely one of them.

I keep chuckling, and eventually Zohra starts to giggle too. She's never been able to stay mad at me, even when I deserve it.

We're nearly at the well when we both see the tree log. It's a log we pass almost daily, and every time, it brings back memories of what life used to be like, when all the kids from the village spent the days playing together. My mother says that it's no longer proper for a girl of my shape to go out and play, that it will be seen as indecent. But even if she did let me play outside, I don't have anyone left to run in the fields with. Most of the girls around my age aren't allowed to leave their homes, and the boys have begun helping their fathers in the fields and shops.

Zohra and I are still allowed to see each other, but even time with her isn't the same as it used to be. She doesn't want to run around anymore; she would rather sit and gossip about the village, sharing all the information she hears from her parents while braiding my hair.

For the first time in my life, I feel alone. Lonely. Even though my little brothers and sister are always around, it seems like I no longer belong in my family—at least not the new me—the bizarre, curvy, grown-up me. This feeling of nowhereness makes me empty inside in a way that I can't explain to anyone, not even Zohra. She seems to be embracing all the changes that I can't.

I wish I could be like that log. It's always been the same—able to fit the tiny backsides of a dozen or so children, squeezed tightly together. We'd sit there taking breaks from running around the village, sharing treats if we had them, munching the nuts and mulberries we'd picked from the nearby woods.

"What are you smiling at?" Zohra breaks my train of thought.

"Nothing. I was just remembering how we used to play around that log," I say as my smile fades. "It looks so sad without us there."

"You're the one who looks sad over a piece of wood," Zohra says. "Besides, I don't think we could all fit on that thing anymore. If you haven't noticed, our backsides have grown a bit." She smirks. "I remember when Rashid found that thing in the woods while we were picking berries and we all had to roll it up here. I think my back still hasn't forgiven me!" Zohra dramatically puts one arm on her back and slouches like an old bibi, and in fact, she looks a lot like her own grandmother when she does it.

I remember that day so clearly, even though it was a lifetime ago. Rolling that chunk of timber, all of us together as a team. It was a grueling task, and we didn't think we could make it, but Samiullah, whose family owns the well and the fields beyond it, he knew we could. Every few feet of progress, one of us would want to stop. But Samiullah wouldn't let us. He kept encouraging us to keep pushing.

He was always the leader out of our little gang of village kids. Some families didn't allow their children to play with us because we were a mixed group—Pashtun children playing with Hazara children—but our parents didn't mind. We were connected through the land and through our fathers—Samiullah's Pashtun father is the landowner, and our Hazara fathers are the farmers.

After we moved the log to its current spot, we all sat on it, picking out on another's splinters. We couldn't believe we'd done it, just like Samiullah said we would.

"Did you hear that Sami's back?" Zohra cuts off my thoughts of the past.

"What?" I don't think I heard the words correctly. Samiullah had left for religious studies—he was supposed to be gone for years. There was no way he was back.

"Yeah, I heard he's back from the madrassa, at least that's what my father told my mother and grandmother last night. He heard it from Kaka Ismail," she adds, throwing her empty plastic jug up in the air before catching it again, sending Afifa into a fit of giggles.

"Sami's father told your father?" I ask, still confused.

"Yeah, didn't your father tell you? Apparently he spoke to them when he came by to check on the fields." This time she misses the jug after her toss. "He didn't last long did he?" She picks it up and slaps the dirt off the plastic.

"What do you mean?" I can't seem to process anything Zohra is saying right now. How is Samiullah back? Why haven't I seen him yet? Why didn't I know he'd returned? We used to be best friends, Sami and I. Could he be around here? We are near his house right now. He could be anywhere on these grounds.

"Most boys don't come back until they're adults with their scraggly beards, telling us all what bad Muslims we are," Zohra says rolling her eyes. "Thank God he left early. Apparently Rashid is still there. Kaka Ismail said he's coming home soon, too, but just to visit. Knowing Rashid, once he finishes at the madrassa, he'll want to hang all of us for being infidels just because he can."

"Don't say that."

"What? We both know he's always been a little dewana." Zohra shrugs her shoulders before crossing her eyes.

I cluck my tongue at her in disapproval while grabbing her jug. Samiullah's cousin has always been a bit rougher than the rest of their family, but he's not crazy. He was a part of our childhood. He was a part of what made us us.

As I walk down the path, My heads spins with Zohra's news. Is Samiullah really home? When he left three years ago, I thought I'd lost my friend forever. Could he really be back?

I look through the trees that guard their house from the well, and a stampede of questions race through my brain: Is he there? Can he see me right now? Is my dress clean? Why didn't I let Zohra braid my hair today? Why does it matter if I let Zohra braid my hair today?

But I know the answer to that last question. I know why it matters.

作品选读（二）

A Land of Permanent Goodbyes

(CHAPTER 3)

By Atia Abawi

CHAPTER 3

Hours passed at the site of their bombed-out apartment building. Most of the survivors could do nothing but watch and weep as the corpses were lined up on the ground-bodies that included Tareq's grandmother and mother.

The moon shone bright as he lay between his mama and *teyta*. Holding their lifeless hands, Tareq tried breathing in his mother's scent one last time, but all he could smell was smoke and dust.

He squeezed her palm, ignoring the sirens that engulfed his neighborhood. Although limp, it was still the same hand that he had held as a timid child when stepping into crowded souks in search of spices and clothes. He stroked the elegant fingers that had caressed him gently, making him feel warm and safe. "I will be okay, Mama, please don't worry. I will take care of my little brothers and sisters just like you took care of us." He looked at her closed eyes with those perfectly arched brows and took in her beauty. Even dead, his mother looked peaceful and gracious. Tareq brought her delicate hand to his mouth, pressing it to his lips ever so gently. A kiss goodbye. A finality he didn't want to accept; no child ever does, no matter their age.

When he looked up, he was brought back into the current chaos, listening to the sounds of wails and the sirens. The man in the white helmet wasn't alone: There were many wearing the same uniform—they all had the same tan vests and tired eyes. Some helmets were brighter, others stained with the gloom of war, a thick layer of death and broken souls.

Tareq spotted the man who had pulled him out—Ahmed—marching forward, carrying something. His headlamp beamed in front of him, making it hard to see what was in his arms. It was when he got closer that Tareq recognized the long dark brown hair bouncing with Ahmed's every step.

"I'm sorry, *habibi.*"

He handed Farrah's wilted body over to her big brother, who rocked the young girl in his arms as he kissed her round cheek. The tears falling from his face cleaned the dust from hers.

"I found her in the room next to where I found you." Ahmed quickly turned and walked away, unable to take the grief. His only way to cope was to keep working and continue digging. He promised this boy he'd help find his family, and right now that's all he could do for the kid.

Tareq went to lay his sister down next to their mother when he spotted the red car still clutched in her hand, Salim's toy that was passed down from Tareq. A Matchbox sedan that would live in Tareq's dreams and memories forever, connecting him to his days here and a life that no longer existed.

He examined the small toy and couldn't find a dent on it. "How did you survive this and they didn't? How?!" With a rage he had never felt before, he threw the car toward the rubble. "How are you whole and not them?" He fell to his knees, crying again.

After more time passed, Ahmed returned to say that he couldn't find any additional survivors. "You should go to the hospital. Before we pulled you out, there were others who were sent there. You will likely get more information if you go there."

Creases surrounded his rescuer's light brown eyes. They were the eyes of an elderly man who had seen too much, the eyes of an old spirit coming toward the end of life. Not the eyes of a twenty-five-year-old who, a few years ago, was studying to be a doctor.

Once the war broke out, Ahmed's plans for his future came to an end. No longer able to study, he decided the only way to help his fellow Syrians was by joining the Syrian Civil Defense—an organization full of men and women who rushed toward the fire while everyone else ran away from it. His mother begged him to stop his work, as they too were now targets, but he told her, "If I can't help my people, I am already dead."

Ahmed convinced one of the men watching what was going on to take Tareq to the hospital and helped him into the small blue hatchback. "I'll take care of your family here," he assured the boy. "Good luck, *habibi. Massalame, Allah ieshfeek.*" With a wave, he closed the door on the kid that he knew he would likely never see again—this was what Syria had become, a land of permanent goodbyes.

• • •

As the car drove down the street, Tareq surveyed the destroyed and dilapidated buildings along the way. What was once considered strong, indestructible construction now looked like a city made of the thinnest cardboard, crumbled by the hands of the devil himself. Tareq shut his eyes and leaned his forehead on the cool glass, unaware of the blood that dripped down his scalp. The physical pain was numbed by the enormous emptiness in his soul.

The middle-aged driver didn't know how to console the teen, so he too stayed silent. When they pulled up to the hospital, Tareq stepped out of the car, strengthened only by the hope of finding someone, anyone from his family who was still alive.

"*Yislamu*," he muttered to the stranger who had brought him there, thanking him, before shutting the car door.

The tears and screams inside the emergency room echoed the sounds from his bombed-out home, but now were contained in what felt like a powder keg of emotions waiting to explode and tear the hospital apart.

The stench was more concentrated. The tang of blood and death was everywhere. There was no escaping the sour odor inside the hospital doors.

A doctor ran over to Tareq, eyeing the blood that trailed down the side of his face. "Come with me!" she demanded, grabbing an arm and pulling him to a room full of other patients, none of whom were critical. Pushing him down onto a plastic chair, she pulled over a tray on wheels.

As she dabbed liquids from her bottles and searched his head, her panic steadied. "You're going to be fine." She took a breath. "I just need to bandage up your head and you can rejoin your family." She instantly regretted her words as the young man's eyes began to well.

"I'm here to find my family," he whispered. The compassion in the woman's face made it hard for him to keep his emotions at bay. Evading her tender gaze made it easier. She began to wrap a bandage around his head. "My youngest sister and brothers, they may have been brought here." His lips quivered and voice trembled while he fixated his eyes on the blue wall. "We couldn't find them. Al Defa'a al Madani told me to come here."

"Can you describe what they look like?" she asked, using surgical scissors to cut the gauze.

"Salim is thirteen, Susan is four and the twins are almost six months. Here, I have pictures." He pulled out the old cell phone his father had given him last year. It wasn't as fancy as the ones some of his friends owned, but it had all the features he wanted, including a camera. The doctor continued to wrap, tuck and bandage as Tareq scanned his photos. He felt guilt and pain as he swiped past the lively, smiling faces of his mother, grandmother and Farrah.

He quickly found a family picture of everyone together, longing for the day it was taken. An afternoon when they'd wanted to go to the park but thought it was too dangerous to leave the apartment. Instead, they had settled for a barbecue on the balcony and laid out a blanket on the living room floor. Eating off the plates set on the ground, with the TV off, just enjoying their time together.

"I haven't seen him"—the doctor pointed at Salim—"but I have seen her and them." She looked at Tareq, who was unable to read her expression.

"Can you take me to them?" he asked, excited to see his siblings. All he wanted at that moment was to kiss and hug them. They needed one another more than ever.

"She's being treated right now, but she will be fine, I promise."

His eyes widened, elated by those words. Susan was going to be okay. Suddenly the emptiness he had been feeling started to fill.

"I will take you to your brothers," the doctor said, this time not sharing any more information.

Tareq followed her down a busy corridor that got quieter as they continued to the end, abandoning the mayhem. The stillness sent a chill up his spine. He suddenly longed to hear the wails of a baby. A sound he spent so many hours of his life rocking and cuddling to stop. They paused outside a light blue door. She put her hand on his back and said, "I'm very sorry," before walking away.

• • •

Tareq stared at the bodies of his baby brothers. His eyes were as lifeless as their small bodies;, which lay on a shared hospital trolley. Ameer wore the white booties their grandmother had knitted for him, and Sameer the yellow. Their pacifiers were still attached to their striped blue-and-white onesies—orange for Sameer and green for Ameer.

Tareq continued to look intently at his brothers, hoping to see their tummies move up and down, like they used to when they would sleep peacefully. He stayed motionless, listening to the clicks of the clock above, losing track of how long he had stood there staring. He didn't know what else to do. His job was to protect them. He was their big brother. He was the one who'd changed their diapers every morning when they woke up. He was the one who'd given them their bottles. He was the one who would dress them, attach their bibs and clip on their pacifiers—orange for Sameer and green for Ameer.

Tareq finally found the courage to move closer. He glided his fingers through Sameer's dark wavy hair and grabbed ahold of Ameer's pudgy hand. It was then that he noticed a spot of blood inside Ameer's nostril. The doctors must have missed it when wiping his sweet face. That one tiny stain was the proof that Tareq did not want to see. His brothers were dead. That blood made it feel instantly real.

"I'm so sorry! Please forgive me!" He began to sob, pressing his face into the unmoving bodies of his little baby brothers. "I'm so sorry!" He struggled to breathe through his wails.

He begged for the forgiveness of his youngest siblings, who wouldn't have been able to answer him even if they were alive. He begged for the forgiveness of his mother, grandmother, and sister Farrah, whose bodies were still lying on the ground, cold and alone. He begged for the forgiveness of God, believing he must have done something to deserve this suffering, to deserve this emptiness.

Tareq felt a hand on his shoulder, jolting him back into the dark and desolate hospital room. He turned to find his father, who immediately held him tight.

"Baba, I'm sorry, I couldn't save them!" Tareq continued to cry.

"Shhhh ..." Fayed said, choking back tears as he firmly held his eldest son while staring at his youngest.

30

(Dima Alzayat, ?—)

迪玛·阿尔扎亚特

作者简介

迪玛·阿尔扎亚特（Dima Alzayat，？—）出生于叙利亚大马士革（Damascus, Syria），在加利福尼亚州圣何塞（San Jose, California）长大，她拥有兰开斯特大学（University of Leicester）创意写作博士学位，现居住在曼彻斯特（Manchester）。她的短篇小说集《鳄鱼和其他故事》（*Alligator and Other Stories*，2020）由“两美元电台出版公司”（Two Dollar Radio，美国）和“皮卡多出版社”（Picador，英国）出版，并入围2021年笔会/罗伯特·W.宾厄姆处女作短篇小说集奖（PEN/Robert W. Bingham Award）、2021年度斯旺西大学迪伦·托马斯奖（Swansea University Dylan Thomas Prize）和2021年詹姆斯·泰特·布莱克纪念奖（James Tait Black Memorial Prize）。

她的故事曾出现在BBC广播4台、《时尚先生》（*Esquire*）、《灵巧杂志》（*The Adroit Journal*）、《草原篷车》（*Prairie Schooner*）、《布里斯托短篇小说选集》（*Bristol Short Story Award Anthology*）、《布里波特奖选集》（*Bridport Prize Anthology*）和《英尼扎甘姆文学杂志》（*Enizagam*）上。她的短篇小说《在坎南之地》（*In the Land of Kan'an*）被艺术家珍妮·霍尔泽（Jenny Holzer）2017年的投影作品《致奥尔胡斯》（*For Aarhus*）收录，并成为2017年霍尔泽在马萨诸塞州当代艺术博物馆举办的展览的一部分。

短篇小说《鳄鱼》（*Alligator*）选自《鳄鱼和其他故事》短篇小说集。作为《鳄鱼和其他故事》中的核心故事《鳄鱼》，是一部关于历史重建和代际创伤的杰作，通过社交媒体帖子、剪报和证言以书信形式讲述了佛罗里达州一个小镇的执法人员对一对叙利亚移民夫妇处以私刑的真实故事。迪玛把这个故事置于美国种族暴力、法外死亡以及这对夫妇的子女及其子女的子女在此后几年里所发生的事情的更大背景下，对美国同化的要求及其局限性提出了挑战。迪玛·阿尔扎亚特的这部处女作通过九个故事，分别探讨了性别、家庭、代际创伤、同化和种族等主题。至关重要的是，这些故事以多种方式唤起人们的流离失所感：作为一个叙利亚人，一个阿拉伯人，一个移民，一个女人。

作品选读

Alligator

By Dima Alzayat

ALLIGATOR

ADELE (1990)

my mother's skirt hair on my father's arms black shoes leather sandals slippered feet across a hardwood floor strawberries pyramid-stacked on trays crates of oranges maybe peach cha-ching cash register louder than my mother's voice cha-ching I'm up off the floor snatched mid-run rest my head against her shoulder my lips on pale yellow cloth moving across the shop her body me with it voice low sweet sings my name *Adele Adele my lucky Adele*

White Man Lynched By Florida Mob

Lake City, Fla., May 17, 1929. — A white man, N. G. Romey, grocer, was lynched near here early today several hours after his wife had been fatally wounded in a gun battle with the chief of police.

A coroner's jury held an inquest in a ditch two miles from here where Romey's body was found. Its verdict was that Romey met death at the hands of parties unknown.

The jury also found that Chief of Police John F. Baker had acted in self-defense in shooting the woman five times after she had fired three shots at Baker, breaking his shoulder blade.

Romey's body, filled with bullet wounds and sitting upright in the ditch, was found this morning. Authorities brought it here. Romey had been jailed last night.

JOSEPH (1964)

Of course we took the children in. We had our own to look after, but they were our kin, George my cousin. He'd left Valdosta after running into some trouble and moved his family down to Lake City. I was doing well there. I had a grocery, not big, but business was steady. He thought he'd do the same, and for a while he did. I didn't ask him to come but I was glad to have them near. Thought it would be less lonely for me and Mariam, the kids too. If there's blame in that for me I'll take it.

For a long time after, I saw their spirits, him and Nancy both. They weren't angry, nothing like that. Came when I was alone and sat with me and didn't speak a word. I saw no sense in telling anyone about it. I didn't want to worry Mariam. Knew it was just my mind seeing things and that with time it would sort itself out. It did then, and I'm sure it will again.

We went to Birmingham after they passed. Not because I was worried. There was nothing to run from. What's done is done, I told Mariam, and we've nothing to get, carrying on like we've been wronged. We'd been in the town nearly ten years. People knew us, shopped in our grocery, said hello on the street. We're no different from them, I told her, and she agreed. She had a good head, that woman. God rest her.

I moved us on account of the kids. Not because I was worried. Just felt it best they grew up somewhere they wouldn't be reminded. It would've confused them, made it harder to fit in. So I waited until we had Samuel back, sold the shop, and left.

STEVEN 'BUBBA' MORELLI (2003)

Dammit. Off he goes. Those pines thick as anything. Is that him there? His tail. Well gone now. That damned wind. Quiet all morning, blowing soon as I spot him, sending my scent through the pines, oaks, every goddamn thing. Should have pulled the trigger sooner. No matter.

He was big. Nine-, ten-pointer maybe. A giant for these parts. Whitetail rack shining and me not a hundred yards away. Can't get a clearer shot at this level. A wonder he didn't pick up my scent sooner. Must be running toward the cypress swamp now, startling the others. I could've pulled the trigger. Damned hand. There go the songbirds again, laughing.

No matter. The rut's cranked up. Weather's cool. More of them on the prowl. Heading toward the swamp, no doubt. Does down there. If I had my stand I would've seen him. That damned Diane. That's fine. I'll head toward the swamp, set up a blind.

Might have had it set up here before I'd seen him if the hand had calmed down. It's better now. Yes. Already stopped trembling.

FLORIDA GROCER LYNCHED

Romey's trouble with the authorities started yesterday when Chief of Police Baker told him that he would have to clean up some rubbish in front of his store. Romey finally agreed to take some of his produce in boxes on the sidewalk inside his store.

Shortly afterward, according to Judge Guy Gillem, Romey telephoned Chief Baker and told him he had placed the produce back on the sidewalk and for the officer to "come back and try to make me move it again."

Baker returned to the store and another argument ensued. Mrs Romey, who joined in the altercation, is said to have procured a pistol and fired three shots at Baker, one of which broke the officer's shoulder blade.

Chief Baker then opened fire on the woman, wounding her five times. She died in a hospital about midnight. Romey was arrested and placed in jail.

Sheriff (Babe) Douglas said a mob forced the lock and bars on Romey's cell. Romey formerly lived at Valdosta, Ga. He went to Florida three years ago after having been flogged by a band of masked men near Valdosta.

June 18, 1929

Dear Governor; —

I am writing you regarding the recent events surrounding the deaths of two citizens under your jurisdiction in Lake City. As you are now well aware, the Romeys met their deaths under reprehensible circumstances last month, and we demand and trust that you will do everything within your power to ensure that justice is served.

Syrian American citizens throughout Florida and elsewhere are outraged, and rightly so, at the brutality with which these lives were unnecessarily taken. Our very trust in the law is shaken, and I have faith that it can be restored only by the dutiful investigation of the men involved in this unforgivable offence.

If an investigation reflects what many Syrian Americans believe, that the policemen involved are at fault, we trust they will be duly held to account. It is only right that we pursue the course of law in this matter, not only to bring some comfort for the relatives of the deceased, but to send a message that no one is above the law.

Most respectfully yours,

WITNESS 1 - NAME WITHHELD (1968)

I'm not saying it's right what happened to that man and his wife, but it's nothing that doesn't happen to us and will again. When that mob came in I kept my head down and told the other fella to do the same. Maybe I saw their faces and maybe I didn't and what difference would it make? Men like that all look the same to me. Eyes too narrowed to see, mouths dried up and thirsty.

I was relieved enough to hear them walk past our cell and stop in front of his. Wondered if they were gonna break the lock or if the sheriff was gonna open it for them. Whether I heard a metal blow or a key turning, I don't know, and if I did or didn't makes no difference now. The other fella in the cell with me kept looking up like he was gonna see something new. He was old enough to know better and I told him so. You want them to take us too? I asked him. You want your mama to see you bruised and swollen and dangling from some damn tree?

They went on for some time hitting that man in his cell and he must've been in an awful state by the time they left. When they'd first started laying into him he was screaming loud and by the time they left I couldn't hear him no more. They had to carry him out and I'd reckon he was all but dead when they did. But I didn't look up and I didn't see nothing.

Re: 2013 Kill Thread	**#43096—11/11/13 11:06 PM**
bama Bubba 10 point Registered: 02/13/11 Posts: 261 Loc: Birmingham, AL	Buck or Doe: 6 pt buck Date: 11/11 Time: 4pm Location: Osceola WMA, FL Stand location details: sitting on the ground in hardwoods bordering a pine thicket Shot distance: 125yd Distance to recovery: 50yd Weather conditions: cool and breezy Equipment used: Mossberg patriot .243 with 95 gr. Federal Fusion, Vortex scope

St. Augustine, December 31, 1840.

Glorious—Forty Indians Captured—Ten Indians Hanged.—Capt. Thompson, of the Walter M., arrived this morning from Key Biscayane, brings a verbal report that Col. Harncy, who had proceeded into the Everglades with ninety men, succeeded in discovering the town of We-ki-kak, where he captured 29 women and children, and one warrior, and killed or hanged ten warriors—(they were perhaps shot in the attack.)

We hope, however, that they were *hanged*, after being caught alive, for belonging to the gang which committed the massacres at Carloosahatchie, and Indian Key, they deserved neither mercy, judge or jury—nothing but an executioner; and the People of Florida have long deplored the unfrequency of such salutary retributive examples. If these Indians were hanged, their people will see we are at last in earnest.

CARINE (1991)

Everyone said to bear the years. Nothing but time will make it better, they said. But time's a stretched rubber band bound to snap right back into place. Lately, she's all I see when I sleep, my mother. Filling my nights with dreams that chase me well into the day.

It didn't help me none that Samuel wouldn't talk about them when they passed. Even the mention of our parents' names made him droop and fold into himself like mimosa leaves after nightfall. I was left alone with it. Over and over I thought of what fears they might've had that day, what thoughts of us they held in their final moments.

For months after, Adele cried for her mama and baba, and I couldn't tell her nothing but that they were off and away working and soon they'd come home carrying sweets and stories. She was only four, the youngest of us all, and no one could bear to tell her. How do you make a child understand something like that? No. It was for the best. Try and help the only one of us who could forget. Not a year passed before she stopped mentioning them altogether and began calling Aunt Mariam Mama even though the rest of us never did. This made Lily mad as a wet hen. 'That ain't your mama,' she screamed until Adele cried and Aunt Mariam and Uncle Joseph had no choice but to lock Lily up in the bedroom until she settled down.

When Adele passed last year I told Samuel it was only right to let Lily know. He just shrugged when I said it but he still tracked down an address, the first I'd had for her in more than twenty years. He left it to me to write the letter and all I said was she ought to come to the funeral even after all this time. Baby Adele ain't a baby no more, I said, but an old lady like us who passed in her sleep.

Well, she didn't come. And I didn't mention the letter to Samuel and he didn't ask, but I know he was thinking what I was, that she was living in Florida again, wondering how she could bear it. Even now I wouldn't step foot in that country. Me, a seventy-five-year-old woman still dreaming of her mama, frightened of waking up with her face singed on my mind's eye, her body bleeding and her belly round and sticking up in the air.

SATURDAY, DECEMBER 7, 1907

COMMISSION IS SPLIT

Members Still Differ Over Restricting Immigration.

SOME UNDESIRABLE ALIENS

Education Best Test.

Judge Burnett said last night that the only solution of the immigration problem is the educational test requiring each immigrant to be able to read and write in his own or some other language. This, he declares, will cut off 75 per cent of the undesirable immigrants, most of whom, in his opinion, come from Asia Minor, Southern Italy, and Sicily.

"Not 60 per cent of these people can read or write," said Judge Burnett, "and it is of the utmost importance to this country that they be shut from our shores. Especially from Sicily, our immigrant is ignorant and vicious. He is coming to the United States on every steamer, and should be stopped."

31

(Ismail Khalidi, 1982—)

伊斯梅尔 · 哈立迪

作者简介

伊斯梅尔 · 哈立迪（Ismail Khalidi，1982—）是一位美国巴勒斯坦裔剧作家、编剧和戏剧导演，其作品涉及巴勒斯坦和现代中东的历史，以及更广泛的种族、殖民主义和战争主题。他最出名的是戏剧《纳布卢斯网球》（*Tennis in Nablus*，2010）和《真相血清蓝调》（*Truth Serum Blues*，2005）以及广受好评的《重返海法》（*Returning to Haifa*），该剧于2018年在伦敦首映。2008年，他还在纽约大学读书的时候就凭借《纳布卢斯网球》获得了两项研究生肯尼迪中心荣誉奖（Graduate Student Kennedy Center Honors）：马克 · 吐温喜剧编剧奖（The Mark Twain Comedy Playwriting Award）和寻求和平剧本奖（The Quest for Peace Playwriting Award）。从那时起，他的剧本开始在国际上制作和展示，并在六本选集中出版。

哈立迪与娜奥米 · 华莱士（Naomi Wallace）共同编辑了一本名为《内部 / 外部：巴勒斯坦和侨民的六部戏剧》（*Inside/Outside: Six Plays from Palestine and the Diaspora*，2015）的选集。哈立迪2010年的剧本《纳布卢斯网球》也被收录其中。他关于1982年入侵黎巴嫩的剧本《萨布拉的崩溃》（*Sabra Falling*，2016）发表在《双重曝光：犹太人和巴勒斯坦侨民的剧本》（*Double Exposure: Plays of the Jewish and Palestinian Diaspora*，2016）中，他的这部戏剧中的两段独白分别被《有色人种演员的独白：男人》（*Monologues for Actors of Color: Men*）和《有色人种演员的独白：女人》（*Monologues for Actors of Color: Women*）收录，这两部选集均由罗伯塔 · 乌诺（Roberta Uno）编辑，由劳特利奇出版社（Routledge）于2016年出版。

节选部分出自伊斯梅尔·哈立迪的戏剧《纳布卢斯网球》第一幕。《纳布卢斯网球》的背景设置在1939的巴勒斯坦。一个巴勒斯坦家庭在如何在外国统治下竞争日益激烈的土地上实现自由和生存方面存在分歧。真实的事件激发了这部"政治悲喜剧"，讲述了阿拉伯人反抗英国占领的悲惨命运，以及帝国主义的弊病和荒谬。《纳布卢斯网球》将幽默、悲剧和丰富的角色组合在一起，编织了一个关于世界即将发生重大变化的史诗故事。

作品选读

Tennis in Nablus

(SCENE 1)

By (Ismail Khalidi, 1982—　)

PROLOGUE

Darkness. A summer night. Nablus, Palestine, 1939. The creaking of wheels on a donkey-drawn cart can be heard, then the cocking of a rifle.

SOLDIER (*Offstage*). Halt! Step down from the carriage with your hands in the air, old man.

(*Out of the darkness Waleed, an old man in a peasant's robe, enters with his hands raised. From the opposite direction a British soldier enter.*)

What's in the carriage Methuselah?

WALEED: *Bidenjan*, your…. highness.

SOLDIER: What?

WALEED: Eggplants sir. Aubergines. I want to take them to the early morning markets up north.

SOLDIER: Eggplants, huh?

WALEED: No relation to eggs though, sir. They are related to the potato and tomato, however. Who would have known that such a dark elegant purple orb was related to the fat lumpy white potato, eh? The world is a mysterious place, sir, and God has a way of making a kind of poetry with his creations, no?

SOLDIER: I prefer to be called "your highness," old man. Now let's see what's in the cart.

WALEED: The word aubergine, for example, "your highness," derives from the Spanish "berenjena" which comes from the Arabic "bidenjan," which in turn is from the Persian "badingan," all derived originally from the Sanskrit, "vatin gameh."

SOLDIER: Bloody fascinatin'.

WALEED: Yes I think so too.

SOLDIER: Why don't you tell me why you're driving up in the dead of night? There'sacurfew you know.

WALEED: Well, because eggplants are in the nightshade family, sir, so it is their custom to move at night. They rot under the sun. But when they travel in darkness they arrive at the market pregnant with the night, full of the whispers of their friend the moon … And this way I sell twice as many as the farmers who transport their produce in the morning heat! Shall I tell you about the harvesting of the eggplant sir? It really is/fascinating.

SOLDIER: Jesus, please don't! Just piss off old man. Be on your way, and stay off the main roads!

(*Waleed bows and exits into the shadows.*)

ACT ONE

SCENE 1

Later that night in an old Palestinian house. There is a table with a typewriter on it. On the back wall hangs an Ottoman sword.

Yusef Al Qndsi enters quietly. He wears a British officer's uniform. He stops and takes in the room. He begins to remove oranges from his various pockets. One after another.

After a moment Anbara enters from behind Yusef. She silently grabs the sword off the wall and places the blade on his neck. He raises his hands and turns slowly to face her. They look at each other for a beat, the sword still near his throat.

YUSEF: Have you escaped from your harem to seduce a British officer such as myself, young lady? (He *sits*)

ANBARA: It doesn't suit you.

YUSEF: Or am I being knighted?

ANBARA: You're in my chair.

YUSEF: This chair belongs to His Majesty King George! I...

ANBARA: Yusef.

(*Anbara touches his face. He rises.*)

YUSEF: Anbara. You … Two years … It's been two—

(*Anbara pushes him back into the chair.*)

ANBARA: Two years. Yes. I know.

YUSEF: … And I've gotten older.

ANBARA: But you've been giving the Brits hell since they released you. At least that's what everyone in Nablus is talking about.

YUSEF: Seven days, nonstop. What are they saying?

ANBARA: Yet after two years apart it took you seven days to make your way to your wife?

YUSEF: Blame the British, not me.

ANBARA: I do. But you must have known they would capture you that day at Tulkarem.

YUSEF: Anbara, I was arrested and exiled because I fought. And I fought because they occupy us.

ANBARA: Simple.

YUSEF: And if it weren't for them I'd be playing the oud for you every night.

ANBARA: I'd like that.

YUSEF: Like I used to. But that life is gone Anbaia. So as soon as I was released I went to work. The revolution can't wait—

ANBARA: Don't talk to me like some young recruit from the hills.

YUSEF: I came as soon as I could.

ANBARA: I've been waiting.

YUSEF: Well. I had to see if I still had it in me.

ANBARA: And? Do you still have it?

YUSEF: Naturally.

ANBARA: I've missed you.

YUSEF: Naturally.

ANBARA: And still so modest. Naturally. (*Beat*) So you've come home to me?

YUSEF: In the flesh.

ANBARA: And who said you could come here, anyway?

YUSEF: You are my wife. This is my house.

ANBARA: And what if I have a guest over and this isn't a good time? Did you think about that?

YUSEF: I can leave.

ANBARA: A young man to keep me company perhapss, a man fleeing out the bedroom window as we speak.

YUSEF: Somehow I imagined this homecoming differently.

ANBARA: That my clothes would fall to the ground the moment I saw you?

YUSEF: For instance.

ANBARA: Perhaps you should be the one stripping down for me.

YUSEF: You haven't changed.

(*She lights a cigarette, takes a drag and then hands it to him.*)

ANBARA: It's dangerous, Yusef, they'll be after you.

YUSEF: Hence the disguise.

ANBARA: You look ridiculous.

YUSEF: But I bet you're dying to hear how I got it.

(*She ignores him.*)

The English, as you know, are formidable opponents, Anbaia: they're ruthless, callous and greedy… *But*!

ANBARA: Tea, coffee or a drink?

(*He nods to the bottle and continues:*)

YUSEF: But… they have one weakness which allows a quick-witted opponent in need of disguise to get their uniforms off their backs quicker than a Turkish prostitute.

ANBARA: And you have experience with such women?

YUSEF: It's a figure of speech, Anbara. Please. Ask me how did it!

ANBARA: No.

YUSEF: Simple. Costume parties. The British will drop everything at the mere mention of a themed costume ball.

ANBARA: I've noticed.

YUSEF: I got the idea when I arrived with the other prisoners to Haifa last week. We docked before dawn and on shore I could see half the officers' corps in costume, returning from a night out. By mid-morning they'd released us and I was on the road, down the coast and then inland, village to village, town to town:.

ANBARA: Like the old days.

YUSEF: Except half of my men from before are dead or in prison.

ANBARA: I've been to my share of trials and funerals while you were gone.

YUSEF: You hate funerals.

32

(Azareen Van der Vliet Oloomi, 1983—)
阿萨琳·范德维里耶·欧卢米

作者简介

阿萨琳·范德维里耶·欧卢米（Azareen Van der Vliet Oloomi, 1983—）是一位美国伊朗裔作家。她曾就读于布朗大学（Brown University）和加州大学圣地亚哥分校（UC San Diego），现在住在芝加哥地区。

欧卢米因其处女作《弗拉·基勒》（*Fra Keeler*，2012）获得2015年的怀廷奖（The Whiting Writers' Award）和美国国家图书基金会“35岁以下5人”奖（National Book Foundation “5 Under 35” Honoree）。她的作品发表在《巴黎评论》（*The Paris Review*）、《格兰塔》（*Granta*）、《格尔尼卡》（*Guernica*）、《炸弹杂志》（*Bomb*）和《洛杉矶书评季刊》（*The Los Angeles Review of Books*）等杂志上。《叫我斑马》（*Call Me Zebra*，2018）被翻译成六种语言，《弗拉·基勒》于2015年以意大利语出版。她的小说《野蛮的舌头》（*Savage Tongues*）已于2021年出版，另一部中篇小说《N》与拿破仑在厄尔巴岛的流亡有关，将于2022年由咖啡馆出版社（Coffee House Press）作为其空间物种系列的一部分出版。

她的2018年小说《叫我斑马》获得了2019年笔会/福克纳小说奖（The PEN/Faulkner Award for Fiction）和约翰·加德纳奖（The John Gardner Award），并入围笔会公开图书奖（The PEN Open Book Award）。

欧卢米是“湮灭、流放和抵抗文学”（Literatures of Annihilation, Exile and Resistance）的创始人，这是一个两年一度的专题讨论会和系列讲座，由克罗克国际和平研究所（Kroc Institute for International Peace Studies）和圣母大学文学艺术学院（College of Arts and Letters at the University of Notre Dame）赞助，重点研

究由领土和语言政治、殖民主义、军事统治和严重侵犯人权的历史塑造的文学，汇集了中东/西南亚和北非作家和艺术家。

节选部分来自其2018年小说《叫我斑马》和处女作《弗拉·基勒》。《叫我斑马》是一部杰出的黑色喜剧，探索了流放、文学、受害者以及暴力和帝国主义构建的人类历史框架，这是一部尖锐而真正有趣的流浪汉小说，将幽默和辛酸结合在一起，讲述了一个新颖而难忘的故事。

《弗拉·基勒》讲述的是一名男子买了一所房子——弗拉·基勒的房子，搬了进来，并开始调查后者的死亡原因。然而，调查很快转向了内部，它试图揭示的现实似乎变得越来越陌生，因为叙述者追求的不是线索，而是思路，往往得出可怕的结论。

作品选读（一）

Call Me Zebra

(Prologue The Story of My Ill-Fated Origins)

By Azareen Van der Vliet Oloomi

PROLOGUE
The Story of My Ill-Fated Origins

ILLITERATES, ABECEDARIANS, ELITISTS, RODENTS ALL—I WILL TELL YOU this: I, Zebra, born Bibi Abbas Abbas Hosseini on a scorching August day in 1982, am a descendent of a long line of self-taught men who repeatedly abandoned their capital, Tehran, where blood has been washed with blood for a hundred years, to take refuge in Nowshahr, in the languid, damp regions of Mazandaran. There, hemmed in by the rugged green slopes of the Elborz Mountains and surrounded by ample fields of rice, cotton, and tea, my forebears pursued the life of the mind.

There, too, I was born and lived the early part of my life.

My father, Abbas Abbas Hosseini—multilingual translator of great and small works of literature, man with a thick mustache fashioned after Nietzsche's—was in charge of my education. He taught me Spanish, Italian, Catalan, Hebrew, Turkish, Arabic, English, Farsi, French, German. I was taught to know the languages of the oppressed and the oppressors because, according to my father, and to my father's father, and to his father before that, the wheels of history are always turning and there is no knowing who will be run over next. I picked up languages the way some people pick up viruses. I was armed with literature.

As a family, we possess a great deal of intelligence—a kind of superintellect —but we came into this world, one after the other, during the era when Nietzsche famously said that God is dead. We believe that death is the reason why we have always been so terribly shortchanged when it comes to luck. We are ill-fated, destined to wander in perpetual exile across a world hostile to our intelligence. In fact, possessing an agile intellect with literary overtones has only served to worsen our fate. But it is what we know and have. We are convinced that ink runs through our veins instead of blood.

My father was educated by three generations of self-taught philosophers, poets, and painters: his father, Dalir Abbas Hosseini; his grandfather, Arman Abbas Hosseini; his great-grandfather, Shams Abbas Hosseini. Our family emblem, inspired by Sumerian seals of bygone days, consists of a clay cylinder engraved with three *A*s framed within a circle; the *A*s stand for our most treasured roles, listed here in order of importance: Autodidacts, Anarchists, Atheists. The following motto is engraved underneath the cylinder: *In this false world, we guard our lives with our deaths*.

The motto also appears at the bottom of a still life of a mallard hung from a noose, completed by my great-great-grandfather, Shams Abbas Hosseini, in the aftermath of Iran's failed Constitutional Revolution at the turn of the twentieth century. Upon finishing the painting, he pointed at it with his cane, nearly bludgeoning the mallard's face with its tip and, his voice simultaneously crackling with disillusionment and fuming with rage, famously declared to his son, my great-grandfather, Arman Abbas Hosseini, "Death is coming, but we literati will remain as succulent as this wild duck!"

This seemingly futile moment marked the beginning of our long journey toward nothingness, into the craggy pits of this measly universe. Generation after generation, our bodies have been coated with the dust of death. Our hearts have been extinguished, our lives leveled. We are weary, as thin as rakes, hacked into pieces. But we believe our duty is to persevere against a world hell-bent on eliminating the few who dare to sprout in the collective manure of degenerate humans. That's where I come into the picture. I—astonished and amazed at the magnitude of the darkness that surrounds us— am the last in a long line of valiant thinkers.

Upon my birth, the fifth of August 1982, and on its anniversary every year thereafter, as a rite of passage, my father, Abbas Abbas Hosseini, whispered a monologue titled "A Manifesto of Historical Time and the Corrected Philosophy of Iranian History: A Hosseini Secret" into my ear. I include it here, transcribed verbatim from memory.

Ill-omened child, I present you with the long and the short of our afflicted country, Iran: Supposed Land of the Aryans.

In 550 BC, Cyrus the Great, King of the Four Corners of the World, brave and benevolent man, set out on a military campaign from the kingdom of Anshan in Parsa near the Gulf, site of the famous ruins of Persepolis, to conquer the Medes and the Lydians and the Babylonians. Darius and Xerxes the Great, his most famous successors, continued erecting the commodious empire their father had begun through the peaceful seizing of neighboring peoples. But just as facts are overtaken by other facts, all great rulers are eclipsed by their envious competitors. Search the world east to west, north to south; nowhere will you find a shortage of tyrants, all expertly trained to sniff out weak prey. Eventually, Cyrus the Great's line of ruling progeny came to an end with Alexander the Great, virile youth whose legacy was, in turn, overshadowed by a long line of new conquerors, each of whom briefly took pleasure in the rubble of dynasties past.

Every one of us in Iran is a hybrid individual best described as a residue of a composite of fallen empires. If you were to look at us collectively, you would see a voluble and troubled nation. Imagine a person with multiple heads and a corresponding number of arms and legs. How is such a person, one body composed of so many, supposed to conduct herself? She will spend a lifetime beating her heads against one another, lifting up one pair of her arms in order to strangle the head of another.

We, the people—varied, troubled, heterogeneous—have been scrambling like cockroaches across this land for centuries without receiving so much as a nod from our diverse rulers. They have never looked at us; they have only ever looked in the mirror.

What is the consequence of such disregard? An eternal return of uprisings followed by mass murder and suffocating repression. I could not say which of the two is worse. In the words of Yevgeny Zamyatin: *Revolutions are infinite.*

By the twentieth century, the Persian empire's frontiers had been hammered so far back that the demarcating boundary of our shrunken nation was bruised; it was black and blue! Every fool knows that in order to keep surviving that which expands has to contract. Just look at the human heart. My own, reduced to a stone upon the double deaths of my father and my father's father, both murdered by our so-called leaders, is plump and fleshy again; your birth has sent fresh blood rushing through its corridors.

Hear me, child: The details of the history of our nation are nothing but a useless inventory of facts unless they are used to illuminate the wretched nature of our universal condition. The core of the matter, the point of this notable monologue, is to expose the artful manipulation of historical time through the creation of false narratives rendered as truth and exercised by the world's rulers with expert precision for hundreds of years. Think of our own leaders' lies as exhibit A. Let us shuffle through them one by one.

When the century was still young, our people attempted the Constitutional Revolution but failed. In time, that failure produced the infamous Reza Shah Pahlavi, who ruled the country with thuggery and intimidation. Years later, during the Second World War, Mr. Pahlavi was sent into exile by the British, those nosy and relentless chasers of money—those thieves, if we're being honest. And what, child, do you think happened then? Pahlavi's son, Mohammad Reza Shah Pahlavi, who was greener than a tree in summer, stepped up to the throne.

Claiming to be the metaphysical descendent of the benevolent Cyrus the Great, the visionary Mohammad Reza Shah Pahlavi anointed himself the "King of Kings" and launched the White Revolution, a chain of reforms designed to yank the country's citizens into modernity by hook or by crook..

It was just a matter of time before the people rose against the King of Kings. Revolution broke out. Mohammad Reza Shah Pahlavi spilled blood, tasted it, then, like a spineless reptile, slid up the stairs of an airplane with his bejeweled queen in tow and fled, famously declaring: "Only a dictator kills his people. I am a king."

The Islamic clergy, whose graves the king had been digging for years, hijacked the revolution, and in one swift move, the monarchy was abolished. The king's absence allowed the revolutionary religious leader Ayatollah Khomeini to return to the country after a long political exile. Khomeini, former dissident, swiftly established the Islamic Republic of Iran and positioned himself as the Supreme Leader. The Grand Ayatollah proceeded to outdo the King of Kings. His line of metaphysical communication skipped over Cyrus the Great; it pierced the heavens to arrive directly at God's ear. The Supreme Leader claimed to enjoy unparalleled divine protection.

How did he employ his blessings? By digging the graves of the secularists and the intelligentsia just as the Pahlavi kings had dug the graves of dissidents, Communists, and the clergy. With one hand, God's victors eliminated their revolutionary brothers, and with the other, they shucked pistachios, drank tea, raided their victims' closets, ate cherries picked from their gardens.

作品选读（二）

Fra Keeler

(5)

By Azareen Van der Vliet Oloomi

5. I was standing there all alone. I thought, this is not the end of it: her singing a song, making a mockery of it all. I paced back and forth on her doorstep. I looked down at my hands, then quickly at the doorknob. My hands were cold. The skin around my knuckles was burning. I thought, I have to get in; I have to go through her door. And if not through her door then a window. I snapped my fingers at the thought. An image came to me of the lamp I had spotted at the end of the hallway. I imagined her cat curving around the lamp, her tail illuminated under the bulb. Warmth, I thought, and light. But I couldn't remember if the lamp was on when I had seen it, or if I had just imagined it to be—a soft, yellow light calling me through her door.

The wind picked up. It was slightly colder than it had been all along. I rubbed my hands together. I stuck my hands into my pockets. I withdrew my hands. I touched one finger to my temple, then another. I looked up at the stars. They were flickering. There was a yellowish hue around the moon. A bird darted across the sky: slick and black and singular. The sky, I thought: infinitely deep, infinitely dark. I wanted to cup my hands around the stars, pluck them out of the sky once and for all.

Suddenly, I remembered the dull, black surface of my dream. Everything burns to ashes. Lives out by whatever machinery, whatever injustice, then burns down to the very surface that held it up. The hand—I thought—the face in my dream! She was getting in the way of everything, her trembling form redoubling itself in my sleep. Wretched old lady, I thought, I will show her. Because in addition to putting up with her in life, I thought, I should not have to put up with her in my dreams.

Better to take a walk around her house, I thought, to take a good look before going in. Certainly her house could be just as deceptive, just as duplicitous as she herself:

one countenance on the outside, another altogether on the inside, with no connection between. I leaned over to scratch my ankles. There were mosquitoes everywhere, flying frantically in the wind. Just as I leaned over to persuade them away from my ankles, the blood drained from my brain. But it wasn't dizziness I experienced. Rather a feeling of disorientation, because just then an image of the club I had dropped in the yard behind my house appeared in front of my feet. How, I wondered, has it made an appearance so suddenly, and directly in front of my feet? But slowly, as I stood up, it all made sense: yes, I thought, the club—it is exactly what I need. I dashed over to my yard and grabbed the club. By now the wind had died down, the night was quiet and still. I thought, nothing could be more perfect than silence on a night like this; the stillness of dying, the silence of death, and a rush of excitement filled my veins.

I returned to her doorstep. I practiced swinging the club. I swung with one arm, then the other. Definitely, I thought, my right arm is the stronger of the two. I was feeling more lighthearted than ever. This is joy, I thought, this is happiness, all my investigations taking form. With a decisive air I jumped off her front steps and turned the corner. I entered her backyard. There I saw a goose waddling away. A goose in her backyard, I thought: under the light of the moon, a goose waddling away! My blood froze. All I could think was: a goose in her backyard, stark in the middle of her yard, a goose. For a moment, I raised the club over my head. Perhaps the goose is an omen, I thought, and my blood started to move again. The bird waddled into the trees, which were slim and silver under the light of the moon. The goose released a loud honk. The sound returned my attention to the world. I found myself standing directly above the goose behind a row of trees. I placed the club down and leaned my weight into it as though it were a cane. I could ring its neck, I thought, looking at the goose. Then it occurred to me: I could spy into her house through the skylight on her roof. Now, in my distraction, the goose waddled away. That is what I'll do, I said to myself, maintaining a line of thought: I will climb directly onto her roof. And a moment later I was standing there, club in hand, staring down at her skylight as I stood on her roof.

Was it real? I thought, and looked down at my hands.

The cat walked cautiously by the wall.

She arched her back, pointed her tail up to the sky. Her eyes narrowed into slits. She began to lick her right paw. The pale pink of her tongue makes a pleasant picture, I thought, against the soft pad of her paw. But the next moment she leaned away from the wall. She wound between my legs, rubbed her body against the club. One moment the cat is cool and distant, I thought, the next all warmth.

I walked over to the kitchen counter. I had dropped the club. The cat followed me. I took a seat on one of the stools. The cat jumped onto the counter. From a distance she inspected my face. I looked out the window. A few leaves ruffled slightly in the wind, gave a small shudder. A bird gave out a low whistle, then took off into the night. Everything went still. Everything went silent. I looked around. The house was quiet, motionless except for the cat. I reached out to touch her and felt her breath against the palm of my hand. Could it be, I thought, and by whose hands? I looked at the club. I had left it leaning against the couch. I couldn't differentiate the club from my hands. Ten fingers, I thought, two hands. I inspected the furniture. Deep reds and browns, floral patterns. Ten fingers, I thought, as I looked at my hands. They could be performing any gesture: playing the keys of a piano, digging soil, folding a napkin.

No, I thought. It couldn't have been. Because certain things are of a category that one remembers. Not a lot of time, I thought, has gone by. Minutes, organized into units. How many minutes had gone by?

I wondered.

An image of the shards came back to me. I watched the skylight shatter as I relived the memory. I looked up to where the skylight had been, then traced the rectangular chunk of sky down through the opening to the floor, where the shards were glistening with late-night rain. I shrugged my shoulders, puckered my lips. No matter, I thought. Because everything has already been done. Everything, I thought, in this room, and beyond this room, everything has already happened and been done with, dealt with. There is no doing, I thought, no matter, nothing left to do in this world. I felt my heart die down. Now the cat was walking among the shards. I thought, she must be taking pleasure, avoiding the sharp triangles, the pointed edges. Because she was extending her paws, licking them intermittently as she tiptoed around the shards. I looked back up at the skylight. One moment, I thought—and then my mind was a flood of memories, because I saw an image of myself standing over the skylight, staring at my reflection, which is to say: I saw myself twice. It was a slight pause in time, an interruption. Everything shattered: tiny bullets of glass flew through the night like shooting stars. Now I could see the shards, a few feet from where I was seated, scattered across her living room floor, and, seated on her stool, a version of myself reflected in the shards, just as I had seen myself, only whole, in the skylight as I stood on her roof.

* * *

I walked out of the kitchen, down the hallway. In her bedroom everything looked wounded. There was a purplish hue on the walls, over her bed, on her furniture. I looked down at my hands. I felt my arms detach from my shoulders. I watched them float away. Could it have been? I thought, and imagined her gaping mouth form an answer. I saw a reflection of myself in the bedroom window. Couldn't I get away? I was standing in her doorway. Was it real? I wondered, and backed away. A moment later I was in the bathroom, kneeling on the tile floor.

I turned the tap, stuck my head under the spigot, scrubbed my neck. Couldn't I have imagined it? The water ran over my head. Her two eyes: icy, blue lakes drifting farther and farther apart from each other as though her face were a humid land being stretched to its limits. I walked back into her bedroom. I left the water running in the bathroom. I turned her body over. A sudden urge. A mass of mangled branches. First to one side—I inspected her back—then the other. There was a streak of blood running from her mouth to her neck. I pulled up her hair. The blood, I thought—looking down at my hands—her wet flesh. I heard the water spill over the tub and spread across the bathroom floor. Lovely, I thought, in this moment, the sound of water pouring over a tub. I pulled the covers over her frame. I walked back to the couch. I left the water running. I thought, let the earth sink.

A sedentary feeling grew at the base of my chest. The cat curled onto my lap. Everything faded. Was it me, I thought, wasn't it me? I heard the water trickle out of the bathroom. I imagined the water being absorbed by the bedroom carpet. Then, as though in the distance, I heard a door slam, I heard voices. I heard a man draw out a roll of tape. I stroked the cat. Everything, I thought again, has already happened, even the end. I heard a loud noise. I felt my body stiffen. The room turned. It spun around. Everything spun with it: Fra Keeler, I thought, the papers, her trembling hand. It was a mere instance. Because one moment—then I felt someone turn me over, clasp a cold thing around my hands—one moment, I thought, and then the next.

33

(Samir Younis, 1985—)
萨米尔・尤尼斯

作者简介

萨米尔・尤尼斯（Samir Younis，1985— ）是一名作家兼演员。他出生在美国得克萨斯州休斯敦（Houston），父亲是黎巴嫩人，母亲是叙利亚–黎巴嫩人。他在范德比尔特大学（Vanderbilt University）获得了西班牙语和社会学的学士学位，并在那里学习了戏剧。之后，他获得了哥伦比亚大学（Columbia University）表演艺术硕士学位。《布朗镇》（*Browntown*，2003）是萨姆剧本处女作。该剧最初是在纽约第一届美国阿拉伯裔人喜剧节（NYC Arab-American Comedy Festival，2003）上的一个小品，由喜剧演员梅森・扎伊德（Maysoon Zayid）和迪恩・奥贝达拉（Dean Obeidallah）创作。电影节结束后，尤尼斯将这部小品改编成了2004年纽约边缘艺术节（NYC Fringe Festival）的一部长篇戏剧，并在该艺术节上获得了"剧本写作全面卓越奖"（Overall Excellence in Playwriting）。

《布朗镇》后来由戏剧传播集团（Theatre Communications Group）在2010年的选集《萨拉姆和平：中东美国戏剧选集》（*Salaam Peace: An Anthology Of Middle Eastern American Drama*）中出版。《布朗镇》是关于为一部关于恐怖分子/恐怖组织的戏剧征集阿拉伯角色的故事，它如实反映了媒体对阿拉伯人的准确描述的需求，以及"9・11"事件后穆斯林在戏剧界受到的歧视。

除了戏剧，尤尼斯还出演过电视剧《初为人妻》（*The Starter Wife*，2008）、《特工队》（*The Unit*，2008）和《海军罪案调查处：洛杉矶》（*NCIS: Los Angeles*，2011）。他还出演了《血肉之躯》（*Ways of the Flesh*，2006）和《窄门》（*The Narrow Gate*，2006）等电影。

节选部分来自萨米尔·尤尼斯的《布朗镇》第1～3幕。《布朗镇》从三个棕色人种的演员奥马尔、马莱克和维杰的角度探讨了文化刻板印象的问题，他们在试镜一个非原创电视电影的时候面临着一个两难的境地："我应该为了钱而扮演那个恐怖分子角色，还是原则上拒绝它？"他们的试镜经历揭示了三位演员都是文化诽谤的受害者和肇事者。

作品选读

Browntown

(Scene 1-3)

By Samir Younis

Scene 1
THE WAITING ROOM

The Wide-Net Talent Casting office in Midtown Manhattan, Tuesday, eleven o'clock A.M. Omar Fakhoury sits perusing Maxim magazine as he awaits his chance to audition for The Color of Terror, a made-for-TV movie. Malek Bizri enters the waiting room, signs his name on a clipboard, sits, pulls out his audition material, and begins quietly mouthing his lines to himself. Though physically animated, he is inaudible. Eventually, he notices Omar and greets him.

MALEK: Omar! What's up, dawg! Figured I might see you here.

OMAR: You, too, man! I saw you come in, but I didn't wanna bug you. You were in "the zone" with your sides over there.

MALEK: It's cool, man. Just some last-second prep work.

OMAR: Nice. So, you staying busy these days?

MALEK: Well you know, just doing the audition-slash-catering thing. Kinda slow right now don't you think?

OMAR: Catering or auditioning?

MALEK: Both, really.

OMAR: Yeah, but it'll pick up soon. The summer's always dead.

MALEK: Hey, I didn't see you on the clipboard. Did you sign in?

OMAR: Oh shit, I forgot.

(*Omar stands, scurries to the clipboard, signs in, and takes an extra moment to scan the names of the many actors who have signed in before him.*)

Karim Fustok, Fawaz Qaddumi, Raj Patel, Julio Ramirez—Jesus, they're seeing all of Browntown for this one!

MALEK: I know, it's crazy, man!

(*Beat.*)

So where have you been? Still doing car shows out of state?

OMAR: Yep. Just got back two weeks ago.

MALEK: What exactly do you *do* at those shows?

(*Omar suddenly launches into a rapid-fire version of his intolerable auto show speech. He has delivered this exact speech a thousand times. Malek may interrupt in the middle of the speech.*)

OMAR: "Welcome to the Subaru display at the Louisville auto show. Subaru offers a complete line of award-winning vehicles, in terms of both safety. and value. Subaru is the only company to offer Symmetrical All-Wheel Drive as standard equipment on every vehicle we sell ..."

MALEK (*Miserable, interjecting*); Dude—enough. I get the picture.

OMAR: Such horseshit. I'm glad to be out of Kentucky, tell you that much. Talk about a red state.

MALEK: You gotta find a new gig, man. That job's sucking your soul.

OMAR: I know, that's why I came back.

(*Beat.*)

So, do you know anything about this TV movie thing?

MALEK: It seems kinda interesting. I finally finished reading the script on the way here and I thought it was *way* better than—what was that last one we both auditioned for a couple of months ago?

OMAR AND MALEK (*Simultaneously*): *Geronimo jihad!*

MALEK: That was it. Ya know, I think Sameer actually booked that one.

OMAR: Really? Good for him. That's great.

MALEK: Yeah, he's in Morocco shooting it right now.

OMAR: Hey, at least they cast Sameer, and not one of those poser Indian guys.

MALEK: Whatever, who cares, man.

OMAR: Is Sameer cool with all the "lu-lu-lu-lu-lu"? (*Mimicking the "crazy Arab" sounds*)

MALEK: Yeah, he's game. They made him grow out a long beard and behead a Dutch journalist.

OMAR: That's ridiculous.

MALEK: I know, but he hadn't worked in a while so ...

OMAR: Glad he's working then. That's an awesome break for him.

MALEK: So what did *you* think of the script?

OMAR: I quit reading it halfway through.

MALEK: Why?

OMAR: I dunno. I wasn't crazy about it. *The Color of Terror!* Just seems like another scary brown-guy movie.

MALEK: Hey, at least the Arab in this one is a *valiant* terrorist.

OMAR: What do you mean?

MALEK: I mean he has heroic reasons for blowing up the supermarket.

OMAR: Heroic reasons?

MALEK: He cared about his family. Al Qaeda was gonna kill his baby if he didn't comply, so Mohammed had no choice.

OMAR: But that's the thing, man. Why is his name *Mohammed*? Why do *all* terrorists gotta be named Mohammed in these movies?

MALEK: Well, Mohammed *is* the most popular name in the world.

OMAR: I know, but it's like these writers have never even heard of another Muslim name. It's always Mohammed! I mean, I'd love to play an Islamic militant named Tarek or Fadi for a change. Hell, I'd even settle for Moustafa.

MALEK: But at least this writer is trying to justify Mohammed's *reasons* for doing what he does.

OMAR: Why should she justify it? Why should anyone? Terrorism is fucked up. Is her *justification* supposed to make me feel better about it?

MALEK: I take that back. She's not exactly justifying his actions, but at least making him more human. And did you notice—they even called him a "freedom fighter" in the breakdowns!? "Freedom fighter." That's some progress right there! You can't be a snob about this shit, man.

OMAR: I'm not, I'm just saying, you gotta draw the line somewhere. For Chrissake, this Mohammed's got four wives, he hates all Jews, he drives a Mercedes that he bought with his family's oil money, and he's conspiring with a guerilla group called "Allies for Allah." They may as well put him on a camel and strap a bomb on to him in the opening scene. This is basically the same shit as *True Lies* or *Not without My Daughter*!. There are consequences for perpetuating these stereotypes.

MALEK: Weren't you in *True Lies*?

(*A beat. Omar's busted.*)

OMAR: Look, all I'm saying is—why can't I—just once—play a normal guy? A paramedic, a musician, a stockbroker, a journalist. Why can't I be the brown John Cusack? You know? Some dude who's just chillin? at Al Bustan, eating some falafel, smoking some shisha and watching all the hot Lebanese chicks stroll by. 1 would kill to play a normal bad guy. Like an ethnically nondescript ...

MALEK: Bank robber!

OMAR: Or con artist—

MALEK: Or serial rapist! That would be awesome… (*Has an epiphany*) You know what? Why don't we just stop bitchin? already and write our own screenplay?

OMAR: About what?

MALEK: I don't know, *good* Arabs.

(*Another young brown actor, Vijay, enters wearing headphones and trendy shades. He drags a noisy, compact rolling suitcase behind him.*)

OMAR: Actually, that's not a bad idea— (*Noticing Vijay*) Oh shit, man.

MALEK: What?

OMAR: Look who just walked in.

MALEK: Who, Vijay? Yeah, so what?

OMAR: That fucker keeps taking our parts.

MALEK: Our parts?

OMAR: He just got cast in *Hijacked at Home and Baby Bomber*s. Don't get me wrong, he's a nice guy. I just don't understand why they keep hiring an Indian guy for specifically *Arab* roles.

MALEK: Cuz he's good! That guy played every mainstage lead at Juilliard.

(*Vijay, unzipping his hooded sweatshirt, conspicuously reveals his Juilliard T-shirt.*)

OMAR: But why don't they just let us represent *ourselves* for a change? We don't need some Indian guy speaking for the Arab community.

MALEK: Oh gimme a fucking break, dude. You're just jealous.

OMAR: I'm really not! I don't want that role! I told you, I'd prefer not to play these terrorist roles, unless they are really high paying. All I'm saying is, if you're not gonna give it to me, at least give it to another Arab. Give it to you. Or to Sameer. Don't give it to some Indian who's ignorant of our culture—

VIJAY (*Takes off his headphones*): Hey, Omar! And, Malek, right?

OMAR AND MALEK (*Awkwardly, feeling busted*): Yeah! Hey, man!

VIJAY: Oh, I'm not interrupting something, am I? Some serious conference?

MALEK: No, not at all!

OMAR: No. It's good to see you, man. You're a busy man these days, right?!

VIJAY: These days, yes. We'll see how long the luck can last.

OMAR: Must be nice juggling two films.

VIJAY: I'm just happy to be working at all! Enough about me. Omar, didn't you just get back from Louisville?

OMAR: Yeah.

VIJAY: So ... how was *Indian Ink*?!

(*An awkward pause.*)

You played the lead guy—Nirad Das, right?

OMAR: Yeah, Nirad, It was a lot of fun, man. 1 was psyched to be in a Stoppard play. His shit is brilliant.

MALEK: *Indian Ink?* I thought you said you were in Louisville to show Subarus.

OMAR: I was, at first. Then Actor's Theatre had an open call and I booked it. So I quit the car show. I can't believe they cast me—the whole Indian thing.

VIJAY: Hey, I'm sure you were great as Nirad.

MALEK: Shit. I wanted to audition for that, but my agent said they were only seeing "straight-up Indians."

OMAR: Well, my guess is they really don't know the difference.

VIJAY: Tell me about it. Ever since I filmed *Hijacked at Home*, it's been one Ahmed after another for me.

OMAR: Go figure.

MALEK: Hey, at least you're working.

VIJAY: Very true. No complaints here.

(*Ann, the casting director for* The Color of Terror*, enters.*)

ANN: Malek Bizri? Right this way.

MALEK: Omar, let's do some brainstorming after this—movie ideas.

OMAR: Sure, if you don't mind waiting for me.

MALEK: Not at all.

VIJAY: Break a leg, man.

34

(Betty Shamieh, 1986—)

贝蒂·沙米耶

作者简介

贝蒂·沙米耶（Betty Shamieh, 1986—）出生于加利福尼亚州旧金山（San Francisco），是一位美国巴勒斯坦裔剧作家、作家、编剧和演员。她毕业于哈佛大学（Harvard University）和耶鲁戏剧学院（Yale School of Drama）。2016 年，她获得了古根海姆戏剧和表演艺术奖学金（Guggenheim Fellowship for Drama and Performance Art）。她曾两次获得纽约艺术剧本奖（The New York Foundation for the Arts Playwriting Fellowship）。2011 年，沙米耶被联合国教科文组织提名为“跨文化对话青年艺术家”（UNESCO Young Artist for Intercultural Dialogue）。

贝蒂·沙米耶是十五部戏剧的作者，其中包括外百老汇首演（Off-Broadway Premieres）《黑眼睛》（*The Black Eyed*，2005）和《咆哮》（*Roar*，2004）。

2012 年，沙米耶根据自己的剧本创作的歌剧咏叹调组曲《领土》（*Territories*）在普林斯顿大学高级研究院（Princeton University's Institute for Advanced Studies）举行了世界首演。作为 2011 年俄罗斯 / 美国 – 俄罗斯总统双边委员会和百灵鸟戏剧发展中心美国季的一部分，她的剧本《再次和反对》（*Again and Against*，2006）被翻译成俄语演出；其剧作《不可能的事》（*As Soon As Impossible*）、《机器》（*The Machine*）和《自由基》（*Free Radicals*）很受欢迎。沙米耶创作并联合主演了她的独角戏《高温下的巧克力》（*Chocolate in Heat*，2001），在外百老汇（off-Broadway）剧院和二十多家大学剧院演出时场场爆满。

沙米耶对戏剧和文学的贡献不容忽视。她一直为《纽约时报》（*The New York Times*）、《美国戏剧杂志》（*American Theatre Magazine*）、《湾区戏剧》（*Theater*

Bay Area）和《国际先驱论坛报》（*The International Herald Tribune*）等报刊做专题报道。她的作品已被翻译成七种语言。

节选部分出自沙米耶的歌剧咏叹调组曲《领土》。受真实故事的启发，伊斯兰领袖萨拉赫·阿尔丁（Salah Al-Din）的妹妹被臭名昭著的法国十字军雷金纳德·德·夏蒂隆（Reginald de Chatilon）绑架。雷金纳德因其独特的折磨方法和勾引女强人的能力而闻名。这部戏剧在妹妹被捕之前、期间和之后流畅地展开，讲述了一个永恒的战争故事。

作品选读

Territories

(Excerpts)

By Betty Shamieh

PROLOGUE

Lights up on Saladin and Reginald on their sides of the stage.

Lights up on Alia in the center of the stage. Alia is wearing a traditional Muslim woman's clothing (not a burka but rather a headscarf, a handkerchief to cover her face except for her eyes, and a light robe).

SALADIN: I will be praised for my chivalry in poems and epics for hundreds of years. It won't only be my people who speak of my valor as a soldier and a king.

REGINALD: I will be a footnote of a footnote. In that footnote of a footnote, I will be called a pirate.

(*Alia takes off her face covering and places it onstage.*)

ALIA: No one will think it worthwhile to write down my name.

SALADIN: The descendants of people who considered me their enemy will praise me too. Dante, Sir Walter Scott, the list goes on.

REGINALD: However, I prefer to think of myself as the Official Royal Plunderer of God's Greatest Gifts in His Holiest of Holy Lands.

ALIA (*As she takes off her headscarf*): I will be known only as one man's sister and another man's captive.

SALADIN: I negotiated a peace treaty with Richard the Lionhearted.

REGINALD: The battle I lost is the reason Richard the Lionhearted had to come.

ALIA: And I am the reason why the battle was fought in the first place, though the chroniclers of our time refer to me as such, not one ever wrote down my name.

SALADIN: When I died soon after putting an end to the Crusades, my men opened my treasury. They found there wasn't enough money to bury me. I had given everything I had to the poor.

ALIA: Fool!

SALADIN: But, my people built me a glorious tomb in Damascus anyway.

ALLA: A tomb with no prayer written anywhere on the walls that mentions my name. A tomb which a French general named Henri Gouraud will enter in 1920.

REGINALD: I love it that he was French like me.

ALLA: Over eight hundred years after we are all dead, Brother, this French general will kick the entrance of your tomb that lies near the Grand Mosque. He will say:

REGINALD: "Awake, Saladin, we have returned. My presence here consecrates the victory of the Cross over the Crescent."

ALIA: And I will know that I was right to do what I did. I, who was just a nameless, faceless woman to everyone except for…

SALADIN: Me.

REGINALD: Me.

The lights focus on Alia. She glances from one man to the other before speaking.

ALIA: Why don't you ask what you want to ask?

SALADIN: Did he rape you?

REGINALD: Should I rape you?

ALIA: I'm not answering that question.

SALADIN: Why not?

REGINALD: Why not?

ALIA: It's a trap.

SALADIN: You're not going.

ALIA: Who are you to decide?

REGINALD: I'm disappointed that you even attempted the trip, actually. Don't you know who I am?

SALADIN: I am the sultan of the Muslim world. Your brother.

ALIA: I know who you are.

REGINALD: And you dared to make the trip anyway. That's naughty. My name, my castle right smack in your way, is not enough to strike fear in your heart. Or that of your monkey brother. Did you hear that? I called your brother a monkey.

ALIA: Which brother?

REGINALD: *The* brother. The only way you could be here is if he allowed it.

SALADIN: No caravan will attempt the trip without my consent. No one will take you if I forbid it.

ALIA: You said "if."

SALADIN: I meant "when."

ALIA: There is so much hope in the world, room for possibility, when a sentence begins with the word "if." If I was the ruler, I'd make a decree! All sentences should begin with the word "if."

REGINALD: If I rape you, I wonder how your brother would react? What would that Mohammedan vow to do to me if I laid a hand under your skill?

ALIA: An I supposed to fear you?

SALADIN: No.

REGINALD: Actually yes.

ALIA: My faith, my God, commands me to go to Mecca.

SALADIN: Since when are you so pious, Sister?

ALLA: Since when have you discouraged me from being religious, Brother?

SALADIN: Since it has become too dangerous. That devil incarnate Reginald has been catching caravans on the road to Mecca.

REGINALD: Of all the caravans I could have captured—

SALADIN: Sister, no one slips through anymore, everyone that passes Reginald's castle has been harassed at the very best and at the worst...

REGINALD: I caught yours.

ALIA: He won't catch mine.

(*The lights go down on Saladin.*)

REGINALD: I heard you called for the one in charge. Welcome to my cozy little home.

ALIA: You speak Arabic?

REGINALD: Would you prefer Kurdish? I could manage, but my Kurdish is rather rusty.

ALIA: Arabic is fine.

REGINALD: I'm so glad, my honorable guest. I wouldn't want you to be in the least bit uncomfortable.

ALIA: Leave me alone. Get out of here now.

REGINALD: Unless I'm mistaken, you are my prisoner and you stay, well, you know, alive only at my discretion, so I decide—

ALLA: There's a funny thing about power. You don't have to declare it if you possess it.

REGINALD: You don't have to, but declaring it is so much fun. Haven't you heard about what I do to caravans?

ALLA: I've heard.

REGINALD: But you came anyway. I'm curious. Why did you even attempt the trip?

ALLA: I'm curious. Where did you leam to speak Arabic?

REGINALD: I learned Arabic the same place you did. Prison.

ALLA: What do you mean by that?

REGINALD: You figure it out, woman.

ALLA: Where is my maid?

(*Reginald smiles.*)

Miriam is her name. It means Mary. She's a Christian, you know.

REGINALD: Arab Christians always side with you Muslims over us. I have a collection of ears I've cut off of their priests and nuns—

ALIA: I'd bet you do.

REGINALD: Then you'd win your bet. Would you like to see it?

ALIA: No.

REGINALD (*Yelling*): Add the ear of the Christian maid to my collection.

ALIA: Are you trying to terrorize me?

REGINALD: No, I'm trying to impress you. Something makes me feel like I will.

ALIA: I do not ask for many favors, sir. She is a defenseless Christian girl.

REGINALD: And, when my men are done with her, she will have a Christian burial. Save your pleading. You will need it for yourself.

ALIA: You won't see me plead for myself.

REGINALD: We'll see about that.

ALIA: I'm too expensive of a hostage to kill.

REGINALD: We'll see about that too.

ALIA: Do you have any idea who you're dealing with?

REGINALD: Yes, I do. Your shield says you are from the family of Izz Al-Din. But you aren't. I know Izz very well, and he says no one from his family is missing: I thought to myself—the only reason someone would pretend to be in his family is if they were from a greater one. I'm very clever, aren't I? But also your retinue told us everything. They betrayed you utterly and rather quickly, I might add.

ALLA: They didn't want to die.

REGINALD: You're wrong there. They wanted to die. They very desperately wanted to die and we wouldn't let them but never mind all that. So, tell me, how is good ole Salah Al-Din Yusuf Ibn Ayyub? Also known as—

ALLA: Arrange a ransom for my return.

REGINALD: Saladin. I haven't yet met the sultan—the famous Kurdish cur-—but I'm sure I'll get the chance. What's your name?

ALLA: My name is five thousand dinars in your treasury if you hum me over. That's all you need to know about my name.

REGINALD: I was told that you were shaking last night. Had a sort of fit. What's wrong? Are you afraid of little old me?

ALLA: Sir, if you scared me, do you think I would have even attempted the trip? This shaking is a condition I have.

REGINALD: That's unfortunate. To not be able to control how you move—

35

(Amani al-Khatahtbeh, 1992—)

阿曼尼 · 阿尔 – 哈塔贝

作者简介

阿曼尼 · 阿尔 – 哈塔贝（Amani al-Khatahtbeh，1992—）美国约旦和巴勒斯坦裔作家、活动家和科技企业家。哈塔贝在新泽西州（New Jersey）长大，父母是约旦和巴勒斯坦裔阿拉伯人。高中毕业后，她进入罗格斯大学（Rutgers University），并于 2014 年获得政治学学位。她是穆斯林女性的博客“穆斯林女孩网”（MuslimGirl.com）的创始人，并因与“穆斯林女孩网”的合作而入选福布斯 30 位 30 岁以下媒体人，还被 CNN 提名为 25 位最具影响力的美国穆斯林之一。

哈塔贝的著作《穆斯林女孩：成年》（*Muslim Girl: A Coming of Age*，2016）于 2016 年 10 月出版。她在这部著作中分享了自己作为一名年轻的穆斯林女性在“9 · 11”事件之后、在无休止的反恐战争期间、在随意的种族主义的特朗普时代的痛苦经历。2001 年 9 月 11 日，9 岁的阿曼尼 · 阿尔 – 哈塔贝在新泽西州的家中目睹了两架飞机撞向世贸中心。同年，她第一次听到种族歧视。13 岁时，全家去了父亲的故乡约旦，阿曼尼得以亲身体验了建立在伊斯兰最纯粹的和平本质上的文化，而不是她在新闻中听到的伊斯兰刻板印象。多年来，西方媒体所谈论的话题似乎都是穆斯林女性，而她作为一名穆斯林女性的声音却被边缘化，因此，她经常以戴头巾作为对抗仇视伊斯兰教的行为。具有讽刺意味的是，受到这次约旦之旅的启发，哈塔贝在 2009 年创建了年轻穆斯林女性的在线社区——穆斯林女孩网（MuslimGirl.com），并组建了一个穆斯林女性团队，开始了致力于行动主义的一生。

节选部分出自阿曼尼的著作《穆斯林女孩：成年》第一章。《穆斯林女孩：成年》是阿曼尼作为穆斯林女孩在青春期的非凡经历，从每天面对的伊斯兰恐惧症，到她创建的成为文化现象的网站，再到 2016 年唐纳德·特朗普当选总统后的美国政治氛围。在打破头巾既不代表激进主义也不代表压迫的神话的同时，她分享了自己的个人经历和作为她在《穆斯林女孩》编辑团队的姐妹作家们的逸事。

作品选读

Muslim Girl: A Coming of Age

(Chapter 1)

By Amani al-Khatahtbeh

The only time I ever cried during an interview was when I was asked to recall my memory of 9/11. Was it for *International Business Times*? *The Guardian*? I can hardly remember anymore. But, surprisingly, I had never been asked that question before, and it caught me so off guard that when I started describing the vivid image seared into my memory, the tears began to fall.

On September 11, 2001, Bowne-Munro Elementary School in East Brunswick, New Jersey, planned to hold its annual Yearbook Photo Day. We were all dressed up and excited for an excuse to leave our classrooms, go outside, and spend the day on our grassy soccer field, against whatever backdrop they had for us that year. There was an electric energy of anticipation when we got to school. Everyone was wearing their best clothes; the boys wore new sneakers and the girls had their hair plaited in cute updos, or their smiles beamed from between bouncing curls. My hair was always frustratingly thick and slightly unruly, but at least Mama tried to brush it straight for me that day, my uneven curtain of bangs resting just above my eyes. I always felt my best on Yearbook Day, if only because Mama was eager to get a new set of photos of me to add to her collection. She took pride in displaying what turned out to be a chronological evolution of my awkward haircuts over the years, in pretty frames among porcelain figurines in the heavy cherrywood cabinet that was only accessible in the dining room on special occasions.

Mama loved Yearbook Day. She had just bought me a new outfit. I was wearing a stiff pair of jeans and a blue shirt—I hated the color pink when I was a little girl and rebelled against expected "girliness" by always opting for blue and green, which is fascinating considering nearly everything I own is pink now—with a black vest over it. I finished the look by slathering on my favorite Bonne Bell Dr Pepper Lip Smacker. I was probably wearing a pair of dress shoes that I couldn't wait to show off. And I remember it was really warm and sunny outside.

From the earliest moments of our first period, however, something was weird. Actually, a lot of things were weird. First of all, it was eerily quiet in our school. The TVs in all of the classrooms, which were usually on the district's cable channel of PowerPoint slide announcements to the background tune of elevator music, were turned off. That morning, the principal didn't deliver our usual morning announcements over the PA system, either. Then, soon enough, we were told by our teachers, almost inconsequentially, that Yearbook Day was canceled. They told us pesticide was sprayed on the fields that morning so we couldn't go outside. I remember feeling confused and a little disappointed, but everyone else just accepted that we would take our pictures another day, so I did, too.

Our math teacher cried so much throughout the morning that some of us thought that someone in her family had died. I remember the class trying to make her feel better while faculty passed through the halls or popped in every now and then in a state of disarray.

"It's okay, Ms. Brady," we said to her when she was hunched over at her desk, her eyes red from the tears, her face contorted like she was hanging on by a thread that could break at any moment. "It's going to be okay!" we cheerfully encouraged her. That only made her cry even more.

Our young fourth-grade minds were not much alarmed by these events, nor did we really think to string them together. How could we? How could we have possibly imagined what was waiting for us?

Our school day finally ended with an unscheduled early dismissal, much to our delight. Somehow, our parents were already informed of this, because when I ran out of school, my mom, who was routinely late to pick me up, was on time and waiting for me. I ran up to the car and Mama leaned over the passenger seat to unlock the door for me from the inside. I opened the door and didn't even have time to climb into the seat before she said, "Amani, something happened today."

"What's up?" I asked, getting in and closing the door beside me.

"You know the Twin Towers?" she asked.

"No—" I responded, confused.

"You know those two really tall buildings that are next to each other in New York? That we were looking at and talking about how huge they were when Dad took us for a drive in the city?"

"Yes," I said, remembering.

"Okay, well, there's been a crash, and they're not there anymore."

"They're not there anymore?!" I asked, trying to understand. "Like, at all?"

"No, honey. They're not there anymore. Two planes crashed into them."

"What? There was an accident? Is everyone okay?" I asked naively.

"Someone drove the planes into them," my mom said, but I still was not processing what had just happened. For the rest of our five-minute car ride home, I kept repeating the same questions, not sure how someone could intentionally fly a plane full of people into a skyscraper full of people, nor that those two towers in the opening credits of my parents' favorite television show, *Friends*, could possibly cease to exist. They weren't there anymore?

When I walked into our home, my family was in the living room, their eyes glued to the television screen. My dad was standing beside the TV and my mother joined him. My baby brothers, Ameer and Faris, then three and four years old, respectively, were in the family room, watching *SpongeBob SquarePants*. My grandmother and Auntie Ebtisam were sitting on the long couch in the back of the room, reacting in Arabic. They were visiting from Jordan and living with us for one year at the time, enjoying their first trip to the United States. My twenty-three-year-old aunt had her elbows up in the air, her fingers at work twisting her waist-length black hair, usually hidden beneath a veil, into one tight strand that she distractedly wrapped around the outside of her ear, which was a habit of hers. They couldn't believe what had happened. "I had just taken them there a couple of days ago," my dad, or Baba as we usually call him, told me. "They looked up at the towers through the sunroof of our car in wonder." Now, suddenly, they weren't there anymore.

But, here, on our TV, there was an image of the Twin Towers with clouds of black smoke coming out of them. I was trying to understand how they got like that, trying to imagine how this could have possibly resulted from a plane crash—and then it happened. The news channel looped the footage—a scene that would continue to loop in my mind's eye, surface in my everyday, for the rest of my life—of two planes crashing into the sides of the towers. My eyes saw it. I was suddenly a witness to an evil that I was not even able to grasp, exposed to a tragedy that I only had the capacity to feel but not comprehend. Whenever the footage appeared in the broadcast, everyone in the room fell silent again, in a trance, probably not far from my own elementary struggle to make sense of what I was seeing.

And then, Baba said something that I didn't understand at the time, but that alerted me to the impact of the day's events beyond two beautiful towers—and, as I later would learn, thousands of people—not being there anymore.

"This is a horrible thing that happened," he told his mother. "And they're going to blame us. And it's going to get much worse."

中国人民大学出版社外语出版分社读者信息反馈表

尊敬的读者：

感谢您购买和使用中国人民大学出版社外语出版分社的 ______________ 一书，我们希望通过这张小小的反馈卡来获得您更多的建议和意见，以改进我们的工作，加强我们双方的沟通和联系。我们期待着能为更多的读者提供更多的好书。

请您填妥下表后，寄回或传真回复我们，对您的支持我们不胜感激！

1. 您是从何种途径得知本书的：

□书店　□网上　□报纸杂志　□朋友推荐

2. 您为什么决定购买本书：

□工作需要　□学习参考　□对本书主题感兴趣　□随便翻翻

3. 您对本书内容的评价是：

□很好　□好　□一般　□差　□很差

4. 您在阅读本书的过程中有没有发现明显的专业及编校错误，如果有，它们是：

____

____

____

5. 您对哪些专业的图书信息比较感兴趣：

____

____

____

6. 如果方便，请提供您的个人信息，以便于我们和您联系（您的个人资料我们将严格保密）：

您供职的单位：______________________________

您教授的课程（教师填写）：______________________

您的通信地址：______________________________

您的电子邮箱：______________________________

请联系我们：黄婷　程子殊　吴振良　王琼　鞠方安

电话：010-62512737，62513265，62515538，62515573，62515576

传真：010-62514961

E-mail：huangt@crup.com.cn　chengzsh@crup.com.cn　wuzl@crup.com.cn
crup_wy@163.com　jufa@crup.com.cn

通信地址：北京市海淀区中关村大街甲 59 号文化大厦 15 层　邮编：100872

中国人民大学出版社外语出版分社